# I heart
## Hawaii

Lindsey Kelk was born and brought up in Doncaster, South Yorkshire, and worked as a sales assistant, a PR exec, a silver service waitress and a children's editor before moving to New York and becoming a full-time writer. She now lives in LA.

Lindsey has written fifteen novels, including the *I Heart* books and the *Girl* series, as well as several standalones and a children's book series called *Cinders & Sparks*. A fan of lipstick, pro-wrestling and cats (although not all at the same time), she co-hosts the beauty podcast, *Full Coverage*, and pro-wrestling podcast, *Tights & Fights*.

You can find out more about Lindsey here: http://lindseykelk.com and on Facebook, Twitter or Instagram @LindseyKelk.

# I heart Hawaii

## Lindsey Kelk

HarperCollins*Publishers*

HarperCollins*Publishers*
1 London Bridge Street
London
SE1 9GF

www.harpercollins.co.uk

A Paperback Original 2019
19 20 21 22 LSC 10 9 8 7 6 5 4 3 2 1

A catalogue record for this book
is available from the British Library

B-format: 978-0-00-823685-4
A-format: 978-0-00-824019-6
Export TPB: 978-0-00-823686-1
US ISBN: 978-0-00-834805-2

Set in Melior by Palimpsest Book Production Limited,
Falkirk, Stirlingshire

Printed and bound in the United States of America
by LSC Communications

For more information visit: **www.harpercollins.co.uk/green**

For Della.
The Jenny to my Angela, Angela to my Jenny.
Without you, there would be no *I Heart*.
Thank you, thank you, thank you.

# PROLOGUE

'Angela? Are you up?'

I was not up. I had no interest in being up.

'Come on. You can't stay in bed all day.'

Slowly, very, very slowly, I prised open one eye as I tried to work out where I was.

The ceiling was too low, the window was in the wrong place and I couldn't hear a single car horn honking. Not to mention the fact my bed was altogether too small and too empty.

'Angela.'

Two taps on the door of my childhood bedroom before it opened, my mum's face popping inside without waiting for an invitation.

'Why aren't you dressed? It's nearly eight.'

Today was the day.

'I just woke up,' I croaked in response, raking a hand through the bird's nest on top of my head. Everything came rushing back: where I was, why I was here, what had to be done today, and the steady thrum of nerves that had been beating in my chest since I got on the plane found its rhythm once again.

'Well, I know we had a lazy one yesterday but you can't lie around in bed all day today. The sooner you get up and start getting on with things, the better you'll feel.'

I pulled the duvet up over my face.

'Come on,' she said, her voice softening outside my blanket fort. 'Kettle's just boiled. I'll bring you up a cup of tea.'

'Thanks, Mum,' I whispered from underneath the covers as the door clicked shut behind her.

From the day you left home, the prospect of waking up in your childhood bedroom was never a welcome one. Best-case scenario, it was Christmas. Worst-case scenario, your life had completely fallen apart. I wondered where my current predicament fell on that scale.

With a groan, I tossed away the duvet and rolled over to stare into the eyes of the Care Bear printed on my pillowcase. It had to have been at least thirty years old but Mum always put it on the bed when I came home, even when it was last minute, even when it wasn't planned. Pressing my cheek against the cool, soft fabric, I sighed. Poor Tenderheart Bear, he had already seen so much in his many years of service and now, here he was, offering his services as a stand-in for the person who should be lying in bed beside me.

Alex.

I glanced over at my phone, thought about it for just a second and then pushed the idea out of my head. No, not yet.

Save the torn-out pages of the *NME* I'd left stapled to the walls, my room still looked exactly the same as it did the day I left. Every time Dad redecorated, Mum insisted they keep the colours the same. Maybe there was a different duvet on my double bed but my Care Bear pillow and the crocheted blanket from my grandmother's house were always there. Same pine wardrobe and chest of drawers. Same dressing table with the same scorch marks from my teenage pyromaniac phase. Terracotta essential oil burner from the Body Shop on the windowsill, pink plastic cassette case sitting beside my incredibly cool zebra-striped ghetto blaster. All this familiarity should have made me feel better but it just made me feel further and further away. Like my years in New York had been a dream. Like I'd imagined Alex and Jenny and James and Delia and Erin and all the rest of it.

As though none of it had ever happened.

'But it did,' I whispered, turning my engagement and wedding rings around and around on my finger and waiting for a genie to appear. 'It did, it did, it did.'

'Only me.'

The door opened again, all the way this time, as my mum marched in bearing a steaming mug of tea and not one, but two, biscuits.

Oh my. Things really were serious.

'The sooner you get up, the sooner you can get this day started.'

'And the sooner I can come back to bed?' I added hopefully.

'Oh, Angela,' she said, sitting down on the edge of the bed and smoothing my messy hair down on the top of my head. 'Don't overreact, you're making it worse than it is. Everything is going to be fine. When has your mother ever steered you wrong?'

This didn't seem like a question that needed answering with a tremendous degree of honesty.

3

'Drink your tea, jump in the shower and I'll have your breakfast waiting. Your dad is raring to go.'

'Classic Dad,' I replied as she walked around the bed and tore open all the curtains. This day was coming in whether I liked it or not. 'I don't know if I can do this.'

I should have known not to push my luck. The sympathetic lift of her eyebrows folded in on itself until it evolved into its final form; Annette Clark's trademark glare. I shrank back against the pillow. It worked when I threw a tantrum in Woolworths when I was three and it worked now.

'Angela Clark, I will not have this attitude,' Mum declared from the doorway, hands on hips, frown on face. 'Downstairs in ten minutes. Today is a big day. You need to be up and dressed before everyone gets here. Whatever you've convinced yourself of, things aren't going to go better with you in your bed, are they?'

With one last forceful look, she closed the door and left me alone. I might have left home when I was eighteen but I would know the sound of Mum's purposeful march down the stairs anywhere with my eyes closed.

And I also knew when she was right.

Stretching my legs, I pushed away my blankets and felt for the floor with my toes.

It was all going to be fine, Mum said.

I put one foot on the floor, followed by the other. There, I was officially standing. The day had officially started. All I had to do was get up, get dressed and meet the day head on.

No turning back now.

# CHAPTER ONE

One year earlier . . .

'I am a woman who has it all,' I said quietly, staring at my own face reflected back in the screen of my iPhone. 'I am a woman who owns her power.'

The version of me looking back rolled her eyes but I went on regardless.

'I am strong, vital and beautiful.'

And tired, emotional and, according to the tag in the front of my pants, wearing my knickers back to front. Although they were clean, so at least there was that.

The affirmations were my best friend, Jenny's, idea. Apparently, if I said them out loud, every day, they would all come true. The more I heard myself say these things, the more I would believe them and then the whole world would believe them too. In theory. But the more I stared at my pale complexion and red-rimmed eyes I couldn't help but think a nice, uninterrupted eighteen-hour nap would be more effective. Also, I wasn't entirely sure I was supposed be reciting them on the toilet at work but I was fairly sure this was the first time I'd been entirely alone since I'd given birth ten and a half months ago.

I took a deep breath and refocused. My attention span was something else that needed some work, along with my short-term memory and my pelvic floor muscles.

'There is nothing I cannot accomplish when I put my trust in the universe,' I said, breathing out.

Jenny said the affirmations would open up my subconscious and allow me to contact my inner goddess, the divine feminine energy, but so far mine was nowhere to be seen. Probably out dicking around with all the other inner goddesses who hadn't got up five times in the night with a teething baby.

Lifting the phone a little to improve the angle of my selfie, I really looked at myself. Jenny said you had to look yourself in the eye when you were doing it and I didn't have a mirror on me. Maybe there was something in these affirmations, after all. Sleep deprivation didn't do much for a girl's dark circles but my cheekbones looked killer. I tapped the photo-editing app Jenny had also installed on my phone and swiped through until I found my favourite filter, trying to snap a picture to send to Alex. Because nothing says I love you like a selfie taken on the toilet.

'Hello?'

Three sharp raps on the cubicle door and I jumped out of my skin. My phone slipped out of my hand, fell between my knees and plopped directly in the toilet bowl.

'Excuse me, do you have any toilet paper in there?'

'Nooooooo,' I breathed, momentarily paralysed

before grabbing handfuls of toilet paper and waving it under the stall door. Yes, I'd just destroyed a thousand dollars' worth of technology but I'd be damned if I would let another woman go for a wee without sufficient loo roll.

'Thanks,' the voice replied, sounding relieved as the paper disappeared. 'Appreciate it.'

'You're welcome,' I replied in a bright, tight voice as I gazed at my phone in the bottom of the toilet bowl, only to see myself looking back. And then the screen went black. I nodded and sighed before rolling up my sleeves and reaching in. I was a strong, vital, beautiful woman with her hand down a public toilet.

Brilliant start to a brilliant day.

The first day in a new job is always nerve-racking. Even if you're in your thirties, even if you've done pretty much exactly the same job somewhere else before, unless you're either Kanye or a complete sociopath, there are bound to be a few first-day jitters. And if you take those jitters and multiply them by the fact you're coming back to work after having your first baby you've got a real, one hundred percent 'shitting it' situation on your hands.

With my waterlogged phone in my pocket, I eventually convinced myself to leave the lavs and made my way across the huge reception of my new office building. I smiled at the pleasing tap-tap-tap of my heels against the marble floor. Heels. In the daytime. It had been so long.

'Hi.'

I beamed at the man seated behind the reception desk. He did not beam back.

'I'm Angela Clark. I'm starting work at Besson Media today.'

Without raising his eyes to meet mine, the man nodded.

'Photo ID?'

Slipping my hand into my ancient Marc Jacobs satchel, I pulled out my passport on the first try and handed it over with a brilliant smile. He looked at me, looked at the passport and looked at me again. Still nothing.

'Fifteenth floor,' he replied, sliding my passport back across the desk and inclining his head towards the bank of lifts across the cavernous hall. 'Take elevator six.'

'Thank you!' I said, tucking my passport away and making the eighteen thousandth reminder to myself to finally get round to applying for a New York driver's licence. I'd only been here the best part of a decade, after all.

But in all that time, I'd never seen anything like this. My old office had been a flash, glass, nineties-tastic monster of a skyscraper, slap bang in the middle of Times Square. If you were into flashing neon signs and an ungodly number of tourists, it was heaven, but this? This was something else. Besson Media had set up shop in an architectural icon. A recently renovated sugar refinery on the edge of Williamsburg, perfectly positioned to give Manhattan a good dose of hipper-than-thou side eye. Alongside the landmark building, we also had our own park, our own sculpture garden, different food trucks every single day and our very own beach. I'd read about the building, and I'd seen it when I walked by, but actually being inside felt so very special. Old red-brick walls and old-fashioned arched windows contrasted against the shining steel of the lifts and the touch screens I saw absolutely everywhere. Stopping myself from swiping wildly, I stepped into the lift, clutching my bag against my hip and grinning at strangers as more people joined me.

'Hi,' I said to the backs of people's heads, shuffling backwards into the corner. 'Hello.'

Ten months at home with a baby was pretty much exactly the same as when someone on a TV show disappears one week and then shows up the next, only to explain they've spent a thousand years in another dimension and no longer know who they were. You don't speak to strangers in lifts, not in New York or anywhere else for that matter. One by one, floor by floor, people piled out until it was just me, all on my lonesome, arriving at floor fifteen.

It was beautiful.

Besson Media was, of course, on the top floor and, unlike the rest of the building, the penthouse level was all glass, giving us a 360-view of New York, Brooklyn and Queens, for as far as the eye could see. Not that anyone's eyes were concentrating on what was happening outside the windows. Everyone already at work in the open-plan office had their eyes firmly fixed on whatever screen was in front of them, a desktop, a laptop, a tablet, a phone. Without anyone to greet me, and not seeing anyone I recognized, I took an awkward step away from the safety of the lifts and into the hub. Perhaps, if I could find my office, I could get settled and then start from there.

'Hello,' I said, waving at a young Japanese woman

with green hair who was studying her laptop intently. She peered back at me from behind gold wire-framed glasses with exceptionally large lenses. 'Um, I'm starting today? I'm Angela Clark. I don't suppose you know where my office might be?'

'We don't have offices,' she replied. 'It's open plan. Hot desk. Set up wherever you like.'

A shiver ran down my spine.

Hot desk? There had been no discussion of hot desks.

'I'm fairly sure I'm supposed to have an office,' I told her, subtly nudging my left breast pad back into place with my forearm. 'I'm going to be running a site—'

'I run a site,' the girl replied. 'I'm Kanako. I run Bias? The fashion site? No one has an office except for the CEO.'

'Did someone say my name?'

The shiver turned into the cold grip of dread.

'Angela, you're here.'

Everyone in the office looked up at once as Cici Spencer, my former assistant, stepped out of the lift. I had to admit it, CEO looked good on her. She strode into her office wearing a sleek Tom Ford jumpsuit with at least twelve grands' worth of floral embroidered Alexander McQueen blazer casually slung on her shoulders. A pair of crystal-studded Gucci sunglasses perched on her surgically perfected nose, which she lifted up to the top of my head to look me up and down. I shifted my weight from foot to foot. I'd agonized over this outfit for days: Anine Bing booties, brand-new Topshop jeans, my favourite Equipment shirt. I was playing with fire wearing a silk shirt while breastfeeding but I'd done a literal

10

dry run and was wearing two pairs of breast pads so I was certain I could get away with it. My ensemble was comfortable, smart, no bold statements but enough style to let people know I was supposed to be there and hadn't got lost on my way to the Target in the Atlantic Mall.

I would never get lost on my way to Target. I loved Target.

'Here I am,' I said as I twisted my engagement ring around my ring finger.

'Here you are,' Cici said finally, lifting the sunglasses out of her silky straight, ice-blonde hair. 'And it's OK, we don't have a dress code.'

I would not rise to her bait. I was the one who had agreed to come and work for my former-nemesis-turned-assistant-turned-sort-of-kind-of-friend  and there was no point acting surprised when a leopard showed its spots. Not that Cici would be caught dead in leopard print these days, far too common.

'I also hear you don't have offices. What's that about?'

'I have an office,' she shrugged, letting her black Valentino tote bag slide off her shoulder and into the crook of her arm. 'Everyone else lives here.' She waved at the mass of desks behind me, randomly placed around the room, some at seated level, some raised to standing. 'Our director of culture said this was the best way to nurture creativity.'

'But where will I put all my stuff?' I asked with a frown. She knew I needed my stuff. It was all essential to my process, from my signed framed photo of Robert Downey Jr to the Hannah Montana Magic 8 Ball I used to make any and all difficult decisions.

'Besson doesn't encourage personal artifacts at the work station,' Kanako recited from an invisible rule-book. 'A decluttered environment promotes a more efficient workflow.'

I felt a dark look cross my face.

'If any so much as thinks the words "spark joy" I'm going home.'

She shrugged and turned back to her computer. 'We all like it this way.'

*We.* There was a 'we' here and I, the new girl, was not a part of it.

'I'm sure I'll figure it out,' I said, my hand never leaving my satchel for fear of my photos of Alex and our daughter leaping out and exposing me to all the world for the hoarder that I was. 'Nice to meet you.'

'Let me know if you need me to show you around,' Kanako said without looking back.

It sounded like a nice thing to say but I could tell what she really meant was 'now go away'.

'I can give you the tour,' Cici offered as a short but beautiful man with a shaved head appeared at her side. 'Do I have time to give her the tour?'

'You have seventeen minutes until your conference call with the investors,' he replied, glancing down at a small tablet.

'Plenty of time,' she replied, shrugging off her bag and her sunglasses into the man's waiting arms. From the look on his perfectly symmetrical face, I had to assume he was her assistant. It was the exact same expression last seen on Bambi, right after his mother was killed.

'I'm Angela,' I said, holding out a hand to the assistant. He looked down at it, his own hands full of thousands of dollars of designer goods. 'It's my first day.'

'He knows who you are,' Cici said, already striding off to survey her domain. 'He's my assistant, he knows everything.'

I really hoped he knew how to write a CV and find a new job ASAP.

'Well, it's nice to meet you . . .'

'Don,' he replied before turning back to Cici. 'I'll put these away and prepare for the call.'

'Thanks, Don,' she smiled as he scuttled away before sighing and lowering her voice. 'It's so hard to find a good assistant. You were so lucky to have me.'

'Remember that time you had my suitcase blown up at Charles de Gaulle airport?' I replied, watching as he ran.

'No.'

It was a blatant lie. That was the kind of memory that kept Cici warm on the cold winter nights.

Before Besson, Cici and I had both worked at Spencer Media, one of the biggest publishers in the world, and a company founded by Cici's grandfather. When she told me she wanted to strike out on her own, I knew she'd find her feet but I hadn't realized just how fast she'd do it or how very big her feet would turn out to be. Within six short months, Besson had become a major player in digital media with some of the highest-trafficked sites in the US. While Cici could never claim to have been one of the world's best executive assistants, she certainly could boast an innate ability to throw her family's money at the most talented people in the industry, which resulted in absolutely brilliant content that was thriving in a market where everyone else seemed set to struggle.

'I'm so glad you're finally here,' Cici said as we made our way around the open-plan office. 'How is baby Ellis? Such a cool name. Alex pick it?'

'Ellis is a cool name but my baby is called Alice,' I answered, following her away from the hodge-podge of standing and sitting desks. 'She's named after my grandmother, actually.'

Fantastic. Now I was not only anxious about my first day at work, I'd also have to spend the rest of the morning wondering whether or not it was too late to change my baby's name.

'How old is he now? Like, three?'

'*She* is ten and a half months, remember? You were there when I took the pregnancy test. How fast do you think babies age?'

'Is that all? I guess they do say time flies,' Cici said with wide eyes. I could tell it was taking an awful lot of energy for her to show this much interest in my personal life and I appreciated it, even if I knew she didn't really give two shits.

'They do and it does,' I replied. 'But I'm excited to be here, back at work. I've been going kind of crazy at home, I can't wait to get stuck in with my site. I've got some really fun ideas—'

'Yeah, I'm sure they're great, that's why I hired you,' she interrupted. 'So this is the conference table where we have most of our editorial meetings.'

She paused in front of a giant slab of crystal, propped up on a metal frame. If Coachella made office furniture.

'The crystal channels your energies and creates a

more harmonious working environment,' Cici explained. 'And it cost thirty-five thousand dollars.'

'Bargain.'

'I got it from an artisan I met at Burning Man.'

'Of course you did.'

It really was just crying out for a ritual sacrifice with unicorn dip-dyed hair and a flower crown.

'Over by the elevators we have our reading rooms, our privacy pods and meditation centre.' She pointed at a row of frosted-glass doors. 'While we encourage all our team players to invest their energy in our open-plan dynamic, we understand sometimes they need privacy.'

'Oh yeah, sometimes,' I agreed, trying not to vom at the term 'team players'. I couldn't help but wonder which Instagram influencer she had hired to do her HR. 'Phone calls, difficult conversations, lactating.'

'Lactating?' Cici reared back as though I'd slapped her in the face.

'Breastfeeding,' I explained, making unnecessary honking motions in front of my own boobs. 'Or pumping, I suppose. I have to pump.'

'Still?' she screwed up her pretty face. 'Isn't it a little old for that?'

'Again, she, and again, not even eleven months,' I repeated, staring at the privacy pods and wondering how many times a day they were used for the very important purpose of crying at work.

'So gross,' she muttered, adjusting her own perfect B cups inside her Tom Ford jumpsuit. 'Anyway, this is where you would do that, I guess. The kitchen is right by the movement studio and the bathrooms, showers and dressing rooms are over there.'

She pointed off in the vague distance as I tried to log all the information. Things like this were more difficult to remember these days but I was fairly sure I'd be able to remember the place where the food was and where I needed to go for a wee.

'And before you freak out and call HR, it's one bathroom for everyone. That way no one can get offended.'

I lit up with a smile. 'Like *Ally McBeal*?'

Cici looked back at me, stony-faced.

'Don't make that reference again,' she warned. 'People know I hired you. Don't make me regret it.'

'I promise you will not be the one with regrets,' I assured her.

This was your choice, I reminded myself. You could have been sitting in your cosy office at Spencer Media right now but, nooo, you had to take a chance, you had to trust your gut and leave. Only my gut had a baby in it when I made that decision. It couldn't be trusted. I should have been stopped.

'And that's it. I'm sure corporate culture went over the basics with you: no official start and finish hours, vacation is taken as and when it's needed. We have a chef on staff to create round-the-clock snacks and beverages for all possible dietary restrictions and no orange in the office. I think that's it.'

'Sorry, what?' I said, tearing my eyes away from the man who had just arrived with a small pig on a leash. 'No oranges in the office?'

'No orange,' she repeated. 'The colour. I hate it so I banned it.'

Brilliant. Starting her own company definitely hadn't sent her mad with power.

'Right. So, is now a good time to discuss my ideas

for my site?' I asked as she started back towards the elevators. 'I have a name. It's going to be Recherché dot com, it's French and it can mean "to search for" or "exquisite", which I think is perfect, don't you? And content-wise—'

'Sounds great, go for it,' she nodded. 'Have the design team get started.'

'How do I get in touch with the design team?'

'They're in the directory,' Cici replied.

'And where is the directory?' I asked.

'On your computer?' she answered.

'And where's my computer?'

'I have to go to my office,' Cici said, folding her arms across her chest. 'I have a conference call.'

'I thought we didn't have offices,' I said as she pressed her fingertips against a touch screen to summon a lift.

'You don't, I do,' she replied. 'If you have any questions, please go talk to corporate culture. Otherwise, get started. I hired you because you're good at what you do so, like, do it?'

The lift dinged softly and I felt a wave of panic wash over me.

'But we haven't actually established what I'm here to do, have we?'

'You know, I think this whole mom vibe is working for you,' Cici said as she stepped into the lift. 'I mean, I get it. Once you have kids, it's hard to not be lame but you've really leaned in to mom-dom, Angela. Maybe you were fighting against this normcore vibe all along.'

Normcore? Did she just call me normcore? Admittedly I wasn't one hundred percent certain what it meant

17

but I was one hundred percent certain I should be offended. What did this woman want from me? Higher heels? Tighter clothes? Should I have whipped out the Sherbet Dip that lived in the bottom of my handbag and pretended it was a gram?

'I'm going to go and find a desk,' I said, smiling politely as the lift doors closed on my smiling CEO. 'I'm so excited to get started.'

Hell hath no fury like a British woman mildly offended.

'Right,' I said, turning my attention back to the sea of desks in the middle of the bright room. Squeezing the strap of my satchel, I steeled myself and entered the fray, looking for an empty desk. Note to self, buy Apple AirPods on the way home. All the cool kids at school had AirPods.

'Work,' I corrected myself under my breath. 'Not school, work.'

Only this felt very reminiscent of my first day in sixth form when absolutely everyone else had Doc Martens and I was wearing Converse and I never, ever lived it down.

Things are different now, Angela, I thought to myself. You're a married woman. Living in New York. You've got a cool job in the media, loads of interesting friends and an actual baby. You are a parent. If you can heave a living being out of your vagina and make it home from the hospital in time to watch *RuPaul's Drag Race*, you can certainly make it through your first day back at work.

I smiled, settling on a desk right by a window that looked out over Lower Manhattan. There, wasn't so hard, was it? And besides, it wasn't the first time I'd thrown myself head first into a situation with no idea what I was doing and I'd always survived before. Just barely on occasion but I'd always figured it out, one way or another.

'This is going to be brilliant,' I said out loud to the city below. 'Just you wait and see.'

# CHAPTER TWO

'I'm home, I'm home,' I wailed as I barrelled through the door, closing it firmly on a day I was keen to leave behind me. 'Sorry, I totally lost track of time and the subway ran local and I had to stop to buy wine and tell me she's not asleep already.'

Dropping my satchel on the dresser by the door, I kicked off my boots and looked up to see the most gorgeous man to have ever lived, holding Alice Clark Reid, no hyphen, the best baby in existence, standing in front of me. Admittedly, there was a chance I was a little bit biased on both counts because they were both mine.

'Hey,' Alex whispered, handing over the milk-drunk bundle of soft, sleepy wonderment. I met his green eyes as I took my daughter's weight and felt my day fall away. 'She's still kind of with us. I just gave her a bottle and we were just about to go to bed. How did it go?'

'I've no idea what I'm doing, Cici is worse than she's ever been, I forgot to lock the door of the privacy pod while I was pumping and so the entire office has already seen my tits *and* I dropped my phone in the toilet before I'd even got into the office,' I replied, checking Alice still had all ten toes I'd left her with that morning. 'Does she look bigger to you? She looks bigger to me.' I rubbed my cheek against her fine baby hair.

'Yes,' he replied. 'She waited until you were gone this morning and, boom, she shot up half an inch. It was incredible.'

I flashed him a look but it was a look tempered with a smile. I already felt so guilty for leaving her and it was only one day. Christ, the next twenty-one years were just going to fly by, weren't they?

'Sounds like you made a good first impression. Did you say you brought us wine?'

'Yes but Alice has to wait until she's fifteen, just like Mummy did,' I replied softly, tilting my head back for a kiss as I continued to stroke Alice's hair. I still couldn't quite believe I had made something quite so brilliant. Admittedly she was occasionally revolting, especially after we gave her avocado for the first time, but for the most part, she was incredible.

'I can't believe I married a teenage alcoholic,' Alex said, grabbing the woodwork around the doorframe and stretching his long, lean body. 'Let's hope she takes after Daddy and doesn't start drinking until she's twenty-one.'

'Yes, let's hope she takes after Daddy and runs away to join a band and shag everything on the Eastern Seaboard for a straight decade,' I muttered, covering Al's tiny ears. 'That'll look good on her college applications.'

Before we met, it was fair to say my husband had sown an entire field full of wild oats but, against all laws of god and man, I really didn't care. Alex was a vision. Tall and skinny with perfectly square shoulders

21

that were made for vintage T-shirts, beaten-up leather jackets and holding onto when we kissed. His skin was so pale, it was practically luminous, and the contrast of his jet-black hair only made his green eyes shine even brighter. And if that wasn't enough to get him laid, he had the uncanny ability to make absolutely everyone he met feel like they were the most important person on earth. Also he was a musician. In a band. In Brooklyn. That made money. Honestly, it would have been more worrying if he hadn't spent a good decade putting it about.

'Slut-shaming your own husband,' Alex said with a dramatic sigh as he leaned against the doorframe. 'Go put that baby to bed. I'm making dinner.'

'I always knew you'd make an amazing wife one day,' I called, doing as I was told and carrying Alice through to her bedroom. Was there anything more erotic than a man making you dinner when you were totally knackered? No, I thought not.

Our Park Slope apartment was easily my favourite place in the entire world. Bloomingdale's, Shake Shack and that random bodega that stocked Jaffa Cakes on 12th Street all ran a close second but, like, home is where the heart is and – more importantly – it was full of the best people and all my snacks.

Our place wasn't as swanky as Erin's West Village townhouse or as cool as Jenny's new Financial District loft but it was my home; all comfy sofas and soft rugs and prints and pictures and things that made me happy. And right in the heart of it all was Alice's room, a.k.a. the nursery of dreams. Alex had painted it four times before we found the perfect shade of pale pink, something that was harder to find than you might think. Of all the hills to die on, the colour of my daughter's bedroom had been a fight so many people had chosen to go to war over. Jenny wanted to paint it blue to defy the patriarchy, Delia said it should be green to stimulate intellectual development, and my mother, despite saying she didn't think it mattered one way or the other, had fourteen litres of Farrow & Ball 'Middleton Pink' shipped over from England in an attempt to instil some regal British backbone into her long-distance grand-daughter. Unfortunately, when we got it on the walls, it looked a little bit like we'd dipped a brush into a bottle of calamine lotion that had gone bad in 1987 but, as far as Mum was concerned, Alice was absolutely sleeping in a nursery painted in a random shade of pink chosen by someone in marketing who wanted to make a quick buck off the royal family.

But far and away my favourite part of the nursery was Alice's wardrobe. It turned out almost all designers made baby clothes. Teeny, tiny versions of their adult togs that were so much more affordable than their grown-up counterparts. There was no way I could spend three thousand dollars on a Gucci sweater for myself but two hundred dollars on a romper for the best-dressed baby in town? Um, yes. Al was already a sartorial masterpiece. Even though all she did was throw up on them. Actually, throwing up was best-case scenario. If I'd done what she did while decked out in head-to-toe Stella McCartney, I'd never have been able to look at myself in a mirror again.

'But it's OK when it's you, isn't it?' I whispered, pulling back the sheets and laying her down gently. Crouching down at the side of the cot, I stared at her through the wooden bars of her tiny baby prison. Every night I wondered when I would get bored of this but it hadn't happened yet. Al turned her head to look at me, fixing me with the same green eyes as her daddy. The spit of Alex, people said – his hair, his eyes, his full lips – but every so often, I could see a flash of myself in there. Usually when she was hungry or angry or both. Which made perfect sense, really.

'So, do you think you're going to sleep through tonight?' I asked with the newfound optimism I'd discovered immediately after pushing eight pounds and six ounces of human being out of my body. Would she sleep through the night? Probably not! Would I keep hoping she might? Yes! For all eternity!

When she didn't reply, just blinked her long lashes at me and gave a sleepy smile, I pulled the covers up over her little legs and thought of all the things I'd learned in the last year that had never even occurred to me before. Like baby pillows. I'd searched high and low. Looked in the shops, I'd checked online, I'd even turned to Etsy, but it turned out babies don't have pillows, only a mattress. Who knew? And then it was the quilt. Some people said they could have quilts, other people said they couldn't. Louisa said she used a sleeping bag but Erin said sleeping bags would be too much in my apartment because it got so hot. My mum said I had a home-knitted blanket and I'd been lucky to even have that . . . Life was a lot easier when the only things I searched for were discount Marc Jacobs handbags and photos of Chris Hemsworth with his top off.

'She didn't really nap this afternoon so she should sleep OK,' Alex said as I tiptoed into the living room once Al was fully asleep. 'We went for a walk around the park but she would not give it up. I think she was hoping to get a glimpse of Patrick Stewart.'

He smiled at me with heavy-lidded eyes, put a glass of red wine in one of my hands, the TV remote in the other then disappeared back into the kitchen. If that wasn't my most intense sexual fantasy, I didn't know what was.

'Her and me both,' I said, setting down the remote and following him into the other room. 'You were all right today, though? I'm sorry I didn't text as much as I said I would. My phone wouldn't turn on so I had to text from my laptop and—'

'You sent thirty-seven texts,' he replied, taking a sip from his own fingerprint-smudged glass. 'How many times were you planning on sending?'

I shrugged, peering into a bubbling saucepan. Ooh, pasta. The deal for now was I would go to the office Monday to Thursday and work from home on Fridays. While he wasn't away on tour, Alex would be home with Al Mondays and Tuesdays and the part-time nanny we shared with Sasha and Banks, a couple from my antenatal group, came by Wednesday and Thursdays so he could, in theory, get on with writing his new album.

In theory.

'Did Graham come over?'

Alex shook his head and snatched his fingers back from the spitting pan.

'He and Craig are gonna swing by tomorrow. We've gotta figure out the set, make more time to rehearse. It's creeping up on us real fast, we've only got three weeks.'

In an attempt to get themselves back into the creative flow of things, the band had announced a hometown show, their first in more than a year, supposedly to try out new material. Only there was no new material. And the show was in less than three weeks. Unless Alex was planning on rocking out some adult-oriented rock covers of 'Baa Baa Black Sheep', he definitely had an uphill struggle in front of him.

'You look so good today.' Alex tossed a tea towel over his shoulder and looked back at me. 'Did you get your hair done or something?'

'I washed it,' I whispered brazenly. 'And then I brushed it.'

'That is so hot,' he replied, leaning over to press his mouth against mine in a decadent red wine kiss. 'You want to blow off dinner and go straight to bed?'

'What's for dinner?' I asked, breathless from the kiss.

'My celebrated spaghetti in sauce from a jar and pre-shredded cheese.'

It really was a difficult choice.

'Will you still love me if I say dinner first and then bed?'

Alex took the spaghetti off the stove and dumped it into the colander that waited in the sink.

'I would love you even more than ever,' he replied, clearly relieved. 'I didn't sleep last night at all and with Al not taking a nap all day, I'm exhausted. I'm so tired I don't even think I could get it up.'

'Oh good,' I muttered as I remembered I hadn't shaved my legs in over a week. Because we hadn't had sex in over a week. Or was it two weeks? Maybe more.

'What's up?' Alex asked.

'Nothing,' I replied, replacing my frown with a grateful smile. 'Hey, do you know what normcore means?'

Even though I'd always thought of myself as someone who prized sleep above almost everything else in life, ever since Alice came along, I had found myself awake at two thirty in the morning, right on the dot. Almost every night, I found myself lying in bed wide awake, even when Al slept straight through. Always looking for a silver lining, I tried to fill these weird little moments of me time with useful tasks, like watching YouTube videos and eating.

'And then she called me normcore,' I whispered into my headphones as I prowled around the kitchen, looking for snacks.

'Well, I don't know what that is but it doesn't sound very nice,' Louisa said, her lovely face looming large on my iPhone screen. 'Tell her to sod off.'

My absolute favourite thing to do with this unwanted gift of useless time was to call one of my best humans in the UK and interrupt her breakfast routine. I watched over Louisa's shoulder as my six-year-old goddaughter, Grace, merrily poured herself a red Le Creuset mixing bowl full of cereal behind her mother's back.

'Do you think my life has got boring?' I asked, dreading the answer to my question. Louisa had known me forever and she wasn't terribly good at sugarcoating.

'If your life is boring, I should take myself down to the glue factory right now,' she replied. 'Listen to yourself, woman.'

'I suppose you're right.' I opened the fridge and pouted at the miserable contents. I would not be reduced to eating a pouch of pureed baby food. Again. 'My life is amazing. This is the first week I've felt like I'm getting myself back, you know? I actually feel like myself again.'

'I remember trying to renew my passport when Grace was six months and Tim came home to find me sobbing on the settee,' Lou replied. 'I was so broken I couldn't remember my middle name. You're definitely doing better than me.'

'I'm not completely on top of it,' I admitted. 'I'm knackered all the time and I can't get through a full set of adverts without crying and I have to unfasten the top button on my jeans by lunchtime every day, but other than that, yeah, I think I'm there.'

'I thought you said you'd lost all the baby weight?'

'This body grew a baby and I will not be fat-shamed by you or anyone,' I replied, trying to look as indignant as possible for someone who had already eaten three Penguin biscuits before calling. 'And for your information, I did get rid of all the baby weight but I replaced it with Christmas weight and the pastries-from-the-new-coffee-shop-that-just-opened-round-the-corner weight. Plus, I feel like everything has moved. Pregnancy is rude, why couldn't it put everything back where it found it?'

'It's all a matter of discipline, Ange,' replied the woman who still weighed exactly the same as she did on her wedding day and tried on her wedding dress once a month, every month, to confirm it. 'Just eat less and move more. Dead simple.'

I was about to give her my best snappy comeback when Gracie splashed an entire four pints of milk into her mixing bowl.

'Does Gracie always make her own breakfast?' I asked innocently.

Louisa glanced over her shoulder then immediately did a double take.

'Oh, fuck,' she grunted, dropping her phone on the kitchen table. I smiled happily at her faux gabled ceiling as the wailing started across the room.

'I'm going to have to call you back,' Lou said, her face sweeping across the screen. 'There's bloody Coco Pops everywhere.'

'Wait, you said you wanted to ask me something,' I reminded her. I'd woken up to several WhatsApp messages, which usually required me to find some bizarre toy like a WTF doll or some such shite that was already sold out in England – but such were the responsibilities of Cool Aunt Angela in America.

'Honestly, I'd forget my head if it wasn't screwed on,' Louisa said while Gracie continued to wail in the background. 'I'm coming to see you!'

'You are?' I opened the fridge and grabbed the pouch of baby food. 'All of you?'

'No, just me,' she explained. 'Tim and I were supposed to be off on a dirty weekend but he's been pulled into a work conference. Figured I'd abuse his air miles and get some quality BFF time in.'

'Sounds lovely,' I replied. 'Clearly Gracie can be left alone to look after herself.'

'Grace is going on a pony camp with her friend Lily and her mummy,' she said loudly. 'If she behaves and stops crying and eats her breakfast like a good girl.'

'I h-hate i-i-it,' I heard Grace stammer through choked sobs. 'I w-want my Coco Pops.'

'What have you given her?' I asked, peering at the tiny, tear-stained face behind my friend.

'Coco Pops,' she replied with a sigh. 'But she wants them in the mixing bowl. Tim put them in there months ago so they could share and now she insists on it every single day. Because some daughters don't realize there's seven quids' worth of cereal and milk in that bowl and some fathers laugh at them every time they do it, which just encourages said daughters.'

'Which ends up with said mothers going completely bonkers,' I finished for her. 'So, I am getting the feeling you could use a weekend away. When were you thinking of coming?'

Louisa's entire face broke out into a bright, happy smile.

'Weekend after next,' she said. 'I've already booked it, had to grab the seat while it was available. I will see you a week on Thursday!'

'A week on Thursday!' I forced the corners of my mouth up into a smile while my heart began to beat faster. 'That is very soon and specific and what were you going to do if we weren't here?'

'Where else would you be?' she scoffed. 'There's no running off all over the world these days, Angela. You've got a baby now. Even if Alex goes off on tour, you're going to be at home, aren't you?'

I sucked in my bottom lip and bit down hard.

'I'm so looking forward to it. I can't wait to give Alice a squidge.' Lou smiled so happily, I couldn't help but smile back. 'Some proper quality time with my two favourite girls.'

Right on cue, Grace began to wail from her spot at the kitchen table.

'My favourite girls other than you,' Louisa yelled, shaking her head at me and frantically waving. 'Say bye-bye to Auntie Angela.'

The call ended abruptly, leaving me all alone in the dark kitchen with a phone in one hand and a pouch of pureed apples and plums in the other. I unscrewed the cap on the pouch with my teeth and squished half of it into my mouth. Alex liked to make his own fruit purees but there wasn't always time and, though I didn't have the heart to tell him, Alice definitely preferred these to his homemade efforts. Also, I knew it was petty but sometimes his perfect father routine was ever so, ever so very slightly grating. No matter what my mother, his mother, fourteen thousand mummy bloggers and Gwyneth Paltrow said, a couple of store-bought processed fruit pouches weren't going to kill her or me.

I pushed the door to Alice's room open, just a fraction. The calming blue light from her humidifier cast just enough of a glow for me to see her peaceful, sleeping face. I smiled and fought the urge to go over and stroke her little pink cheek.

'I will always let you have a mixing bowl full of Coco Pops for breakfast, even if Daddy says no,' I whispered, closing her door and tiptoeing back into my bedroom. I plugged my phone into its charger and slid under the covers, curling myself around Alex's sleeping body and burying my face in the nape of his neck, waiting for sleep to come back to me.

# CHAPTER THREE

'So do you think it's better to split the site into sections or just use tags?' I asked Ramon, head of design, as we stared at three different screens, each showing a dummy mock-up of my new site on Wednesday afternoon. 'Maybe a floating menu at the top of the page—'

Before I could finish the thought, my screen froze and the disembodied head of our fearless leader appeared in front of me. Cici, the great and terrible.

'Can you come up to my office?' the head requested.

'Now?' I asked. 'I'm in the middle of something.'

The head smiled.

'Hit the penthouse button in the elevator, it'll bring you straight up.'

The head disappeared.

'Don't go anywhere,' I said to Ramon as I gathered my notebook and a pen. 'I'll be back in a minute.'

'No, you won't,' he replied. 'But I agree you need a drop-down menu. I'll figure it out.'

\*

'You decided to keep things low-key in here then?' I said as Don let me in, only stopping to pick my jaw up off the floor. Cici shrugged, seated in what had to be a custom-built chair behind what had to be a custom-built desk. Although it wasn't really a chair, more of a throne that had mated with a tube of Ruby Woo lipstick on the set of a Lady Gaga stage show. A huge, glossy pop of colour in the otherwise all-white office with views out over the East River. She'd always been destined for an office like this, I realized, high in the sky and looking down on New York. She was born for it.

'What's up, boss?'

She gave a happy shimmy as I sat myself in one of the butter-soft white leather chairs on the opposite side of a crystal desk.

'I do love hearing that,' she said, nodding when Don appeared with two glasses of water and placed them on the coasters before scurrying away without a word. 'Here's the thing. It's been a really fun six months doing literally everyone's job for them but I need someone else to oversee the editorial because, like, I don't want to do it any more. I really like being the CEO but I don't want to have to deal with all the, you know . . .'

'People?' I suggested.

'Exactly,' she agreed, slapping the air for not getting it as quickly as I did. 'The people. And the actual work. It's really not my thing. Someone else needs to deal with the day-to-day running of the sites. I don't have the time to sit in editorial meetings, pretending to give a shit.'

There was an argument to be made that honesty wasn't *always* the best policy. I'd known Cici for years but that didn't mean I was always ready for her blunt-ness. All the diplomacy genes had gone to her identical twin, Delia, in the womb but what Cici lacked in subtlety she made up for in . . . well, nothing good.

'Someone has to give a shit,' I told her. 'You're ultimately responsible for what you're putting out.'

'Exactly, that's the problem. I hire people because they are the best at what they do but they're always asking for my approval on every last little thing. It's a huge turn-off,' she sniffed. 'So we're creating a new role to deal with it.'

I straightened up in my chair as far as my high-waisted jeans would allow. I'd made a mistake abandoning my maternity jeans already and I knew it.

'I'm hiring a VP of content.' She leaned back in her lipstick throne and fixed me with her steady gaze. 'What do you think?'

Biting my lip, I considered my answer. I thought it was a great idea but I also knew I didn't want to do it. I left my last job when it became too corporate and I wasn't ready to sign up for an even bigger, even more management-y role. I wanted to come in, write stories I cared about and go home at the end of the day, wondering why my brain made up words like manage-ment-y. I wanted to see my husband, hang out with my friends, put my baby to bed every night and still have time to binge on Netflix and eat an entire pizza. Taking on a bigger job would put all of that at risk, especially the Netflix and the pizza, and I just wasn't having it.

'I think it's brilliant,' I said, trying to come up with the most gracious rejection I could. Cici was not someone I wanted as an enemy. Again.

'Right?' she said, letting out a sigh of relief. 'So, you

might think this is crazy but you were the first person HR suggested for the role.'

'Me?' I gasped with fake surprise. There were no Oscars in my future.

'Yeah but I told them you wouldn't be interested so they found someone in the London office. I interviewed her yesterday and she's starting next week.'

Oh.

'They were all crazy about hiring internally, and obviously you have experience at this kind of thing, but I know it's not what you want to do,' Cici said, tapping her finger aggressively against the trackpad on her computer to bring it to life.

'No,' I agreed, fighting my FOMO. 'It's not what I want to do.'

But it would have been nice to have the chance to turn the job down.

'You're going to love Paige,' she went on, eyes scanning her inbox as she spoke. I could tell her attention was already elsewhere. 'You guys have a ton in common. She's British, you're British. She worked at Spencer UK, you worked at Spencer US.'

I raised an eyebrow.

'She's a little younger than you,' Cici said as she tapped away at her keyboard. 'And she comes from more of a fashion background so she's, you know, cool. And she has really great ideas. And hair. Fantastic hair. So not, like, everything in common, I guess.'

I'd never heard Cici be so complimentary about anyone. For the first year I'd known her, she would only refer to me as the 'girl who turned men gay', which wasn't even true. All I did was encourage a very famous, supposed shagger of an actor to come out, which was, in hindsight, a total blessing in disguise. These days we'd just post a 'hashtag live your truth' pic on Instagram with seventeen rainbow emojis and no one would say a single thing about it, but back then it was kind of a big deal.

'Since you did the whole London to New York thing, I'd love for you to help her out for the first few weeks,' she said, forcing her features up into a cheerful smile. 'Make sure she settles in right.'

Oh good, another job for me. So, on top of looking after my actual baby, I now had to babysit a younger, more fashionable, more senior version of myself who had better hair as well.

'I can't wait to meet her,' I replied, focusing on the giant Andy Warhol original behind her desk. Even though Cici was right, I wasn't interested, for some godforsaken reason, tears were burning at the edges of my eyes. My emotional response to any given situation had been out of control ever since I found out I was pregnant. Alex had already banned me from watching any and all reality TV after finding me in floods of tears after my favourite bladesmith was eliminated on an episode of *Forged in Fire*.

'I can't wait for her to start dealing with all these whining editors,' she replied, leaning her head to the left and digging her fingers into her shoulder with a pretty grimace. 'I have legal meetings all day and I don't want to have to OK another feature on leather pants for summer, yes or no.'

'Is everything OK?' I, a whining editor, asked, my tears disappearing as quickly as they had arrived. 'With the company, I mean?'

'Everything is great,' she nodded. 'But the investors

need to hear me say that a thousand times a day and I don't appreciate a bunch of old men in suits assuming I don't know what I'm doing just because I'm young and beautiful. They're a nightmare,' Cici groaned, pressing her perfectly manicured fingertips into her temples. 'I'm, like, you gave me the money, I'm doing my job, now go away please.'

'Oh, I can imagine,' I said with an uncomfortable chuckle. I could not *even* imagine. 'What's a few million dollars between friends?'

'Exactly. I should have funded this whole thing myself. It's just all so *much*.'

I was well aware that Alex and I were a lot better off than most people. But for the most part, my money went on impossibly dull, everyday things Cici wouldn't have been able to fathom. The last thing I'd funded myself was a chocolate croissant.

'Jumping from assistant to running an entire company is a lot,' I reasoned. 'But you know you're doing an incredible job, everything is going so well.'

'I know,' she replied without a hint of even false modesty. 'And you would think I'd have more to do now but I really don't. When I was your assistant, I had so many different things to do every day. Like, a thousand dumb tasks.'

I resisted the urge to point out how few of those tasks were ever actually completed.

'But now it's bigger-picture stuff. I don't have so many things to do but the things I do have are intense. Sometimes it's exhausting, all this power.'

She closed her eyes and smiled like a shark, only Cici Spencer was a thousand times more dangerous than any Great White.

'I'm sure you went through this when you were younger. I mean, people don't talk to you like you're dumb now, do they? It's terrible that we should have to wait until we're in our forties to be taken seriously, totally sexist.'

'Cici,' I said, clearing my old crone throat before I spoke. 'I'm not in my forties. You're three months older than me.'

'Oh, Angela.' The look on her face was one of pure horror. She waved a hand in front of her own visage to make sure I knew just what had offended her so greatly. 'What happened?'

For just a moment, I allowed myself to revel in the memory of that one time I'd punched her at a Christmas party. It wasn't an act I was proud of but it was something that gave me great comfort in trying times. Like this.

'Remind me to get you a certificate for Botox for your next birthday,' she said, still utterly aghast.

'So, work on Recherché is going well,' I said, attempting to redirect the conversation before I lamped her. I looked young for my age, everybody said so. Not that it mattered but still. 'We should be ready to go live in a week or so.'

'Awesome, sounds great, can't wait to see it.' She held up her hand to quiet me as she stared directly at my face. 'Are you *sure* you're only thirty-five?'

'I'll be back downstairs if you need me,' I said, standing up to leave. 'I'll try not to bother you in the meantime.'

Because really, if you'd already punched someone once before, did it really count if you punched them again?

# CHAPTER FOUR

'I thought you'd stood me up,' I said, manhandling Jenny in a massive hug after she'd run down the street, fifteen minutes late for our dinner reservation. 'Again.'

'That was one time,' she told me, shame-faced and shiny-eyed. 'I'm a busy gal. How is my favourite baby?'

'Ask me when my scalp stops throbbing,' I replied as I pressed my fingers into my temple. Alice was going through a grabbing phase and I did not care for it one bit. 'Alex says you can't see the bald patch but I don't trust him.'

Jenny peered into my hair, giving it a thorough check. When you couldn't trust your husband not to lie, only a best friend's opinion would do.

'You're good. It's red, though. She's getting strong.' She linked her arm through mine and started leading me down an exceptionally murdery alleyway. I hadn't seen Jenny in forever but that didn't mean I wanted to be led to my untimely death just to get in some non-baby friend time.

The sun was setting and we were deep in the middle

of an industrial area I had never been to before and, god willing, would never visit again. According to Google Maps, the address Jenny had given me didn't exist and so I'd already let myself into a lumber store, a ceramics studio and something they'd told me was doggy daycare – but, since I hadn't seen a single dog or dog-related item, I was fairly certain had been a meth lab. Alex would be so annoyed if I got killed the week the nanny was off.

'Where are we?' I asked as Jenny rapped three times on a bright red door.

She turned back to look at me over her shoulder, with a half-smile on her face and dark brown eyes full of mischief. 'Are you ready for an adventure?'

'I'm ready for my dinner,' I replied, pressing a hand against my empty belly. 'Seriously, I'm starving. You promised me a feed, Lopez.'

'I promised you an *experience*,' she replied. The red door opened and a tall, very serious-looking Asian man appeared. He was wearing an exquisitely cut black suit, black shirt and black tie and I suddenly wasn't sure my absolutely adorable blue Faithfull shirt-dress and shiny white Converse were going to pass the dress code.

'Welcome to Fukku Rain to Shinkā,' he said, looking us both up and down and frowning at my choice of shoe. I was correct. 'You have a reservation?'

'Lopez, for two,' Jenny said. 'Riverside.'

'Riverside?' I whispered as the man nodded once and held open the door. 'Is that some sort of password?'

'Not quite,' she whispered back. 'Relax, this is going to be a night you will never forget.'

I immediately tensed up from head to toe. When

40

Jenny promised an unforgettable evening, someone either usually ended up at karaoke until three a.m., face first in the bottom of the Bellagio fountains, or moving to Los Angeles. And given that the last thing I'd done before leaving the house was apply calendula cream to my cracked boobs while Alex quietly sulked about me going out, none of those options seemed particularly favourable.

'Not to be a Debbie Downer but I can't be out super late,' I said. Managing expectations was key with Jenny. 'Alex is exhausted from being at home with Alice all week.'

'Angie, it's Wednesday,' she whispered as we followed the host through a heavy black velvet curtain and into a tunnel so dark I couldn't see my hand in front of my face. 'And Monday was a holiday so you weren't even at work.'

'Well, he's tired and I don't want to take the piss,' I said, stumbling over something unseen. 'Are you sure about this?'

'Positive,' her voice confirmed somewhere in the darkness ahead of me. 'You're gonna flip.'

'Only if I don't fall first,' I corrected. 'I've got a bag full of Ikea tealights at home, I'd have brought some if I'd have known.'

'We have arrived.'

The darkness was split by a sliver of something like daylight as the host pulled back another black curtain at the end of the tunnel.

'Please, choose your vessel.'

I blinked as my eyes adjusted to the light and then again to make sure I wasn't seeing things. As far as I could tell, we'd only walked a few feet but somehow we had been transported to another world. I took a step forward onto a rickety wooden dock that jutted out over an actual river. Flowing water ran all the way around the room, surrounding a miniature island that was covered with full-size cherry trees, and dotted between the trees were a number of tiny tables, glowing with the light of a dozen candles. So, they didn't need my Ikea tealights after all.

'Well?' Jenny said, nudging me towards three little wooden rowing boats tied up to what looked like an ancient dock in front of us. 'Choose your freaking vessel.'

'We have to row to dinner?' I asked, as a tiny bird flew past my head. They had birds? Inside? Inside birds on purpose did not seem like the kind of thing that would get you a good grade from the New York department of health and safety. 'Jenny, is this the actual Gowanus Canal? Because you know that water has gonorrhoea, right? I mean, they tested it and everything—'

'Roberto will row the boat,' the host explained with a small bow, gesturing towards what was quite clearly a male model, wearing nothing but a pair of gold swimming trunks. Either someone's encyclopaedia had its pages stuck together or they'd been doing far too much coke when they came up with the idea of this place.

'We'll take this one.' Jenny pushed me down the dock and hopped into the boat, spreading her gorgeous scarf-print dress around her on her seat. 'Angie, can you take a picture?'

She leaned forward to hand me her phone before positioning herself in the boat, lifting her chin and reclining seductively.

'I'm real sorry but we don't allow photos inside the forest,' Roberto explained in a thick Texan drawl. Holding my breath, I waited for Jenny to scratch his eyes out but, instead, she simply sat up straight and nodded, her face a study in seriousness.

'Of course,' she said, snatching back her phone and shoving it deep into her quilted Gucci camera bag. 'Totally get it.'

What was going on? Jenny was OK with being told she couldn't take photos? Everyone had officially gone insane. I looked down at the water and saw something dart underneath the boat.

'I'm sorry I don't want to panic anybody but I think I just saw something in the water.' Most likely gonorrhoea, I thought to myself. 'It looked like a fish?'

'Most surely was, Ma'am,' Roberto replied as he nonchalantly adjusted his package. 'How else are you gonna fish for your supper?'

'Jenny.'

'Angie?'

My heels were already starting to hurt, my stomach was howling with hunger and I was almost certain one of the tiny birds had already shat in my hair.

'Have you brought me to a restaurant where I have to catch my own fish before I can eat?'

'Technically, only if that's what you order,' she replied, hitting me with her biggest, brightest smile. 'But I ordered ahead so that is what you're going to do, yes.'

'I am going to die,' I muttered, gripping Roberto's arm tightly as I boarded. 'I cannot believe you brought me here.'

'You're so welcome,' Jenny said happily, taking my

43

hand and completely missing my point. 'It was not easy to get a reservation, believe me. But nothing's too good for girls' night, not for my Angie.'

I eyed her suspiciously. She was definitely up to something.

'I'll bet you one hundred dollars that one of us falls in the water before the night is over,' I replied, entirely unamused as we rowed across the moat. 'There's no way we're getting in and out of a place that serves booze *and* has a moat without one of us ending the evening piss-wet through.'

'Jeez, would you relax?' she huffed. 'This is the hottest restaurant in the world right now, it's booked up for months. Someone at work offered to get me into the Met Gala if I gave them our slot tonight.'

'Are you serious?' I asked. 'You passed up tickets to the Met Gala so we could fish for our dinner in Gowanus?'

Jenny shook out her lion's mane of chocolate-brown curls as the boat completed its brief journey and hit dry land. 'It isn't what it used to be,' she muttered as Roberto the golden-trunked gondolier helped her out of the boat. 'It's all Kardashian-Jenners these days. At best, you get Rihanna. Who tried to get a reservation here and couldn't, by the way.'

'Here we go again,' I replied, wobbling up and out. 'When will you stop the one-upmanship with Rihanna?'

'When she admits I gave her the idea for Fenty Beauty,' Jenny snapped. 'You were there, you know it's true.'

'If you're talking about the time you were so wasted you lunged at her when she was leaving Philippe

Chow and told her she was really hot and she should "do something with makeup", then, yes, I was there.'

With a dismissive huff, Jenny turned on her heel and walked off up the dock and into the forest.

The restaurant whose name I had already forgotten was beyond. There was lush green grass beneath my feet, a dusky sky complete with fluffy clouds above my head. I didn't understand it and I didn't care to. Now I was out the murder tunnel and on dry land, the only thing I could think about was food. I ducked to avoid a head-on collision with a passing butterfly as a beautiful redhead in full Geisha get-up tiptoed through the cherry trees towards us.

'Good evening, ladies,' the woman said, bowing her head slightly. 'We are so pleased you could join us on the island. I have you at one of our riverside tables this evening. Please follow me.'

At least the 'Riverside' bit made sense now.

I didn't dare ask if her ensemble was cultural appropriation as we followed her to our table because I was fairly certain it was and I was too hungry to get thrown out. She led us down a winding pathway through the trees until we reached a small table, right next to the water. I could see other tables dotted around the forest but the perpetual twilight meant I couldn't quite make out anyone else's face. I made a mental note to have a nose when I went to the toilet, just in case there were any proper celebs in attendance.

'Wait,' I said, clutching my non-existent pearls as Jenny took her seat and immediately started fannying about with the fishing pole resting next to her chair. 'Where *are* the toilets?'

'Our lounge is through the forest and over the

bridge,' the waitress replied, waving a graceful arm over yonder. 'It is gender neutral and paperless. Tonight we will start with our signature cocktail and feel free to begin fishing at your leisure. Please let me know if you require assistance on your journey.'

With a soft smile and a gentle nod, she disappeared back into the trees.

'This place is so very you,' I told Jenny, allowing her to believe it was a compliment. The restaurant, like my friend, was the very definition of the word 'extra'. 'What happens if I don't catch a fish? What happens if I do catch a fish? And what does she mean by a paperless toilet?'

'Half of me never wants to know and half of me so does. There's no menu, by the way. Everything other than the fish you catch is *omakase*, chef's specials, OK?'

'Not really but sure,' I replied, trying not to stare into the water. There. Was. An. Actual. Fish. 'So, I haven't seen you in a million years. What's going on with you?'

There was a time when I knew absolutely every thought that went through Jenny's head. Back when we lived together and spent all our nights watching *America's Next Top Model* and mainlining Ben & Jerry's, there wasn't a single second of a single day when I didn't know where she was, why she was there and what or who she was doing. Even when I'd moved in with Alex, we'd still managed to see each other all the time but, ever since Alice had come along, the amount of time I had to hang out with my friends, even my best, best friend, had been obliterated.

'Everything. Everything is going on,' she said, grabbing her napkin and flicking it out onto her lap. I did the same, knocked a pair of chopsticks off my plate and watched them roll onto the floor, down the bank and into the river. The evening was off to an excellent start. 'I've finally figured it out. I know how I'm gonna become the next Oprah.'

Jenny had been plotting to dethrone Ms Winfrey ever since we met. There was not a single woman on this earth who owned as many self-help books, went to as many workshops or generally went around giving out unsolicited advice. Not that I was complaining about her fabulous fairy godmother routine, it always worked out a treat for me. Well, almost always.

'Tell me everything.'

Jenny's beautiful face lit up with an excitement usually reserved for sample sales, Tom Hardy and other people's dogs.

'I'm starting a podcast!' she said, throwing her arms in the air, narrowly missing what looked awfully like Alec Baldwin's face by roughly three millimeters. 'Isn't it the greatest idea you've ever heard?'

'Oh my god, it is!' I gasped as she did a happy dance in her seat, inching ever closer to the edge of the water. I utched my own chair a few inches back towards safety. 'You're a genius.'

'So, I was running a few days ago and listening to a podcast and I was, like, dude, I should have a podcast! And now I'm officially a media mogul.'

'To be honest, I expected a more dramatic story,' I admitted, one eye on the fish that was having a good poke around at my submerged chopsticks. 'Does it have a name?'

Jenny tapped her fingers against the table in a mini drumroll.

'It's called . . . "Tell Me About It with Jenny Lopez",' she announced. 'I'm going to interview interesting people and get them to, you know, tell me about stuff. I already asked a bunch of people. It's going to be amazing.'

'I am so excited for you,' I said, meaning it completely. This was so entirely perfect for her, I couldn't believe we hadn't thought of it sooner. A microphone, a platform and a completely captive audience? She'd be president within a decade.

'I still have a few things to figure out.' She smiled at the waitress as she returned with two tall glasses of clear liquid that did not look even slightly like proper food. 'Like a studio and an editor and all the marketing, social media and graphic design. But other than that, I'm good to go.'

'Other than that,' I said, ignoring the tiny warning bells that had started ringing.

'And I don't know if you would know this but do you have any idea how you actually get a podcast online?' she asked, not a trace of irony on her face. 'Do I just send it to the podcast people and they do it all?'

Ring-ding-ding-ding-ding.

'Podcast people?'

'Ladies, this is a Chu-Hai Spritz,' the waitress said, setting the glasses down on the table. A fat lychee bobbed around in the top of each cocktail. 'Your first tastes will be out soon.'

I really hoped my first taste would be a full pizza.

'So, you're starting a podcast but you don't know how to record a podcast, market a podcast or share a podcast?' I asked.

Jenny shook her head and pushed her drink away.

'Is that lychee in there? I hate lychees. Oh, and I'm taking over EWPR while Erin and Thomas are in London. I guess I'm going to be really busy over the next few months.'

I grabbed my cocktail and took a deep, much-needed drink. 'I didn't know Erin and Thomas were planning a trip to London. How long are they off for?'

Jenny's eyes widened for a second.

'She hasn't told you?' she said, her voice lifted by surprise. 'They're moving. Thomas got transferred, they're leaving right after July Fourth.'

Erin wasn't just Jenny's boss at Erin White Public Relations, she was also one of our best friends. This was a lot to process on an empty stomach. I glanced off into the forest to see where our waitress was hiding. Just how much trouble would we get into if I broke out the emergency mini Twix I was hiding in my handbag?

'It's supposedly only for a year,' Jenny added. 'But she wants me to take over completely while they're away. Acting president.'

And to think I'd guessed it would take her another decade to earn that title.

'I'm gutted Erin is leaving but, Jen, that's amazing,' I said as she looked away, the big smile that had been on her face only a moment ago fading. 'Isn't it?'

Jenny ran her fingers through her curls and attempted to tuck her hair behind her ears as she took a deep breath in. It stayed in place for approximately three seconds before springing free as she breathed out, doubling in size as the curls bounced around her gorgeous face.

'I'll kill it, I know I will,' she said, more to herself than to me. 'But there's so much going on and, I don't know. I never even really wanted this job, you know? I fell into it by accident and now I'm running the show? There's so much I wanted to do this year, there's the podcast, we just moved into a new place and, I don't know. Other stuff that I can't do if I'm running a company.'

I reached across the table for her hand and put on my most supportive face. There was nothing I wouldn't do for my best friend. Except give her my secret Twix.

'You know I'm here for you. Anything you need, you've got it.'

The very second the words left my mouth, I knew I would regret them.

'There is one thing,' she said, turning back to face me with a different, more determined expression. 'I have a huge problem that needs fixing ASAP and I desperately need your help. You know Précis Cosmetics?'

I nodded. I did know. I had stolen loads of it from her office. Lovely lipsticks, terrible mascaras and EWPR's biggest account since forever.

'They're launching a new mascara.'

Good news.

'And we're hosting an influencer event for them in Hawaii.'

Bully-for-the-influencers news.

'And I have to go because Erin is house-hunting in the UK and my account director just quit to go and run a Christmas tree farm in Pennsylvania with her girlfriend.'

Oh god. I-know-exactly-where-this-is-going news.

I pulled my cocktail closer and sucked on the paper straw.

'What can I do? The last few years have been tough on people,' she replied with a shrug before pulling her phone out of her bag. 'Whatever, that's not the point. The original plan was, we were gonna take a bunch of YouTubers from around the world to Hawaii to promote it, but it turns out maybe one of them tweeted something about Nazis and maybe another one of them fat-shamed some chick from *America's Got Talent* and, the short version of my very long story is, the brand disinvited all the Americans and I have one week to find five people to take on an all-inclusive trip and I know I've barely had time to hang out lately but I'm going to make it up to you right now because you're totally coming with me on this trip.'

I continued to suck on my paper straw until my drink ran dry.

'May I refresh that for you?' the waitress asked, appearing out of thin air.

'Yes, you may,' I replied as she scooped up my glass and rested it on a small wooden tray. 'Jenny?'

She shook her head as she scrolled through her impossibly full inbox.

'Do you want something else?' I asked.

'Just a seltzer,' she replied with a sweet smile. 'I have a shit ton of admin to do when I get home.'

Even though I'd said I didn't want to be out late, it still stung to know I wasn't her only plan for the evening. While the chances of rolling out of our favourite karaoke bar at three a.m. were slim to none, it would have been nice to think it was still on the table.

'Come on, Angie.' As soon as the waitress was gone, Jenny hurled herself across the table, stretching out her arms until her phone almost touched my face. 'Look at this, tell me it's not heaven. Come through. Come through for your old pal, Jen.'

'Jenny, you're insane,' I said, slapping her phone away but not before I caught a glimpse of the photo she was trying to show me. Blue skies, white sand and a turquoise ocean that looked a million miles away from the East River. 'I can't just up and disappear to Hawaii. I have a baby and a job and, on top of that, Louisa is coming to stay next weekend.'

'That's perfect!' she said, snapping her fingers. 'Louisa can come too. Now we only need to find three other people. Anyone else unproblematic you can think of?'

'We're not coming,' I reiterated. 'What about Sadie? Précis would love that.'

'I said unproblematic,' Jenny replied, shaking her head. 'I had dinner with her last week and she was super excited because someone on Twitter said she was peak white feminism and she retweeted it thinking it was a good thing.'

'OK, so not Sadie,' I agreed. 'What about Eva from Evalution? She was at Spencer but she's gone back to doing YouTube full time. I'm almost certain she's entirely unproblematic. I can ask her if you'd like?'

'That would be amazing,' Jenny cheered, flicking through more photos. Oh, it did look pretty. 'So that's you, Louisa, Eva and we still have two open seats.'

'Four open seats,' I said. 'I'm not coming. And I haven't even asked Eva yet.'

'Angie, baby,' Jenny slunk out of her seat and crept

around the table, crouching down by my side. 'Just think about it. You, me, cocktails even more delicious than this one. Sun, sea, sand and a ton of free makeup.'

Hmm. I did enjoy free makeup.

'And it would be so great for your new website. I could set you up with an interview with the amazing woman who founded the brand, you could write travel pieces about Hawaii and we'll have make-up artists and a photographer there the whole time, taking millions of photos of you looking super awesome.'

I also enjoyed looking super awesome.

'Can't you imagine it?' she sighed, stretching her arm skyward to paint an imaginary picture. 'You, me and Louisa, sat on the deck of your private villa, sun slipping over the horizon with nothing but the warm, blue waters of the Pacific Ocean for as far as the eye can see. And then, at the end of the day, you hop in your personal hot tub and go to bed.'

I held a hand against my chest, my breath caught in my throat.

'Uninterrupted sleep,' Jenny whispered seductively. 'For five whole nights.'

The foul temptress.

'Jen, honestly, I can't,' I said, shaking myself to shatter her spell. 'If someone had told me having a baby would mean turning down a free trip to Hawaii, I'd have considered getting a dog instead, but she's ten months old now, it's a bit too late for me to do anything about it.'

'Bring her.'

I arched an eyebrow. 'Really?'

'No, not really,' she sighed. 'We're not insured for babies and I really don't know how I was planning to get out of that one if you'd said yes.'

I closed my eyes and chased any thoughts of white sandy beaches, cocktails served in coconuts and big, empty king-size beds out of my mind.

Jenny flopped down into the grass and sighed. 'I know it isn't as easy as it was before but come on, Angie. You could at least *ask* Alex. You could at least *find out* if you could take the time off of work. We used to have so much fun and now I never even see you.'

There it was. *Used to*. We used to have fun. And I'd looked up what normcore meant: it was just a sneaky hipster word for boring. Was that me from now on? A Used To Be person?

'I know this is a lot to ask but it would mean so much to me, for work and as a friend.' Jenny pushed herself up onto her knees, hands clasped together in front of her chest, her gorgeous silk scarf-print dress spread out around her like a sexy Gucci picnic blanket. 'Please, Angie, won't you just think about it?'

'Jenny,' I whispered.

'Yes?' she replied.

'You're awfully close to the edge of the water.'

'Oh shit!'

Jenny looked over her shoulder, losing her balance as she twisted. All at once, I grabbed for her hand as she grabbed the fishing pole stuck in the grass at the side of my seat, only for the line to suddenly come to life and pull her flat down on her face. Jenny had a bite. She landed flat on her stomach, her face inches away from the water as I launched myself out of my chair, rugby-tackling her around the waist and anchoring my friend to dry land.

'Let go of the fishing rod!' I yelled as whatever was

on the other end of the fishing line splashed furiously in the water.

'Don't let go of me!' Jenny screamed, thrashing around as though she was about to dredge up Moby-Dick. 'It's pulling me into the river!'

'It's not Jaws,' I shouted back, hoping that was true. I was scared, excited and still very hungry but even I didn't think I could eat an entire shark. 'Let go!'

'Here's your drin— oh, crap!'

But Jenny did not let go. And the waitress, delivering my fresh cocktail, did not see us sprawled out on the riverbank. I glanced upwards just in time to see the look of shock on her face as she tripped over Jenny's wildly kicking legs. She was not dressed for speedy reactions, her reflexes severely hampered by her heavy silk kimono and traditional wooden sandals, and before anyone could do anything she went flying. The cocktails went first, sailing over our heads and into the river. With one arm still wrapped around Jenny's waist, I threw the other up in the air, trying to catch her as she fell, but it was too late, she was already as good as gone. A swoosh of silk, a desperate cry and, finally, a very, very loud splash.

'Get off me!' she shrieked as Jenny and I attempted to pull her back onto the island. The river was only about knee-deep but that hadn't stopped her getting soaking wet from head to toe.

Across the way, Roberto the Rower and the man who had shown us down the dark, dark tunnel jumped into one of the row boats, manically trying to reach the waterlogged waitress.

'Are you all right?' I asked as she crawled out of the water. Jenny picked up one side of her sodden kimono and tried to wring it out with a helpful smile. The waitress waved her away, Jenny ducking just in time to avoid a damp slap.

'No, I'm not all right,' she yelled. 'Look at me. What the fuck were you doing on the floor?'

'What is happening?' The host from the front door stormed up the path, straightening his tie as he blustered onto the scene, Roberto and his gold trunks bringing up the rear.

'We really don't want to make a big deal about this,' Jenny said, clearing her throat and dusting herself off as she stood up. 'So we'll take a round of free drinks and everything's cool.'

The host fixed her with a steely glare the likes of which I hadn't seen since my mother caught me sneaking in through the living room window at three a.m. after I lost my keys at Peter Jensen's seventeenth birthday party.

'The sanctity of the forest has been disturbed,' he said calmly as the waitress hurled herself against Roberto's naked chest. Out of everyone, he didn't seem too mad about it. 'You need to leave.'

'You're kicking us out?' I replied, indignant and, more importantly, still starving. 'You're serving booze and charging people hundreds of dollars to play hook-a-duck in the arse end of Brooklyn and you didn't expect anyone to fall in, ever?'

'Angela Clark, you savage,' Jenny breathed in my ear before turning to the waitress with a sympathetic smile. 'We're really super sorry.'

'I'm not even a waitress,' she wailed. 'I'm an actress, this isn't what I do. I have six thousand followers on Instagram.'

Jenny looked over her shoulder at me, impressed.

'Wanna come to Hawaii?' she asked as the waitress turned out her pocket and dropped a tiny goldfish back into the river.

'Just get out before I call the cops,' the host ordered. 'Roberto, take them out the back.'

'Your loss, lady.' Jenny threw her hands up over her head and turned on her gorgeous red patent heel as we were escorted off the premises. 'For real, I can't give this trip away.'

'Come on,' I muttered, considerably less keen to make eye contact with the other diners than I had been when we arrived. Being marched through the kitchens and kicked out into a dustbin-filled alleyway was not how I'd envisioned my evening ending. 'Dinosaur BBQ is around the corner. Let's go and eat some proper food.'

'OK but you owe me a hundred bucks,' she said, curtseying at Roberto as he shrugged and then slammed the door in our faces.

'I do?'

'You bet me a hundred bucks that one of us would fall in the water by the end of the night,' Jenny replied, impossibly pleased with herself. 'And neither of us did.'

'Hmm.' I linked my arm through hers as we turned the corner back onto 3rd Avenue. 'I suppose I do. Look at us, growing as people.'

She grinned and gave my arm a squeeze.

'If you come to Hawaii, I'll let you off?'

I couldn't help but smile. 'If I pay for dinner will you shut up about Hawaii?'

'No, you're totally coming, doll. The sooner you accept it, the better.'

At least she'd been right about one thing, I thought as we walked on, arm in arm towards a plateful of pulled pork. It had certainly been a night I'd never forget.

# CHAPTER FIVE

Light was already beginning to seep in around the curtains when someone decided to lean on their car horn right outside my bedroom window at six a.m. on Thursday morning. I hated to start my days feeling homicidal but this was the price I paid to live in New York; occasionally, people were thoughtless dicks. Presumably there were thoughtless dicks everywhere but the horn honking really seemed much more prevalent here than anywhere else I'd ever been. Whether I liked it or not, I was awake and I knew the intelligent thing to do would be to stay awake. Either Alice or my alarm would go off by seven anyway and the extra hour would be meaningless, I'd feel worse than if I got up now. But I wasn't intelligent, I was exhausted. As I rolled over onto my side, pulling the duvet up under my chin, Alex curled around me, pressing himself into my back and giving me another bone to deal with.

'Alex,' I breathed into my pillow as he ran his hand under the covers, down my arm, my waist, my hip, tiptoeing his calloused fingertips across my leg and tracing circles on my thigh. 'I'm tired.'

He didn't say anything. Instead I felt his warm body moving against the curves of my back, his fingers sliding upwards under the edge of my shorts.

'It's so early,' I mumbled, smiling into my pillow.

'You don't have to do anything but lie there,' Alex replied, lifting my hair up at the nape of my neck and pressing his lips against my skin. 'Unless that sounds really creepy and you would like to be more actively involved.'

'That sounds like a very workable plan,' I replied, giving in as his hand slipped between my legs.

It had been a while since this had happened. And by 'a while' I meant more than month. I thought I knew what tired was before I had a baby – living with Jenny was hardly a relaxing experience, after all – but this was something else entirely. Motherhood utterly consumed me, mind, body and spirit. For the first six months, every ounce of my existence had gone into Alice and now, as I tried to pull back pieces of my life, I was even more exhausted than before. No matter what the baby books said, it was almost impossible to get yourself in the mood when you were so exhausted you felt like you were in a medically induced coma every time your head hit the pillow. No matter how hot your husband might be.

'Alex, wait,' I whispered, my voice catching in my throat as he pulled my T-shirt up over my head and the world turned pink for a moment as I untangled myself from the fabric.

'What's wrong?' he asked, stopping immediately.

Wrangling my T-shirt back down, I offered him my best apologetic grimace.

'I need a wee.'

Really I *had* to start working on my Kegel exercises.

'Give me two seconds,' I said, all arms and legs as I scrambled out the bed, running to the bathroom on tiptoes. A quick wee, a rinse around with mouthwash and, bloody hell, I thought as I caught sight of myself in the mirror, maybe we'll go for a once-over with the micellar water, given that I got approximately none of my mascara off before I went to bed. Motherhood meant multitasking and I was well into my second cleanse, sitting on the loo, when I heard Alice start.

'No, no, no,' I chanted, dropping pads of used cotton wool in the bin. 'Please go back to sleep. Mummy needs to get some.'

Looking down at my shorts and knickers, a pool of pale pink fabric on the bathroom floor, I sighed. My sleeping clothes were a sad state of affairs. I picked up the greying granny pants with my toe and tossed them in the trash, right on top of the cotton wool. So brazen for six o'clock in the morning.

As I washed my hands and combed my fingers through my bedhead, I realized Alice had stopped screaming.

'Thank you,' I said as I slicked on some lip balm. 'Mummy appreciates it more than you'd know.'

Except what Mummy didn't know was that Alice had only stopped crying because Daddy had brought her into bed.

'Alex,' I said from the bedroom doorway.

'She was crying. I couldn't leave her,' he said,

bouncing her up and down on his knee. 'I'll make it up to you later.'

With a frustrated sigh, I padded back to bed, sliding under the covers. It was true, Alex Reid was the greatest dad of all time. He had taken to fatherhood like a waitress to water, throwing himself head first into all things Alice from the very first day we'd brought her home. He was the one who said we didn't need a full-time nanny when I went back to work, he was the one who cleared out Barnes & Noble's parenting section, and I would be lying if I said he hadn't done more than his fair share of dirty nappies and three a.m. feeds. He'd even built a chute that ran out of her bedroom window and down into the bin so I could chuck her dirty nappies away without having to go outside in the winter. But the fact of the matter was, for one person to be the best at something, someone else had to be the worst.

Alex was a natural parent, I was not.

And it didn't feel good.

'Here she is,' he said, waving a sulky bundle of baby in my face. Softly shaking my head, I forgot my frustrations and snuggled into the family hug. Even though she was sleeping in the nursery, I loved how she almost always found her way into our bed in the mornings, all grumpy and fidgety and half-asleep.

'She always reminds me of you when she first wakes up,' Alex said, pulling the covers up over his long legs.

'Thanks,' I replied, running my fingertip along her tiny ear as her big green eyes watched me, cheeks flushed with crying. 'She always reminds me of you when she cries, it sounds like you singing.'

'Thank you for that vote of confidence two weeks out from my first show in forever. My baby's gonna be a rockstar.'

Stretching until my back cracked, I smiled and shook my head. 'Auntie Jenny says she's going to be a YouTube sensation.'

'Over my dead body,' he said instantly. 'She's going to be a rockstar. Or an astronaut. Only choices on the table.'

'What if she wants to do something really important with her life?' I countered. 'Like write amazing novels that are never appreciated in her lifetime? Or start an underground feminist magazine? Or open a cat café?'

'Also acceptable options,' Alex replied as Alice poked the blanket with great concentration and babbled to herself. We were so close to her first words I could feel it and every single atom of my body wanted that word to be 'Mummy'. I knew it wasn't a competition as to who she loved the most, but I also knew it totally was.

'Jenny wants to take me to Hawaii,' I said, resting my head against his chest with my eyes closed, synching my breathing with the reassuring thud of his heartbeat.

'And I was going to offer to take you to breakfast. Why does she always have to one-up me?'

'Because she's Jenny?' I suggested.

He nodded sleepily. 'When does she wanna go?'

'Next week,' I replied. 'For five nights.'

Alex and Alice both looked at me with their matching big green eyes and laughed.

'Sure. Classic Lopez.'

'It's a work thing, all expenses paid, fancy private

resort on one of the little islands,' I said, rolling onto my back and catching Alice's tiny toes in my hand. Alex closed his eyes and smiled. 'I told her I couldn't go.'

I looked over to check for a reaction but in the pale dawn light of our bedroom his face was perfectly still and his eyes were shut. He wove his fingers into my hair, running them from root to tip and then back again, sending happy shivers down my spine.

'You don't want to?'

'I would love to but I have work,' I reasoned. 'And Louisa is coming to stay and, you know, I have to keep a human being alive.'

'I don't know, Angela.' The corners of Alex's mouth turned upwards in a smile even though his eyes stayed closed. 'I think I can survive without you for five nights.'

'Ha ha, I meant Alice,' I said, propping my head up in my hand. Alex stayed exactly as he was, his chest rising and falling evenly with every breath. 'Although you would also be a concern.'

'I'm not the one who leaves their hair straightener on three times a week,' he reminded me. It was a harsh but fair point. 'If I had the opportunity to go to Hawaii on Lopez's dime, I would go. You'll be gone what, five days? Me and Al can cope on our own. You managed when I was gone for the weekend.'

'Yes but that was different,' I argued, reaching for a hair band from my nightstand and automatically pulling my hair up in a ponytail. Once the hair was up, that was it. I was officially awake.

Alex opened one eye and raised an eyebrow. 'How exactly?'

Don't say because I'm her mother, the voice whispered in my head, do not say because you're her mother.

'Because I'm her mother.'

Alex closed his eye and grinned. Alice said nothing.

'If you wanna to go, you should go,' he said through a yawn. 'When this record is finally finished, we'll definitely have to tour, and I'm not a parenting expert but I hear babies are a lot less trouble than toddlers, so consider this my pre-emptive apology for all the times she throws a tantrum when I'm off playing some rando festival in Germany two years from now. You were fine on your own, I'll be fine on my own.'

I rubbed my thumb against the band of my engagement ring and scooped Alice out of his arms, resting her against my chest.

'When you went away, I spent the entire weekend in my pyjamas,' I muttered, gazing down at my baby. 'I didn't shower, I only slept for six hours the whole three days and I took her to the emergency room when her spit-up was blue.'

'What was it?'

'I was so tired, I forgot I'd given her blueberries,' I said, stroking her delicate head. 'She was fine.'

'If she spits up blue, I'll shoot you a text,' Alex promised. Cradling Alice carefully, I reached for the edge of the curtain, pulling it back on what looked to be another extremely sticky day. Did Hawaii get as humid as New York? I imagined it was less of a concern if you were sitting on a beach in a bikini.

'I don't know,' I said, letting the curtain fall back into place, a shaft of daylight fading in and out across Alex's face. 'I can always go when she's older. Hawaii isn't going anywhere, is it?'

'Can't promise that,' he said with an uncertain shrug. 'Climate change is a real thing. Which reminds me, you have to start separating the recycling, babe.'

'I'm going to tell Jenny I can't go,' I said, thinking out loud and mentally listing all the reasons not to jump on a private jet to a five-star resort with my very best friends for five nights in paradise. 'I can't leave you two on your own. It's not fair.'

'Obviously, I would miss you, it's like we never have any time together, but that shouldn't stop you from going.' He turned over and covered his eyes with his forearm.

Well, that was considerably less encouraging.

'And, if I have to, I can always get my mom to come and help out.'

He could do what? I sat bolt upright, suddenly wide awake.

His mother? Just when I was starting to think about going . . .

'It's not that I don't like his mum,' I ranted into my phone the second I left the house. 'It's more that my entire body rejects the very concept of her existence.'

Louisa growled in agreement. 'So what you're saying is, you're not that close?'

'At our wedding, she asked me if I was marrying Alex for a green card. When I said I wasn't, she asked if I was pregnant. And then, when I was pregnant, she bought Alex a home paternity test, "just to make sure",' I replied, peeling off my denim jacket as I walked. It was only the end of May and summer was coming on strong. It seemed as though we were skipping spring and going straight into a three-month-long heat wave again this year. 'Every time they come over, she spends the entire visit telling me everything I'm doing wrong then goes, "I suppose that's the British way", before walking off in a huff.'

'If she's not careful, the British way will be me giving her a kick up the arse,' Lou said. 'And I thought Tim's mum was bad.'

'I don't know, what's the worst present you've ever had from Tim's mum?' I asked.

'Oh, I don't know.' She clucked her tongue as she considered. 'Probably the time she accidentally bought me a vibrator. The man in the shop convinced her it was a back massager. That was a bit awkward.'

'Alex's mum bought me a lifetime subscription to Weight Watchers for Christmas. While I was pregnant.'

Louisa gasped.

'And his dad's no better. They never gave a shit about Alex until we had Al and now they can't keep away, even though all they do is go on about how amazing his brother is and he's not, he's the worst human alive.'

'I already believe they're awful,' she laughed. 'No need for hyperbole.'

'He's an estate agent,' I said, pausing to check traffic before running across 8th Avenue. '*And* an amateur magician.'

'He must be kept away from Alice at all costs,' Louisa replied gravely. 'Have you considered a moonlight flit? Change your names and move back to England?'

'Yes,' I admitted ruefully. 'I actually have.'

'Well, far be it from me to tell you what to do but I do have to say, the idea of a weekend in Hawaii isn't the worst thing I've ever heard,' she said carefully. 'Not that I wouldn't be extremely happy to spend the weekend in New York with you and Alex but this trip does sound like a bit of a dream come true, doesn't it?'

I knew I shouldn't have told her.

'I've got to go,' I said, checking the address in the mysterious email I'd received a week ago. 'I've got a meeting before work and I'm already late. They bloody love a breakfast meeting around here.'

'It's hard to stay on schedule when you've got a baby,' she said. 'I'm sure they'll understand.'

'Keep your fingers crossed,' I said as I climbed the steps of 585 11th Street. 'It's some super exclusive mummy and baby club. They emailed me and Alex said I should meet them. He seems to think I need more mummy friends.'

'And so do I,' Lou replied. 'You can't keep refusing to socialize with other mums just because they sing different words to the "Wheels on the Bus". It's not good for Alice.'

'I'm not refusing to, it's just weird.' I shuddered at the memory of my one morning with the Park Slope New Parents group. Dairy-free, gluten-free, caffeine-free and fun-free. 'The groups here aren't like they are at home. I feel like I'm about to join a cult.'

'Then don't drink the Kool-Aid,' she instructed. 'And if you see any pictures of Tom Cruise on the walls, run for the hills.'

'Noted,' I said, pressing the doorbell and hearing a gentle chime echo on the other side of the door. 'Speak to you later.'

I slipped my phone into my satchel, gave my

underarms a surreptitious sniff and straightened my shoulders. Even though I was a grown woman with her own child and a husband and a job and a mortgage, whenever I was confronted with a group of women, especially mothers, I always felt like I was back in Year Seven, delivering a message to the sixth-form common room.

According to their website, The Mothers of Brooklyn, or M.O.B., was a non-profit parenting group, 'dedicated to supporting mothers and children through emotional support and growth', and according to their Twitter feed, they would be doing this by getting half-priced manicures at Gloss nail salon every Thursday morning from ten until two. The manicures I could definitely get behind, but the rest of it sounded a bit much.

After what felt like forever, a tall slim brunette opened the front door. She was impeccably dressed for eight thirty in the morning, wearing sky-blue Jesse Kamm sailor pants, a white silk T-shirt and a colourful statement necklace made of oversized crystals that Alice would have destroyed in seconds.

'Yes?' she said, giving me the same look I gave to the people who knocked at my door with a clipboard in their hand.

'Oh, hello,' I said, overcome with the utter certainty that I'd knocked on the wrong door. 'I'm supposed to be meeting Perry Dickson, I'm Angela. Angela Clark?'

The woman forced a smile onto her face and opened up the door fully, a cool blast of air conditioning making a break for the sweaty street.

'You're Angela Clark.' It sounded more like a threat than a question or a statement. 'I'm Perry. Please do come in. We've been expecting you.'

We? Gulp.

I followed her through the foyer into a huge, airy living room, full of tasteful, elegant furniture that was perfectly lit by crystal-clear floor-to-ceiling windows that let in the blinding sunshine. It looked just like my apartment. If you knocked out every wall of every single room, painted the entire thing a bright, clean white and never allowed a human being to touch a single thing.

'This place is gorgeous,' I said, head on a swivel as we carried on walking, striding across the stripped wooden floors and through a doorway at the end of the room. 'You have a beautiful home.'

'This isn't my home,' Perry replied with a solid bark of a laugh. 'This is our office, our clubhouse, shall we say.'

The only club I'd ever been a member of was the Take That fan club and I had a sneaking suspicion Perry was neither a Mark nor a Robbie girl. I squeezed my denim jacket, wishing I'd worn something more formal. I loved my little leather flip-flops and pink cotton Zara sundress but, compared to Perry's sophisticated ensemble, I felt as though I'd just trotted in from the morning milking. Which, I thought, absently squeezing my deflated boobs with my forearms, I sort of had.

'Here we are.'

I walked through to another high-ceilinged room, this one opening out into a stunning conservatory, full of lush green plants I hardly dared look at. I could kill a cactus by simply looking at it and I counted at least three orchids in Perry's collection. Best to keep my distance.

'Morning, everyone,' I said, raising a hand in a hello. Four other women dotted around the room smiled and nodded in response. Each and every one of them was just as perfectly put together as Perry. These were not women who were worried about sweat stains or subway mess or baby puke. If the townhouse hadn't been enough of a giveaway, their immaculate presentation did it. I was out of my depth and trapped in a room full of Cicis that had spawned and I couldn't work out for the life of me why on earth I was there.

'This is Nia, Danielle, Avery and Joan,' Perry said, each woman raising a diamond-bedecked hand as her name was called. 'We're so happy you could join us.'

'That's always nice to hear,' I replied as I sat down, keeping one eye on the other women. They hovered at the edges of the room, poised and graceful, as though posing for an unseen photographer. It was all very unsettling, not least because there was literally no sign of a single baby in this supposed mother and baby group. I couldn't see one piece of plastic or wipe-down surface anywhere. I no longer owned anything that couldn't be cleaned with a baby wipe. 'I'm sure it's my baby brain acting up but I can't remember how you said you got my details originally.'

'No, that's because we didn't say,' she replied as one of the other women presented us with glasses of sparkling water before resuming her original position.

Gulp.

'You didn't?'

'We didn't,' Perry confirmed. 'We're very discreet. And as the head of the membership committee, I personally select women for the group who are a good fit for our community.'

And I had been selected? Me? Teenage Angela who never got picked for dodgeball was very excited but adult Angela was more than a little wary.

'Let's get to know each other a little better,' she suggested. 'You work at Besson Media?'

'I do,' I confirmed, sitting on my shaking hands. 'Well, I just started but I was at Spencer Media before that.'

'And you're a writer.'

Perry's smooth face barely moved as she spoke.

I nodded, crossing my legs at the ankles to hide the chipped nail polish on my big toe. This was not a chipped pedicure kind of a gang, I could tell.

'We have a lot of contacts in the media,' she said. 'And a few of our members are in publishing.'

'Oh, I'd love to write a book one day, it's always been my dream,' I told her, a happy smile on my face as I rambled on. 'I used to write children's books, ghost-write actually. I would write the books that went with kids' films and TV shows. You might have read some of them actually, they were dreadful obviously, but don't hold that against me.'

This is not the time for verbal diarrhoea, I whispered to myself. Cut it out, Angela.

'What is it you do?' I asked, very aware of the sweat patches under my arms.

'Hedge fund manager at YellowCrest,' Perry said as though telling me she ran the corner shop. No wonder The M.O.B. had a five-million-dollar brownstone as their clubhouse. Erin's husband worked at YellowCrest and Erin's husband made literally millions of dollars a year.

'Or at least, I used to. I gave it up after Mortimer came along.'

'Mortimer?' I squeaked. Please let it be the name of her dog, please let it be the name of her dog, please let it be the name of her dog.

'My son,' she replied with a smooth smile. 'He's my second, he's almost eighteen months now, and Titus, his big brother, will be three next month. Two sons under three, oof, what a challenge. There's simply no way to manage a full-time job and two children, although I was heartbroken to leave.'

'Right, must be tough,' I said, trying to work out just what exactly Perry had done to her face. Her forehead was perfectly smooth, her cheeks very slightly overinflated and there wasn't a single visible pore on her skin. While I very much supported people doing whatever the hell they wanted to their own faces, something about Perry's work just looked off. She looked ageless and not in a good way. I'd have placed her anywhere between thirty-five and fifty, there was just no way to tell.

'We're so excited you're interested in joining us,' Perry said, glancing over at the other women who promptly left their positions and came to join us on the sofas, her smooth face void of any visible signs of said excitement. 'We do some magnificent work here and we're always on the lookout for quality members. Between the support we give each other and community outreach, if you're accepted into The M.O.B., I think you'll find being part of our group quite rewarding. Although I should mention membership is select – not everyone who is invited to meet with us ends up making the cut.'

'And I'm always excited to make new friends,' I lied, so pleased to know they might still reject me even though I hadn't asked to join in the first place. 'So what's the deal? Coffee mornings, jumble sales, playdates, that kind of thing?'

'I don't know what a jumble sale is but I am quite sure the answer is no,' she replied, brushing her silky brown hair over her shoulder. 'We're an exclusive network of elite women, come together to lift each other higher. I will admit we are somewhat selective about the women who join our collective but that's to preserve the quality of our experience. We strive to stimulate our intellect and grow our spirit in all that we do.'

Oh god, it *was* a cult.

'Right, one question,' I said, slapping my thighs and making everyone jump. 'Where do the kids come in?'

'Kids?' Perry looked confused.

'Yes, your kids,' I said. 'Where are they while you're, you know, stimulating your intellect?'

'This isn't a mommy and me class,' she replied as the other four women laughed. 'The B.O.B.s aren't always here.'

'B.O.B.s,' I repeated slowly.

'Babies of Brooklyn,' Perry clarified.

'That's what I thought,' I said, leaning back against the sofa. 'Just wanted to make sure.'

'The goal is to create an empowering network for our children from an early age,' she said, flicking an invisible speck of dust from her trouser leg. 'I've worked with a social psychologist and several corporate counselling experts who agree it's essential for children to begin forging the right kinds of bonds right from birth. They are the next generation of leaders, after all.'

'Do you not worry that's a lot of pressure to put on

a baby?' I asked gently, a vision of Alice being sworn into the White House passing through my mind.

Perry stared right back at me.

'No,' she said.

I waited for the rest of the sentence for a moment before realizing that was it.

'Oh, OK.' I looked down at my flip-flops and wondered how fast I could run in them. This was clearly not the group for me.

'The networking isn't just for Alice,' Perry said, leaning forward and gripping my knee with her coffee-coloured nails. 'We want to raise these children in an environment of powerful women. A tribe is only as strong as its weakest member.'

'Christ almighty,' I whispered.

'I'm sure we all have a busy day ahead of us so let's get things moving,' Perry said, sitting back and clapping her hands. 'I'm going to ask you a few questions and then we'll play a little game.'

Please let it be Hungry Hungry Hippos.

'In how many classes is Alice currently enrolled?' Danielle, a striking woman with tightly curled black hair, asked from the sofa beside Perry.

'Classes?' I stared back blankly.

'Music class, baby yoga, dance, swim, is she learning any languages?' Nia replied. Nia was a tall willowy blonde who looked as though she should be playing Reese Witherspoon's best friend in at least seventeen movies.

'Maybe art class?' suggested Joan, the gorgeous black woman sitting on my left with poker-straight hair that fell all the way to her waist. My hair was in a bun, secured by a scrunchie. I was a monster.

'Or sign language? Or ballet? Mind and body sensory stimulation?'

'She's not even one yet,' I replied, making a mental note to find out what the hell mind and body sensory stimulation was and avoid it at all costs. 'She isn't in any classes.'

Joan sucked the air in through her teeth as though about to give me a quote for a new carburettor.

'What's her hashtag?' Perry asked, tapping away on an iPad that had appeared from nowhere.

'Hashtag?'

'For social media,' she clarified. 'My boys are "hashtag MorTitus", for example.'

Oh dear god, those poor children. As if their real names weren't already going to get them beaten up when they got to school.

'My husband isn't a massive fan of social media so we don't really put pictures of Alice online all that much,' I said slowly.

All the women looked at each other.

'If that's the choice you've made, that's the choice you've made,' Perry declared. I had a feeling it wasn't the only choice that had been made. 'Perhaps we should skip along to the game and get this over with.'

'You know, I have to get to work,' I said, fiddling with the buttons on my denim jacket. A universal 'I'm going to leave now' gesture. 'This has been so lovely but—'

Before I could stop her, Avery, a delicate redhead with reflexes like a cat, had snatched my handbag from the floor and upended it on the coffee table. My phone clattered onto the marble tabletop first before it was buried in piles of my secret shame. A bag of

M&Ms, three tampons, one out of its wrapper, a dried-up pen with a missing cap, lip balm, lip gloss, eyeliner, a manky old mascara, two more lip balms, my MetroCard and, even though this wasn't my baby bag, two open packs of baby wipes.

I opened my mouth to protest as the women began pawing through my belongings but nothing came out. It was worse than the time Karen Woods nicked my diary in Year Nine and read it out loud in registration so the entire year group heard how I was worried about my left boob coming in bigger than my right one. Nia screwed up her delicate face as she held a loose Percy Pig up for inspection.

'I wasn't going to eat that,' I said quickly.

I was absolutely going to eat it.

'What we carry with us is who we are,' Perry said sadly as she inspected a half-eaten Special K bar. 'What do you think the content of your purse says about you, Angela?'

'I think it says I have a baby and a full-time job and no time to sit cleaning out my handbag,' I replied. My cheeks burned as the five women picked over my belongings, tutting and sighing and occasionally throwing in an 'Ew' for good measure.

'How cute!' Avery held up a key ring in the shape of the Empire State Building. 'You know, I've never actually been.'

'My husband took me when we first started dating,' I said, compelled to explain in spite of myself. 'He gave me that before he went away on tour a few years ago.'

'Tour?' There was a very definite sneer on Avery's face as she raked through my makeup, tossing eyeliners

77

and lipsticks all over the coffee table. 'What is it that your husband does?'

'He's in a band,' I told her, grabbing a precious packet of Sour Patch Kids out of Avery's hands. 'I don't know if you've heard of them, they're called Stills.'

All five women froze.

'Stills?' Perry repeated, her grey eyes suddenly open wide. 'Your husband is in Stills?'

I puffed out my cheeks and nodded slowly.

'Is it Alex or Craig?' she demanded before looking at the other women to explain. 'Graham the bassist is gay.'

Oh god, I thought as the colour drained from my face. She'd shagged one of them, hadn't she?

'Alex,' I replied, my voice barely above a whisper.

As my voice grew quieter, Perry's elevated to an all-out screech.

'You're married to Alex Reid?' she squealed.

'Yes?' I replied.

Perry turned on Nia with savage stare.

'Why was this not in her background check?' she hissed. 'Unacceptable.'

Nia shrank back, visibly quaking in her overpriced boots, and I wondered how many lashes she'd be getting after I left.

'Do you know Alex?' I asked, afraid to hear the answer to my question.

'I don't know him, know him, but I love him,' she said so quickly I could barely understand her. 'That is, I love Stills. They're my favourite band. I've seen them at least ten times. I've been to every tour they've ever played. I once went to Texas to see them play at South by Southwest. Imagine, me in *Texas*.'

A quick look around the room confirmed that neither Nia, Danielle, Avery or Joan could even conceive of such a thing.

'Angela,' Perry said. 'I have to meet him.'

And just like that, Perry the investment banker and grown-up Mean Girl turned into a squealing teeny-bopper who had a crush on my husband. But on the upside, at least she hadn't shagged him.

'They're playing here in a couple of weeks,' I said as casually as I could manage. 'Trying out some new material.'

Perry gave a sharp nod and Danielle, Avery and Nia began shovelling my belongings back in my handbag while Joan pulled out a Google Pixel phone and began tapping away at the screen.

'If you're looking for tickets, the show sold out as soon as they announced it,' I said. 'Sorry.'

'Angela,' Perry leaned forward and gripped my knee so tightly my foot sprang out and kicked Avery square in the shin. 'Can you get us tickets?'

'I don't know,' I gasped, wincing as I pried her fingers off me. 'I can ask.'

'I would do anything to go to that show,' she said, opening her eyes so wide I could see white all the way around her pale grey irises

'Anything?' I replied, more frightened than interested.

'Anything,' she confirmed. 'Forget the membership process, you're officially in The Mothers of Brooklyn.'

'Which is very nice of you,' I said as I grabbed my bag back from Nia, immediately reaching in to find my phone, my thumb hovering over the emergency call button. 'But really not necessary. I really do have to go, as lovely as this has been.'

It hadn't been lovely, it had been intimidating, humiliating and ultimately terrifying, and for the first time since I'd met Cici Spencer, I couldn't wait to get to work.

'We'll work it out,' Perry said, following as I stood up out of my seat. 'There has to be something.'

'I will ask,' I promised, not even sure if I meant it. 'Nice to meet you all.'

The M.O.B. stared after me as I dashed out the room, walking quickly through the big white room and breaking into a run as I hit the steps to the street.

'You need to socialize with other mothers more, they said,' I muttered as I turned onto 8th Avenue and flagged down a passing yellow cab. I couldn't get far enough fast enough on foot. 'You need more mommy friends, they said.'

Hurling myself into the back seat, I rummaged through my bag to make sure everything was there before tearing into the packet of M&Ms, inhaling them by the wild-eyed handful. There wasn't a single thing anyone could offer that would make me go through that again. They could send all four of the Chrises to my house, oiled up and shirtless, each bearing a different Chanel handbag, and I still wouldn't be swayed.

I never wanted to see Perry Dickson again as long as I lived.

# CHAPTER SIX

'I'm not saying she's obsessed but I am saying, if I ever get home from work and seem a bit off, please just check it's me and not Perry Dickson in an Angela skinsuit,' I said, pushing Alice's pushchair through Park Slope. It was Friday and I should have been 'working from home' but Cici had called an emergency meeting and demanded I attend. On my first Friday working for her. Definitely not a power trip.

'Maybe we should come up with a safe word,' I suggested. 'Like, if I seem taller than usual, ask me what I want for dessert and if I don't say rhubarb, she's got me locked in the attic of that bloody mansion on 11th Street.'

'I thought our safe word was peanut butter,' Alex replied through a mouthful of doughnut.

'Your safe word is peanut butter,' I said, flushing at the very thought. 'I don't have a safe word, I'm English.'

'Rhubarb it is,' he agreed simply. 'Perry Dickson, huh. Is she hot?'

'Yes,' I admitted grudgingly. 'And she's got some very nice trousers.'

'You've got nice trousers too,' Alex said, resting his hand on the top of my arse. 'I can put her on the list for the show if you want me to.'

And there I was, hanging on the horns of a true moral dilemma. I did not want Alex to put Perry Dickson on the list for his show but I knew if I did, it would make her incredibly happy. It was a selfless act that would make someone else's day, earning me many karmic brownie points, but it would also mean spending another second of my life with Perry Dickson, something I had vowed never to do.

'Maybe,' I said, staying non-committal until I'd consulted wiser minds on the matter, i.e. Jenny. 'I'll let you know.'

Hanging back on the edge of the street, we waited until the light changed before starting to cross 7th Avenue to the subway station. Besson's offices might be cool but they were not convenient. I had to get the G to Lorimer and then the L to Bedford and, even then, it was still a fifteen-minute walk. Thankfully, the humidity had broken and the weather was civilized again, even if my commute wasn't. As we crossed, I fished around in my satchel, digging around for my MetroCard and trying my best not to think about all those women from The M.O.B. rummaging through my things. Just as I caught the edge of the travel pass with my fingertips, my bag slipped off my shoulder, hanging precariously between me and the pushchair for a second.

'Alex, watch out!' I cried but it was too late. The bag fell, hitting Alex hard in the back of the knee and knocking him off balance, the strap wrapping round his leg and sending him face first into the road.

'Oh my god,' I yelled as Alex groaned, the contents of my bag rolling on the street around him. I pushed Alice to the safety of the pavement and stamped the brake on before turning to help Alex up to his feet, the two of us stumbling to safety right before the light changed, leaving my bag at the mercy of the traffic.

The strap had snapped.

The strap of my Marc Jacobs satchel, my first and only true bag love, had snapped clean in two.

Pushing my hair behind my ears, I looked right, then left, then right again, preparing to run out against the light to retrieve my poor bag as it sat waiting patiently for me in the middle of the road.

Until a taxi came tearing around the corner and ran right over it.

'My bag,' I gasped.

'My ankle,' Alex moaned.

'Waah,' Alice added. She was absolutely fine but understandably wanted to be part of the excitement.

'Are you OK?' I asked my husband as I tried not to cry. I was worried about him, of course, but he was clearly in one piece and this was my *bag*. My precious, beautiful, wonderful bag. Unable to tear my eyes away from the carnage, I choked back a sob as I saw it lying there in the middle of the road, flat as a pancake, haemorrhaging tampons, breast pads, loose change and tubes of lip balms that had rolled away from the scene of the crime and into the gutter.

'I don't think anything is broken but my ankle does not feel good,' Alex said, wincing as he touched his leg. The fall had torn his paper-thin vintage jeans and there was a nasty gash on his knee. 'What the hell happened?'

'My bag broke,' I said, the simplicity of the statement not nearly covering the enormity of what had just happened. A bus hurtled down the street towards the victim and this time I had to look away. Rest in peace, little bag. 'We should go to the hospital, you've got to get it looked at.'

'I'm fine,' he insisted before howling in pain the second he tried to put weight on his left foot. 'I take it back, I'm not fine. ER it is.'

'Right, yes, let's do that,' I nodded before realizing the light had changed again. 'Just a sec.'

I dashed into the crosswalk, scooping up my flattened satchel, smashed phone and as many of my other belongings as I could. My keys and wallet seemed to have survived unscathed but everything else was a goner. I couldn't even look at the packet of salt and vinegar Squares that were scattered all over the street. My last bag of them as well.

'Don't be upset,' Alex said, leaning against the push-chair and holding out a hand for the wreckage of my bag. 'I'll bet I can fix it.'

'We should fix you first,' I said, wiping away a tear as I cradled my first bag baby in my arms. My first human baby was no longer crying but looked understandably confused by what was going on. One day you will understand, I thought sadly, but I hope I will be able to spare you this pain. 'There's that walk-in clinic on 5th Avenue, it's closer than the hospital.'

'You're going to be late for your meeting, go, I'll be OK.' Alex hopped along using Alice's pushchair as a makeshift crutch. I shoved the remains of my bag into the shelf under her seat and gave him an unconvinced once-over.

'Yeah, I don't think so,' I told him, glancing down at the open wound on his knee. 'They can wait ten minutes. I'd prefer to know you didn't bleed out on the way if it's all the same to you.'

With half a smile on his even paler than usual face, Alex rested one arm around my shoulders, keeping the other hand on the handle of the pushchair while Alice sang happily to herself, entirely unmoved by the drama unfolding around her.

'Angela Clark,' Alex said, hobbling down the street, very, very slowly. 'What did I do to deserve you?'

What did I do to deserve this? I replied silently as I spotted the puff from my lost-forever Chanel powder compact, blown up into the air by another passing car. It certainly felt like punishment for something but – oh, wait a minute.

'This isn't exactly the time for it,' I said, sliding my arm around my husband's waist and staring up at the sky. Someone up there was taking the piss. 'But when you get home, if you could add Perry Dickson to the guest list for the show, that would be grand.'

'Sorry I'm late,' I called, emerging out of the lifts at Besson forty minutes later. 'Minor emergency, crisis averted.'

Cici, Kanako and the rest of the editors were sitting around the crystal conference table. One by one, they each turned to look at me, all of them with the same expression on their faces.

'So, this is Alice,' I said, pointing to the baby hanging from my chest.

Alex and I had made it to the walk-in clinic, only to find out there was a two-hour wait to see a doctor. Convinced he wouldn't survive a trip to the emergency room at the hospital down the block, I agreed to pop on the papoose, take Alice to my meeting then jump in a cab to come back and collect him once they'd strapped him up. The intake nurse had assured me he'd be fine and quietly promised they'd keep him in what she referred to as the Man Flu wing until I returned.

I hated the papoose, Alice just hanging there, arms and legs waving wildly, bursting out of my chest like the alien in, well, *Alien*. And, as someone who went arse over tit more often than the average bear, it didn't feel safe.

'She doesn't look like you at all!' Cici said, almost smiling as I found a seat at the table. 'Are you sure she's yours?'

'Unless they pulled a watermelon out of me and then switched it with this, yes, I'm pretty certain,' I replied. I pulled out a bag of rice crackers and handed one to Alice, praying to anyone or anything that might be listening that she would be quiet through the meeting.

'And why is she here?' she asked. Besson Media was supposedly a parent-friendly workplace. It said so on our website! We were even getting a crèche! Just not before Cici got the executive spa I'd heard her discussing with the building owners the day before.

'It's a long story,' I said, forcing a smile onto my face. 'But the short version is, my handbag broke then Alex fell over and I had to take him to the doctor for an X-ray and the wait was so long I couldn't leave her there and I didn't want to miss the meeting and, actually, that's the whole story. Sorry.'

'Thanks for making me wish I hadn't asked,' Cici replied. 'Will it behave?'

I looked down at my little girl who looked back with an angelic smile.

'I reckon we should just get started,' I replied, committing to nothing.

'Fine,' Cici said, never taking her eyes off Alice. 'I have an appointment in the city in an hour so I'll keep this brief. We've hired someone to manage the day-to-day running of all your sites. She's going to be overseeing content, developing new ideas, that kind of thing.'

According to the panicked murmurs and uncomfortable glances that ran around the table, no one else had been informed of this change in command.

'I'll still be here,' Cici added, even though she was already mentally gone from the meeting, scrolling through emails on her phone as she spoke. 'But once she starts in two weeks, you'll all report into our new vice president of content, Paige Sullivan.' She turned and called out imperiously, 'Paige?'

Cici Spencer was a good-looking woman, tall and slim with surgically perfected features, but even I felt myself go full goldfish when Paige Sullivan stepped out from the closest privacy pod. While Cici was a hot cross between a china doll and a bitch, Paige was absolutely lush. Long blonde hair fell around her face in loose curls, full lips painted old Hollywood red pouted at the room and her simple fitted black shift dress only emphasized the curves that made even married me question my sexuality.

87

She wasn't only a taller, cooler, younger me. She was a blonde, British Jenny Lopez. Cici had found a way to clone me and my best friend and breed a new and improved version to replace us both.

'Good morning,' Paige said, joining Cici at the head of the table. 'So great to meet everyone, I'm looking forward to booking in some one-on-one time with you all next week so we can get acquainted before I start properly. I think I recognize everyone, except for possibly the baby.'

'She's just interning for the day,' I replied, scooping regurgitated crackers off the crystal desk before Cici could see them.

'If anyone has time to chat now, I'll hang around but, if not, I will book out some time in the diary and we'll talk later on,' Paige said, a friendly smile on her beautiful face. Immediately, everyone stood up, practically running back to their desks. Cici might be a brilliant CEO but she was not a talented manager. People did not like surprises in the workplace unless they were pastry-based.

'I have to go,' Cici said, dropping her phone into an alligator-skin Birkin. 'So I guess I'm leaving you with Angela. She's developing a new site right now but she used to be editor of *The Look* magazine at Spencer.'

I gave the pair of them a small salute to confirm these facts.

'She also turned James Jacobs gay, accused me of abducting her friend's baby and punched me in the face at a party one time.'

'Happy memories,' I said, a rictus grin frozen on my face. 'Thanks, Cici. I'll see you tomorrow.'

She stopped and stared. 'Tomorrow?'

'At your birthday party?' I replied. 'That is tomorrow, isn't it?'

'Yes but I didn't invite you.'

There was absolutely no filter on the woman, none whatsoever.

'Delia invited me,' I said, methodically rubbing my hand up and down Alice's front. 'You know, your twin sister? With whom you share a birthday?'

With an actual out-loud groan, Cici rolled her eyes and gagged. 'Really? I hate when she mixes business with my personal life. I've told her a thousand times, you don't make friends with the staff. This is just like the time she took our old nanny to tea at The Plaza. Who cares if it's her seventieth birthday? You know I can't go there any more?'

'Must be a nightmare for you,' I said, wishing Alice could puke on command. In that moment, I'd have held her over those suede thigh-high boots without a second thought. 'Should I return your gift?'

'Angela, I'm sure your being at the party will be a gift in itself,' she replied, jabbing the button on the bank of elevators as though she could will it to come faster. 'Your appearances usually end in some kind of drama and I didn't book entertainment.'

'I know who you are!' Paige said, as Cici melted away into the lift. 'You're Angela Clark!'

'Oh god,' I replied, squeezing Alice's feet. 'Is that a good thing or a bad thing?'

'Actually, we have friends in common,' Paige explained, sliding into the chair beside me and shaking one of Alice's sticky fingers. 'You know my friend Tess, Tess Brookes?'

'Yes, of course, the photographer,' I replied, relaxing right away. 'I haven't seen her in forever.'

I could not have been more relieved. If Paige was friends with Tess, no matter what wicked qualities she'd displayed to impress Cici so much, she couldn't be all bad. Tess was one of the nicest people I knew so Paige had to be at least half decent.

'She's helping me house-hunt,' Paige said, one finger still trapped in Alice's grasp. 'Apartment-hunt, rather. I can't believe how expensive flats are here. As much as I'm enjoying crashing at Tess's place, I don't think her boyfriend loves having me around.'

'I don't think boyfriends ever really do.' I thought back to all the times Jenny had ended the night face down on my and Alex's sofa. 'If I hear of anything, I'll let you know.'

'It's been a total whirlwind, getting the job, moving so quickly,' she said, shaking her finger loose from Alice's grasp. 'It's nice to know there's going to be at least one friendly face when I get started.'

I glanced over my shoulder at the rest of the office, working hard to look as though they were working hard at their standing desks.

'They're all pretty nice once you get to know them,' I said, before silently adding, 'I imagine.'

'I'm off to look at another walk-in wardrobe masquerading as an apartment,' Paige said, checking her watch. 'See you in a couple of weeks.'

I waved goodbye and she stepped into the lift, the doors sliding shut and whisking her away.

'She was all right, wasn't she?' I said to Alice, handing her another cracker before helping myself to one. 'I'm almost excited about working with her.'

For her, corrected the unhelpful voice in my head. You'll be working *for* her.

'Whatever,' I muttered, heaving myself out of my chair with accompanying sound effects. 'Shall we go and see if IT can lend us a phone?'

Blinking, Alice hurled her half-eaten rice cracker in my face.

'Don't give me that, you bloody love that phone,' I muttered, picking the cracker off my stripy T-shirt and dropping it in the bin as I passed through the kitchen. 'Although, if your dad asks, we definitely don't do screens when he's not watching.'

Truly, I was a terrible mother.


'Look, I know we need to get back to the clinic but it's been a very traumatic day.'

Alice looked up at me from her papoose, disapproval all over her face.

'I've never noticed it before but you do have a look of your grandmother on occasion,' I told her, looking away. It was one thing to be judged by other adults but it was quite another to get the side eye from your own infant.

Safely tucked away in the corner of Milk Bar on Metropolitan, I snaffled another mouthful of Milk Bar Pie under my daughter's disapproving gaze.

'It's too sweet for you,' I said, licking the gooey caramel filling off my spoon. 'And Daddy doesn't like you having sugar.'

She gave me a look as if to say he didn't like her watching old episodes of *Teletubbies* on YouTube either but that didn't stop me turning it on every time he was out the house.

'That's just as much for my enjoyment as yours,' I told her with a sniff.

Even though I knew we should have gone straight back to the clinic and sat with Alex while he waited for his X-rays, the call of the Milk Bar Pie was too strong. Alice was too young for me to explain why but I made a mental note to ask her future therapist if this might have any lasting effects.

This was how I'd imagined New York motherhood. Café-hopping with my baby strapped to my body in an overpriced, ergonomic papoose and paying six dollars a pop for a slice of overpriced, hipster dessert. The two-dollar cup of weak tea I could do without but I was the one who chose to live in America and so we made do with what we had. Maybe we'd make it a tradition, I thought. Maybe we'd come here every week, sharing something sweet when she was old enough, until she was so big she wanted her own piece. Once upon a time I couldn't have begun to imagine life with a baby. Now, I couldn't even conceive of the fact that, one day, my baby would be a grown-up.

Staring out the window, I watched as people went about their day outside the café. Williamsburg had changed, grown up, and I wasn't sure I liked it. Everyone looked like everyone else, all the originality chased out of the neighbourhood by developers with deep pockets. It was crazy to think what it would cost to live around here these days. The artists' lofts had been replaced by skyscrapers, all the bars we used to go to chased out in favour of fancy restaurants with fourteen-course tasting menus. This city was a living thing, constantly changing, moving, growing. Today I was paying six dollars for a piece of pie but, a couple of years ago, I wouldn't have wanted to walk down this street on my own.

Everything in New York changed so quickly. Most of the shops and restaurants in Union Square had either closed or moved in the last few years; Coffee Shop shuttered a year ago, Republic was gone and even the massive Toys 'R' Us on the east side of the square had shut up shop. But it didn't matter, I realized as I patted myself down, making sure I still had my MetroCard, keys and wallet, bereft without my bag. New York was bigger than any one shop, any one restaurant. It wasn't a middle-aged divorcé buying a sports car, shaving the hair off his bum and having it implanted into his scalp, it was the most thrilling, electric city on the planet and, when one door closed, seventeen more opened, even if they were a few subway stops further east and cost twice as much in rent.

The phone I'd borrowed from the not-at-all-happy IT team at Besson rattled across the table, pulling me out of my moment. Setting down my fork and rubbing my hands on the legs of my jeans, I swiped at the screen to see who had tracked me down on WhatsApp, expecting Alex's photo to fill the screen.

Perry bloody Dickson.

Alice began to fuss as the phone continued to buzz. My heart told me not to answer but my head was convinced Perry wasn't the kind of woman to take no for an answer and I was terrified if I didn't pick up the call I'd find her waiting on my doorstep when I got home. It didn't matter that I hadn't given her my address. If Jenny could find out where Taylor Swift lived and print her full address, phone number and personal email in my birthday card, Perry Dickson could certainly find me.

'I'm not going to answer it,' I told Alice who was just about to pop an arm out of her socket, trying to answer the call. It was longest twelve seconds of my life. When the screen finally went black, I breathed out, waiting for the inevitable voicemail message.

'Angela, it's Perry Dickson,' she said, as if I hadn't immediately put her contact details into my phone the second I'd left the meeting. You didn't go around letting people like this sneak up on you if there was any way to get a head start on them first. 'We heard about Alex's accident and I wanted to call to see if there was anything we could do.'

How had she heard about Alex falling over a broken handbag and skinning his knee? Had the world suddenly run out of news? Seemed bloody unlikely, given the state of things.

'I'd love to send my personal chef over to take care of you but if your housekeeper would be offended, say the word and I'll think of something else.'

'My housekeeper?' I mouthed. Alice kicked me right in the boob, presumably because she had just found out other babies had been born into families with housekeepers and personal chefs.

'Hopefully this won't mean Stills has to cancel the show on the fourteenth, I'm so looking forward to it. Call me when you get this, love to Alex.'

Ha. So that was it. She was really calling to check on the tickets to the Stills show. That didn't exactly explain her network of Park Slope spies but at least I didn't have to worry about her showing any genuine concern.

Alice began to nod, her head lolling forwards as she drifted in and out of sleep. Against her sleepy will, I pulled her out of the papoose and turned her round, ignoring her grumblings and dodging the tiny, flying baby fists as I worked her legs back into the holes. The second she was settled, the babbling stopped. Her eyelids flickered, long black lashes settling against her cheeks, and she was out for the count.

'Come on,' I whispered, one hand holding the fork that was hanging out my mouth, the other curled around Alice's back. 'Let's go and check on the invalid.'

I felt a smile forming on my face as I screwed up the napkin I'd had in my lap and dropped it on my plate. I could cope with all the madness as long as there were moments like this, just me, my girl and six dollars' worth of sugar. I didn't need five-star trips to Hawaii, personal chefs or designer handbags, I already had everything I could ever want and more. For at least a moment, I was officially FOMO-free.

'Let's see how long that lasts,' I mumbled, leaving the café and flagging down the first passing taxi, headed back to Park Slope, Alex Reid and a proper cup of tea.

# CHAPTER SEVEN

'Look at us, out of the house together at the same time without the baby,' I said, squeezing Alex's hand as we walked into Cici and Delia's birthday party.

'I know,' he replied, squeezing back. 'Just a couple of devil-may-care, crazy kids out on the town on a Saturday night.'

It was exciting, even if one of the crazy kids had to wear a pair of Spanx shorts over a Spanx bodysuit just to fit into her dress and the other one had insisted on bringing his crutch because he wanted to drink and couldn't take the hardcore painkillers his doctor had prescribed.

We were so rock and roll, it hurt. Or at least my rib cage and Alex's ankle did.

The party was at Delia's townhouse on the Upper East Side, which was about as far away from Brooklyn as Alex could travel without his head exploding, but the unobstructed view of Central Park at sunset from her edge-of-rooftop terrace made the forty-dollar Uber and twenty-dollars-an-hour babysitter (plus twenty dollars for dinner and twenty dollars for her cab fare home) worth every penny.

'Can you see food?' I asked, after I'd finished totting up everything I'd spent just to get out the house. That did it, I was definitely getting drunk. I started scanning the rooftop, searching for trays of anything.

'I don't think I've worn this since Graham's wedding,' Alex said as he slid one finger under his collar and strained against the stiff white cotton and his skinny black tie. 'And I see a bunch of guys here not wearing suits. I thought you said this was a formal thing?'

I smiled and straightened his tie before brushing his black hair out of his eyes. 'That's not technically true,' I said. 'You asked if you needed to wear a suit and I said yes. You didn't ask why you needed to wear a suit.'

'So why did I need to wear a suit?' he asked, wrapping his arm around the waist of the black satin Reformation wrap dress Jenny had 'borrowed' for me from the sample cupboard at work.

'Because I think you look really hot in a suit.' I grabbed two glasses of champagne from a passing waiter and handed one to him with as big a smile as I could muster. 'And I'm a monster.'

'Tricking a man into wearing irresponsibly sexy clothing for your own benefit, Angela Clark, you are a monster,' Alex murmured into my hair as he took the glass before clinking the rim against my own. 'I hope you're happy. What if these women can't control themselves around me? What will you do then?'

For a split second, I panicked. What if anyone from The Mob was here? There really was a chance I'd be sleeping with the fishes if Perry saw the way he filled out a tux. But no, we were safe. Out on a Saturday night, all dressed up and, if I had my way, half an hour away from getting very tipsy and a couple of hours away from a bloody good seeing to.

'Oh, shit, who is that stud?'

As usual, we heard Jenny before we saw her.

'Aw, it's only Reid, never mind,' she said, flipping her curls over her shoulder. 'How's it going, Hopalong?'

'Lopez,' Alex leaned in for a kiss on the cheek and got an enormous, full-body hug in return before she released him and turned him over to her gigantic, bearded husband. 'Mason.'

The men engaged a manly half-hug while Jenny fussed with my hair and took out her phone for a selfie.

From the top of her head to the tips of her toes, Jenny was a vision. In spite of the earlier summer downpour, she was wearing sky-high, black patent strappy sandals and a fitted black velvet mini dress that was so short, I really hoped she'd had a recent wax. The high neck and long sleeves balanced out her bare legs and a sequined snake ran all the way down from the neck to the hem, glinting gleefully in the low lights of the party.

'So, Mason,' I heard Alex say over my shoulder. 'I see you're not wearing a suit . . .'

'Look up,' Jenny ordered, wrapping her arm tightly around my shoulders. 'Chin down, half-smile, there we go.'

She snapped a dozen or so pics before releasing me from her vice-like grip and turning her attention to FaceTune. 'Good work, we're cute.'

'That dress is amazing, where's it from?' I asked as

she expertly swiped and smoothed our photo. Clearly not quite cute enough.

'Valentino,' she replied, utterly preoccupied. It seemed like editing my dark circles was taking up most of her energy. 'And can I just say, I'm so sorry about your bag. I know how much that ugly old thing meant to you.'

'You helped me buy that ugly old thing,' I said, contending with a fresh rush of grief.

'Yeah, ten years ago. It was time for it to go. Now we can get you something new, maybe a Chanel.' Jenny breathed in sharply at the very thought. 'Hey, did you hear Cici got the food guy from *Queer Eye* to cater the party? My friend said something about him being her date.'

'That poor man,' I replied, immediately searching the crowd for the stars of my favourite show. 'I know there's a clue in the name but does she realize he's gay?'

'You think that would stop Cici Spencer from trying to get what she wants?' Jenny clucked. 'Erin told me she got Leonardo DiCaprio to escort her to their sweet sixteenth.'

I shook my head, watching all the beautiful people pass by. 'That's just a rumour, Delia told me. It was actually Jake Gyllenhaal.'

'Goddamn, I wish I was that rich,' she sighed. 'I'd hire Ryan Gosling to come over and organize my closet.'

'Is he known for his organizational skills?' I asked.

Jenny flicked away a smudge of mascara from underneath my eye.

'Who cares?' she said, smiling at my corrected

makeup. 'I just want to lie on my bed and watch him touch my things.'

I couldn't argue with a plan like that.

'Angela!'

The worst thing about identical twins is that they're identical. I gripped Jenny's arm as a statuesque blonde wearing an absurdly beautiful beaded gown parted the crowds and moved towards us, her sparkling, silver dress shimmering with every step.

'I'm so glad you're here,' she said, leaning in for hugs and kisses, immediately outing herself as Delia, the good twin and our hostess.

'And I'm so glad you're you and not your sister,' I said. 'Happy birthday.'

'It must be amazing to go through life without getting that reaction,' she replied, tucking a long loose wave behind her ear. 'I can't imagine what it's like to live in a world where Satan isn't walking around town, wearing your face.'

'Cici couldn't be Satan,' Jenny said, taking two glasses of champagne from a passing waiter, handing one to the birthday girl. 'Didn't he start out as an angel? She's been evil through and through since birth.'

Delia clinked her glass against Jenny's in agreement.

'I've been meaning to call you,' Jenny said, nursing her drink as Delia threw hers back. 'I am planning the most exciting trip ever and I really want you to come. We're going to Hawaii next Thursday and I've got a seat saved just for you.'

'Jenny, I wish I could. I haven't been to Hawaii since I was a teenager,' Delia said with a mournful sigh. 'My godfather has an estate on Lanai and we would go every year. When we were kids, Cici and I would run around naked and practically live in the ocean. It's heaven.'

'Wait,' Jenny said, shaking her head. 'Is your god-father Bertie Bennett?'

Delia gave her a quizzical smile. 'Uncle Al to me, but yes, how did you know?'

'How did I not know this? That's where we're going!' she shrieked. 'We're staying at Hala Lanai. Bertie is a client of EWPR and he's friends with the brand owner and he said we could host there and, oh man, now you've gotta come.'

'But I can't,' she replied, the regret evident all over her pretty face. Even though Delia was no stranger to a bit of Botox, unlike her sister she could still actually express emotions. 'I've got so many big meetings coming up this month, there's no way I could take off.'

'Angela's coming,' Jenny bargained.

'No, I'm not,' I countered.

'Angela, if you can, you must,' Delia insisted, grabbing hold of my hand. 'Truly, it is the most beautiful place on earth. And I heard Uncle Al was thinking of selling. I hate to think who might end up buying it. It's such a special place.'

'Couldn't you buy it?' I suggested as my FOMO began to raise its ugly head. 'You're loaded.'

'Not private-estate-in-Lanai loaded. My mom told me Bill Gates tried to buy it from him once and Uncle Al said no.'

'Maybe if you could convince Cici to run around naked on the beach again, the pair of you could pull in a few bucks,' Jenny said. 'There's totally a market for it.'

Gross, but she wasn't wrong.

'I'm so insanely jealous,' Delia said, finishing her champagne with a second sip. 'Things are so crazy with the business and I haven't had a vacation in forever. You're going to have the most incredible time.'

'Except I'm not going,' I reminded them both, taking the tiniest sip of champagne. A sniff of the barmaid's apron and I was anyone's these days, which was great when I was safely tucked up on the sofa with all the Harry Potter movies and a glass of rosé but less impressive when I was at a very fancy party full of very fancy people. The last thing I needed was for Alex to be holding my hair back while I hung off the roof and chundered six floors above Park Avenue.

'Angela, is it true?'

Before anyone could make me feel any worse, Erin stepped out from the crowd. I couldn't help but give her a big sniff as she leaned in for a kiss. Erin was the closest thing our group had to a proper grown-up and she always smelled reassuringly expensive.

'Is what true?' I asked as the waiter swung back around, refreshing Delia's glass of champagne, handing a new flute to Erin and giving Jenny's legs a thorough appraisal. I, apparently, was invisible.

'That you've been invited to join The Mothers of Brooklyn?' Erin demanded.

Jenny and Delia gasped.

'Oh, shit, Angie, for real?' Jenny's eyes were so wide, I had to check over my shoulder to make sure Ryan Reynolds wasn't standing behind me. 'This is epic.'

'Big if true,' Delia confirmed. 'I had a friend who applied to join but they turned her down because she didn't meet their criteria. She cried about it for weeks.

And however you feel about her dad, Ivanka has gone through an awful lot lately.'

'I heard Michelle Williams tried to join,' Erin added in hushed tones. 'And they met with her but she failed their test and that's why she moved upstate.'

'I love *The Greatest Showman*,' I replied. 'Maybe Michelle wants to start her own group with me?'

'Of course you do,' Erin sniffed. 'But that isn't very Mothers of Brooklyn either so keep it to yourself. So, is it true? Did they really ask you to join?'

The three of them crowded around me, eyes wide, mouths slightly parted, vibrating with anticipation. Exactly the same way the waiter had looked at Jenny's legs.

'First, you're all freaking me out,' I said, taking a sip of my champagne for courage. 'And second, how did you even hear about this? I thought the first rule of Fight Club was, we don't talk about Fight Club?'

'My friend Andrea is in it,' Erin explained. 'Perry Dickson sent an all-members email out asking about you and she recognized your name.'

Interesting. And terrifying. I still hadn't replied to Perry's voicemail and, every time I went home, I was half expecting them to be waiting on my doorstep in long red capes with the hoods up.

'Angela, you have to join,' Jenny said, putting down her champagne to take both of my hands in hers, just in case I didn't realize how bizarrely desperate she was. 'The Mothers of Brooklyn are one of the most powerful parenting groups in the city. They'll get you into all the right parties, they'll introduce you to all the right people and then you can take *me* to those parties and introduce *me* to those people.'

'Shouldn't it be more about Alice?' I suggested, prising my hand away. When Jenny put down booze, I knew things were serious. 'It's a parenting group, isn't it?'

'Oh, sure,' she said, flapping her hands around in the air. 'Make it all about Alice, as usual. What about me, Angela, what about *me*?'

'It would be so good for Alice. Perry's sister-in-law is Lorraine Dickson,' Erin interjected before I could give Jenny the slap she was so dearly asking for.

I gave her a blank look.

'She's one of the top preschool consultants in New York,' she said, not bothering to hide her exasperation. 'It cost me five hundred dollars just to get a meeting with her when we were trying to get Ariana into Horace Mann and then it was twenty-five hundred an hour for her to work on the application.'

'Didn't Ariana go to the West Village nursery?' Delia asked.

Erin took a long sip of her champagne.

'Yes.' Erin's voice was brittle. 'We didn't get into Horace Mann.'

'So you're telling me I should join this group of weirdos just because they're related to someone who could potentially not get Alice into a preschool I couldn't afford to send her to in the first place?' I said. 'Great. Good to know.'

She pressed her lips together, looking about ready to throttle me. 'I'm saying you should join because they have power, Angela, they have reach. I would have happily left the West Village and moved to the back of beyond if I thought I would have been invited to join.'

Only a woman who had lived in Manhattan for her entire life would consider Brooklyn the back of beyond.

'You know,' Delia added, lowering her voice to a hushed whisper. 'I happen to know Perry has very strong political connections.'

My glass hovered in front of my lips as I raised one eyebrow. Delia would know, the New York real estate billionaire club was very small.

'My green card is totally legit,' I informed her, trying to remember exactly when it needed to be renewed. 'You can't undo those. Can you?'

'I don't think you want to be on the wrong side of her, that's all I would say,' she said carefully. 'I know some of the people they know and they're not to be messed with.'

'It's just not for me. I went in thinking we would just have a lovely chat and instead they emptied my bag all over the table and—'

'Angela, no!' Erin cried, clamping her hand over my open mouth and almost breaking my front teeth with one of her diamond rings. 'You're not supposed to tell us anything that happens in a M.O.B. meeting!'

'They're a bunch of frustrated former CEOs, not the Illuminati!' I argued, slapping her arm away from my face. 'Besides, they don't want me, they want Alex. As in, they literally want him. Perry Dickson was about to kick me out the door before I mentioned who I was married to and then she practically peeled off her knickers and threw them in my face.'

'Ew,' Jenny muttered. 'Thanks for the visual.'

'You would not have cared for it,' I said, glancing over my shoulder at an oblivious Alex. 'Someone needs to throw those women an Ann Summers party. There's a fortune to be made.'

'One, I don't know what an Ann Summers party is, and two, you need to do whatever it takes to become part of that group,' Erin warned, feeling around in her gold Fendi evening bag for her phone. In just a few flicks, she was three years deep into some woman's Instagram and holding a group photo in my face. 'Who do you see here?'

'Alex's number one fan, for starters,' I said, pulling my head backwards as she shoved the screen right up against my nose. 'And I think that's Nia but I can't tell because she doesn't look like she's fifteen minutes out of a lobotomy so—'

'In the middle,' Erin thundered, tapping the screen with her long but so tastefully painted acrylic nail. 'In the middle of the photo.'

'In the middle?' I took the phone from her and held it at arm's length, waiting for my eyes to refocus. 'Oh. Is that Beyoncé?'

'What the fuck?' Jenny squealed, grabbing the phone out of my hand to look for herself. 'Angie, you gotta get in with these people. Next you'll be telling me they've had Oprah round for afternoon tea.'

'She was at their Fourth of July party last year,' Erin said, skimming through the feed and landing on a photo of the big O.

'You're joining,' Jenny replied, my opinion irrelevant. 'I want to meet Chrissy Teigen.'

'Chrissy Teigen doesn't live in Brooklyn,' I replied. 'Why would she be there?'

'They obviously made an exception for her because this is Chrissy goddamn Teigen,' Jenny said, waving

Erin's phone in my face. 'Angela Clark, please. Please do this for me. I'm taking you to Hawaii, remember?'

'No you're not, remember?' I said, turning my attention to Erin in a desperate attempt to change the subject. 'So, I hear you're moving to London and leaving me with this monster for an entire year? Why, Erin? Why?'

'Because Thomas has been sleeping with a woman at work and he can't afford to divorce me so we're moving to another country to "try again",' she replied, making bunny ears with her fingers before taking a sip of champagne. 'Would you rather chat about that?'

My jaw dropped. 'Christ, Erin, I'm so sorry,' I said, lowering my voice and taking a step closer to my friend. My first instinct was to wrap her up in a hug but the last thing I wanted was to upset her any more. Erin was not a public crier. That was one of my specialities. Well, mine and Jenny's. And often both of us at once. 'Are you OK?'

Of course she's not OK, I told myself, what a stupid question to ask. I'd been cheated on, I knew how much it hurt. Once the trust was gone, it was difficult even to look at the other person, let alone—

'These things happen,' Erin said, cutting in on my internal monologue. 'Do you know if they're serving food tonight? We didn't eat before we came out and I'm starving.'

I looked at my friend, no idea what to say. Erin was one of the most fierce women I had ever met, in both the literal and *America's Next Top Model* sense of the word. She was strong, capable and impossibly resilient but to so easily brush off something like this set off so many alarm bells in my head, it sounded like New Year's Eve up in there.

'Do you want to talk about it?' I asked quietly. 'We could go somewhere if you like? I don't have to stay.'

Erin smiled, the tiny smile lines she allowed her aesthetician to leave on her otherwise flawless face crinkling up at the corners of her eyes. That was what was wrong with Perry's face, I realized, no smile lines. That and the fact she was completely out of touch with reality but there was no injection to fix that. As far as I knew.

'There's nothing to talk about,' Erin said, only a shadow of sadness showing in her eyes. 'I hate to say it but I wasn't even really surprised. It's not unheard of, is it? If anything, I'm more upset by the cliché of it all.'

I felt my un-Botoxed brow creasing with concern. How could she be justifying his behaviour? Didn't he realize Erin was incredible?

'New York men are used to getting everything they want,' she said, looking away as she delicately scratched her nose with one slender finger. 'There aren't many who will turn it down when it's offered to them on a plate. They're all the same, Angela.'

Without even thinking, I turned around to look for Alex. He was exactly where I'd left him, laughing and joking with Mason, tie already loosened, top button of his shirt undone. I still couldn't get over how handsome he was.

'Is Cici wearing Givenchy?' Jenny asked, handing Erin her phone and cutting in on our hushed conversation. 'She is. She's wearing ten thousand dollars' worth of Givenchy to a house party for a non-major birthday.'

We turned to see my boss glide into the room.

'Jenny, you're wearing Valentino, what's the problem?' I reminded her, wondering how much she knew about Erin's situation and, more importantly, why she hadn't told me. It wasn't like Jenny was known for being the soul of discretion.

'Correction,' she whispered. 'I'm wearing borrowed Valentino. That dress is couture, it must have been made for her. I have never been so jealous in all my life.'

Regardless of what the dress had cost, it was breath-taking, even by Cici's standards. At first glance, it was a simple black dress with white panels, long sleeves and a high neck, beautifully cut, but nothing to get too excited about. Until she came closer and I realized the nude patterned panels were actually cut-outs. The glowing white fabric was actually her skin and there was an awful lot of it on display. With her pale corn-silk hair piled up on top of her head, Cici shone in the spotlight, ensuring all eyes were on her.

'I know she's literally the worst but is it me or do you kind of want to do her too?' Jenny asked. 'Not that I want to jump on the sexual fluidity bandwagon but she could definitely get it.'

'Mason would be delighted,' I replied. There was no version of reality that would ever see me having lustful feelings for Cici Spencer.

'Mason *would* be,' she whispered back. 'And so would Alex or any other red-blooded living man. Christ, is that chick wearing Givenchy too?'

I followed her gaze over to another blonde making her way across the roof terrace.

'That's Paige,' I said, raising a hand to wave her

over. 'My new boss.' Oh yes, in fact Cici was now my boss's boss. Without lifting a finger I had managed to slide two notches down the pecking order from my old job.

'I already hate her,' Jenny said through a forced smile as Paige bounded over on what looked like a tiny pair of silver stilts. 'Oh my god, I love your dress.'

'Thank you,' Paige swished her hips, the sharp pleats of the material shimmering under the spotlight like an iridescent oil spill come to life. A thick metallic belt that matched her shoes made the most of her tiny waist and a strategically placed cut-out gave the tiniest suggestion of under-boob, before the dress flowed over her shoulders and fluttered down her back like a pair of butterfly wings. 'I was a bit worried I might have overdone it but I see I'm in very good company. Is that Valentino?'

Without even realizing, Paige had won Jenny's loyalty forever. My best friend reached out a hand and grabbed Paige's arm.

'What are you doing on Thursday?' she asked.

Paige pursed her lips, thinking. 'Um . . .'

'Cancel it,' Jenny ordered. 'You're coming to Hawaii with me and Angela.'

'I'm not going,' I reminded her. 'And Paige can't go either, she's starting a new job, she's got to find somewhere to live—'

'Perfect! The people who are subletting our old place are moving out of my old apartment two weeks from today,' Jenny said, snapping her fingers, the deal as good as done.

Paige looked at Jenny with an expression on her face I remembered from the first time I met my very own

110

fairy godmother. She had a knack for appearing in people's lives right when they needed her, and new-to-New-York Paige definitely needed her. I made myself smile so they could all see how delighted I was about the idea of my new boss, the younger, cooler, taller me, moving into my first apartment and going on a once-in-a-lifetime dream holiday with my best friend.

'If it's in my budget, I'd love to look at it,' she said. 'And, well, Hawaii sounds lovely but I just moved and hopefully I'm about to get a new apartment so I should save my money—'

'It's free!' Jenny exclaimed, her enthusiasm level stuck on 'slightly overexcited'. 'Hawaii, not the apartment, that is. It's a press trip so it won't cost you a penny and you will lit-er-all-y never get a chance to experience anything like this ever again, as long as you live. You get the last seat.'

It was so unlike her to underplay things so much. Wait, did she say last seat?

'Last seat? Who else is going?'

'Eva confirmed this morning, thanks for the intro,' she replied while Paige continued to stare at her in polite alarm. 'And I was gonna save it as a surprise but, since you keep insisting you don't want to come, I might as well spill the news. James is coming.'

'James Jacobs?' I asked.

'James Jacobs?' Paige echoed, only louder and at a higher pitch. 'The actor? Oh, I love him!'

'Dollface, he will love you too,' Jenny insisted. 'Before Angela turned into my mom, the three of us got into some serious situations, right, Angie? Remember that night in Vegas? Paige, I can already tell you and I are gonna get along great.'

'But why is James going on a press trip to promote mascara?' I shouted over all the squealing as two women who had just met joined hands and bounced up and down on the spot. 'It doesn't make any sense!'

Jenny threw one arm around Paige and the other up into the air. 'It doesn't have to make sense, he's A-list, baby. But if you think those lashes of his are one hundred percent untouched, you're living in a dream world. It's perfect, boys in beauty are so hot right now.'

'*So* hot right now,' Paige confirmed. 'Jenny, I don't want to overstate anything but I think you might be my favourite person I've ever met.'

I frowned and took another sip of my champagne.

'Paige, I know we just met,' Jenny took a deep breath and composed herself, which only served to escalate Paige's giddiness. 'But I am offering you a trip to paradise. Only an idiot would turn it down.'

It was all too much. First my bag breaks, then I find out Thomas is cheating on Erin and now the younger, hotter, cooler version of me sweeps in and takes my old apartment, my new job, my friends *and* my dream holiday? No. Bloody. Way.

In the little black leather clutch bag I had tucked under my arm, I could feel my mobile vibrating. Pulling out, I answered it right away, not recognizing the number and immediately assuming it was the babysitter, telling me she'd burned the house down.

'Hello?'

'Angela, Perry Dickson.'

The sneaky mare, calling from a different number to make sure I picked up.

'Checking in on you and Alex,' she said. 'Did you get my last message?'

'I did.' I did a 360-turn to make sure she wasn't about to jump out of the crowd and surprise me. 'Sorry, I've been so busy, I haven't had time to call you back.'

'Not at all, not at all,' she said with a forced laugh. 'How is Alex?'

'In agony,' I lied as he and Mason made their way back over from the bar.

'Oh, that won't do at all,' Perry gasped. 'You must go and see Dr Pentland. Louise is an orthopaedic surgeon and one of our founder members and I'm sure she'd be able to help.'

'Uh-huh,' I replied as Jenny introduced Paige to the boys. Slowly, still listening, I made my way over towards them.

'I thought perhaps you'd be at the Spencer girls' birthday party this evening?'

I glanced around the party, looking for her spies. They had eyes everywhere in this city, what choice did I have?

'Just a quiet night in on the couch,' I said with a grimace as someone turned the music up a notch. 'Watching a very loud film.'

'If Alex is well enough to be left alone, perhaps we could get together this week to discuss the next steps in your joining us here at The M.O.B.?' she said, seemingly buying my nonsense. 'Would Thursday morning work for you again?'

'This Thursday?' I repeated. 'I would love to but I can't.' I could feel myself starting to panic. This woman was tracking me all the way around NYC.

'You can't?' she asked, doubtful.

'No,' I told her, waving a hand to get Jenny's attention. 'I'm – er – I'm, I'm going to Hawaii on Thursday.'

'You are?' Jenny asked, full of glee.

'You are?' Alex asked, full of something else entirely.

I considered my options. Stay home, meet with Perry Dickson, go to work, try not to murder Erin's husband then spend a sweaty weekend touring New York's most humid tourist traps with Louisa?

Or . . .

'Yes,' I said to all of them. 'I'm going to Hawaii.'

# CHAPTER EIGHT

'I can't believe we're going to Hawaii!'

Louisa squeezed her hands into little fists, leaping around as though she was auditioning for the *Flashdance* reboot I hoped they never considered making. I'd been waiting for her jetlag to kick in since she arrived but she'd seemingly been saving every ounce of energy from the last seven years for this exact moment. It was exhausting.

'Neither can we,' Alex replied coolly, bouncing Alice in his arms as we all crowded in the hallway, waiting for our taxi to the airport on Thursday morning. He had dressed her in my favourite outfit, a little green floral dress from Ralph Lauren that had an adorable Peter Pan collar and matching bloomers. I'd looked high and low for a matching dress for myself, but no, Ralph did not understand mothers at all.

'I'll be back on Tuesday,' I told him, clutching at Alice's warm little foot and pushing away the unpleasant feeling that had been growing ever since I'd agreed to this stupid trip. 'And you can call any time if you need me. I mean, call me anyway. And text, no matter the time. Anything at all, I want to know about it.'

'Angela, it's fine,' he said, leaning on his crutch and staring past me out the open door. 'We'll get by. I did tell you to go, didn't I?'

I looked up at him as I kissed her hands, nibbling on her fat little fingers. Even though he was saying the right things, Alex didn't look terribly happy. But it was a once-in-a-lifetime trip! And all my friends were going! And he *had* said I should go. Even if that was before he hurt his ankle and needed to use a crutch. With a baby.

'Technically, it's work, not a holiday.'

Cici had given the trip the all-clear provided I was ready for the launch of my site in a week's time and, since I was already well ahead of schedule and desperate to be convinced I'd made the right decision, I'd let Jenny convince me I'd be able to do all manner of work-related activities once we were on the island. Interviews, travel articles, product reviews . . . and if the work bits didn't work out and I ended up spending the entire trip sat on the beach getting mildly to moderately intoxicated with my friends, that could work too.

I slid my hands around Al's waist and gently prised her out of Alex's arms. She smelled like baby powder and her blankets and – very, very slightly – like the packet of salt and vinegar Hula Hoops I'd eaten over her head while Alex was in the shower. She smelled like heaven. My precious little girl. My tiny, perfect love. My angel, who I had never left for longer than a working day before, and was it just me or was she

116

totally giving me side eye right now? My heart squeezed itself until I was almost certain I was having a heart attack.

'This is a terrible idea,' I said, breathing hard. 'I'm not going.'

'The car is here,' Louisa said, panic in her voice, hula in her hips.

'I don't think I can leave her,' I shook my head as Al babbled nonsense at her aunt. 'It's too soon.' She reached out an arm to stroke my cheek and I felt a single fat tear roll down my cheek. 'See? She doesn't want me to – ow! Alex!'

'I think she's OK with it,' he said, carefully unclamping her hand from around the hair that was left in my temple and taking the world's tiniest sociopath back into his arms. 'I think she wants some alone time with Daddy whose hair she never pulls.'

Somehow, my heart sank and sped up at the same time. The car was outside, our flight left in two hours and then it was five whole days away. I hadn't been further than the island of Manhattan on my own since Alice was born and now I was going to disappear all the way to Hawaii because of FOMO? Just what exactly was wrong with me?

'Angela, our car is waiting,' Louisa said, rolling her giant suitcase back and forth on the creaky wooden floor and pulling the door open wider. Now there was a woman who had no such qualms but Gracie was six going on whatever age kids decided they were going to be YouTube superstars.

'False alarm, not our car,' she corrected. I peered out.

A slim, black-haired woman was climbing out of a

black town car, dragging an enormous overnight bag with her.

'Alex?'

'Mom!'

Passing Alice to me, he abandoned his crutch and jogged down the steps to help her with her bag.

'She called last night to say she'd try to stop by today,' he called over his shoulder.

'With a packed bag?' I replied, squeezing Alice more and more tightly until she squeaked in protest. 'At the exact same time our car is due to leave for the airport?'

'There's my little girl,' Mrs Reid dropped her bag at her son's feet and ran up the steps to snatch Alice from my arms. Her name was Janet but we were still very much on a 'Mrs Reid' basis. It was fun, kept me on my toes.

'Wow, that's a big bag for a spur-of-the-moment visit,' I said.

'I figured you'd have left already,' Mrs Reid said, still addressing Alice instead of me.

'Ange, that one is definitely our car,' Louisa gave me a pleading look as she pulled the strap of her document pouch over her head, keeping her passport, photocopy of her passport and her exceptionally safe pre-paid travellers' credit cards close to her chest. 'We don't want to be late for the flight.' She lowered her voice. 'You can tell me how awful she is on the way to the airport.'

'Can you tell your mommy how excited you are to see your grandma?' Janet said, talking about me but not to me. She blew happy raspberries against Alice's cheek as she squeaked with delight, not even attempting to pull a single hair out of her head. The traitor. Mrs Reid pulled something out of her pocket. A bow? She was putting a bow on my child?

'She doesn't like things on her head,' I said, attempting to swipe it away but Janet was too quick.

'I think it gives her some panache,' she replied, spinning out of my reach. 'And how else will people know she's a little girl?'

'I'm going to take my suitcase out to the car,' Louisa said, giving Janet a sharp smile. 'We don't want to be late to the airport.'

'No,' Janet agreed readily before wandering off into the living room and making herself at home with my pride and joy. 'You don't want to be late to the airport.'

'Mom's going to stay the whole weekend,' Alex announced, holding the door open for Louisa to squeeze out with her giant case. 'How great is that? I told her about you leaving and my accident and she offered. I couldn't say no.'

He should have asked, I thought. I could have helped him.

Our driver honked his horn.

'We gotta go, lady!' he called through the car window. 'Let's move it!'

'OK, OK, I'm coming,' I said, heaving my suitcase down the steps and into the boot of the car.

'Have a great time,' Alex said, sticking his hands in his jeans pockets at the top of the stairs, not even offering to help. His mum stood in the front window, pulling a theatrically sad face and making Alice wave goodbye.

'There's tons of milk in the freezer and you shouldn't need any nappies or anything but if we do run out, get the Huggies, not the Pampers. They don't stay up when she starts crawling,' I called before hopping in the back seat of the car beside Louisa. Perfect, it smelled like stale coffee and cigarettes, the official perfume of the New York City Taxi and Limousine Commission. 'I love you!'

But Alex had already closed the door.

'Ready to go?' Louisa asked, clutching her passport holder in her sweaty hands.

'Ready as I'll ever be,' I said, taking one last look at my husband, his mother and my daughter playing happily in the front room without me as we pulled away. 'Let's go.'

And off we went.


I rested against the edge of the terrace and gazed out at the ocean. A cool breeze was blowing across my face but doing nothing to help convince me I wasn't dreaming. Hala Lanai was set on a hill, a little way above the beach below, giving me the perfect view of the cove. The shoreline curved round in a gentle swoop, creating a private bay with soft white-crested waves that lapped at the white sand. The water shimmered, shifting from bright, light turquoise all the way into deep, dark indigo as the waves swept away from the shore. Way off in the distance, the ocean blended with the sky at the edge of the world.

'Ange, I just saw a dolphin.' Louisa threw her arm out, jabbing at the air in excitement. 'An actual bloody dolphin just jumped out of the sea, I swear.'

We were so far from Skegness, it was scary.

'I feel like I'm losing it,' I replied, rubbing my eyes as a dolphin and his friends leapt out of the water right in front of us and then disappeared under the waves.

Tearing herself away from the terrace, Lou backed into the villa. With a happy sigh, I grinned as she hurled herself across the enormous bed in the middle of the room. Just like Jenny had promised.

'The room's not too shoddy,' she said, face down in the mound of pillows. 'It'll do for me.'

'I've stayed in worse,' I agreed, eyeing the thick, white sheets and eight different pillows.

'You mean that time we went to Ibiza after our A levels?'

The mere mention of that trip and I could taste the cinnamon Aftershock, dodgy kebabs and the tongue of that awful boy with the tribal tattoos who thought the Harry Potter books were based on a true story.

'My mum put all my clothes on a boil-wash the second I walked through the door,' I said with a near nostalgic smile.

'My mum burned mine,' Lou said as she rolled over, disappearing into the big, fluffy pillows. 'Can I stay here? I don't think I've got the energy to walk all the way next door.'

'Yes, after travelling half the way around the world, the ten steps to the next villa are what's going to finish you off,' I said, running my hand over the walnut dresser, hand-painted screens and the absolutely massive telly, before peeking into the bathroom. 'But since there's a big basket full of personalized swag in the bathroom, I think you might want to go and get your own.'

'I'll see you in a bit then,' Lou grunted as she rolled off my bed, grabbed her suitcase and ran out the villa.

'Dinner's at seven,' I shouted, checking the time on the antique clock by my bed. 'Don't fall asleep!'

'I can be ready to do the school run in five minutes flat, I could be ready to meet the Queen in an hour,' she called before the door slammed shut behind her.

I padded across the hardwood floors and stepped back out onto the balcony. The sun was low. We were only an hour away from sunset, and the light, bright blue sky was streaked with pink, already tarting itself up for the night ahead.

'Something you should be doing too,' I told myself. Who knew what kind of glamazons would be at dinner. Jenny said Précis had invited influencers from all over the world and I was doing my best not to worry about it but, after my experience with The M.O.B., I was more than a little bit anxious about having to make new friends.

I pulled out my phone to check the time in New York. If it was six p.m. in Hawaii, it was eleven p.m. in New York. Alex would probably be awake but I didn't want to wake Alice by calling. That said, it might wake his mum up too . . .

'Be the bigger person,' I told myself, peeling away my plane layers and tapping out a text.

'I am grateful for each and every gift of experience life sends my way,' I whispered, settling into a sun lounger in nothing but my bra, knickers and the lei they had given us at the airport while I waited for Alex to reply. If you couldn't really get stuck into your affirmations in Hawaii at sunset, when could you?

'This road is mine and mine alone and I will travel in grace and power.'

I smiled as I watched the sun slip away until there

was nothing left but a slash of orange reflecting off the far-away seas, and breathed out, full of nothing but gratitude, peace and the Toblerone I'd eaten on the way over. Snide in-laws and sulky husbands aside, this was setting itself up to be the most perfect trip of my entire life.

Because what could possibly go wrong?

# CHAPTER NINE

'Lou?'

I knocked on the door of the neighbouring villa an hour later, as gussied up as I was capable of getting. My hair was clean, my face was presentable and I was wearing my favourite new outfit: flat leather sandals paired with a buttercup-yellow midi dress from Paul & Joe that had little covered buttons running from the low sweetheart neckline all the way down to the fitted-but-not-so-fitted-that-I-couldn't-eat waist. I had taken button-up tops for granted until I had to breastfeed but now they were right up there next to skirts with pockets on my sartorial preferences chart. You never knew when you'd need to pop out a boob and Alice did not enjoy being stuffed under a jumper, let me tell you.

'Lou, are you ready?'

When she didn't bound out the door, ready and waiting, I tried the handle.

'Someone still lives in the suburbs,' I muttered to myself when it opened immediately. 'Come on, you tart. If we're late Jenny will beat us with two very large sticks.'

But Louisa wasn't coming to dinner. Louisa was passed out, fast asleep on top of her bed, happily buried in a nest of pillows. Jetlag had finally claimed its victim.

'This is all for karma points,' I whispered, pulling a blanket off her sofa and carefully laying it over her legs. I had to be out of the red by now.

Creeping out of the room, I closed her door and ventured back out to the main house, prepared to brave the welcome dinner alone.

My timing was perfect. The exact moment I walked into the gorgeous main house of Hala Lanai, the attention of the assembled masses was squarely focused on Jenny, who was tapping a spoon against a crystal champagne flute at the front of the room. And what an assembled mass it was. There had to be around twenty of the most gorgeous creatures I'd ever laid eyes on, all milling around the open-concept living room. A sweet-smelling fire was burning in the fireplace and women who could easily have passed for models were draped on endless squishy-looking seating options that had been positioned around the vast but still cosy room so that each and every perch had a view of the Pacific Ocean. Instead of walls, the house had sliding slabs of glass, all the better for dolphin-watching or seeing who was hanging out in the cliff-edge infinity pool. It didn't feel possible that this could be someone's home but I would very much have liked it to be mine.

'Aloha, everyone!'

The excited chatter in the dining room died down

as Jenny climbed on top of a coffee table to give her speech. I gave her a quick wave which she returned with a wink before getting back to business.

'My name is Jenny and it's my great honour to be your host this weekend. We're all here to celebrate the new True Soul mascara from Précis Cosmetics which I hope you all found in your bathrooms this evening, but most importantly we're here to have a great time. We're super lucky to be staying at Hala Lanai, a private estate belonging to the one and only fashion legend, Bertie Bennett, so please relax and enjoy yourself, but remember this is also someone's home, so no shoes on the soft furnishings is what I'm saying.'

Cue half polite laughter and half girls removing their shoes from the soft furnishings.

'When you get back to your rooms after dinner, you'll find a couple more treats and a schedule of events for the next few days. We've got a ton of fun stuff planned for you guys but if there's anything at all that you need, just grab me or Jesse or Sumi—'

Two girls I recognized from EWPR raised their hands to identify themselves.

'And we will hook you up with whatever your heart desires.'

Jenny climbed down from the coffee table, landing delicately on her four-inch heels as I considered my heart's desires. A good night's sleep, an uninterrupted bath and Richard Madden delivering me breakfast in bed and then politely asking about my day while I binge-watched an adult-appropriate TV show should do it.

'Oh,' Jenny held up a hand to silence the excited early burble of conversation while she finished her thought. 'And please use "hashtag True Soul" and "hashtag ad" in all your social posts otherwise I'll have to hunt you down and kill you. Thanks, guys!'

It was nice to see that work Jenny was very much the same as regular Jenny.

Everyone clapped our appreciation and or fear as dozens of waiters appeared from all corners of the room, some passing out different foods on skewers and others filling a long candlelit dining table that was set on the patio outside.

I looked around for faces I might recognize as Jenny worked the room, and eventually found my former co-worker Eva, lounging on a daybed in front of the pool outside.

'Hey!' She sat up as I approached, a cheerful grin on her face. 'You're here!'

'I'm here!' I confirmed happily. Eva was a ridiculously young and ridiculously successful YouTuber who was also ridiculously nice. The three things rarely went together so I made an effort to be especially appreciative of her. Not only because I liked her but because I wanted to be spared should she ever go to the dark side. Even technophobe me knew better than to get on the wrong side of a YouTuber.

'So,' I said, nodding at the elaborate eyebrow brigade all around us. 'Do you know who all these people are?'

'I do,' she confirmed, her honey-blonde afro bobbing as she nodded. 'I see Lily from London, that's Pearl and Darcy, they're from the UK too, sister vloggers. They do fun lifestyle stuff. I definitely saw Elodie and Violet earlier, I met them on a trip to Paris one time, and I think someone said there were some people here from Germany and Switzerland. Précis is big there, makes sense.'

'I didn't realize there would be so many people,' I said, leaning against her chair and wishing I'd made more of an effort with my makeup. What was I thinking? This was a beauty trip. A slick of lip gloss and a powdered nose was not going to cut it.

'Jenny said we'd all be breaking up into smaller groups after tonight,' Eva shrugged. 'This place is so huge, we probably won't see half of them again.'

'I would be fine with that,' I said, watching one of the French vloggers position herself on the edge of the infinity pool for a photo, hanging over the cliff and pouting into her own camera. I couldn't watch. Death by selfie.

'Be still my heart. If it isn't my old beard, Angela Clark.'

Instead of giving me a hug like a normal person, James Jacobs scooped me up off my feet and tossed me over his shoulder before I could even turn around.

'Put me down, you big knob,' I squealed upside down, watching him extend a hand to a perplexed Eva.

'Beard?' she asked.

'Long story,' I replied, pinching the tender spot on the back of his arm until he put me down. 'Don't ask.'

'The first time we met, I tried to seduce Angela into being my pretend girlfriend so no one would know I was gay,' James said, following up his handshake with a kiss on each of Eva's cheeks. 'But her overpowering femininity convinced me to come out instead.'

'You're such a cock,' I grumbled before grudgingly accepting a real hug.

'No, I *like* cock,' he corrected. 'And thanks to you, now everybody knows it.'

Even when he was being a tit, you couldn't help but love that man. Breaking off the hug, I wrapped an arm around his waist and leaned my head on his shoulder. Big blue eyes, curly brown hair and a jaw so square it made Superman look like a total puss. He looked like a movie star. Probably because he was one. And it was especially nice to have your gay husband around when your real one was ignoring your calls.

'That's crazy,' Eva grinned. 'Why did you have to pretend you weren't gay?'

'Angela, I don't know this girl but I'm obsessed with her,' James said, squeezing my shoulder, a delighted look on his face. 'God, I wish I was coming out now, it's a much better time for it. Career killer back then, love, Hollywood thought no one wanted to go to the pictures knowing they were fantasizing about a poof. But everyone's queer these days and no one cares in the slightest, it's wonderful. Still plenty of actors in the closet, though.'

'Really?' Eva's head popped straight up like a millennial meerkat. 'Like who?'

He held up his whiskey and winked. 'Let me put a couple more of these away so I can claim plausible deniability tomorrow.'

'You auditioned for *Hamilton* in London then?' I asked.

'Too fucking right, I did,' he replied. 'Now, is Lopez bullshitting or what? Does she really know Bertie Bennett?'

I nodded, eyeing the passing waiters like a hawk and grabbing a pineapple skewer as soon as they came close enough. 'He's one of her clients. He designed her wedding dress, she didn't tell you?'

'All I remember about Jenny's wedding was waking up in a room that wasn't mine,' he said, smiling at the memory. 'But I'm sure she looked divine. Have you met him?'

'No,' I replied, wondering who exactly he'd hooked up with. 'But Jenny says he's amazing. There are so many mad stories about him getting up to shenanigans with super celebs back in the day. I once saw a photo of him carrying Debbie Harry around Studio 54 on his shoulders and I was not unimpressed.'

'He *is* amazing and, let me tell you, all the mad stories are true.'

I turned my head to see Paige appear, glowing from head to toe in a white silk slip, held together by tiny ties at her shoulders. Why was I the only one who looked as though they had spent the last fifteen hours travelling, I thought, giving my own pallid cheek a pinch. I'd done everything the internet said I was supposed to, I'd even used a sheet mask on the flight from New York to Honolulu and scared Louisa half to death when she woke up from a nap.

'You've met him?' James asked, dropping me like a hot rock and turning his attention to Paige.

'He's the absolute best,' she nodded. 'The sweetest gentleman, he'd do anything for anyone. He told me an incredible story about the time he made a dress for Princess Margaret and how they ended up getting rat-arsed in Buck House before the Queen came in and gave them all a bollocking. I didn't quite believe it until I found a photograph of Princess Margaret wearing the dress.'

'My kind of man. I'm James, friends call me Jim,' he said, lighting up as Paige shook his hand. 'Pleasure to meet you.'

'Of course I know who you are,' she said with a pretty laugh. 'Paige Sullivan, I'm the new vice president of content at Besson.'

'Is that right?' James cast his eyes from Paige to me. I chomped down on my last piece of pineapple and desperately looked around for more. 'Which makes you, what, Angela's boss?'

'Oh,' Paige answered. 'I suppose it does.'

'Has anyone seen the pineapple man anywhere?' I asked, covering my mouth with my hand.

'No but I can smell drama,' James whispered in my ear.

'I'm amazed you can smell anything over that after-shave,' I replied curtly.

'It's Tom Ford,' he shot back, horrified.

'Smells like piss,' I hissed.

Before we could exchange any more cutting insults, Jenny sailed over on a cloud of a more classy perfume and a good night's sleep.

'Hi, hi, hi. Everyone looks amazing,' she said to everyone, standing on tiptoes and bending down for assorted hugs and kisses. 'Angie, cute dress.'

'It's yours,' I held out the fabric for everyone's approval. 'Remember? You said it made you look fat so you gave it to me.'

'I know.' She chomped on a chip, glancing around the room. 'Looks great on you, though.'

'We really shouldn't judge ourselves on how we look in our clothes.' A dark-haired English woman with a cut-glass accent forced her way in between

131

James and Jenny, giving everyone within spitting distance a filthy look. 'Your self-worth shouldn't be tied to how tight your jeans are.'

'It isn't,' Jenny replied with a very serious look on her face. 'It's tied to how loose they are.'

The woman let out a tiny sigh before flicking a strand of her expertly waved hair over her bronzed shoulder. I hadn't seen her on the plane, I had no idea who she was and it was quite clear that she had no idea who Jenny was. I couldn't believe La Lopez was about to let a hair toss that snide pass by unacknowledged.

'I think that's very sad,' the woman declared, waving a glass of champagne around in the air in front of her. 'I think we should all accept the universe exactly as it is.'

She had a smile on her face but I noticed Jenny's fingers were curled into tight little fists at her sides. I was prepared to bet there would still be fingernail imprints in her palms in the morning.

'Couldn't agree more,' Jenny replied evenly. Her first true professional test of the trip and she passed with flying colours. 'Can I get you something to eat?'

'Perhaps.' The woman turned up her tiny nose and winced. 'I don't eat fried foods, red meat, sugar, carbs, dairy, gluten or pulses.'

'Just as nature intended,' Jenny smiled. 'We haven't met yet but I'm guessing you must be Lily?'

'Lily Lashgasm,' she confirmed with a nod. I flicked my eyes up to James, looking for silent confirmation that it was a stupid name. 'I arrived a while before you all but don't worry, I shan't tell Précis there was no one here to meet me.'

'Except for the entire seventy-five-person staff for a twelve-room hotel,' Jenny muttered over her shoulder before collecting herself. 'I'm so sorry, Lily. It's entirely my fault, we were out collecting the other girls from the airport. I spoke to your team at Content in London and we're all super sorry for the mix-up.'

'I shall let it go this time,' Lily replied with feigned grace. 'Since we're all new friends.'

'I imagine "her team" were so happy to see the back of her, they sent her out early,' James whispered into my ear before turning his million-dollar-movie-star smile onto the group. 'I propose a toast. To old friends and new, to the games afoot and to the spirit of *ohana*.'

'*Ohana* means family,' Jenny added, looking around for a glass to join in the toast.

'Yes, yes, we've all seen *Lilo & Stitch*,' I replied. 'What's he talking about, the games afoot?'

'Oh, nothing, just some activities the brand suggested,' she said as she stuffed her face with a piece of pineapple. 'You'll like them, it'll be fun.'

I couldn't quite put my finger on why but for some reason, I just didn't believe her.

'So happy this is going to be our little gang for the next few days.' Jenny raised a bottle of water she grabbed from the table into the air as I looked around at the familiar and not so familiar faces. Eva, Paige, James and Lily. I wondered if there was an opportunity to make one trade. 'It really is going to be incredible so try to get some rest tonight. I want to see you all at breakfast, bright and early in the morning.'

'No problem,' James replied, chugging his whiskey. 'It's impossible to get drunk in Hawaii, you know?

Something to do with the altitude and the quality of the air.'

'And I'm happy to see you're putting your theory to the test,' she said, watching as one of the waiters replaced his glass without even asking. 'OK, gotta go check on some stuff.'

'You can't stay and have a drink?' I asked.

Jenny let out one loud laugh. 'I wish,' she scoffed. 'First night, there's so much to do. I'll be back soon, I promise.'

Avoiding me again.

'Soon,' I shouted after her as James necked his second drink. 'Be back soon.'

After a couple of cocktails, a mountain of Hawaiian pork and a vegan veggie bowl prepared especially for Lily, everyone seemed a lot more relaxed than they had when they arrived. Sitting on a sun lounger by the pool, I stared off at the pitch-black horizon, wondering how far away the next closest human being might be.

'Angela Clark, you should go to bed,' James stated, walking straight into the end of the sun lounger and snapping me out of my sleepy stupor.

I looked up to see his trademark curls were flopping all over the place and, for some reason I didn't care to know, his Hawaiian shirt was unbuttoned halfway down to his belly button.

'Do you need me to carry you, you messy bitch?' he asked, slurring every single word.

'No, do you need me to carry you?' I replied, picking up the key that had dropped to the floor the second he pulled it out of his pocket.

'Yes please,' he said with a hiccup. 'I've no idea where my room is.'

'Starting as we mean to go on,' I said, using all of my five feet and five inches to support all six feet six of him. I looked around for someone to help but Jenny was AWOL, Paige had gone to bed ages ago and Eva was deep in conversation with one of the French girls, leaving me to drag the nominee for Best Actor in a Drunken Stupor back to his room all by myself.

'Don't mind me, totally OK here on my own,' I muttered, stumbling under the weight of the giant man. 'Thanks, friends.'

'Word of warning, I might vomit,' James whispered.

'Thank you for letting me know,' I replied, pulling away from his boozy breath as we staggered back towards the villas.

It took fifteen minutes to find his villa, which, we discovered after trying every single lock on every single door, was directly opposite mine. Once I'd run James through practically all of Alice's evening routine (save the nappy change) I left him snoring with a glass of water and bottle of Advil on the bedside table, along with a note that said I'd taken the chocolates Jenny had left in his room as penance.

Back in my own villa, I locked the door behind me with a happy sigh. Someone had been in to turn down the giant bed and leave a pair of beautiful white cotton pyjamas with my initials embroidered on the chest pocket.

'I'm living in an Instagram story,' I whispered, yanking my dress off over my head and pulling on the pyjamas as fast as humanly possible. Free PJs, two boxes of chocolates and a massive bed all to myself. Women had killed for less.

With James's chocolates in one hand and my phone in the other, I slid open the doors to my terrace and settled down to resume my staring. The sky and the sea were completely black with nothing but a slim streak of reflected moonlight running across the waves to cut through the night. I couldn't imagine how anyone wouldn't be completely in love with this place and understood entirely why Delia was so upset at the idea of Bertie Bennett selling up. Who would willingly let this place go? It was the closest I'd ever come to heaven on earth and I'd been on the Cadbury's *and* Ben & Jerry's factory tours.

It was midnight in Lanai, five a.m. in New York. Alex would definitely be asleep now. A sudden pang hit my heart as I swiped through my favourite photos of him and Alice, wishing they were with me. With a tiny sigh, I snapped a shot of the sky and sent it as a text along with a half-dozen heart eyes emojis, hoping he knew how much I already missed him. Hoping he already missed me.

With a yawn big enough to swallow the entire island, I shuddered in my seat and a wave of complete exhaustion slapped me right in the face. My second wind had died down, there was no third wind. It was time for bed.

'Hello, jetlag,' I muttered, eyes still skyward. I might have missed travelling and jumping on planes over the last couple of years but the debilitating tiredness that had taken me over was not something I'd been especially yearning for. Alex and Alice were five thousand miles away but, as I trudged back inside with legs like lead, my bed felt even further.

I rolled my head from side to side, hoping to loosen

the tight muscles in my neck but it was definitely a job for a professional. One of the girls from Précis had said something about an onsite masseuse. Maybe I could do that instead of the First Annual Lopez Games. Sliding underneath the cool, crisp sheets, I plugged in my phone and set an alarm to make sure I had time to call home before my day began. Now, hopefully I wouldn't have any trouble falling asleep and all would be . . . my eyelids slipped over my dry eyes and everything else disappeared.

Pitch black, absolute silence, pure bliss.

# CHAPTER TEN

When I woke up on Friday morning, I felt like a new woman. After an entire night of uninterrupted sleep, I couldn't remember where I was, how I'd got there and really had to think for a moment before I could remember my own name. Who was this decadent madam who slept for nine hours straight with several different kinds of pillows and woke up with her hand in a box of chocolates? Me. It was me. And I had never been happier.

'Gross,' I muttered to myself, licking the melted chocolate from my fingers. 'I am so gross.'

I reached over for my mobile, swiping it out of its slumber to find a text from Alex. Rubbing the last specks of sleep out of my eyes, I opened the attached image to see his mother manhandling Al beside the lake in Prospect Park. My child was wearing a patterned pink outfit that had one hundred percent not been purchased by me and had what looked like a giant blue carnation sprouting out the middle of her forehead.

Gorgeous. I gritted my teeth as I typed. You both OK?

Three dots appeared at the bottom of the screen before swapping places with a thumbs up emoji. Hmm. Alex was not someone who usually went in for emojis.

Can I call and say hi? I said, cradling the phone in both hands as I typed.

Three more dots hovered at the bottom of the screen as I wiggled my toes awake. Quick chat with Alex, nice hot shower then breakfast. All without a tiny human screaming if I didn't take her with me from room to room, what a bloody treat. For the first six months, if I was home and she was awake, I had to be in Al's eyeline at all times or she would scream the house down. I couldn't even go to the toilet on my own without a tiny chaperone. But when she hit nine months, something happened, and now she was constantly trying to lose me. I couldn't so much as blink without her disappearing behind the sofa or crawling off into another room. For a brief moment, I'd considered putting a bell on her but Alex said it was cruel so I had to take it back to the pet shop.

The three grey dots were still rolling along at the bottom of my screen when I threw back the covers and crossed the room to open up the French doors to the terrace. Oh no, it was even more gorgeous in the morning than it had been in the evening. What a shame.

My phone buzzed in my hand.

Not a great time. I'll try you later.

'It's not a great time,' I said out loud, placing the phone on my nightstand with a concerned frown. 'He'll try me later.'

No point in trying to read too much into it, I told myself, it just wasn't a great time. To talk to his wife, the mother of his child, the love of his life who he missed so much he couldn't even breathe. Not a great time. His mum was visiting so it seemed unlikely that he'd filled the house with groupies the moment I'd walked out the door. Unless his mum had a stranger take that photo of her and Al and sent it to Alex who sent it to me to throw me off the scent because he was already embroiled in a sordid affair with Perry Dickson.

'Definitely not overreacting,' I muttered to a small red-crested bird that cocked its head at me on the edge of the terrace. With an agreeable chirp, he fluttered his wings and took off, soaring down towards the infinity pool and the beach beyond. Holding my hand over my eyes to shield them from the sun, I saw dozens of men and women running back and forth across the patio, skimming the pool, sweeping up leaves. Someone said Bertie Bennett employed more than a hundred people on the estate, one way or another, and he'd even paid for kids of his employees to leave the island and go to university or found them jobs in his various businesses. Everyone talked about him like he was some kind of saint: Santa Claus but make it fashion. It seemed difficult to believe anyone could love their boss that much but, watching them all as they laughed and smiled and set the table for breakfast, everyone certainly looked happy. Perhaps I'd been working for Cici for too long. It had been almost an entire week, after all.

As the table filled with fruits and pastries and other delicious things, my stomach began to rumble loudly. Mmm, breakfast. I wondered what Alice had had for breakfast. Had Alex remembered to use the yellow spoon? No one had been able to work out why but she always ate more when we used the yellow spoon. I'd know if he'd pick up the bloody phone.

'Food first, worry later,' I decided, slapping my growling stomach.

It was a system that had never steered me wrong before.

Replying to Alex with a thumbs up of my own, I decided to turn all of my attention onto Paige. While I had no interest in taking part in any of this, if I was going to be forced into organized fun, I'd rather be forced into it with someone who hadn't spent a good chunk of the previous evening explaining why Piers Morgan wasn't all that bad when you got to know him.

The ocean lapped the shoreline lazily with a line of tall, palm trees watching over us as we walked single file down a narrow stone staircase behind the house and across Bertie Bennett's private beach. It was all too perfect, like a child's drawing of the seaside. Bright colours, bold lines, happy, smiling faces.

And Jenny Lopez had found a way to ruin it.

Standing with her back to the water, Jenny paced up and down in front of myself, Louisa, Paige, Eva, James and Lily. Before heading off to bed, I'd suggested to Jenny that Lily might prefer to enjoy her time on the island with the rest of the Brits but the rest of the Brits had beat me to it. Seemingly, they'd had more than enough of her on the plane ride over and made Jenny swear to keep her out their way for the entire weekend. Clever bastards. Everyone else had been whisked away on a tour of the island, leaving us at Jenny's mercy, lined up like we were waiting for the first annual Précis Cosmetics Hunger Games. I would *not* volunteer as tribute.

'Good morning, everyone,' Jenny barked, a sarong

tied around her waist and a very shiny whistle hanging around her neck – part drill sergeant, part island princess. Why would she need a whistle for some 'fun games'? Why had we been separated into teams? And why was I on a team with a woman who the night before had described Piers Morgan as 'not that bad when you got to know him'? I looked down the line at Lily and frowned.

'Before we start, I want to introduce you to a very special guest who just arrived here on the island,' Jenny said, speaking into an invisible microphone. 'Founder of Précis Cosmetics, Camilla Rose!'

We clapped politely as an exceptionally attractive older woman strode across the sand towards us. If anyone could sell me a face full of slap, it was this human. I quietly wondered whether or not she could teach me how to cover up my permanent dark circles with something other than Polyfilla while she shook everyone's hand. Good grip, soft skin, top marks. Seemed like a nice woman.

'Hawaii has been a second home to me,' Camilla said in an oddly lilting accent that was impossible to place. 'I hope you'll find the same joy and inspiration here that has always come to me. To better acquaint you with Hawaiian culture, Jenny and I have come up with a few games to get us all in the vacation spirit.'

'What kind of games?' Louisa asked, wringing her hands behind her back. Lou had never been especially fond of PE but you try taking a cricket ball to the head during a particularly agro game of rounders in Year Seven and see how much you like it.

'Nothing too heinous,' Jenny replied as she rubbed her hands together.

'What do the winners get?' Lily asked.

'An afternoon of massage and pampering.'

'And what about the losers?' James gave me a pointed look for some reason.

'We'll think of something dastardly,' Camilla replied with a wicked grin. 'This will be fun but it will not be easy.'

With nothing nice to say, I said nothing at all. Imagine dragging people a third of the way around the world and then forcing them to play stupid games when they could be getting shmammered on piña coladas. I was wrong, she was not a nice lady, Camilla Rose was very obviously a sociopath. I once read an article about how sociopaths often had great skin, something to do with a lack of stress hormones, and even though that article had literally no science to back it up this was more than enough evidence to convince me they were onto something.

'Hula dancing is a traditional Polynesian dance that originated here in the Hawaiian islands,' Camilla said. Me, Lily and Louisa pulled on blue T-shirts as Jenny handed them out; Paige, James and Eva were wearing pink. 'Even though it may look improvised, every movement in the hula has a meaning and the dances were passed down through generations as a way of telling the stories of their ancestors.'

'I've always wanted to learn to hula dance,' Lily said, busting out a few hip swivels in the sand. 'Do we get a grass skirt as well?'

I was considerably less excited, tortured by inescapable visions of myself thrusting around in a coconut bikini like Baloo in *The Jungle Book*.

'No, because we're not learning to hula dance. Yet,' Jenny said. 'First you have to tackle hula *hoops*.'

I had a horrible feeling she didn't mean the crisps.

One of Jenny's assistants slapped her way across the beach in a pair of Précis-branded flip-flops, carrying six silver hula hoops, and handed them out, one by one. It was so weird. I couldn't remember the last time I'd held a hula hoop, let alone tried to use one – no, wait, that was a lie. I had a sudden vision of Jenny and I arsing about in FAO Schwartz one afternoon after one too many lunchtime cocktails and being asked to leave. No wonder that place had shut down, they had no sense of humour.

'When Camilla Rose says "Hula", I'm going to start the stopwatch,' Jenny called, brushing a stray curl behind her ears as the breeze blew her hair around her face. She'd only been here a couple of days and she was already glowing with a golden tan, a smattering of adorable freckles over her tiny, snub nose. 'Whoever is still going after sixty seconds gets two points.'

'I don't want to be a bitch about this,' Lily said, immediately sounding like a bitch. 'But I really want to win this. So, be good, yeah?'

'I hula hoop with my little girl all the time,' Louisa said, dipping from side to side to warm up. 'No problemo.'

'And I haven't hula hooped *since* I was a little girl so I'm promising nothing,' I replied, throwing up an OK sign.

'If you can floss, you can hula hoop,' Eva called.

'Floss?' I was confused. What did flossing your teeth have to do with hula hooping?

All at once, Jenny, Eva, Louisa, Paige and James began swinging their arms and hips in opposite directions, as though they were drying their bum with a towel only the towel was missing. They looked insane.

'Are they all having a seizure at the same time?' Lily asked, a worried look on her face.

I'd missed out on so much due to my post-pregnancy mental fug; Pete and Ariana, cold-shoulder tops, the actual royal wedding (slept through the entire event) but I was fairly sure this was one thing I could live without. Camilla Rose held one arm up in the air and all flossing ceased immediately.

'On your marks, get set, hula!'

Paige, James, Eva, Lily and Lou picked up their hula hoops and began swinging their hips wildly. I looked at the big shiny hoop in my hand and thanked assorted deities that Alex wasn't here to see this. At some point I wanted Alice to have a little brother or sister and seeing me attempt to hula hoop could be enough to turn him off for life.

'Angela, you gotta start!' Jenny yelled. 'Don't make me disqualify you.'

'Oh god,' I muttered, holding the hoop at waist level and closing my eyes on the scene. How hard could it be? I flicked the hoop and began twisting my body as fast as possible. Almost at once, it all came back to me. Sun on my skin, sand in between my toes and a crappy little piece of plastic looping around my waist. This wasn't so bad after all.

'Bollocks!' James shouted as his hoop rattled down his hips and landed in the sand. 'There, now you all know the truth, I have no rhythm.'

'There goes the *Dirty Dancing* remake,' Jenny said with a fake sad smile. 'You suck, Jacobs. Everyone else, forty seconds to go.'

Forty seconds.

I closed my eyes again and concentrated, my tongue poking out the corner of my mouth. I'd always been good at this as a kid and now I was in the swing of things, I had a flashback of me and Lou, hula hoops spinning on every part of our body; ankles, wrists, neck. I wondered what had replaced that skill in my brain. Probably some very important Taylor Swift song lyrics or the choreography to the chorus of 'Single Ladies' that was always such a hit at weddings.

'Lily is out!' I heard Jenny yell. 'Twenty seconds.'

I can actually do this, I thought to myself, undulating wildly, faster and faster and faster. Maybe I could start a hula hooping exercise class. It had to be good for the obliques and god knows people will pay for anything if they think it'll make them skinny.

'Goddamn it!'

I opened one eye and saw Eva's hoop in the sand.

This is it, I realized, I'm actually a master hula hooper. My whole life had been building towards this moment where I suddenly realized I was always meant to hula hoop. My hips spun faster as Jenny began the final countdown and I threw my hands up over my head, victorious, just as I looked down and saw a name flashing up on my phone.

Perry bloody Dickson.

'Five, four, three . . .'

One second was all it took. The momentary lack of concentration broke my stride and, before I could do anything to stop it, my hoop rattled down my hips, sliding all the way down my legs and landing in the sand with a soft thud.

'Two, one and that's it!' Jenny shouted. 'Louisa and Paige, you're our winners. Two points to each team.'

Ignoring Lily's colourful torrent of abuse, I dived for my phone just as Perry's face faded away.

'Tut-tut, phones away for the challenge,' Camilla called, swooping in and snatching my phone out of my hand just as the voicemail alert came through. 'Everyone hand over their devices, this is an analogue-only morning.'

'Over my dead body,' Louisa gasped, madly shoving her iPhone X down the back of her knickers. 'How does she think we're going to cheat at hula hooping with our phones?'

'Definitely a sociopath,' I decided with narrowed eyes as Camilla placed everyone's phones into a big, branded tote.

'OK, who feels like throwing an axe?' Jenny asked, holding the weapon up in the air.

'Me,' I replied, raising my hand. 'I do.'

I had a very good feeling I was going to be a natural at this one too.


'And it all comes down to the final competition,' Camilla Rose declared as both teams lined up at the edge of the ocean.

My nose was tingling from being out in the sun for too long and the rumble in my stomach suggested we must be very close to lunchtime. Since the hula competition had ended in a draw, our team managed to snatch back two points in the axe-throwing competition but we lost the limbo and the pineapple peeling, although I was thankful points were the only thing we lost after Louisa almost managed to take her thumb off, removing the core from her last pineapple. So far, this was not turning out to be the relaxing trip Jenny had promised. We'd already had Eva in tears and Paige was soldiering through a nasty turned ankle. I was not someone who believed competition brought out the best in people and this morning had done nothing to persuade me otherwise.

'Our last challenge harks back to the days of the Hawaiian people's oceanic adventures,' Camilla said. 'One member of each team needs to swim out to the pink buoy, grab the silver streamer and swim back to shore.'

'I'm not doing it,' Lily declared. 'I've got lash extensions in, the seawater will ruin them.'

'And you know I'm not a good swimmer,' Louisa said, shaking her head decisively. 'Ever since I nearly drowned at Jason Simpson's swimming party.'

'You did not nearly drown,' I said with a sigh, stripping off my T-shirt to reveal my black one-piece swimming costume. The sooner I got this over with, the sooner I could have my phone back and see what that lunatic wanted. 'You swallowed a mouthful of water because you were diving for bricks with his brother and showing off.'

'I almost died!' she protested. 'I was sick for hours.'

'Yes, I know, all over the back seat of my dad's Ford Sierra,' I replied. That car had never been the same. 'Whatever, I'll do it.'

'Me and you then, is it, Clark?' James strode up towards me, flexing his muscles as he walked. 'I don't want to put you off but I should mention I spent two months training with professional swimmers for *Aquaman*.'

'You weren't in *Aquaman*.' I said, tying my hair up in a bun.

'Bastards cut me out,' he muttered. 'Eight hours a day flopping about in a bloody tank and they turned my character into a talking dolphin.'

'How is it fair that I have to swim against him?' I asked. 'Surely that's cheating?'

'Sorry,' Jenny said with a not-sorry-at-all shrug. 'Take it up with your team captain.'

We'd been here less than twenty-four hours and there was already no love lost between Jenny and Lily. She hadn't stopped complaining from the moment we got here. The food wasn't right, the birds outside her room were too noisy, the moon was shining directly through her window, the slope of the bath was too steep for her exceptionally long neck. The last one had been my favourite. All the better for Jenny to strangle her if she didn't pack it in, I thought to myself as she pulled a tiny brush out of her handbag and combed her eyelashes, without a hint of irony, in front of everyone.

James dropped down into the sand, putting on a one-armed push-up show for his new friends while I ignored the creaking noises coming from my knees as I shook off my shorts. I wasn't having it. James did not get to win just because he was bigger, faster and had voiced an animated superhero dolphin. I'd always been a pretty good swimmer when I was younger, I definitely stood a chance. The water wasn't that deep. I could see the bottom almost all the way out to the buoy as we stepped into the sea, tiny waves lapping at our ankles. I could definitely do this.

'On your marks!' Jenny shouted.

'I'm going to have you, Clark,' James said with a grin.

'Get set!'

'May the best man win,' I replied, eyes on the prize.

'Go!'

The second Jenny gave the command, I gave James a hard shove, knocking him off balance and sending him face first into the sand.

'Cheat!' he wailed. 'She cheated!'

'He slipped!' I shouted as I ran into the waves. 'Sorry, James.'

The water was cold against my sun-warmed skin as it hit my body. I folded my arms over my chest before ducking down to submerge myself and start swimming. I should be on the beach right now, I thought, sweeping my arms through the water towards the buoy, I should be on the beach in my swimming costume and drinking a cocktail out of a pineapple. Was that too much to ask? My arms burned from the unfamiliar effort as I reached the buoy, grabbed my silver streamer and turned around. Right behind me was professionally trainer swimmer and very angry man, James Jacobs.

'I can't believe you cheated,' he gasped between strokes.

'I can't believe you didn't,' I replied, sailing right on by.

The swim back was harder as I pushed against the tide, clinging to my streamer for dear life. Paddling as though my life depended on it, I heard Louisa and Lily screaming my name from the beach. I was almost there, switching from swimming to wading as the bottom of the ocean became the beginning of the beach, when I felt someone grab hold of my ankle.

'Not today, Satan!' James screamed.

'Stop making me do things I have to apologize for later!' I shouted back, kicking hard until I felt something solid.

James fell backwards into the surf but I scrambled through the water on my hands and knees, hurling myself at dry land like a beached whale. I was starting to understand how that happened, I realized as I lay panting in the sun, listening to Lily and Louisa cheer my name. Swimming was exhausting, beaching yourself was definitely the easier option.

'Blue team are the winners!' Camilla Rose announced. 'Even though I'm not entirely sure I approve of the tactics used to secure the victory.'

'I am sorry,' I said, still panting for air as James collapsed on the beach beside me, silver streamer still in his mouth. 'I don't know what came over me.'

'Human nature,' he said, flopping face down in the sand. 'We adapt so quickly. Remember the last Harry Potter film? One minute they're running around trying to free house elves, the next they're carrying their twin's dead body out on a stretcher. You looked into the heart of darkness, darling, and it looked back.'

Rolling onto my back, I squinted up into the blue sky before it was blotted out by the silhouette of Jenny Lopez.

'Congrats,' she said, swapping the silver streamer for my mobile phone. 'This thing has been blowing up. I thought you said you weren't joining The M.O.B.?'

'She called again?' I asked, sitting upright and drying my hands on the edge of Jenny's shorts.

'She called so many times,' Jenny replied, pulling the fabric out of my hands. 'What does she want? Does

151

she want to come meet us? Can she bring Beyoncé with her?'

'I don't know,' I said, putting my phone on Do Not Disturb and refusing to think about it. 'And I don't care.'

'I still think you're going to regret this,' she sang as everyone started back towards the staircase and back up to the house.

'And I think you're going to regret forcing me to play *American Ninja Warrior* when you promised me a relaxing holiday,' I told her, whacking her on the arse as we walked. 'What are we doing now?'

'You,' Jenny said, whacking me right back. 'Are going to get lunch and then hit the spa. I have to work. Also, have you been working out? Your ass feels like steel.'

'You're a terrible liar,' I reminded her. 'Really? You have to work?'

She nodded, pulling her hair up into a ponytail as if to drive home the point.

'If I didn't know better, I'd think you were avoiding me,' I said lightly. 'What happened to you, me, a cocktail and the hot tub?'

'We'll do that later,' she promised before picking up her pace and racing off to catch up with her assistant, Sumi, at the front of the group. 'Enjoy your massage!'

'What's up with her?' Louisa asked, falling into step beside me.

'I don't know,' I replied, watching as she ran off. 'But I'm definitely going to find out.'

# CHAPTER ELEVEN

'Hello?'

'Am I glad to hear your voice,' I sighed as I sank into the sun lounger outside my room ten minutes later. 'How are you? How's Al? Is she there, can I talk to her?'

'Angela?' he yelled into my ear. Drums and guitars crashed in the background as I held the phone away from me and put Alex on speaker.

'I'm at rehearsal, I can't hear you. Can I call you back?'

'Oh,' I replied, deflating slightly. 'Where's Al?'

'At home with my mom.'

Oh Christ. I just knew that woman was out buying Alice more rubbish I'd have to accidentally destroy next time I did a load of washing. If I came home and she'd pierced my daughter's ears, I'd be piercing her face. With my foot.

'It's gorgeous out here but Jenny's being weird,' I shouted over the escalating noise in the background. Craig had drunk too much caffeine, I could totally tell. 'I think she's avoiding me.'

'Ange, I'm sorry, we're right in the middle of this, can I call you back? We're doing a song with Johnny Jefferson at the show and he's only around to rehearse tonight,' he explained. 'And I can't hear a damn thing.'

I listened to the noise in the background. Didn't sound like Johnny Jefferson to me. Sounded like a girl.

'Who else is there?' I asked. 'Can you put me on speaker? Can I say hello to everyone?'

'It's just us,' he replied. 'And we're working.'

'Weird, sounds like a woman's vocals down the line,' I said, wincing as I said it. I sounded like a suspicious idiot and I knew it.

'Yeah, Cara is here too,' Alex said. 'Anyway—'

'Cara?'

'You know Cara.'

I did *not* know Cara.

'She's opening for us, we're doing a whole thing all of us together at the end of the show,' he said before sighing loudly. 'Ange, I can't hear shit. I'm hanging up now. I'll call you later.'

'I love you,' I called loudly.

But he was already gone.

Well. So far, so shit, I thought as I lay back on the sun lounger.

'Go to Hawaii, everyone said,' I muttered, scrolling through my text messages to find nothing from no one. 'You'll have an amazing time, everyone said.'

But instead of lapping up the gorgeous blue skies and sweet ocean air, I was worried about a grumpy husband, confused by an evasive best friend and, quite frankly, terrified of how James might go about getting his revenge. At least Louisa and I had the afternoon at the spa to look forward to, I reminded myself. Please, universe, distract me from my own nonsense. It was almost impossible to worry about anything when you were slathered in oil and getting a nice rub-down from hopefully a very attractive man named Sven.

'You're being irrational,' I said out loud before taking myself back inside for a shower. 'You've had too much sleep, too much time to think and you're being irrational. Everything is going to be all right.'

And I very nearly believed it.


'And then what did he say?' Louisa asked when I relayed my conversation with Alex an hour later in the lounge at Hala Lanai spa.

'That he couldn't hear anything and he had to get on with work,' I replied. I wrapped my fluffy spa robe tightly around myself and sulked. I had not done a good job of convincing myself to cheer up even though I had done an excellent job of eating a burger at lunch. But here we were, in Bertie Bennett's private spa, and I was determined not to ruin the afternoon for myself. Every time you opened a door on the estate, it was another piece of heaven. When Camilla had said we were getting massages, I'd imagined someone coming to my room with one of those fold-out-pasting-table-type things, but no, that was not the case. Behind what seemed like the perfectly normal door of a perfectly normal villa, we'd found a dimly lit lounge, complete with huge, squishy sofas, big fluffy blankets and pillows, pillows and more pillows for us to wait on while they prepped the massage rooms. Serene spa music played over hidden speakers, accompanied by a distant rumbling. When I pulled back the blind that covered a window, I discovered the rumbling came from the waterfall outside. Just in case we wanted to act out our own Herbal Essences ad.

'I'm sure it's nothing,' Lou insisted gently, bringing me back to the here and now. 'He *was* rehearsing, wasn't he? You *could* hear the music in the background, couldn't you?'

'Yes,' I admitted. 'But why would he be weird about this Cara woman being there? And why would he say I know because I definitely don't. The only Cara I can think of is Delevingne.'

Sitting on the opposite sofa, her profile etched out against the five candles she'd positioned all around her, Lily closed the magazine she was pretending to read and sat up, excited.

'Maybe it is Cara Delevingne?'

I turned to look at our previously silent team captain. Couldn't have got her massage at a different time, could she? Of course not.

'Is that supposed to make me feel better?' I asked.

'Just a suggestion,' she replied, picking up the magazine and flipping through the pages theatrically.

I twisted my wedding ring around and around on my finger. It was so frustrating. I'd never doubted Alex before. Why did these ideas have to sneak into my head when I was a million miles away? Louisa pulled my hands apart and fixed me with a gentle stare.

'Look, Angela, when I thought Tim was cheating on me, there were so many signs. He was working late, Gracie was taking up all my time and we weren't having sex at all. Every conversation we had was about the baby. He felt like he wasn't getting any attention and I just felt weird, like I didn't know who I was any more. You haven't had any of that, have you?'

'No,' I replied, grabbing a handful of freshly baked miniature macadamia nut brownies from the coffee table in front of us. 'Absolutely none of that applies to us in the slightest.'

I stuffed three brownies in my mouth and chewed madly.

'And Tim wasn't even cheating, it was just some stupid attention-seeking flirtation. I was hypersensitive and his precious male ego was bruised. Maybe he's a bit annoyed that you went away and maybe you're feeling a bit insecure about yourself. That's all normal for a new mum and dad.'

'Unless he *is* having an affair with Cara Delevingne,' Lily said. 'You're married to the lead singer from Stills, aren't you? He's fit.'

'Ladies?'

The door to the treatment room opened before I could put Lily through it, face first. A pretty Hawaiian woman wearing loose pale pink trousers and a T-shirt waved us through the door into an even darker, circular room, lit only by a couple of candles. The whole building was made of wood and this had fire hazard written all over it but I was ten seconds away from a two-hour massage and if Bernie Bennett wanted to play fast and loose with health and safety regulations, who was I to tell him otherwise?

Inside the room, I saw two more women in identical outfits and three massage beds, positioned so that the heads of the beds pointed into the centre of the room.

'We're all getting our massages together?' Louisa asked before I could.

'Yes,' confirmed the first woman. 'Today, the three of you will be experiencing traditional *Lomilomi* massage, a spiritual massage practice from the islands of Hawaii. It is a massage conducted with prayer and intention that has passed down through healers in our communities for centuries, connecting your body and your soul.'

'Sick,' Lily said, unfastening her robe and dropping it to the floor. 'You need us naked, yeah?'

Need or not, Lily clearly had no concerns with stripping off in front of strangers and, for the first time since we'd met, I was a little bit jealous of her. Not because her body was perfect (even though it was) but because she really didn't seem to care what anyone thought about her.

'However you are most comfortable,' the therapist replied, unmoved by her charge's naked stretching. 'We will step out for a moment. Please make yourselves comfortable under the blankets, face down on the beds.'

I slipped out of my robe and quickly hopped under the blankets on the closest bed while Lily threw herself into a thankfully bum-to-the-wall downward dog.

'So good to stretch before a massage, don't you think?' she said, looking up at us from underneath a curtain of glossy brown hair.

'Just get on the bloody bed,' Louisa grunted. Motherhood had done nothing to improve my friend's patience and I for one was grateful. 'And Angela. Alex is not having an affair with Cara Delevingne, you know he isn't. What's really bothering you?'

'I don't know,' I admitted, shuffling down the bed until my face was safely slotted into the cushioned cradle. 'It's not one thing, it's a lot of little things. Going back to work, missing Al. I just feel off. And Jenny is definitely avoiding me, have you noticed?'

'She's been here the whole time,' she replied, tucking her hair behind her ears to keep it out of the cradle attachment. 'How is she avoiding you?'

'She's avoiding being on her own with me,' I corrected. 'And now that I think about it, she has been for ages.'

'Go on then,' Louisa said, giving in to my paranoia but making it very clear she was humouring me at best. 'Convince me.'

'Before she invited me on this trip, I hadn't seen her in ages,' I started as the treatment room door opened and three pairs of feet crept quietly across the floor. 'And she hasn't been over to see Al in months. She's always got an excuse not to come over. Seriously, it's been months. Al doesn't even know who she is. Even Mason pops in sometimes, on his way home from CrossFit competitions. He's obsessed with her and yet Jenny is never around these days. It's all I can do to drag her out for coffee.'

'Maybe she hates your baby?' Lily suggested. 'Maybe your baby's awful.'

'Please be quiet,' Louisa instructed. 'Jenny is a busy woman, Angela, and obviously we know Alice is an angel but some people don't connect with babies as well as others. Jenny might not want to share you with Alice when you've actually got time to spend with each other. Not to mention the fact we both know how she feels about travelling to Brooklyn – although as someone who has to drive forty minutes to the nearest Waitrose, I have no sympathy for that.'

Truly, Louisa lived a life of suffering. I said nothing about her standing weekly Ocado order and went on with my list. I shuffled my boobs up and down on the table until I was comfortable. I was so excited to go up a cup size when I was pregnant but, silly me, I hadn't taken massage comfort into account. Thank goodness I didn't have my own spa at home and wouldn't have to worry about this again for some time.

'Something is definitely up, Lou, I can just tell.'

'Maybe she's cutting you out,' Lily said, offering another unrequested opinion. 'Maybe she's trying to ghost you but you won't take the hint and she brought you out here to tell you she doesn't want to be friends anymore.'

'Shall you tell her to shut up or should I?' I muttered into the bed.

'Shut up, Lily,' Lou said. 'I'll admit, it sounds like she's maybe being a little bit weird. You know I'm always going to be a little bit jealous of her, keeping you all to herself in New York, but really, Angela, if I'm being honest, this all sounds like new mum paranoia. You've got so many real things to worry about, you start inventing new ones to distract yourself. Jenny is not avoiding you and Alex is not cheating on you.'

Next she'd be trying to tell me Cici wasn't the devil and Perry Dickson wasn't the head of a secret Mafia-like organization, intent on recruiting me or setting my feet in concrete blocks and dropping me in the bottom of the East River.

'Oh, I've worked it out!' Lily's excited voice carried across the quiet room quickly and clearly. 'What if Alex is cheating on you with Jenny?!'

'Shut *up*, Lily!' Louisa and I said at the exact same moment.

'Perhaps we could perform the rest of the massage in silence,' the therapist suggested.

'Good idea,' I replied, gritting my teeth as she dug her elbow underneath my shoulder.

'You've got a number of knots I would like to work on,' she whispered into my ear while Lily and Louisa made much happier-sounding noises across the room. 'Try to breathe, this might be uncomfortable for a moment.'

I opened my mouth in a silent scream as she pressed even deeper.

'Is that too much pressure?'

'No,' I squeaked, in absolute agony. 'Feels great actually.'

'Fantastic,' she replied. 'I can go a little deeper then.'

As tears formed in my eyes, I scrunched my hands into tight fists and tried to remember my breathing exercises from when I had Alice. When would I learn? When I asked the universe to distract me, I'd been thinking something more along the lines of such complete and utter bliss that I couldn't feel my toes, not the most excruciating experience since I'd forced a human being out of my vagina. At least at the end of that I got a baby and the special bar of Dairy Milk that Alex had been hiding in his guitar case for a month.

'You're OK?' the therapist asked again, digging her strong little fingers into my neck.

'Oh, yes,' I replied, silently trying to atone for any and all sins. This was surely the end. I was going to die from this massage. 'Great, thank you.'

If there wasn't a bar of chocolate waiting for me at the end of this, someone was going to be in serious trouble.

# CHAPTER TWELVE

After our Friday afternoon massages, I'd plunged myself directly into my hot tub and refused to get out until I could move without sobbing in agony. The massage therapist had found knots in muscles I didn't know existed and never needed to know about ever again. Thankfully, James was not just an actor, he was also a walking pharmacist. Ever the caring friend, he supplied me with a trusty Canadian muscle relaxant (he swore this was truly a muscle relaxant from Canada and not a euphemism) and, before I knew it, I had slept right through the special showing of his latest film they'd put on for the entire group in Bertie Bennett's screening room and didn't open my eyes until Louisa started battering down my door on Saturday morning, screaming something about a cat sanctuary.

Hawaii had *everything*.

'My name is Louisa and I love kittens!' Lou wailed, flat on her back in the middle of a lush, green lawn, half an hour away from Hala Lanai, and surrounded by dozens upon dozens of happy cats and kittens. And I'd thought Bennett's place was heaven. 'Jenny, please have one of your assistants move all my stuff here. I'm never leaving.'

'I thought you were never leaving the estate?' I said. The air smelled of freshly cut grass and tuna and I wasn't mad about it. 'Or the first-class cabin on the plane? Or that little shop that sold those macadamia nut truffles at the airport?'

'This wins,' she replied, picking up a little white cat with a black tip on its tail and holding it above her face. 'This wins everything.'

'Bertie Bennett own this place too?' James asked as he rattled his fingers across the grass while a grey and white tabby shook his bottom in the air before pouncing on him.

'He supports it,' Jenny replied from her perch. 'I think it's the only thing on the island he doesn't own. Angie, what is wrong with you?'

'I think my neck is broken,' I whined, gingerly pressing a finger against my flesh. 'That masseuse tried to kill me yesterday.'

'Mine was lovely,' Louisa said, rolling her head from side to side. 'I don't know what you're complaining about.'

'You know Angie, she loves to complain,' Jenny laughed, stretching out her vowels while summoning a small army of kittens. I was desperately trying to cling to the single, little black cat that had shown the slightest bit of interest in me and she already had more kittens than she could possibly stroke in one lifetime.

'I do not,' I grumbled, looking over at Louisa, who

was eyeing Jenny with very little subtlety. Sherlock Holmes, she was not. I'd hoped to find time to talk to her about whatever was going on but, what with having spent fifteen hours asleep and then being herded onto a minibus immediately on waking, I hadn't had the chance. Nor had I been able to speak to Alex who, in spite of his promises, most certainly had not called me back. One meagre photo of Alice done up like a mini drag queen version of season two Carrie Bradshaw and that was my lot. Even if I could not be sure whether he was shagging a supermodel or not, I knew I was definitely in the dog house. Or cat house, as was more appropriate. Wait, didn't that mean brothel?

'Will you take a photo of me?' I asked Jenny, carefully pulling my phone out of the arse pocket of my denim shorts and handing to the closest human within reach. 'Alice loves kittens.'

'Gracie loved kittens when she was Alice's age,' Lou said. 'But now it's pony this and pony that. We should never have caved and got her the guinea pig.'

'Does she still have the guinea pig?' Jenny asked, framing my portrait just so.

'We don't talk about the guinea pig,' Louisa said sombrely. 'Which is one of many reasons she's not having a pony.'

Jenny flipped my phone from horizontal to vertical while I attempted to wrangle the black cat into the cutest possible pose.

'Angie,' she said, staring at the screen. 'Perry Dickson is calling you again.'

'Ignore it,' I called, my focus on the wriggling cat. It was like trying to hold water. 'I'm really not interested in anything she has to say.'

And I was sure I'd find out what she wanted when I got home and found a horse's head in my bed.

'But what if she wants to invite you to a fabulous party?' Jenny said, backing away with my phone still in her hand. 'Delia told me they had Adam Levine perform at their Fourth of July picnic last year and you know he's on my hall pass list. Mason would *at least* have to let me shoot my best shot.'

'Jenny,' I said with a gentle warning, releasing the kitten to gallop wildly across the lawn. 'Please give me back my phone.'

But she didn't. Instead, she kept walking further and further away.

'She left a voicemail. Let's just listen to the voice-mail,' she pleaded, already tapping in my passcode. 'Someone should. What if it's a death threat? You'll need to know so we can get you into the witness protection programme.'

'Give me my bloody phone,' I shouted, rising to my feet and chasing her across the lawn as she set off in a sprint with several of her kitty minions in hot pursuit. I tried to give chase but it was very difficult to run in flip-flops and every time I got near her, one of the kittens threw itself under my feet, kamikaze-style. I'd narrowly avoided standing on three different tabbies by the time I gave up as Jenny tried, and failed, to shin up a palm tree.

'Give me the phone,' I panted. I was so bloody out of shape. 'She probably just wants tickets for Alex's show.'

'She's calling again!' Jenny cried with glee as she slid all of two feet back down the tree and hit the floor with a thwack. 'Angela Clark's phone?'

'You did not just answer my bloody phone?'

When would I learn it was utterly pointless to expect Jenny Lopez to behave like a reasonable, average human?

'Oh, hi Perry. This is her friend Jenny, she's right here, let me hand you over.'

Jenny passed me the phone with the look of someone giving out an Oscar for Best Dickhead before scooping up one of the mewing kittens and waving its little paw in my face.

'Talk to her, talk to her, talk to her,' Jenny chanted, making the cat punch the air in time.

'Hello, Angela speaking?' I said, turning my back on the gang.

'Angela, Perry.'

What a shock.

'Angela, darling, I've been trying to get a hold of you for days.'

'I'm so sorry,' I said, my neck seizing up again at the sound of her voice. 'I'm in Lanai on a press trip. It's been so hard to get to the phone.'

'Lanai? Wonderful! There's a little restaurant down by the water that's divine. It's been in the same family for decades, you must go. I'll send you their details.'

'Thanks,' I replied while Jenny and her kitten waltzed in front of me. 'Was there anything else?'

'I don't want to rush you with your decision about joining us,' she said slowly, even though I did not believe her in the slightest. 'But I did want to talk to you about something else. I was talking with a dear friend a few days ago and he mentioned he was looking for women writers with an interesting point of view and I immediately thought of you. So he read some of your work and he's very interested.'

'That's very sweet,' I said, pulling away as Jenny brushed the purring kitten's tail against my face. 'But I'm so busy with work and Alice and I don't think I have time to take on any freelance.'

'Not freelance.' From the tone of her voice, Perry didn't care for the term. 'Luka is a publisher at Cooper & Bow. He wants to talk to you about writing a book.'

'A . . . a what?'

'A book,' she repeated. 'Anyway, I'll text you his number and you must give him a call first thing on Monday. I told him you'd call Friday and then I couldn't get hold of you but, since you're in Lanai, I'll forgive you. Bring me a pineapple. *Mahalo!*'

'*Mahalo*,' I said softly, slipping the phone back into my pocket.

'What did she want?' Paige asked from her seat underneath a sweeping banyan tree.

I turned back to the group, Louisa, Jenny, Paige, James and two hundred cats waiting on my announcement.

'She wants to introduce me to a publisher at Cooper & Bow,' I said as I sat on the floor with a bump. I was feeling very light-headed all of a sudden. 'They want to talk to me about writing a book.'

'This is freaking exciting, Ange,' Jenny exclaimed, placing her kitten carefully on the floor before giving me a hug. 'She got you a meeting with a publisher? That's huge!'

'She got me a call with a publisher about possibly having a meeting,' I corrected, too scared to get my hopes up. 'Which is very nice of her.'

'You can write my life story,' James suggested as he tried to pick an aggressively keen white cat's claws out of his Gucci T-shirt. 'Did you see I've been voted the gayest man to have ever been born in Sheffield?'

'Twitter is a very cruel place,' Louisa said, patting his hand.

'Are you going to call the publisher?' Jenny demanded. 'Like, right now, please? So we can all listen?'

'Yes, on Monday morning,' I replied, even though the thought of having to sit on this for forty-eight hours was agonizing.

'So exciting, AC,' Paige said from her perch under the tree. 'You should film a writer's diary for the website. I bet loads of people would love to know how a book gets made.'

For a moment there, I'd almost forgotten Paige was actually my boss.

'That could be a good idea,' I said, lying down in the grass and holding out my hand to a curious tabby. A book a book a book a book. 'But it's only one phone call at the moment, nothing to get excited about.'

But it was, though. A book. I could write a book. It was so exciting, I hardly dared think about it, let alone talk about it.

'I want to know about your new website,' Louisa said, tapping a finger to test her sunburned nose and promptly changing the subject. She always had been able to read my mind. 'What's it about?'

'Oh, the website is going to be brilliant,' I said, relaxing as I made a grab for a fat black kitten that wasn't fast enough to get away. Recherché was easy to talk about. It was the one area of my life that was completely under control. 'It's a mix of all the things women like us care about, reported in a clever, compassionate way. So there's fashion and lifestyle but also news and culture and anything that's important really.'

'And who's boning who?' Jenny asked. 'Because that is so important and it's super hard to find a reliable source.'

'That's because no one is getting banged any more,' James told her. 'It's pitiful. This generation of celebs is the dullest ever assembled. All they do is work out and go to bed early and care about things. They always know their lines, they're always on set early and if that wasn't bad enough, they're all *sober*.'

'What a bunch of monsters,' I said to the fat black kitten.

'It's offensive,' James sniffed.

'Surely not Timothée Chalamet, though?' Louisa rolled over on her front to stare him down before he could answer.

James nodded with great knowing. 'Utterly boring. But Armie Hammer can call me by any name he likes.'

'There will be celebrity stuff,' I said, rerouting the conversation before he shattered all of her celebrity dreams. 'But it's all going to be positive. I want it to be a place where people can come for five minutes or however long they have and go away feeling better about themselves, not worse.'

'I'll get you all the insider info from my next film,' James promised. 'If there is any. It's all very top secret, you know.'

'Finally making your move on the Bond franchise?' I asked.

He turned and gave me a sly wink.

'You are not,' I challenged. 'There's no way you've kept that to yourself for the last two days.'

'Oh, you should see your faces,' he said, bursting with laughter. 'Hardly. It goes woman Doctor Who, black Bond and then possibly, if you're very lucky, implied homosexual superhero. It's another DC film. So no, I can't introduce any of you to Chris Hemsworth.'

Jenny crawled over and gripped his shoulders with her blood-red nails.

'I give you so much,' she hissed through gritted teeth. 'And you give me nothing.'

'I was thinking,' Paige said, pulling her feet in towards her as a tiny tortoiseshell started attacking the strap of her sandals.

Biting my lip, I looked over at the boss. No good ever came from a sentence that started with 'I was thinking'.

'I love your message for the website but how would you feel about being more visible?'

'Visible?' I asked, clinging to my black kitten as he tried to wriggle away.

'It seems like such a waste to have you hiding behind the computer when you could be on the screen,' she said. 'You should be the face of Recherché, show the readers the woman behind the content. We should be sharing your incredible life with everyone.'

'Ooh, what a good idea.' Lou threw her a thumbs up. 'I'd watch it.'

'You're the only person who watches my Instagram stories as it is,' I said before turning back to Paige. 'I'm a writer, not a presenter. I don't think I'd be comfortable chatting away into a camera, trying to convince everyone how brilliant I am. I'm not Lily.'

'That's exactly why you should be doing it,' she

said, pulling her feet up onto the bench. 'It's going to be amazing, Angela.'

It *is*? I really didn't like the way she was talking as though this was already happening. The black kitten mewed, straining against my arms before jumping up onto my shoulder. He snuffled against my ear, preferring his pirate's perch to my lap.

'Let's put together an introductory video while we're out here,' Paige suggested, shaking her foot until the kitten scampered away. 'See if we can't come up with something we both feel good about.'

Leaning against James's knees, Jenny pushed her hair out of her face and peered at Paige. 'Honey, why are you sat up there? All the best kitty action is down here.'

'Oh, no,' she said with an apologetic smile. 'I don't really get on with cats. I'm having a lovely time, though.'

'Are you allergic?' Louisa asked while James sorted through the various kittens that were rubbing themselves against his beard. 'Like Lily?'

Was there anything on this earth Lily wasn't allergic to?

'Don't think so. I've just never really been too fond of them,' she said, shirking away as one of the cats hopped onto his back legs and rested his front paws on her thigh. 'My gran had this big Persian thing when I was little and it hated me.'

'More of a dog person then,' James said before stooping down to pick up one of the orange cats and lifting it over his head to re-enact the opening scene of *The Lion King*.

'Not an animal person in general,' she said, shaking

171

her head. 'I even killed my Tamagotchi when I was in school.'

'Note to Angie, don't ask Paige to babysit,' Jenny said, unwrapping a piece of gum and smacking it loudly. 'Man, how great is this? Paige just walked into this super cool job at Besson, Angie is getting a book deal, I'm about to become the greatest podcaster of all time and James is going to be some sort of super gay dolphin in the *Aquaman* sequel. We're like a media power fam.'

Louisa sat stiffly in the middle of us all, stroking a massive ginger tom cat with a static smile on her face.

'The dolphin isn't gay,' James muttered. 'He's pansexual.'

'James Jacobs the pansexual dolphin,' Jenny declared. 'Angie, we've found your book title.'

'Perfect,' I said, watching as a particularly ferocious-looking tortoiseshell ran full pelt across the lawn to attack James's leg, clawing all the way up to his crotch.

'Even cats can't get enough of me,' he yelped. 'Get it off!'

'Can't,' Jenny said, rolling away from his legs and popping her gum. 'They're protected, it's a cat sanctuary. They're allowed to do whatever they want.'

'Is that true?' Louisa asked, her frown breaking for a moment as James ran off in wild circles, several of the cats giving chase.

'Nah,' Jenny replied. 'I kinda just want to see how this plays out.'

Settling back against the sweet-smelling grass, we all watched James trying to outrun half a dozen cats, wailing as he went.

'Do you ever think, how did I get here?' I said with a big smile on my face.

'Every time I get an Uber,' Jenny agreed. 'It's like, I got in, I looked at my phone and then hello! I'm in Bushwick, what?'

'You never go to Bushwick and that's not what I meant,' I said. 'Stop ruining my nice moment.'

Rubbing her hand against her stomach, she looked at her watch and frowned.

'I have to head back,' she said, rising to her feet. 'There's drinks and snacks in the cooler and you're all paid up for the next hour. I'll send the bus back for you, OK?'

'Where are you going?' I asked, jumping up to follow her.

'Gotta take care of some stuff back at the estate for the rest of the guests. Don't sweat it.'

'I'll come with you,' I offered. 'Wait for me.'

Jenny bundled her hair into a knot on the top of her head and smiled. 'Nah, stay with Louisa and the kitties. I have admin stuff to deal with.'

'Jenny,' I said, reaching for her hand and lowering my voice. 'I know you're going to say I'm being stupid but I feel like you're avoiding me.'

'You're right,' she replied, shaking me off. 'You're being stupid. I wish I could spend the whole trip hanging out but it's turning out to be more work than I'd anticipated. Maybe I should have moved to Pennsylvania to work on a Christmas tree farm. I'll see you at dinner!'

'See you at dinner,' I replied before turning my attention to the little black kitten from before who was pawing at my leg. 'You're too young to understand but that was a perfect example of someone being shifty,' I explained, picking him up and cradling him in my arms like a Bond villain. 'Also, you are a cat so it does not matter to you.'

In my back pocket, my phone buzzed with a text. Hoping it might be Alex, I pulled it out to see a message from Perry with Luka Pierce's contact information. I was to call him at nine a.m. Monday, Lanai time, to discuss ideas for a possible book.

'What do you reckon?' I said to the kitten, who looked back at me with clear, untroubled sea foam green eyes. 'The Gayest Man in Sheffield does have a ring to it, doesn't it?'

The kitten said nothing.

'Yeah, you're right,' I sighed. 'I'll come up with something else. I'm not throwing away my shot.'

But I am going to stop listening to the *Hamilton* soundtrack all the way through every single day, I thought as I returned to my friends. It really couldn't be healthy.


There was no part of Lanai that wasn't decent enough to look at but Bertie Bennett's beach at sunset was something special, even by Hawaii's standards. Leather flip-flops dangling from my fingers, I snuck away from the dinner table where James and Paige were happily cackling at each other's jokes and made my way down the stone staircase carved into the cliff. In spite of Jenny's promises, she hadn't been at dinner. Instead, Camilla Rose had taken over duties as host and Jenny wasn't answering my texts. I'd expected the beach to be empty but, instead, I found Louisa sitting on the sand, watching the waves pull back and forth.

'I thought you went to the loo,' I said, lifting the hem of my long floral Zimmermann dress as I sat down beside her. I was definitely more of a jeans and T-shirts kind of a girl these days but I was enjoying moonlighting as a fancy fashion influencer for the weekend. Even if Jenny would be taking all these dresses back with her to EWPR on Tuesday morning.

'I did but I had to get away from Lily,' Lou admitted, patting the sand at the side of her. 'She's doing my nut in. She kept going on about making her own organic lube and I couldn't finish my dinner.'

I swallowed, very keen to keep my chicken tacos down.

'It's gorgeous down here, isn't it?' she said. 'Like a painting.'

'And a long way from Ibiza,' I agreed, thinking back to the last time we'd sat together on a beach at sunset.

Even though Jenny was one of the greatest humans I'd ever met and I couldn't imagine a better man to be married to than Alex (most of the time), there was something about my oldest friend that soothed my soul. We had been together for all the big moments in life: our first periods, our first kisses, that time I crashed my mum's Mini in the Asda car park and lied about it. We'd been side by side through it all (metaphorically at least – Louisa got her period three months before I did). I'd never really thought about how important she was until I couldn't see her every day but even though we now lived oceans apart, she was still there, a constant thread in my life. There were more colours in our tapestry than I could name.

'Did you manage to speak to Alex?' she asked.

I dug my fingers into Bertie Bennett's white sand until my hands were buried up to my knuckles.

'No,' I said, burrowing down until I felt the powdery sand get wet. 'Not yet.'

Lou stretched out her legs, her feet silhouetted against the fading sun.

'If I'd have left Gracie with Tim when she was a baby, I would be either one baby or one husband down today,' she said. 'I know that's not very cool to admit but Tim's useless at being on his own with her, Ange, and I think most of them still are. It's brilliant we're all talking about men taking on more of a share of childrearing and they absolutely should but please know that Alex is not the norm. He might have said he was happy for you to pop off to Hawaii with your mates but, come on, surely he didn't think you'd actually go. *Of course* he's annoyed.'

'I honestly, honestly, honestly didn't think he would care,' I said, searching myself to check that it was true. Alex never lied, never played games, never said things he didn't mean.

Lou gave me a challenging look.

'I really didn't,' I said softly. 'I was wrong.'

She sniffed loudly and then cleared her throat. 'Have you, you know,' she said, nodding at my ever-present phone. 'Sent him any pictures?'

'Loads,' I said, opening up the photo app and scrolling through my camera roll. 'Here's the sunset and here's the cats and here's my room—'

'Not what I meant,' Lou said. 'Have you sent him any photos of you?'

She raised her eyebrows and placed more emphasis on the 'you' than I was comfortable with.

'Ohhhh,' I said. 'You mean?'

'I mean,' she confirmed. 'I know it sounds silly but with Tim travelling so much, it sort of sometimes helps.'

I balked at the thought of Louisa and Tim exchanging sexts. When I thought of the hassle we'd had getting Louisa's first passport photo for that bloody Ibiza trip, it's a wonder Gracie had even been conceived.

'I know, I know,' she muttered, pushing the sand between us into a tiny mound. The world's smallest sandcastle. 'But you know how men are, they love a visual. And I'm not saying I think he's right to behave shittily but I can understand why Alex would be a bit annoyed with you. Why not send him a little pic? Cheer him up a bit and remind him what he's missing.'

'He's been missing it for longer than the three days I've been away,' I said, adding to her heap of sand. 'Unless he's getting it from Cara and then he's not missing anything at all, is he?'

'Don't make me give you a slap,' she warned. 'Alex Reid is not cheating on you. Ever. He just wouldn't. How about a little hot dogs or legs action?'

I looked down at my legs, shins still bruised and battered from the Lanai Olympics the day before.

'All right,' I conceded. 'But can we send your legs instead?'

'This might be something for you to work on back in your room,' she sighed, giving up and flattening the sandcastle. 'You don't have to go full-on *Playboy* centrefold. It's just a picture, Angela. It'll make him smile.'

She had a point. Alex had the most wonderful smile in the world, quick to come and slow to leave, his grin made you feel like nothing in the world could be all that bad. It still made me all tingly when I said or did something that made him laugh.

'Maybe I'll do it when I get back,' I bargained. There was booze in my room and I wasn't nearly drunk enough to stage a porno shoot on the beach with my best friend. 'I hate feeling like he's mad at me. Do you think I've been taking him for granted?'

'Yes,' she replied immediately. 'And I want to give you some sort of feminist award for it but I also don't want you to lose your husband. I'm so happy he's so good with Al but I saw this happen to loads of my friends at home. The only thing is, it was usually the other way around.'

I lay back in the sand, staring up at the palm trees that swayed overhead. 'He's so brilliant with her, I feel like I'm in the way half the time. He was a natural from the beginning, Lou, you wouldn't have believed it. I was useless and he did everything. I remember sobbing in the toilet when we brought her home because he changed her nappy in less time than it took me to get one of those massive sanitary pads they give you to stick to my knickers.'

'Such a magical time,' Lou said with a sigh. 'I really hate women who go on about those beautiful first few days. Mine were hideous. I was so sore I couldn't bear to have a wee and Grace screamed non-stop. I couldn't believe it when I went round to see my friend Jessica's baby. Two days after giving birth and she was up in the kitchen, cooking a full Sunday dinner.'

'What a bitch,' I breathed.

'Parenting is hard,' Lou went on. 'And everyone says it's so cool to admit you're struggling and it's OK to confess that you're having a rough time on the internet but no one has any practical advice about what to do to help. It's easy to put up a pretty pastel Instagram post venting to strangers but it's a lot more complicated to ask your friends for help when you don't even know what help you need.'

'Alice doesn't even want to breastfeed any more,' I said, pressing my boobs back together as they tried to escape from opposite sides of my body. 'I wanted to do the entire twelve months but she's not interested. I don't know if you've ever spent more than ten minutes trying to force your boob into your child's mouth while she's crying for a bottle but, let me tell you, it doesn't feel good.'

Lou grinned. 'The glamour of parenting. This is what you should be talking about in your videos. How are you doing being away from her?'

'Mostly all right,' I said, sitting up and fiddling with my engagement ring. 'I miss her more than I thought I would but I'm coping. Does that sound awful?'

Fierce loyalty burned in her eyes.

'Nothing you can say would sound awful to me,' she replied. 'I know it feels like you can't win right now but you're doing brilliantly. People will judge you whatever you do so get used to it, babes, this is motherhood. Constantly feeling a bit shit about every decision you ever make for the rest of your life.'

We sat quietly for a moment, watching the sky. The sun looked heavy, resting against the edge of the ocean and strung up by candyfloss clouds. Before I'd passed out last night, I'd caught a glimpse of a furiously beautiful sunset, fiery reds and burned oranges setting the sky alight, but tonight it was powder pale pinks and blues, turning grey at the edges of the evening. A much gentler choice.

'I hope you're having a nice time,' I said, pulling my dress down over my bare legs. As the sun slipped lower, the air became cooler and it was very nearly cardigan weather. 'I know it can be a bit much when everyone's together.'

Lou gave a short, soft laugh. 'You mean earlier at the cat place.'

I nodded. I meant earlier at the cat place.

'Jenny wasn't having a go, I know,' she said. 'But it is sometimes strange. You're all out here living these big, exciting lives and I'm at home trying to work out why the Sky box didn't save *Love Island*.'

'And please know that while you're doing that, I'm at home trying to work out how to watch *Love Island* in the first place,' I replied, deadly serious. 'I'm in New York, you're in Surrey, James is in LA, but we're all living the same life at the end of the day, we're all just as happy and as miserable as each other.'

'I don't know,' Louisa said as she untied her pony-tail and let her blonde hair fall over her shoulders. 'I think James might be a bit happier than most people. He's got a pool.'

I thought about it for a moment. Pool yes, but he'd told me he hadn't eaten a pizza in seven years so there were still sacrifices to be made.

'I love Jenny, you know I do,' she added, her cheeks reddening as she went on. 'But I don't think Paige and I are destined to be soulmates. She seems very nice but I think she thinks I'm a bit basic.'

When we were younger, Lou was always the more outgoing one but, as we got older, the happy, carefree version of my friend I'd grown up with had been replaced by someone far more insecure. It seemed wrong to me. Weren't we supposed to get more confident as we got older?

'Someone called me normcore last week,' I said, still bristling at the memory. 'You're not basic and I'm not normcore. We're awesome.'

'Maybe. When I was sixteen, I would have thought we were. If we could go back and tell our sixteen-year-old selves we would be doing this one day,' she said, leaning back to rest on her elbows, 'do you think we'd believe us?'

I watched the sun drop lower into the ocean and wondered what teenage Angela would have had to say about this. When I was sixteen, I mostly worried whether or not Anton Morris would find out I had a crush on him, when I'd get my braces off and why my boobs weren't exactly the same size. The boob one still bothered me from time to time.

'The full *Bill & Ted*?' I asked.

'The full *Bill & Ted*,' she confirmed.

'I don't know if I'd even heard of Hawaii when I was sixteen,' I admitted. 'But no, I don't think I would believe us. Would you?'

'When I was sixteen, I would have believed anything,' she said with a smile. 'But this might have been a bit of a stretch.'

And yet here we were: living out a dream we didn't even know we had. It got me thinking; where would we be twenty years from now?

Lou sat up and shivered, wrapping her arms around her legs. 'I'm getting a bit cold, do you want to go back in?'

'No.' I stood up and stared out at the ocean, hands on my hips. 'Louisa?'

'Angela?'

'Have you ever gone skinny-dipping?'

She looked up at me from the beach and laughed a loud throaty laugh. I looked back down at her, determination all over my face.

'Oh,' she said as she recovered herself. 'You're serious. No, I bloody haven't and I'm not doing it now.'

'Yes, you are.' I slipped the straps of my dress over my shoulders before the moment was gone. 'This is a once-in-a-lifetime trip, isn't it? When are you going to get another chance to swim naked in the ocean on a private beach in Hawaii? If we don't do this now, we'll regret it for the rest of our lives.'

'Or, we'll be sat in the old people's home talking about that time we got our kit off on the beach and all these Instagram models saw our sad post-baby knockers.' She crossed her arms across her chest and settled in. 'I'm not doing it.'

But it was too late for me to change my mind. Shaking off my dress, I unsnapped my bra, stepped out of my knickers and made a run for the water. This was it, I was doing it. I, Angela Clark, the girl who managed to change in and out of her swimming costume and PE kit without flashing so much as an arse cheek for the entirety of secondary school, was naked on a beach. I felt so *Breaking Dawn: Part One*, only without the vampire husband who was about to knock me up with his undead love child that would need to be delivered by his chomping it out of me. So nothing like *Breaking Dawn: Part One*, really.

'The water isn't even cold,' I shouted back up the

beach as I stepped into the water. 'Louisa, get in here, it's amazing!'

'Not a bloody chance,' she shouted back. 'And you're the one who thinks sexting is tacky!'

I strode out into the shallow bay until the water was up to my waist, feeling like a goddess. As soon as my stretch marks were all covered, I was happy. This was great, I decided, I was at one with the ocean, communing with mother nature, connecting to the divine whatever it was Jenny kept going on about in meditation class.

'Oi, Clark, nice tits!'

Arms clasped tightly to my chest, I swivelled around to see Louisa, Paige and James all standing on the beach, laughing their backs off.

'Oh, fuck off,' I shouted. 'I'm having a nice time.'

'Wait for me, I'm coming in,' James called back and he unbuttoned a third Hawaiian shirt and wriggled out of his trousers.

'If he's going in, I'm going in,' Paige said, wrangling her enormous earrings out of her ears.

Holding her breath, Lou scrunched up her face, FOMO personified.

'Sod it!' she yelled. 'I'm coming in in my knickers but I'm coming in.'

Moments later, James belly-flopped into the water, displacing half the Pacific Ocean with a splash the likes of which I'd only ever seen at Alton Towers, while Paige and Louisa followed in his wake.

'I fucking love this place,' James shouted at the top of his voice, sweeping his arm across the top of the water to create another almighty arcing wave that came splashing down on top of the rest of us. Louisa's hair was saturated. 'I love you and you and you and I love my life and I love Hawaii!'

'Is he high?' Louisa asked, doggy paddling over to me.

'Weed is legal here!' he crowed before panic crossed his face. 'Wait, is it?'

'I don't think so, no,' I replied as he did a swan dive under the water, grabbed Paige's legs and pulled her under with him. 'But we love you anyway.'

In fact, in that moment, other than Alex's mother and the fact I sort of needed a wee, I couldn't think of many things in the world that I didn't love.

# CHAPTER THIRTEEN

'Where were you last night?' I asked Jenny as I arrived outside the main entrance to Hala Lanai at eight thirty on Sunday morning.

When I got back to my room after our skinny-dip adventure, I'd found a new package of surprises on my bed. A baby-pink boiler suit embroidered with my name on the back, a pink helmet and an updated schedule that said breakfast would be delivered to my door at seven thirty and I was expected outside, on time, in my new ensemble. Even though I looked like a bottle of baby lotion had made a baby with a KwikFit Fitter, I did as I was told.

'Busy,' Jenny replied, counting people onto the three baby-pink open-top Jeeps parked out front of the estate. 'I heard you had fun?'

'Would have been more fun with you,' I told her, noticing that everyone else had accessorized their outfit in some way. Eva was wearing hers open with a bikini top underneath, while Paige had the top of her boiler suit pulled down and the arms tied around the waist to show off her black racer-back tank. Even Louisa had rolled up the sleeves and popped the collar when she wandered out into the driveway.

Jenny laughed but I saw the tension in her face, the split second before she could push it away. 'Natch, I'm the best. Now get your ass into the car. We need to be at the ranch in a half-hour.'

'Ranch?' I asked as she climbed into the back seat of one of the Jeeps and hauled me up after her. 'Why are we going to a ranch?'

Jenny laughed as Louisa and I fell backwards into our seats, the driver not waiting for us to find our seatbelts. 'Where else are we going to get the horses?'

Horses? I should have tried harder to get through to Alex, I thought, grabbing the roll cage around the Jeep before we took off. It would have been nice to talk to Alice before I met my untimely end.

'Aloha, everyone.'

'Aloha,' we chorused, lining up alongside the Jeeps like we'd just got off the bus on a school trip. But instead of Hampton Court Palace or Alton Towers, we were standing in front of something very different. An actual, bloody volcano.

'My name is Kekipi and I work with Bertie Bennett.'

A short, stocky man with black hair, brown eyes and a quirked eyebrow that could only mean trouble stood before us. He was wearing a nice black shirt, nice black trousers and, even though I'd always said I would never approve of sandals on a man, Kekipi was pulling them off. There was something about him that made you want to bundle him up in a hug and never let go. He had an open face, wildly gesticulating hands and eyelashes so long and thick you could have hung Christmas ornaments off them. Really, he should have been the one advertising the bloody mascara for Jenny.

'I manage his estates, amongst other things, and since it meant a free trip to Hawaii, I volunteered to check in on you all.'

I tried hard to concentrate on our tour guide and take in the stunning scenery that lay beyond but all I could really see was a line of horses, all saddled up and impatiently stamping their feet. Just biding their time before throwing me over a cliff, I could tell.

'Lanai is a very small island with only three thousand inhabitants,' Kekipi went on, waving his arm with a flourish. The man had missed his calling as what my nana would have called, 'one of them dollybirds off that gameshow'. 'The island is only eighteen miles wide and has no traffic lights or stop signs, which makes it a treat for joyriding, though if you tell Mr Bennett I said that, I will deny it to the very core of my being. Legend has it that the island was inhabited by the god of nightmares before he was killed by a young chief from Maui who was sent here as punishment. Of course, there was no one else here to verify this and, as far as we know, the young chief did not manage to catch it on Snapchat, so we just have to take his word for it.'

How fascinating, I thought, never once taking my eyes off the horses.

'Today, we will be venturing into *Keahiakawelo*, also known as the garden of the gods, an area of the island covered with fascinating rock and lava formations that the islanders claim were created when the gods dropped pebbles from their gardens in the skies above,' Kekipi said, quirking that eyebrow even higher. 'The garden's famous lunar-like landscape was also, like so many of the best things in life, influenced by a bet. Two *Kahuna* or priests, one from Lanai and another from Molokai, challenged each other to keep a fire burning on their respective islands. The one who kept it burning for the longest would be rewarded with great gifts from the gods.'

'Is there a single story in history that doesn't boil down to a dick-swinging contest?' Jenny asked.

'No,' he replied. 'Not a single one.'

'So these priests pulled up the whole island and burned it?' Paige asked.

'Basically,' Kekipi nodded. 'Don't judge them too harshly, they didn't have Netflix. Now, it's said that *Keahiakawelo* is the best place on all of Lanai to connect with the gods and, if you listen hard enough, you will hear their message to you. Your mission, should you choose to accept it, is to ride your horse up this hill to the Garden of the Gods, where I will be waiting with a good meal and a stiff drink or two, which should make it easier to hear what those pesky gods have to say for themselves.'

'And when Kekipi says "should you choose to accept it", he means, this is absolutely one hundred percent what you're doing,' Jenny added. 'We'll meet you at the end for the feast. Have fun, everyone!'

'You're not coming?' I asked, grabbing her arm as she climbed back into the Jeep.

'Fuck no,' she replied with wide eyes. 'The last time I rode a horse, I looked like I'd been on a super successful date with the entire roster of the New York

Knicks. Me and farm animals don't mix, dollface, I'll see you at the other end.'

'Well, me and my post-birth bladder aren't convinced we'll get along so well with Black Beauty over there, either,' I said, pointing at the giant horse with my name embroidered on his saddle. 'Can't I just come with you instead?'

'Angie, baby,' Jenny gave me a wicked smile as her driver gunned his engine. 'This is an incredible once-in-a-lifetime experience. It would be cruel of me to deny you this moment.'

'So incredible, you're not going to bother?' I asked.

'The perils of being in charge,' she said with a sigh and a hair flip. 'See you up there, boo.'

And with that, the driver honked his horn and they drove away.

'Come on, Ange, you'll be fine,' James yelled, already astride his horse. 'Stay close to me. I took Western riding lessons for that Quentin Tarantino film.'

'You got shot in the first scene,' I replied, eyeing my new four-legged friend with great suspicion. He seemed no more interested in me than I was in him.

'I was still in it,' he shouted back. 'Get on the horse and shut your yap.'

'Really, Angela,' Louisa called, hopping up onto her pretty brown pony with the greatest ease. 'These horses do this all day, they'll do all the work. All you have to do is not fall off.'

'She says it like it's easy,' I said to the horse, who huffed in agreement.

With the assistance of not one, not two but three stable hands, I wedged one of my feet into a stirrup and heaved myself up onto the horse's back, flinging my other leg over until I was in something like riding position.

'I don't like it,' I wailed, shutting my eyes and gripping the reins so tightly the leather cut into my palms. 'I'm too high.'

'Or not high enough?' James suggested.

'Come on, Angela, you can do this,' Paige said as the group began to trot away. How was it everyone knew how to ride a horse but me?

'I've already dislocated a hip,' I muttered, not quite ready to open my eyes. It was a little bit late to regret turning down riding lessons when I was twelve but, at the time, I'd had a choice between horse riding and ice skating and there was a boy at the ice skating rink who looked exactly like Mark Owen and even before I understood why, I was a slave to my hormones.

'You're going to end up with a broken back because you were dick-led even when you were pre-pubescent,' I scolded myself. 'I cannot believe I'm going to die on a horse in Hawaii.'

'You're not going to die,' James scoffed, circling his horse around to face me. 'You'll fall off and break a leg at best. Maybe a hip. Maybe.'

'Oh good,' I said, holding my breath and tensing every muscle in my body as the horse began to trot off after the others. 'Nothing to worry about then.'

'Nothing to worry about at all,' he agreed.

Half an hour later, I was very nearly almost close to enjoying myself. Louisa and Paige were hanging back with me, one in front and one behind, while the others galloped off, racing like mad things up the hill. My horse, Alani, was actually all right. Even though he

190

was enormous and muscular and I could tell he was just dying to cut loose, he kept a very respectful old lady pace. I couldn't feel my bum any more but I wasn't especially scared, either. I was officially chalking it up as a win.

'I can't believe we're here,' Lou breathed as we rounded another corner and gazed out on the Lanai landscape. 'Look at the ocean. I've never seen so many shades of blue.'

As we rose higher up the rocky road, I could see the shoreline in the distance and the outline of another island a few miles away across the ocean. On the other side of us was a science fiction landscape, cast in every single shade of red and brown that had ever been conceived. Just when I thought I'd seen enough neutral brown eyeshadow palettes to last a lifetime, Lanai could have come up with a hundred more. Other than the wind and the rhythmic rapping of the horses' hooves, it was utterly peaceful.

Until my phone started ringing.

'Shit, it might be Alex,' I said, fumbling around in my not-Marc-Jacobs bag, clinging to Alani's reins and trying to keep my balance. I pulled out my phone and swiped to answer without looking at the caller.

'Hello, Angela speaking?' I said, awkwardly holding it to my ear, everything tight and tense again.

'Well, I would hope no one else is answering your phone. I haven't got long, we're going to Lynette from the badminton club's daughter's wedding but only the night do because we weren't invited to the service. I told your father we shouldn't bloody go at all, after we invited them to your wedding, but he's insisting so I suppose we're going. I suppose you did cancel on the day. Now where's my delicious granddaughter?'

'Mum. Now's not a good time.'

'That's all right, I don't want to talk to you,' Annette Clark replied. 'I want to talk to Alice.'

'No, I mean, she's not here,' I said, pulling a panicked face at Louisa, trying to mouth my issue without falling off the horse. But Louisa was too busy dreamily gazing at the landscape and actually enjoying herself to attempt to help in any way.

'Wherever are you?' my mum asked. 'I have to say, it's not a very good connection. You're not on your own in the park, are you? I've told you not to go in there without Alex, not after I got flashed by that pervert.'

'He wasn't a flasher, Mum, some men just wear their trousers very low these days,' I explained for the millionth time. 'And I'm not in the park, I'm in Hawaii.'

It was never a good sign when my mum went silent.

'Are you still there?' I asked, praying to the teenage chief who fought the nightmare god that she wasn't.

'What do you mean, you're in Hawaii?' she screeched.

'Oh god, even I heard that,' Louisa whispered, kicking her horse into gear and riding off a little way in front. 'Good luck, Angela. Don't tell her I'm here!'

'Louisa is here with me,' I replied instantly as my oldest friend flipped up her middle finger and rode away. 'We're away for the weekend. It's a work thing, Jenny organized it.'

'And where is my grandchild while you're off gallivanting around *Hawaii*?' she demanded, spitting out the name of the state. I wasn't quite sure what Hawaii specifically had done to raise her ire but I was certain I was going to hear about it.

'She's at home with her father,' I said. 'She's perfectly fine. You can call Alex if you want to talk to her. He'd love to hear from you.'

It was a lie but it was all I had.

'Oh, she's perfectly fine, is she?' Mum replied, on a roll now. 'Left alone with Alex while you're gadding around with the girls? Has he even had her on his own all weekend before?'

'He's not a random babysitter I got off the internet,' I argued, tightening my grip on Alani's reins. 'He's her father and he's perfectly capable of taking care of her for one weekend. Besides, his mum is staying with them.'

As soon as the words were out of my mouth, I knew I'd cocked up. Annette Clark vs Janet Reid had been, I hoped, a never-to-be-repeated event. It was the Foreman vs Ali of our times, The Rumble in DUMBO. They met at our wedding and, it was safe to say, it had not gone well. It all kicked off when Janet asked if my mum was my grandmother, which my mother promptly followed up by asking Janet where she had bought her wig. After that it was snide comment after snide comment until they ultimately exchanged addresses. They now sent each other passive-aggressive Christmas cards every year; I was fairly sure my mum only kept sending physical Christmas cards in order to keep tabs on her list of mortal enemies.

'We would have come over to look after her, you know,' Mum said in a dangerously quiet voice. 'There was no need for that woman to get involved.'

'That woman is her grandmother,' I pointed out, as much as it hurt to stand up for Janet. 'And Alex's mum. And, you know, lives an hour away rather than an international flight. It was all very last minute, Mum, don't worry about it. Everything is absolutely fine. I'll be home again on Tuesday and it'll be like I was never away.'

'Except for everything you've missed,' she said with a theatrical sob. 'Everything changes so quickly when they're this little, you'll barely recognize her when you're back. And you know she'll not want to feed if she has a few days off.'

Instinctively, I pressed my forearms against my boobs and realized I hadn't expressed that morning. Or the night before. And I wasn't leaking. Uh-oh.

'Mum, I need to go,' I said, refusing to let her know she'd struck a nerve. 'I'm on a horse.'

'Don't lie to me, Angela Clark,' she replied. 'You can just say you've got something better to do than talk to me and your father.'

'Don't bring me into it,' I heard Dad yell in the background. 'I'm waiting to bloody go, I've got the engine running. We'll never get parked at the club if we're the last to arrive.'

'No, I really am on a horse,' I said as Alani snorted loudly to confirm my story. 'And it sounds like you need to go anyway.'

'Do you know how old you were before I left you alone with your dad?'

I thought back for a moment. How old was I when he set the garden shed on fire letting off the leftover fireworks that time? No, wait, Auntie Vera was there that time.

'Five?' I guessed.

'Fifteen,' Mum shouted gleefully. 'And that was only because I had to go and stay with Marilyn from

194

the library after she had her hysterectomy and you were doing your mock GCSEs! You don't leave a baby on its own with a man, Angela. This is what happens when you live so far away, you're doing it all wrong.'

'I am not doing anything wrong,' I argued, even though I did remember the time she was talking about. Dad burned the shepherd's pie she left so we ended up having fish and chips and putting the wrappers in the neighbour's bin so Mum wouldn't find out.

'I think we need to come out to see you,' Mum declared. 'When are you back? I don't like this running around and abandoning the baby with strangers, Angela, it's not good for her. You're a mother now and a mother is a mother all the time. Not just when you feel like it. This is New York, isn't it? You wouldn't behave like this if you were at home.'

Kekipi might have sounded convincing but I wasn't altogether sure the god of nightmares had been *entirely* banished from this island.

'You can't come and visit,' I said loudly. In the distance, Louisa's horse sped up. 'We're busy. Until Christmas.' I wasn't even thinking about what I was saying, words flew out of my mouth in something like sentences only to be batted away by my mother's tuts and sighs. 'And for the last time, she's not with strangers, she's with her father and her grandmother and I am allowed to do something other than take care of a baby for the next fifty years.'

'Well, that's a fine attitude to have,' she replied. 'I don't know why you bothered having a baby in the first place, Angela, I really don't. You couldn't go back to work fast enough, you practically hurled that child at a nanny, and now you're off on your jollies, leaving Alex holding the baby. That poor boy.'

I didn't know what was more shocking, my mother's 1950s attitude towards childrearing or her sudden attack of compassion for Alex. Actually, I did, it was definitely the latter.

'Alex is fine.'

'Is he?'

I bit down on the inside of my mouth. Too close to the bone.

'I can't think of a single man who would be "fine" with his wife traipsing off on holiday leaving him alone all weekend,' Mum said.

'I can,' I heard Dad reply. 'When are you going? I'll drive you to the airport.'

'OK, this has been a lovely chat but I've got to go,' I said as they started bickering. 'Have a lovely time at the wedding.'

'Angela? I'm not finished—'

But she most certainly was.

I swiped at my phone screen, trying to end the call, accidentally pulling on Alani's reins at the same time. He flicked his head over his shoulder, as if to make sure I meant it, then before I could blink he broke out into a gallop, hooves thudding along the ground, mane streaming out behind him, leaving me clinging to his back with every ounce of strength in my being as my phone slipped out of my hand and under his feet.

'Stop!' I wailed, trying to pull on the reins without falling off the saddle. Someone was getting a Thighmaster for Christmas and that someone was me. 'Alani, slow down!'

But strangely enough the horse didn't understand

English or at least he was choosing not to. We tore past Louisa, my bag slapping against me over and over as I bounced up and down in the saddle, before whipping around a corner and bringing the rest of the group into view.

The rest of the group and the edge of a cliff.

Closing my eyes, I held on as tightly as I possibly could. I knew if you were in a car accident, you were supposed to go limp, something I had practised many thousands of times while travelling in a New York cab, but it was very hard to relax on the back of a runaway horse. Even if I had wanted to breathe, I couldn't, because every time Alani's feet struck the ground, the air was knocked out of me. My surroundings were nothing more than a blur.

'Angela!'

I heard someone screaming my name but I had no idea who it was. All I knew was the wind in my face, overwhelming fear and an unpleasant smell − I couldn't in all confidence say whether it was coming from me or the horse.

Without warning, without slowing down, Alani skidded to a halt and whinnied loudly. Slowly, I cracked open one eye. In front of me was a large picnic table, fresh fruit, bottles of champagne and the terrified frozen faces of my friends and strangers. With a happy head toss, the horse neighed once, trotted over to the table and helped himself to an apple.

'Angela, are you OK?' Jenny asked, still not moving.

'I dropped my new phone,' I whispered as Kekipi prised the reins out of my hands. James grabbed hold of me around the waist and peeled me off the back of the horse.

'We'll get you another phone,' she assured me. I clung to James's neck, not altogether sure my legs would work. 'What happened?'

'My mum called,' I replied, shaking from head to toe.

'That is enough to make anyone bolt,' she said, full of understanding.

Kekipi thrust a glass of champagne into my hand as I tried putting one foot on the floor. 'I've got a flask in my bag if you need something stronger,' he whispered.

'I think I'd rather go back down in the Jeep if that's OK,' I said, finally making eye contact with my apple-munching nemesis. Alani looked exceptionally pleased with himself for someone who'd been three feet away from Thelma and Louise-ing the pair of us into the Pacific Ocean not two minutes earlier.

I drank my champagne with shaking hands while everyone fussed around me. Was this my message from the gods? And if so, just what exactly were they trying to say? Never take a phone call while riding a horse? Core strength is key? Or maybe they were simply siding with Annette Clark. Maybe the gods of Lanai agreed that I was a terrible mother, so bad that I needed to be hurled into the ocean by a runaway horse.

'Here, sit on these.' Kekipi handed me a pair of ice packs. 'Your backside is going to be black and blue tomorrow.'

'Thank you,' I whispered as he exchanged my champagne glass for a cocktail of fresh fruit juice and whatever he was hiding in his flask. 'My backside appreciates it.'

He gave me a solemn wink and went back to the

table, leaving me sitting on the dusty floor, pressing ice packs against my bruised arse, drinking undeclared alcohol and staring out at the ocean to ponder my failures as a parent, a wife and as a daughter.

Well, I thought, if nothing else, I certainly had a story to tell now.

# CHAPTER FOURTEEN

Jenny hadn't told us where the evening's activities were happening but it wasn't difficult to guess. After an afternoon sat on an ice pack, working on my laptop, I met Louisa outside my villa at exactly seven o'clock. We were dressed in gorgeous designer dresses that had been delivered to our villas, and followed the sound of music and laughter.

We wove our way through the villas and out towards the main building. The whole pool area was covered with flowers, leading us down the stone stairs to the beach where a bonfire burned brightly and dozens of men and women were dancing in traditional Hawaiian dress, huge, happy smiles on their faces.

'This is all for us?' Louisa breathed. 'Oh, Angela, this is insane. It's not real life.'

'You're right,' I reminded her. 'It isn't. It's a press trip that was organized for a bunch of millionaire kids on YouTube who weren't allowed to come because they haven't learned one of life's easiest lessons: Nazis are always bad.'

'Tim was in a total mood when I called,' she said, sticking out her tongue to protest against her husband's sulking. 'Did you manage to get through to Alex?'

'I called from the room phone but he didn't answer so I emailed him to say my phone was out of order,' I breathed in. Was that pork? Smelled like pork. 'He hasn't replied yet.'

'You told him your phone is out of order?' Lou quirked an eyebrow as Jenny waved to us from the middle of a circle of hula dancers. 'Angela, it got trampled by a horse that ran you halfway up a volcano.'

'Yes, well, that feels like more of an in-person story to me,' I replied, gingerly pressing the soft spot at the bottom of my back. Kekipi had been right. I looked as though I'd been indulging in at least seventy-five shades of grey and my backside was going to be a billion shades of bruised by morning. Thank god I'd already got my skinny-dipping adventure out the way.

'Welcome to the Précis luau!' Jenny sang, her hair piled high up on top of her head, every inch of visible golden skin shining like lava. She looked as though she'd taken a bath in highlighter, and knowing Jenny, that was quite possible. 'Tonight is the absolute high-light of our trip, a true celebration of everything Hawaii has to offer. And like, really great cocktails. If everyone could take their seats, the show is about to begin. Time to celebrate True Soul mascara!'

'Hashtag ad,' I whispered to Lou.

'Hashtag True Soul,' she replied, utterly earnest.

'Love your dresses, ladies.' Paige danced her way over in improbably high heels, her off-the-shoulder frock fluttering in the breeze as she moved. 'How's your arse, AC?'

'You definitely want to ice it,' James said with a knowing nod as he trotted up after his new BFF. 'When I did my first intensive riding class for that Billy Buskin film, it was so bad I was filling my trunks with ice cubes in the end.'

'There are millions of men and women all over the world fantasizing about you,' I sighed. 'If only they knew.'

With that, someone turned up the music and I noticed there was a stage where the pool used to be. A dozen dancers in traditional Hawaiian costume began to twist and swirl and my drink began to kick in all at once. It was all beautiful and all so very much.

'Angela, I've been thinking and I've had an idea,' Louisa said, eyeing the elaborate cocktails in Paige's hand as she moved towards one of the round tables. 'We should get utterly twatted.'

'That's your idea?' I asked. 'Get smashed?'

'I'm talking you hold back my hair and I'll hold yours, blackout, Ibiza holiday hammered,' she suggested, slapping the back of her hand against her palm to emphasize her words. 'How long has it been since you've been properly drunk?'

'I'm pretty much tanked after two glasses of rosé at the moment,' I confessed. 'And I've got my phone call with the publisher in the morning. I'm not sure this is a good idea.'

'It's the greatest idea of all time,' she said confidently, grabbing two cocktails from a passing tray and nodding towards James's table. 'In two days we're going home, you'll have Alice back, a job to do and a book to write, not to mention a broken bum. This is a no-brainer. Let's get sloshed.'

I considered the suggestion for a moment. It would be so unprofessional of me to get smashed on a work trip, let alone irresponsible and downright immature. But at the same time, if I was just a little bit tipsy, I wouldn't be worrying about my husband, my baby, my job, my mother, all the pictures of my boobs that were floating in the cloud from my failed sexy solo photoshoot I'd invested an hour in the night before (and still not sent to Alex) or the fact that my bum really, really, really hurt.

'I will have one drink,' I confirmed, clinking my drink against hers. 'And that's all.'

What harm could one cocktail do, after all?

The show was amazing. I'd learned all about Hawaii's history, eaten a tremendous amount of pig and been treated to the sight of James storming the stage to join in with the hula and looking like a complete plum. All in all, it had been exactly what I'd hoped this trip to Hawaii would be. Louisa was right, sometimes you just needed to get a little bit tipsy. Not as often as I did when I was twenty-six, but there was definitely a time and a place and the place was Hawaii and the time was now.

'Hello madam.'

I pushed my hair out of my face to find Kekipi, wearing nothing but a grass skirt, sitting in Louisa's chair. When had she got up? I looked at my cocktail and tried to remember if it was my second or third. I'd said one but Lou kept filling it up and I wasn't drunk so it was fine. Probably.

'How are you feeling?' he asked, filling up my cocktail from a jug in the middle of the table. 'Bit like you've been gangbanged by an entire rugby team?'

'I've never been gangbanged by an entire rugby team,' I replied, shifting carefully in my seat. 'But I would imagine it feels something like this, yes.'

'You're still young.' Kekipi produced a single white tablet from where, I did not care to know, and pressed it into my hand. 'And you need one of these. It will fix you right up.'

'What is it?' I asked, holding it between my thumb and forefinger and squinting at the writing on the pill.

'It's *not* heroin,' he said.

'Is it illegal?'

'Not *everywhere*,' he replied.

It was good enough for me. I popped the pill into my mouth and washed it down with my drink. Almost at once, the throbbing in my tailbone seemed to lessen.

'Thank you,' I said, finding my smile all at once. 'Do you think one will be enough?'

'Oh, I would say so,' he laughed, planting a kiss on my forehead. 'Have a fabulous evening.'

'He is so nice,' I said to absolutely no one. 'So considerate.'

And I could have sworn the pineapple in our table's centrepiece winked back at me.

Once the luau had ended and everyone was milling around the stage, snapping pics with the dancers, I took myself off for a quiet, tipsy wander.

Leaving everyone else locked in conversation, I wandered off, away from the pool and down the stone staircase to the beach, planting myself in the sand, away from the fire. I could still hear the party over the soothing swell of the evening waves, cresting in and rolling out, but it felt at a safe distance.

'I wish Alex was here,' I said to no one in particular. 'It's too beautiful for just me to see.'

It'd be hard for him to be here when he isn't even talking to you, the voice in my head reminded me.

'Shut up you,' I muttered, sticking my snout back into my drink. 'No one is interested in what you have to say.'

'My apologies, Miss.'

I looked up to see a tall, gorgeous shirtless man hovering over me, holding a coconut. All the better for bashing me over the head with.

'Oh, not you,' I said, scrambling to my feet, ready to apologize to my would-be attacker. 'I'm sure everyone wants to know what you have to say. I'm so sorry.'

He laughed, shirtless, and held out his hand, still shirtless. Without knowing quite what else to do, I shook it and stared back at him, somewhat alarmed.

'Did you enjoy the show?' he asked.

I nodded, trying not to look directly at his nipples. 'Yes, it was very good.'

'Glad you enjoyed it. I'm Kai,' he said. 'I love your accent. Where are you from?'

Now, I was married but I was not blind or dead. He was totally flirting with me. Half-naked, and flirting.

'England,' I replied, tucking my hair away behind my ear. I didn't want to lead him on but I didn't want to be rude either. Plus, I was drunk. 'But I live in New York now, with my husband. I'm Angela.'

'That's cool,' he said, rolling back his shoulders and

flexing his pecs. I blinked. Did I just imagine that? 'I've always wanted to visit New York. And London, man, that would be so great. Is it just like it is on TV?'

'Depends what you've seen,' I said. Was it normal for someone to have that many muscles in their stomach? Didn't people normally talk about a six-pack? Because I could count at least eight and he wasn't even clenching. 'But I'm going to hazard a guess and say no.'

'Wow, you're just dashing all my hopes and dreams tonight, aren't you?' He ducked his head before looking back up at me with huge brown eyes.

'That's pretty much my thing,' I replied, glugging my drink back as quickly as possible. 'Are you from Lanai?'

'Oahu,' he answered, resting one hand on his naked hip. I noticed his loincloth was riding dangerously low, which was also when I noticed he was wearing a loincloth. 'I moved here to get away from it for a while.'

'I've never been to the Oahu but, if you needed to get away from there, I'm going to hazard another guess and say New York and London might be a bit much. Besides, how could you leave this? It's paradise.'

'That is true,' Kai said, his eyes on the horizon. I followed his gaze and saw little lights way, way off in the distance on a neighbouring island. 'But I do sometimes wonder what else might be out there for me.'

'No one knows how far you'll go,' I commented wisely.

He looked back at me, a confused expression on his face. 'Why have I heard that before?'

'*Moana*,' I said, sucking on my straw before clearing my throat. 'I have a child.'

'You look way too young to be a mom.' Kai took a step closer and I took a deep breath in, very aware of how far down the beach I had wandered. There was no one around us, not a single soul. What if he wasn't from the show? What if he was a Hawaiian serial killer who preyed on tourists who wandered away from the group and got lost on the beach and he worked on his abs especially hard to distract them because no one ever got mad at hot serial killers? I'd watched three episodes of *The Fall*, I still fancied Jamie Dornan, I knew how this worked.

'Well, it is quite dark out here,' I babbled, looking over his shoulder for an escape. 'And I am wearing a lot of makeup and also—'

'Oi! Clark!'

I blinked, looking up the beach to see James charging across the sand with his trousers rolled up around his knees.

'Are you harassing this terribly handsome young man?' he asked, barging in between myself and Kai with a hollowed-out coconut cocktail in his hand. I watched as he tried to get the straw from his drink into his mouth three times in a row and failed.

'Oh my, is that a loincloth?'

'It's a traditional *malo*,' Kai replied, setting his shoulders and puffing out his chest. 'As worn by Hawaiian warriors.'

James looked at me and looked back at Kai before spluttering with laughter. 'Is he cracking on to you?'

'No!' I cried, my head beginning to spin. 'Absolutely not.'

'Is this your husband?' Kai asked. 'I'm sorry, sir, we were just talking. Have a beautiful evening, both of you.'

And with that, shirtless Kai and his loincloth scrambled away, up the beach and back towards the villas. Not a serial killer, just a horny youth. Probably still out to take advantage of drunk tourists who didn't know better, though.

'Oh my god, Clark, I can't take you anywhere,' James said, shaking his head in faux disappointment. 'What would Alex say?'

'Alex would probably tell him it's weeks since I've put out and not to bother,' I admitted. 'Having a baby is no good for your sex life.'

'So glad I decided against it in the end,' he said with as much sympathy as he could manage. 'Well, that and the whole, you know, actually having to raise a child. Speaking of children, that poor boy was enchanted with you. What's your secret?'

'Give him a couple of drinks, he'd be enchanted with you too,' I mumbled, turning the coconut upside down to confirm it was, in fact, empty. 'Me and Louisa are getting twatted, won't you join us?'

'Louisa is already well on her way,' he replied. 'She and Paige are doing fireball shots with Kekipi. Who is married, in case you were wondering.'

'I wasn't but that's good to know. Are there more drinks up there?'

'There most certainly are,' James confirmed before squatting down in front of me. 'Come on, I'll give you a piggyback up the beach.'

Pulling a hair elastic off my wrist, I tied back my hair and climbed up on his back. Look at that, I was practically a pro.

'Oh!' I squealed as he stood. I'd forgotten quite how tall he was until I was clinging to his neck and reliving the trauma of almost being thrown from a horse less than twelve hours earlier. 'Don't drop me!'

'Don't choke me,' he gasped as I loosened my grip around his neck ever so slightly. 'That's more of a second date thing, babe.'

'Do you ever not have a sex joke to hand?'

'I don't think so,' he huffed. 'It's a gift, really.'

'You must be so proud,' I muttered into his thick curly hair, my voice bouncing up and down as he jogged along the beach. Whatever was in those cocktails had not agreed with me in the slightest. And there was the small matter of a mystery painkiller Kekipi had given me to take into account . . . 'Can you put me down now, please, I think I'm going to vom.'

'Your wish is my command.'

As James bent down, I let go of his neck and felt my flip-flops hit the sand. My new friend Kai was nowhere to be seen but everyone else looked as though they were having exactly the right amount of fun for a Saturday night luau in Lanai. As advertised, Louisa and Paige were knocking back shots at a bar manned by Kekipi while Jenny's assistant Sumi and Lily were learning to hula dance on the stage. Jenny, Camilla Rose and everyone else all had smiles on their faces and drinks in their hands. This was exactly what I'd dreamed of, this was exactly what I'd wanted.

'As much as I support your pissed-up plan of action,' James advised, 'I think we should find you some water. A dehydrated hangover in paradise is not a pretty sight, take it from a professional.'

'Fail to plan and you plan to fail,' I slurred, slapping his cheek. 'Actually, I could murder a pizza.'

'Christ almighty, Angela, how much have you had?' he marvelled. 'If this is motherhood, I've changed my mind. Sign me up for half a dozen babies right now. You're behaving like an extremely cheap date tonight, even for you.'

'I'm fine, I've had maaaaaybe, three cocktails,' I said, swatting his hands away from my face. 'And my bum was hurting so I took a tiny little painkiller Kekipi gave me.'

'What kind of painkiller?'

I didn't know.

'I don't know,' I said. 'But I'm not in pain so it worked.'

James grimaced.

'From what I've gathered about Kekipi, it was either a Nurofen Plus or a Quaalude.'

'Well, my arse doesn't hurt any more so I'm happy,' I said before slapping James on the backside and tottering over to Louisa and Paige. 'Helloooooo.'

'Oh, you're hammered,' Paige grinned. 'AC, I didn't think you'd be such a lightweight.'

'I'm so glad you're my boss,' I said, ignoring her protestations and folding her up in a messy hug. 'I think it's brilliant. I think you're brilliant. You'll do so well, better than I could have done at that job anyway.'

'Um, thank you?' Paige broke away from the hug, holding my hands in front of her. 'Are you sure you're all right?'

'I'm brilliant,' I said, letting go of her hands and doing a quick twirl to prove my point. 'I'm out with my friends, I'm living my best life, I'm following my dreams, I'm the woman who has it all!'

Paige gave an awkward laugh as Kekipi poured a tall glass of water and placed it in front of me on the bar.

'Have you tried the mascara yet?' I asked. 'It's properly shit.'

'You're so funny,' Paige replied loudly, looking over at where Camilla Rose was standing talking to Eva, not ten feet away. 'Are you sure you feel OK?'

'Yes, yes, yes,' I insisted. 'I feel great. I wish I had my phone, though. I want to take pictures of us. Can you take pictures of us and send them to me? I dropped my phone earlier when I was on a horse. It ran right off, it did.'

'Yeah, I know,' she said, pulling out her phone as I ran my fingers up her arm and tweaked her nose. 'I was there.'

'What pose are we pulling?' Lou asked, pulling herself up straight as soon as she saw the camera. I wiped my fingers underneath my eyes to remove any errant mascara and pouted towards Paige.

'Hula,' I said, striking a pose. 'But make it fashion.'

'You should do a video,' Lou said. 'You look gorgeous in that dress. You should do a video for your website.'

'I agree,' Kekipi said, pushing the glass of water closer toward me. 'You should drink this and then you should do a video.'

I took the glass with a sigh and gulped it down. Who knew water could be so delicious?

'Are you recording?' I asked as I fluffed up my already fluffy hair. The humidity in Hawaii was no friend to us fine-haired folk.

'I'm recording,' Paige replied. 'Go for it.'

'Hi,' I said, tossing my head at the camera. 'I'm Angela Clark, editor of Recherché dot com, and I'm just like you. I'm a mom, I'm a wife and I'm career woman and, you're probably wondering, how does she do it?'

'I know I am!' Kekipi yelled. 'Tell us how you do it?'

'It's easy,' I said, pouting at Paige's phone. 'The truth is I'm tired all the time. I run on sugar, caffeine and the dream of what the inside of my eyelids used to look like. Plus, I'm constantly on the verge of weeing myself and I haven't had sex in weeks.'

'Tell us more!' Kekipi demanded with glee.

I leaned in towards the camera and gave it my best James Jacobs trademark smoulder.

'Once, I stopped at my friend's house while she was out to change my baby's nappy and her dog took the nappy bag out the bin and ran all through the house, showering shit over three floors. It took me two and a half hours to clean it up, the baby wouldn't stop crying, I had to ride the subway smelling like rancid baby poop and the dog hasn't been right since.'

'Maybe we should try this tomorrow,' Paige suggested. 'I don't think this is quite the tone we're going for.'

'Follow my adventures on Recherché dot com to see my real life, my amazing friends, gorgeous husband and see what motherhood in New York is really like,' I said, throwing my arms up in a flourish. 'Good luck getting your pushchair on the subway, not going to happen. Oh, you're out longer than you were planning to be and need to feed your baby? Enjoy hiding in the stock cupboard in that nice Starbucks on 23rd Street.

212

And you know what won't fit you ever again? All your clothes! It's fabulous!'

'Yeah, let's call it for now,' she replied, lowering her phone.

'Are you sure?' I asked, arms dropping to my sides. 'Because I have at least . . .' I paused to count on my fingers. 'Seventeen more tips.'

'Perhaps we should dance,' Kekipi suggested, hopping around the bar and taking my hands in his. 'The hula has been superlative but perhaps it's time for something a bit more lively.'

He waved over at someone back in the dining room and, as if by magic, a thudding bass line began to echo from hidden speakers and my hips began to move all of their own accord.

'I love this song!' Louisa shouted, throwing her arms up over her head and spinning around, making her dress float out all around her like a soft, silken cloud.

'Me too!' I agreed. 'What is it?'

'I don't know!' she replied. 'I never want this night to end.'

'Me either,' I called, wrapping my arms around her neck. 'I love you so much.'

And just for a moment, everything was perfect.


But it was only for a moment.

'Angela, are you sure you're OK?'

I looked up from my position, slumped in front of the toilet bowl in my villa bathroom.

'I'm fine,' I shouted back to Jenny, drawing out the middle of the word so they'd know I really meant it. 'I'm just going to wash my face and then go straight to bed.'

I looked across the room to the enormous mirror and pressed my fingers to my lips.

'I'm not going to wash my face,' I whispered, swearing my reflection to secrecy. 'I'm going to throw up.'

'I think I'd feel better if I could get in there and see you, boo,' Jenny called through the door. 'Open up for me, will you?'

With a heavy sigh, I rolled over and crawled to the door, pressing the lock inwards and opening it, just a crack. Jenny and Paige peered inside the bathroom, looks of concern on their faces, while James waved his iPhone in my general direction, Louisa clinging to his back like a baby koala bear.

'Take Louisa home,' I ordered, pointing at my friend but not quite aiming my accusatory finger in the right direction. 'She's drunk.'

'Babe,' Jenny replied. 'Seriously?'

'Why aren't you drunk?' I demanded, slapping the floor tiles. 'What happened to a weekend of cocktails and sand and other things I don't remember I'm so tired?'

'I'm not drunk because I'm working,' she said with a roll of her eyes. 'Some of us have a CEO to entertain as well as your drunk ass.'

'I am fine.' I wagged a finger at her from the floor and fought back a barf. 'I'm going to wash my face, clean my teeth, possibly employ a tactical vom, and then I am going to sleep like a baby. Although not my baby because she does not sleep that well. I'm going to sleep better than my baby but just as good as someone else's.'

'Someone should stay with her,' Paige said. 'She's wrecked.'

'This isn't wrecked,' Jenny replied. 'She's not even singing yet. When she starts performing *Les Mis* from start to finish, that's when we worry.'

'I'll stay,' Louisa whispered, struggling to form her words. 'I'll make sure she's OK.'

'You're staying with me,' James answered. 'Someone else is going to have to make sure this one makes it through the night.'

'I'm closing the door now,' I said, reaching up for the door handle and managing to grab it on the second try. 'Good night, friends. I love you so much.'

Ignoring their protestations, I closed the door and locked it behind them, before crawling back to the toilet. I breathed in, breathed out and stared at the inside of the lid.

'Villeroy and Boch,' I said out loud. 'That's a funny name for a toilet.'

Turning around to rest against the cold, tiled wall, I picked up the receiver of the telephone situated next to the lav, my fingers hovering over the keypad before I committed to dialling. After a couple of false starts, I heard the line connect and somewhere across the ocean a phone began to ring.

'Hello?'

'Alex,' I whispered. 'It's me.'

'Ange,' he replied with a yawn. 'Are you OK?'

'I broke my phone on a horse,' I explained. 'And I can't milk myself any more. But I didn't kiss the man without a top on, James will tell you.'

'Got it,' he murmured. 'You're drunk.'

'I am the tiniest bit tippish,' I replied, deeply, deeply offended. 'Because I hurt my bottom on the same horse.'

'Babe,' Alex's voice was croaky and possibly not as pleased to hear from me as I would have liked. 'It's three in the morning and you're not making a ton of sense. Can we talk tomorrow?'

'No, it's later,' I argued. 'It's really late here so it's morning in New York.'

'I'm looking at my watch,' he replied. 'It's three-oh-seven. Which means it's ten-oh-seven in Hawaii.'

Oh my god it was so early. I was a monster.

'But when you called from Japan we talked forever,' I said, unexpected tears edging into my voice. 'And I was so tired and I got on the wrong subway and I woke up in Bay Ridge but I wasn't mad at you.'

'What are you talking about? I'm not mad at you, I'm just tired. And I haven't been to Japan in years,' he said. 'Angela, are you OK? Is Jenny with you?'

'Lou said I should send you a picture of my tits but it was depressing,' I huffed. 'Do you want me to send you a picture of something else instead?'

He did not reply.

'Who's Cara?'

'Oh Jesus,' Alex groaned down the line. 'Seriously? You're pulling this when you're the one who went to Hawaii and left me on my own with the baby and a broken ankle?'

'It's not broken,' I said, a little too quickly. 'And you told me to go. You said I should go.'

He was quiet for a moment before I heard him take a deep inhale and exhale slowly.

'I know I did,' he replied. 'But I guess I thought you wouldn't really go.'

'And now you're mad at me.'

'And now I'm frustrated,' Alex corrected. 'I'm frustrated that I can't get around as quick as I'd like because of my busted ankle, I'm frustrated because the show isn't coming together as well as I want and I'm frustrated because you're not here. But I'm not mad at you. But maybe I'm taking my frustration out on you and I'm sorry.'

'I shouldn't have left you,' I whispered, closing my eyes and wishing he was there with me. 'I miss you so much.'

'I miss you too,' he said. 'Don't let this ruin your trip. I'm good, I'm fine.'

He was fine, I was fine, we were fine. I smiled and rested my face against the side of the cold bath.

'Is Alice all right?'

'Alice is amazing,' he replied with a definite smile in his voice. 'She did the craziest forward roll thing today, I sent you a video. You didn't see it?'

'But the horse broke my phone,' I hiccuped. 'And I left Alice alone because I'm a bad mum.'

'You're not a bad mom.'

'Mum.'

'You're not that drunk if you can correct me,' he said with a smile in his voice. 'Fine. You're not a bad *mum*.'

'My mum says I am,' I told him, twisting one of the strands of the bathmat all the way one way and then all the way the other. 'She says I shouldn't leave Alice alone with you until she's fifteen.'

'Angela, if you got wasted every time your mom raised a question about the way you lived your life, you'd be permanently tanked. I'll admit that I'm a little confused about this horse stuff and why it had your phone but I would like to go back to sleep now. You're a great mom.'

'Mum.'

'Goodnight, Angela,' Alex said. 'Call me when you wake up tomorrow. After you've had coffee and a bucket of Advil.'

'Will you stay on the phone with me until I fall asleep?' I asked.

Somewhere, a very long way away, I knew he was smiling and shaking his head at the same time.

'Yes. But now I'm awake, I have to pee so I'm taking the phone to the bathroom with me.'

Our marriage was the stuff dreams were made of.

'OK, I have to switch to the phone in the bedroom,' I said, placing the handset on the floor, very, very carefully and then crawling out of the bathroom and through into my dimly lit bedroom. I paused. Someone was on the bed. Creeping as quietly as I could, I pushed up on my hands and knees to see a mass of golden-brown curls spread out across one of the king-size pillows.

It was Jenny, eyes closed, under the covers like Goldilocks.

'Jenny,' I whispered. 'Are you awake?'

'No,' she muttered. 'Get your ass to sleep.'

'I want to talk to you,' I hissed. 'I know you're avoiding me.'

'I'm here to make sure you don't choke on your puke in your sleep,' she said without moving. 'Not listen to your drunk-ass bullshit. Would I be here if I was avoiding you?'

She had a point but I was still very certain I did too. I had evidence! I'd put together a case! Only I couldn't quite remember what it was . . .

I rolled myself onto the bed. The firm pillow-top mattress barely budged as I clung to the edge.

'I'm going to say goodnight to Alex,' I whispered loudly. 'Do you want to talk to him?'

'No,' she replied. 'I'm asleep.'

'OK,' I said and picked up the phone on the bedside table.

'Hey.' Alex was waiting on the end of the line. 'You in bed?'

I nodded.

'Are you nodding instead of talking?' he asked.

'Yes,' I confirmed. 'I really miss you.'

'I really miss you too,' he whispered back. 'Now go to sleep.'

'Will you sing for me?' I asked.

'Angela, go to sleep,' Alex crooned quietly. 'It's three o'clock in the morning, our daughter will be awake in two hours and I'm really, really fucking tired.'

'That's a good one,' I said, stifling a yawn. 'Number one smash worldwide.'

Cradling the handset close to my face, I closed my eyes and smiled.

'I love you,' I whispered.

'I love you too,' Alex said. 'Goodnight, Angela Clark.'

I was asleep before he finished his sentence.

# CHAPTER FIFTEEN

Even though I had assured Alex I was OK before I went to sleep, when my alarm went off the next morning, I most certainly was not. I was just about to throw the alarm clock through the French doors and straight into the ocean when I remembered why I'd set it in the first place.

Luka Pierce.

I had to call Luka Pierce at Cooper & Bow Publishers with the worst hangover anyone had endured in millennia. Jenny was already gone, her pillow covered in mascara, and a note on the desk informing me that I owed her a new pair of shoes. Couldn't wait for the memory as to why to come back to me. Forcing myself into the bathroom, I peed, cleaned my teeth, gipping with every brush stroke, and poured myself a huge glass of water from the glass bottle of Evian in my mini fridge. Setting out a pad, a pencil and a stray strip of Advil I'd found in my suitcase, I settled myself down at the desk and prepared to make the call.

It took some people years to find a way into the

world of publishing. I'd been emailing agents and exchanging cards with editors for years and never had so much as a LinkedIn request. But just like that, Perry Dickson pulled one string and here I was, calling a publisher who actually wanted to talk to me. If I hadn't wanted to throw up quite so badly, it would have been a dream come true. I was such an idiot.

'Luka Pierce.'

'Hi, Luka, this is Angela Clark,' I said, taking slow, shallow breaths. 'I had a message from Perry Dickson asking me to call you.'

'Angela, right, right.' The voice on the other end of the phone snapped to attention at the mention of Perry's name. 'How's it going?'

'Going great, going great.' I lied. There was no need to overshare during a first chat. 'How are you?'

'Great, thanks for asking.'

Small talk, brilliant, loved it, couldn't get enough.

'Perry gave me a call to say you were interested in writing a book,' Luka said. 'Tell me about it.'

Fuckity-fuck-fuck-fuck.

'Um, I've been writing for a long time, all my life really,' I said, catching sight of my face in the mirror. Good job this wasn't a video call. 'I'm from England originally. I used to write children's books when I lived there, then I moved to New York and I've been working more on the journalism side of things for the past two years. And blogging, you know, I love to blog.'

I love to blog. Why didn't I just tell him I'd carried a watermelon?

'That's great,' he replied. 'And the book you're working on now?'

The book I was working on now? There was no book.

Perry *bloody* Dickson.

'Yes, my book,' I said, scrambling for a plot to a book that did not exist. Usually I wasn't too bad at bullshitting my way through important conversations but every door in my brain was bolted shut and, no matter how hard I knocked, none of them would open. 'Well, it's fiction, it's about a woman in New York.'

'OK.'

'And she is English,' I said, wincing at myself in the mirror. Shit shit shit shit shit. 'And she shows up with nothing, has to start from scratch.'

'Would I be right in thinking this is kind of auto-biographical?' Luka asked.

I opened up my laptop, blinking at the bright white of the search page, and quickly searched Luka's name. Publisher of his own imprint at Cooper & Bow, specializing in contemporary fiction.

'It's definitely fiction,' I said quickly. 'Inspired by true events of recent times. So contemporary fiction.'

Oh yes, how could he resist a pitch like that?

'Could be interesting,' he replied. 'What do you have ready right now?'

'Right now?' I stuttered. 'I'm actually in Hawaii on a press trip, it's for work. But I could get something over to you for next week?'

'That works,' he confirmed. 'I already took a look at some of your online work and it's good, I liked it. It's relatable, it's funny. But you never really know whether or not someone has a book in them until they write it, if you know what I mean.'

'I do know what you mean,' I said, no idea what he was talking about. 'Thank you so much, Luka.'

'If Perry thinks you have a book in you, I want to read it,' he replied. 'God knows she was right about Michelle Obama.'

'Right,' I squeaked.

'I'll let you get back to your work trip.' Even though I couldn't see him, I could hear the inverted commas he put around his words. 'And you'll get your pages to me a week from today. Looking forward to it, Angela, I can't wait to see what you have to say.'

'Neither can I,' I said as he ended the call and left me staring at my laptop. 'Neither can I.'

Lanai was the most magical place I'd ever been in my entire life. The sky was painted with shades of blue I'd never seen before, the sand felt like baby powder between my toes, the rainforests were Disney movies come to life and every tree, every flower, every plant and every person all looked as though they'd been through an Instagram filter that turned saturation up and misery down. It was an all-consuming, magical paradise that dealt only in joy-inducing fever dreams of bliss.

Which made dealing with the worst hangover of your life even more painful.

'You'll feel better if you eat something,' Louisa insisted as I sat in a makeup chair, resisting the urge to eat her.

At some point while I'd been on the phone with Luka, Jenny and Paige had agreed Monday morning would be the best time for us to take a bunch of photos for my website. Everyone else was doing something on a boat (I wasn't sure what because I was throwing up when they told me) and we had the estate to ourselves for a couple of hours. I'd begged and pleaded to be let off but they would not have it. Proof, if ever it was needed, that they hated me. Tess, the photographer, and Rachel, the makeup artist, had only arrived that morning and the poor things had their work cut out for them.

'You need to drink more coconut water,' Paige replied, art-directing from a lounge chair beside the pool. 'That always does the trick for me.'

'Nah, she needs grease. Bacon, egg and cheese, doll,' Jenny said. 'I'll call the kitchens and see what they have.'

'What I need is to go back to bed, watch seven episodes of *Friends* with a cup of tea, a can of Pepsi, a glass of water, and quietly cry until my head returns to its normal size,' I whispered. Even speaking in a normal voice was too much.

'You can't go back to bed,' Lou said, pulling down her sunglasses to give me the full force of her glare as she lounged back on her sun bed. 'This is our last full day, you have to make the most of it.'

'The fact you're not hungover is genuinely offensive,' I replied, taking short shallow breaths.

'The fact I'm not hungover is largely due to the fact I didn't take an unknown pill from an unknown man,' she said sternly. 'That doesn't stop being a real thing just because you're over thirty.'

'He isn't an unknown man,' I mumbled, flapping my arms up and down against my billowing skirt. 'He's . . . oh god, I've forgotten his name.'

'Kekipi,' said Jenny, Louisa, Paige, the makeup artist,

224

the photographer and the photographer's assistant, all at the same time.

'Angela's right, he's not a stranger. I've known him for ages.' Paige peered at me over the top of her tiny sunglasses, her red-lacquered lips puckered up into a tight frown. 'And I still wouldn't take anything he offered me.'

The thudding in my head drowned out her words as Rachel, Précis Cosmetics' head makeup artist, fussed around me.

'I'm so excited about your book,' Louisa said. I instantly regretted telling anyone about my phone call with Luka but I'd been worried if I didn't tell someone I wouldn't remember it and then I'd be right up a certain creek without a paddle. 'Any idea what the book is going to be about?'

'No idea,' I told her, rearing away from a black kohl pencil. 'Literally, no clue.'

'I'm not worried,' Jenny declared, a glass of fresh-pressed orange juice in her hand. 'You could write a dozen books without even blinking. What I'm curious to know is where this puts you with Perry Dickson and The Mothers of Brooklyn?'

'When The Mob does you a favour, you usually have to do them one back,' Louisa said in a grave tone. 'Although I will admit the only frame of reference I have for this kind of thing is the first two seasons of *The Sopranos*. It was too tense for me after that.'

'They're not the actual Mafia,' I said. 'I don't think they're going to ask me to bump off Kim Kardashian and chuck her into the East River.'

'I might,' Jenny said. 'So over her.'

'All I would say is, I know this is very exciting, but

you don't want to take on too much,' Lou warned, spritzing her shins with not enough sunscreen. 'You've only just started back at work and it's not that easy to juggle a job and a very demanding baby.'

'Not to mention Alice,' added Jenny, holding out her hand for a silent high five from Lou.

Rachel stared at me, a huge palette of different-coloured concealers in her hand.

'What do they do?' I asked.

'Fix this,' she said, waving a hand in front of my face. 'Hopefully. I'm a make-up artist not a miracle worker.'

'Thanks,' I grumbled. 'Do we have to do this now? I should be in my room writing.'

'You can write on the plane,' Jenny said from underneath her huge parasol. 'Stop whining and let that woman do her job.'

'Thank you,' sighed Rachel, dabbing a brush into a worryingly bright shade of peach cream concealer. 'She's worse than my kids.'

I looked down at her with forced surprise.

'Hungover often, are they?'

'All toddlers are just tiny drunk adults,' she replied, tapping the makeup under my eyes. 'How old is yours again?'

'Almost eleven months,' I said, looking upwards. My eyeballs felt like they'd been licked clean by a rabid badger in the night.

Rachel smirked as she took a step back. 'You've still got all that to look forward to then.'

'Angie, you look amazing,' Jenny shouted, waving a rapidly melting ice lolly at me. 'These pictures are gonna be bomb.'

'You would never know she spent half the night puking in a bin,' Louisa said in admiration. 'Well done, Rachel.'

'I'll know,' Jenny muttered darkly as Rachel took a bow. 'I will always know.'

I couldn't even begin to guess how many times in my life I'd said, 'I'm never drinking again', but for the first time, I thought it might be true. Motherhood was an amazing experience but it also took away as much as it gave; important things like your independence, the ability to wear leather leggings without second-guessing yourself and now my tolerance for alcohol. Not that I'd ever been a heavyweight in the drinking department, but what had happened in my bathroom between four and six a.m. had been like something out of a horror movie. I didn't know about Bertie Bennett selling Hala Lanai any more. If he had any sense, he'd burn the place down and start from scratch.

'It's not that I don't love the makeup and the dress,' I said, checking myself in the mirror and finding a much hotter version of myself staring back. Hotter and surprised. 'But I'm not sure how this ties in with what I'll be writing. If I saw someone looking like this telling me about her life as a mum, I wouldn't find her relatable, I'd find her punchable.'

'You want relatable but you also want aspirational,' Paige explained, standing behind Tess as she set up for the first shot. 'For instance, take Jennifer Aniston.'

'I could totally take Jennifer Aniston,' Louisa muttered behind her sunglasses. It was then I realized that the reason she wasn't hungover was because she was still drunk.

'This will be the first and only time anyone has ever

compared me to Jennifer Aniston in my entire life, so please go on,' I nodded, motioning for her to continue.

'She's a megastar,' Paige went on as we all studiously ignored my friend. 'She's absolutely gorgeous and she's got to be worth millions, hasn't she?'

'Probably billions,' Jenny said. 'She owns a bunch of real estate, like half of LA.'

'And she's still completely relatable,' she said, adjusting the neckline of the insane gown she'd trussed me up in. 'Even though she's Hollywood royalty, I always feel as though we'd get on. Like, if you met her at an airport bar, you'd be sharing a bottle of white wine within fifteen minutes while she solved all your life's problems. Perfect mix of aspirational and relatable.'

'And she was married to two of the hottest men I've ever seen with my eyes,' Tess added. 'Ross wouldn't stand a chance.'

'Lou, we just came super close to passing the Bechdel test,' Jenny said sadly. 'But since we didn't, I'm all in. Fuck marry kill, Brad, Justin and Ross. Angie, you first.'

Paige beckoned me over and I tottered around the pool in a pair of dangerously high Gianvito Rossi crystal-embellished heels. High heels, designer dresses and swimming pools did *not* mix.

'So you want me to be Jennifer Aniston?' I said, allowing her to fuss around me, feeling like a second-hand Girl's World.

'You've got it,' Paige replied, biting her lip as she fluffed up my skirt.

'Jennifer Aniston, if she lived in Brooklyn and was English and worked for a website for a living?'

'Spot on.'

'But who also lounges around next to private swimming pools in Hawaii in a thousand dollars' worth of dress?'

'That's at least ten thousand and you're going to have to trust me,' Paige said. 'Now shut up and smile.'

No matter how awful I felt or how uncertain I was about Paige's plan, I was still me and, if there was one thing I knew about myself, it was that Angela Clark liked pretty dresses and this, *this* was a pretty dress. Acres of delicately sequined, powder-blue tulle floated around me as I moved into place. A tight strapless bodice, which somehow put everything back where it once belonged, nipped me in at the waist before flowing out into a long Disney princess dream of a dress. I would have gladly fucked, married and killed Brad, Justin *and* Ross for this frock if I hadn't already been wearing it.

'This is the way forward, AC,' Paige said, hands on her hips. 'I know what I'm doing, that's why I'm the VP of content.'

She was so sure of herself, I almost began to doubt my own feelings. I had to find out what star sign she was. Presumably it was the same as Jenny or Kris Jenner or Donald Trump.

'You've got a lot on your plate, haven't you?' she went on. 'Let me do my job and help you.'

'So, what now? I just stand around while Tess takes pictures?' I said, awkwardly slapping the railing of the main pool's diving board while Paige peered over Tess's shoulder.

'Yep. Walk around, try some stuff, do what feels right.'

'I was quite clear that what feels right is a *Friends* marathon in bed,' I mumbled as I attempted to pull myself together. 'And would also help with some essential What Would Jennifer Aniston Do research.'

'These look gorgeous, Angela.' Tess followed me as I tottered around, trying to keep the hem of the dress off the wet floor. 'Really stunning, Angela.'

'You're amazing,' Paige yelled, as though the louder she shouted the more likely I was to believe it. 'You're gorgeous, you're clever, you're funny, you're killing it at everything you do. You're the Carrie Bradshaw of mums.'

Jenny pushed her aviator sunglasses onto the top of her head, squinting at my creative director.

'But, like, if we're being brutally real, wasn't Carrie Bradshaw a selfish, narcissistic monster who used her friends and abandoned all her ideals for a total asshole who messed her around for ten years?'

Louisa and Paige went as white as the very fancy 800-thread count sheets on the Hala Lanai beds.

'I don't know if you've been keeping up with the reruns,' Jenny said, her words tailing off. 'It's not a show that has aged super well is all I'm saying.'

'Jenny,' I said, making a slashing motion with my hand across my throat. 'Not everyone is ready for that kind of truth.'

'Ah,' Jenny said, picking up her cup of coffee and taking a sip. 'Next you'll be telling me she shouldn't have ended up with Aiden.'

'I'm going to pretend you didn't say that,' Paige said, grabbing her giant iPhone Plus from the little wicker table next to Louisa. 'AC, I'm going to take some behind-the-scenes video to go on the site. So, you know, just be yourself.'

'Be yourself' fell into the same category as 'try to relax'. Easier said than done.

'What does that mean?' I asked, suddenly static.

'You know, be funny,' she replied, holding the camera in front of her face. 'Quirky. Be adorable.'

I frowned, too aware of my arms and legs. The dress felt too tight and my make-up felt too much and I really, really did want to go back to bed.

'Quirky means you're weird but you're cute,' I said, angling one arm behind my back and the other up over my head, no idea what I was doing. 'And you're not allowed to attempt adorable once you have a baby of your own. It was in the secret rule book they gave me when I left the hospital.'

'I don't know, just be you,' Paige shouted back, very close to losing her temper. Interesting. 'Do Angela stuff.'

'What's Angela stuff when it's at home?'

'Breaking my husband's hand at my wedding,' Louisa suggested.

'Punching a girl on stage in Paris,' Jenny added.

'Losing my daughter in New York on Christmas Eve.' Louisa again.

'Falling in the Bellagio fountains,' Jenny began counting off examples on her fingers. 'Cancelling your last-minute wedding at an even later minute, attending a black tie gala dressed as someone from *Game of Thrones*, pole dancing in Las Vegas in an elf costume. You need more?'

'No, I think that's quite enough,' I said, sniffing and turning back to the camera. 'Everyone's done mad stuff, you know. It only sounds more mad because you're saying it all at once.'

231

'Sure,' Jenny agreed, standing up and slipping her feet into her fluffy slides. 'We've all gone to LA to interview an actor and ended up getting photographed eating his face at Chateau Marmont.'

'I know that was Angela but, if I didn't know better, I might say that one is more likely to be a "you" thing, Jen,' Louisa said. 'No offence.'

'Thank you,' she said with a smile, placing a grateful hand on Louisa's arm. 'That totally sounds like something I would do, doesn't it?'

'Right, let's get you out of that dress and into the next look,' Paige ordered. 'Leave the Elie Saab on the hanger and do the striped, sequined Saint Laurent.'

Striped, sequined Saint Laurent? Finally something I could wholeheartedly get behind.

'Christ on a bike, are you stripping off again?' James wandered out of the main house as Rachel helped me out of the blue gown, leaving me standing on the travertine tiles in my knickers. 'Jenny, all this female nudity is making me feel very hashtaggy.'

She presented her cheek as he worked his way around the women by the pool.

'Which hashtag?' she asked. 'There are so many you could choose from.'

'I'm not sure yet. Let me see what's trending and I'll jump on whatever bandwagon is doing best.'

Holding a towel up over my bare midriff, I gave an unsympathetic sniff.

'I don't know what to tell you, Jim. I'm sorry you're so offended by the female form.'

'It's not so much the female form as you,' he said before handing his sunglasses to Jenny. He peeled off his Balenciaga T-shirt, eliciting the world's most feeble wolf-whistle from Louisa, kicked away his Off-White flip-flops and, without warning, broke into a run, coming straight at me as fast as he could.

'James, no!' I wailed as I realized what was happening, altogether too late to do anything about it.

Six foot something of matinee idol launched itself off the ground, tackling me around the waist and hurling us both into the swimming pool. I heard myself scream right before we hit the water, only to have my protestations cut off by the impact. The shock of it all knocked the breath, and very nearly the wee, right out of me.

'I told you I'd get you back!' James spluttered, both our heads breaking the surface at the same time. 'That's for trying to drown me on the beach on Friday.'

'You're evil,' I panted, wiping my eyes and leaving long sooty black trails on the backs of my hands. 'And honestly, this really is the worst mascara ever made. I thought it was supposed to be waterproof?'

'Supposed to be,' Jenny agreed, holding out her hand to drag me from the water. 'Whatever. We both know it sucks but you got a free trip to Hawaii out of it so maybe don't be a dick?'

'Smile for the camera!'

I wiped my hand over my eyes and saw Paige waving from behind her phone. Oh good, she was filming the whole thing. And there I was, worrying I wouldn't be able to relive the moment over and over for all eternity.

'Jenny, any chance we could go for another ride on the horses this afternoon?' I asked as Paige backed away quickly, pocketing the offending device.

'Nope,' she replied as I wrapped myself up in a towel and looked longingly at the striped, sequined

Saint Laurent. My makeup was ruined, I was sopping wet, and this photoshoot was clearly well and truly over. 'We have one last group activity and then it's all free time until we leave, baby.'

'But we're bloody leaving tomorrow,' I said as Louisa wailed with dismay in the background. Truly there was so little difference between my actual child and my friends after they'd had a few, it was alarming. Rachel was dead right on that one. 'I really should try to find time to work on the book proposal. Any chance I can sit this one out?'

'You won't want to,' Jenny assured me with a worrying grin on her face. 'We're gonna get your creative juices flowing. It's all going to be very spiritual.'

The closest Jenny came to spiritual was making an annual pilgrimage to the designer outlets at Woodbury Common.

'Oh my god,' I watched her gleeful expression grow as I hopped up and down on one foot, trying to get the pool water out of my ears. 'You're taking us to drop acid or something, aren't you?'

'Oh, Angie,' Jenny laughed as she walked away towards the main house. 'I can't believe you think I would do something like that to you. Again.'

Truly I had the best friends in the world.

# CHAPTER SIXTEEN

My hair was still wet when I met up with the rest of our group two hours later. A quick shower, a massive coffee, half a bacon sandwich, a five-minute chat with Alex and Alice, visual confirmation of him throwing his mother's latest headband monstrosity directly into the bin, and I was a new woman. I closed my eyes, tilting my face upwards to feel the warmth of the sun on my skin. Bliss. Whatever this next activity Jenny had planned, it would be over in the next couple of hours and then I would settle myself down and write like the wind. My unrequested benefactor, Perry, had left me another message, checking in on my phone call with Luka and casually wondering exactly how many backstage passes she could get for Alex's show. But I tried not to worry. Perry and The M.O.B. were something to think about when I got home, not when I was safe on an island, thousands of miles away.

'Any idea what's going on?' Lou asked in a hushed voice.

'Not the foggiest,' I answered. 'Maybe we're doing an art class or something? She said it was creative.'

Before anyone else could come up with a better suggestion, a small wooden door creaked open behind us. I turned to see an opening in an old, vine-covered wall I hadn't noticed before. One by one, the other half of the group poured out, Pearl, Darcy, Elodie, Violet and the rest, each and every one of them in floods of tears.

'Is it too late to make a run for it?' I asked, grabbing Louisa by the hand.

'Yes,' Jenny replied, sticking her head out of the door. 'Don't even try it.'

'Where are we going?' Paige asked, frowning at Lily as she took out her camera to film the other girls.

'Inside your soul,' Jenny replied in an eerie voice. 'And, in a more literal sense, into this garden.'

'This garden is a very special place,' Kekipi explained, as we filed inside, Louisa crossing herself as she went. 'It was built and cared for by Jane Bennett, Bertie's wife, before she passed. Jane had a spot like this on each of their properties, somewhere to hide away when their parties got a little too much.'

'Did that happen a lot?' Eva asked.

Kekipi turned with an eyebrow arched so high, it could almost be considered his hair.

'Honey, too much was just the beginning.'

Last through the doorway, I wasn't expecting much. Both of my parents were big fans of the National Trust but when you've seen one walled garden, you'd seen them all. And I had seen so very many fancy gardens, because what teenager didn't like being dragged around Clumber Park during the school holidays?

But this? This was something else entirely.

I didn't know the names of many flowers. Roses, daisies, peonies and that was about my lot. My dad was the hands-on gardener in the family and even he couldn't keep a daffodil alive for more than one season, but what I did know was that this garden was extraordinary. Behind the stone wall, hidden from the rest of the world, was something so perfect I didn't even know how to describe it. The lush green lawn was surrounded by hundreds of plants, bushes and trees, blooming with flowers in colours I'd never seen before. There were baby-pink trumpets that faded into a soft coral at their edges, star-shaped blossoms so saturated they were almost neon, tall palm trees, short shrubs, red, blue, green, yellow and every colour in between. It was magical, there was no other word for it.

'They say the eyes are the window to the soul,' Camilla Rose announced, closing the door to the garden behind us. 'To celebrate our new mascara, we'll be taking a look into our own souls.'

Another woman entered through the wooden door. She was wearing a lot more tie-dye that I was usually comfortable with and, since Jenny had a blanket ban on white women with culturally insensitive hairstyles, I had to assume she and her blonde deadlocks were with Camilla.

'This is Truth,' Camilla said, waiting for us all to settle down on the grass with our blankets before she began. 'She is going to be our spirit guide this afternoon.'

'I really like the garden but I think I'm ready to go back to my room,' James whispered into my ear.

'Thank you, Camilla,' Truth said, lowering her head

and pressing her hands together in front of her heart. 'I am grateful for you.'

I bit my lip as I caught the look James gave Jenny across our circle. This was definitely going to go well.

'I'd like everyone to take a mirror from the centre of the circle,' Truth instructed, waving at a wicker basket full of pale pink hand mirrors. 'Now settle into a comfortable position. We're going to spend some time getting to know ourselves a little better.'

'Angela, I'm serious, if she tries to make us look at our vaginas, I'll be over that wall like a rat up a drainpipe,' Louisa hissed.

'They're not going to make you look at your vag in front of everyone,' I whispered back before glancing over at Jenny. 'But if they do, I'll give you a leg up then you pull me over, yeah?'

'First, we're going to take a deep breath and find our silence,' Truth cast Louisa and I a warning look before resting her palms on her knees and closing her eyes. I took a mirror and cleared my throat, suddenly overcome with the urgent desire to laugh. 'Now, you're going to make contact with yourself in the mirror.'

'Bloody knew it,' Louisa said under her breath.

'I'm having Sixth Form French trip flashbacks and I don't like it,' James growled.

I squawked loudly, turning my hysterics into a cough. 'Sorry,' I squeaked. 'Something in my throat.'

'Open your eyes and make contact with yourself,' Truth repeated. 'I want you to look at your reflection as you would your lover or your best friend. I want you to show yourself love and compassion and desire because you are a strong, powerful, beautiful soul.'

238

And now I knew where Jenny had got her sodding affirmations.

'Now, I want you to look into your eyes,' Truth said. 'That's all. Just stare into yourself and look for something deeper than the now. What do you see?'

I took a deep breath and sighed, holding the pink mirror up to my face. Blue eyes, bit bloodshot but no more than to be expected given the circumstances. My eyebrows needed plucking, something Jenny would likely mention before the end of the day, and my right eyelid seemed fractionally lower than the left. Hmm. Weird.

'You're not looking for imperfections,' Truth called, somehow reading my mind. 'I want you to find your own truth. I want you to learn something new about yourself.'

Find something new, I told myself, find my truth. I already knew I had blue eyes. But had the ring around my iris always been so dark? And had I always had those tiny green flecks? I'd read something somewhere that your baby leaves its DNA in you after she's born, so you're actually physically altered by becoming a mother. I wondered if it was possible Alice had left the green flecks. They were almost the same colour as her eyes, as Alex's eyes. I spent so much time searching for myself in her but I'd never thought to look for her in me.

A sharp sniff at the side of me broke my concentration. Glancing over my shoulder, I saw Jenny wiping away a tear, before realizing, to my surprise, I was crying too. Christ, this woman was good.

'Today we are going to learn that we are all enough, exactly as we are,' Truth said as we lowered our

239

mirrors, all of us with damp, misty eyes. Well, all of us except Lily. 'I would like everyone to tell the circle one thing they are afraid of. Our fears hold us prisoner. They build walls between our soul and the next when the reality is, we are all one. Fear, shame, hatred, these are false constructs designed to disempower us. There is nothing to be afraid of in this universe once we all understand that very simple fact. Now, who would like to share something that scares them?'

Strangely enough, no one volunteered to go first.

'I guess someone has to start,' Jenny said, wiping away a tear. 'Eva?'

'Thanks, Jenny,' Eva grumbled. 'Um, I guess I'm afraid I'll never find a boyfriend.'

'And why is that?' Truth asked.

'Because I haven't had a boyfriend in, like, two years?' she replied.

Our spirit guide nodded encouragingly.

'And why is that?'

'Because I go on dates and they're great but then it never turns into anything serious?'

'And why is that?'

'I don't know,' Eva said, her confident voice beginning to break. 'Because New York is full of cute skinny white girls and I'm not a cute skinny white girl? And my mom always said I'd end up alone if I moved to the city and none of these guys I go on dates with want anything long-term with me, they just want to date a black girl for a hot second and I'm afraid my mom was right.'

With that, she burst into full-on, body-rattling hysterics.

Louisa reached out, took my hand and squeezed

it tightly while Truth closed her eyes and breathed out.

'And why is that?'

'Because why would they?' Eva croaked through her tears.

'Do you believe everyone else here deserves love?' Truth asked, opening her eyes.

She nodded.

'Then you must realize you also deserve love,' she said. 'Your mother speaks out of fear, you believe her because of fear. Love is on its way to you but it won't arrive until you're ready.'

'Maybe I'll reinstall Bumble,' she sniffed, wiping her face with her sleeve. 'Thanks.'

'Gratitude is beauty,' Truth replied, smiling at the group. 'Now, who's next?'

Everyone stared at each other, in stony silence.

James broke it first.

'I use humour as a defence,' he wailed.

'My life is boring,' Louisa sobbed.

'I feel selfish for missing my old life since I had Alice,' I admitted.

Everyone turned to look at Lily.

'What?' She sat up, shoulders prickling. 'I don't have anything.'

'Nothing?' Eva asked, smearing her supposedly waterproof mascara across her face. 'There's nothing you're afraid of?'

She sighed and rolled her eyes, lips pursed in concentration.

'Red meat?'

'We'll come back to you,' Truth said kindly. 'Now, let's close our eyes and fold over into child's pose. If anyone isn't familiar, raise your hand and I'll assist you. After a quick breath break, we'll delve deep into our fears and work on overcoming them, together.'

Rolling forward, I stretched my arms out ahead of me and pressed my face into the grass. It smelled gorgeous, like any other grass I'd smelled before was an inferior imitation. Charlie Red to Chanel No. 5.

'Breathing in for ten,' Truth said, her voice moving around the garden above me. 'And breathing out for ten.'

A quiet, scuffling sound at the side of me was enough to break my concentration and I looked up to see Jenny crawling over to the door and out of the garden.

'Breathing in for ten.'

Truth's choice of hairstyle aside, all this self-help bollocks was right up Jenny's alley but she hadn't offered anything up to the group. She might seem fearless but I knew there were lots of things Jenny was afraid of. Open-water swimming, giant subway rats, doing her taxes on time, she could have said any one of those things but, no, she stayed silent.

'Breathing out for ten.'

Enough was enough. Hadn't she promised me a fantasy weekend of the two of us hanging out in a hot tub, getting rat-arsed and indulging in some serious BFF time? Wasn't the fact we'd barely seen each other over the last few months the actual guilt trip stick she'd used to beat me into coming here? This was the final straw. The proverbial camel's back was well and truly broken and I was determined to get to the bottom of whatever was going on.

Slowly, stealthily, I waited until Truth's back was turned before crawling off my blanket, across the grass and out the door. I staggered upright, rubbing the feeling back into my thighs, and set off for the villas at a brisk pace.

'Jenny!' I called, catching sight of her curls bouncing along the path ahead of me. 'Jenny, wait.'

'Go back in the garden,' she ordered without turning round. 'You're missing the session.'

'*You're* missing the session,' I countered, picking up my pace until we were shoulder to shoulder. 'What's going on?'

She stopped in front of her villa, her whole body shaking with sobs.

'I'm totally OK,' she said, holding her key in a shaky hand. 'I just didn't want to do it.'

'You look it,' I replied. 'Jenny, what's wrong?'

'Low blood sugar?' she muttered. 'For real, go back to the garden. You don't wanna know how much I spent bringing that crackpot out here.'

I took the key out of her hand and opened the door to the villa, guiding her inside while she swept away the last few tears. Her villa was exactly the same as mine. If I'd invited fourteen backpackers to bunk down and leave their shit absolutely everywhere.

'I'll be good to go in a minute,' she insisted, shutting herself in the bathroom as I picked up a thong from the arm of her sofa. I had forgotten what a joy she was to live with. Poor Mason. 'And don't touch anything, I know exactly where everything is!'

'How?' I asked myself, taking in the piles of paper, makeup, clothes, room service plates and Précis-branded everything, from Swiss exercise balls to sanitary towels. Picking up a particularly nasty-looking napkin with my fingertips, I turned to drop it in the bin by the desk. And that was when I saw it. Wrapped in a bag, wrapped in tissue, it was barely visible at the bottom of the bin but, once I had seen it, I couldn't pretend I hadn't.

'Jenny?' I marched across the room, not sure what I was going to say but knowing I had to say something. 'Jenny, open this door right now.'

I banged on the door until it flew open, a fresh-faced Jenny on the other side. She pushed past me, an easy smile on her face as though the last two minutes hadn't happened.

'Jesus, Angie, what's wrong with *you*?'

'Why is there a needle in your bin?'

Jenny stopped in her tracks, frozen still with her back to me.

'I don't know what you're talking about,' she replied without turning round.

'OH, ALL RIGHT,' I said in a very loud voice that could possibly have been considered shouting. 'I must have imagined it. Shall we empty the bin out and have another look?'

I dashed at the bin but not before Jenny intercepted me, pushing me onto her sofa and jumping on my back, leaving me face to face with the stray pair of knickers.

'Let go, let go!' I begged. 'I don't know if you wore those or not but this is gross.'

With an exasperated sigh, Jenny rolled off my back and onto a huge pile of Précis-branded towels at the other end of the settee.

'Please don't jump on my back again,' I said, slowly sitting up and chucking her knickers on the floor. 'But you've got to tell me why there's a needle in your bin.'

'You're gonna be mad because I didn't talk to you about it, but it's really no big deal,' she said, dropping her head against the back of the settee. 'Mason and I are trying for a baby.'

I squealed so loudly, she actually had to cover her ears.

'No big deal? Jenny, that's a *huge* deal! I'm so happy, it's brilliant news,' I shrieked, rolling on top of her in a half-hug, half-human-blanket situation. And then I realized what she was saying. 'Isn't it?'

'Things haven't been as easy as we'd hoped,' Jenny's voice was too quiet and precariously soft. I sat myself upright as she pulled up her T-shirt to reveal a swollen, bruised belly. 'So we're doing the IVF thing.'

I didn't quite know what to say. I hadn't seen her in a bikini this whole trip, she hadn't had so much of a sniff of booze here, or at Delia's birthday party or at that ridiculous fish restaurant, and I wasn't sure if this was why she hadn't bothered with the horses, but, either way, I couldn't blame her.

'Hurts like a bitch,' she said as she traced the blossoming yellow bruise on her normally taut stomach. 'And I still have another week to go. Twelve thousand bucks and we don't even know if it'll work.'

Jenny was trying to get pregnant. Jenny was doing IVF. What I wanted to say was, 'Why didn't you tell me?' but I knew this was not the time.

'I'm sure you're doing everything right,' I said instead, stroking her hair back from her face as new tears appeared. 'Are you seeing Dr Laura?'

She nodded. 'She's been amazing. Anyone else would have told us to keep trying for another six months but I knew something wasn't right and she ran all the tests right away.'

Carefully, I pulled a rustling chocolate bar wrapper out from underneath and dropped it over the side of the settee, praying it was clean before I sat on it.

'It's Mason. He has "low sperm motility" and, man, if I didn't want to make a thousand jokes,' she added with a weak smile. 'It's, like, the only thing he has not found funny in the entire time I've known him.'

'I can see why,' I said. 'Oh, Jen, this must have been so hard for both of you.'

'I know you won't say anything but please don't say anything,' she pleaded, wiping her face and taking a breath. 'I wanted to tell you so bad but Mason is still being weird about it and don't be mad but I was kind of jealous that you got pregnant so easy and, fuck, I feel so stupid saying that out loud. It's the hormones, right? It's got to be the hormones.'

'The great thing about this is you can blame literally everything on the hormones for months,' I replied, mustering a real smile for her and remembering what Louisa had said to me on the beach. 'And you don't need to feel guilty for feeling the way you feel. You can tell me anything, I won't judge and I won't share it with a soul.'

Yanking her shirt back down, she pulled up the leg of her shorts to reveal another big bruise. 'It's gross, right?'

'That's exactly what my arse looks like,' I promised without offering to share the proof. 'I will never forgive you for putting me on that horse.'

'I'm so sorry, babe,' Jenny said, laughing a lot louder than necessary. 'Wow, that feels good. Mason is gonna be so mad but I'm so glad I told you. I'm sorry, I totally tried to gaslight you. I was avoiding you but I promised him I wouldn't say anything. This is why I was so stressed about this trip and Erin going away. We already started treatment, how can I take over the company for a year if I'm pregnant?'

'Did she tell you about Thomas?' I asked.

She nodded. 'I threatened to rip his dick off.'

'And what did she say to that?'

'Erin?' she shrugged. 'I don't know. That's what I said to Thomas.'

Jenny never had been one to beat around the bush.

'Erin aside, would you want to take over the company?'

She pinched her shoulders together before letting them drop, her face uncertain.

'I don't know,' she said slowly. 'I'm good at my job and the money is nice and the perks are awesome but it isn't what I'd wanted to do.'

'No,' I replied. 'You wanted to be Oprah.'

If I'd been talking to anyone else, I'd have sounded like I was taking the piss but this was my real-life fairy godmother, Jenny Lopez. There was nothing she couldn't do if she put her mind to it.

'It's not like I'm not happy.' She turned her face away to look out the window and I couldn't work out if she was trying to convince me or herself. 'But it gets to a point where I can't stand the thought of spending my life selling another shitty mascara to women who do not need another shitty mascara. And yes, I'm talking about the shitty mascara that is all over my face right now.'

'So glad we came all the way to Hawaii for you to

tell me how great it is,' I said, waiting to see if there was anything else she wanted to say.

'It fucking sucks,' Jenny declared, turning back towards me with zebra stripes down her cheeks. 'And I hate it.'

'Plus there's your podcast,' I reminded her, reaching for a pack of makeup wipes from on her coffee table. 'Did you manage to get in touch with the podcast people?'

'You're making fun of me but I did,' she replied with a sniff. 'And you're right, there is my podcast. And hope against hope, a baby. But I don't want to let Erin down, she's going through so much.'

'We're all going through so much,' I told her firmly. 'Erin wouldn't want you to be unhappy.'

Jenny nodded even if she didn't look as though she believed me.

'Will you be my first guest?' she asked, her eyes lighting up for the first time in days. 'We can tell my listeners how we met and how you're super inspirational and how you broke that guy's hand and how you run your own website and everything.'

'Maybe we'll leave the part about the hand out,' I suggested. 'But yes, of course, I would love that.'

It was a lie, I couldn't think of anything worse, but I badly wanted to be a good friend and I didn't know what else to do.

'It's still crazy to me that you have a kid,' she said with a sigh, collapsing against me, her curls tickling my nose. 'I don't mean that in a bad way. I think you're an amazing mom. It's just I forget and then I remember and my brain can't always process it.'

'That's funny,' I replied, smiling. 'That's exactly how

I feel. Apart from the amazing bit. Pretty sure an amazing mum doesn't nip off to Hawaii for the weekend.'

'I'm pretty sure any mom that could, would,' Jenny corrected with a laugh before lowering her voice to a more curious tone. 'What's it like?'

'Being a mum?'

'Yeah.'

'It's really hard,' I said, trying to think of something honest but encouraging that covered every emotion and experience I'd been through in the last twenty months. 'And it's not anything like I thought it would be. I'm in love with her. When I'm holding Al and I look at her and she looks back at me, it's everything. Even if it's only for a moment, which it usually is because she'll be screaming blue murder ten seconds later, but it's a completely different feeling to anything else in the world. It's amazing and terrifying, all at once.'

'Kinda sounds like this one time I did mushrooms in the desert,' Jenny said with a happy sigh. 'I was convinced I'd turned into a cat and, I gotta tell you, it was scary but I was pretty happy at the same time.'

'Yes,' I agreed, plucking a wipe from the packet and cleaning her cheeks. 'That's definitely a good story to tell when we're discussing parenting.'

'I'm so glad we talked about it,' she said, brown eyes glassy with tears again. But this time they looked like happy tears. 'I'm excited but I'm so afraid I'm gonna fuck it up.'

'There you go,' I replied, folding her into a hug. 'Not even knocked up yet and already a natural. You're both going to be brilliant.'

And of that, I was sure.

# CHAPTER SEVENTEEN

When Jenny had to leave to set up for our farewell dinner, I didn't want to waste a single second. Laptop under my arm, I set off for the only place on the entire estate where I wouldn't have my door knocked down by my friends, be thrown in a swimming pool or accidentally adopt seventeen kittens. Jane Bennett's garden.

But I wasn't the only one who was looking for some peace and quiet.

'Oh, sorry,' I said as I opened the door and spotted someone sitting at the back of the garden. 'I didn't know anyone was in here.'

The garden's lone resident was an old gent I hadn't seen before. He raised a hand in greeting, his three-piece suit, white hair and white beard seeming quite at odds with his exotic surroundings. He looked exactly like Father Christmas if he was about to give away his daughter at her wedding. Miracle on Hala Lanai.

'Not at all,' the man said, rising to his feet and

waving me inside. 'Please come on in. I was just leaving. I've told them not to keep this place locked up when we've got guests. Janey would have wanted you all to visit.'

Even though I very much felt as though I was intruding, I stepped into the garden, so curious. He was so familiar but I just couldn't place him.

'Yes, yes. My Janey loved showing off her garden. I remember once, she gave Stevie Nicks some cuttings to take home with her,' he chuckled to himself as he strode over to hold out his hand. 'Got the poor girl in all kinds of trouble at the airport. No one would believe it was just a piece of a ginger plant. Can't think why. Nice to meet you. I'm Al.'

'Angela,' I said, shaking his hand. Good, solid hand-shake, hearty smile and he smelled excellent, like a very classy granddad who might have popped by the aftershave counter in House of Fraser on his way to your house. 'My daughter's name is Al.'

'Really?' he asked, crumpling up his already weather-worn features. 'Well, anything goes these days, I suppose.'

'Short for Alice,' I corrected myself with a laugh. 'I call her Al but it's actually Alice.'

'Ahh, I see,' he nodded. 'Al's an abbreviation for myself as well. It says Albert on the old birth certifi-cate. Emphasis on old.'

A huge sunny smile took over his face and all the years fell away. I knew who he was at once.

'Albert,' I said slowly, everything finally making sense. 'Oh god, of course. You're Bertie Bennett?'

'Guilty as charged,' he said with a short, stiff bow.

'Oh my god,' I gasped, placing my laptop on the

floor. Bertie Bennett. I was in the presence of a bona fide legend. All the stories I'd heard about him came rushing back and I took another look, picturing the hair and beard as chestnut brown and imagining Debbie Harry on his shoulders. Yep, definitely him. 'I'm so excited to meet you. Thank you so much for having us. Your house is incredible.'

He waved away my fussing with a jovial smile and sat back down in the deckchair. I folded myself up on the floor in front of him, legs crossed as though I was waiting for storytime. Which I was.

'Apologies for not introducing myself earlier,' said Al. 'Your little troop seemed as though you were having such fun.'

'I've had an amazing time,' I confirmed. 'I don't know how you ever bring yourself to leave.'

'That's what I'm trying to muster the courage to do right now. You caught me on my way out. I have to fly to Milan this evening, I'm afraid,' Al replied, looking none too happy about it. 'Duty calls. Although if I recall my flight plan exactly, it's Honolulu, New York and then Milan. Which is why I don't get back here as often as I used to. Too much buggering around for an old goat like me.'

'Not so old,' I said with a smile he returned and raised with a laugh. There was even more to notice in the garden this time around, tiny birds darting around from tree to tree, butterflies hovering above the colourful plants. 'Although I would think the best course of action would be not to leave in the first place, then you wouldn't have to come back.'

Al nodded, reaching up to rub the petal of a pale orange plant between his thumb and forefinger. 'Very tempting, very tempting,' he said, plucking the petal and popping it in his breast pocket. 'We bought this spot a very long time ago, back when most of the island was a pineapple plantation, but now Janey's gone and I'm at work again, it's a little much. Between this place and the house in Oahu, there aren't enough months in the year for me to make the most of them both.'

'Oh,' I replied with wide eyes. He had two Hawaiian houses? I was definitely in the wrong job. 'Must be a nightmare.'

'We all have our cross to bear,' he said, laughing. 'Oahu is more of a home, this is the fantasy spot. It's easy to lose yourself in a place like this, you forget about the rest of the world very quickly. Makes it very dangerous.'

'And that's before you take into account runaway horses and piña coladas,' I commented. 'But it really is such a beautiful place. Surely someone would bite your hand off for it?'

'Know anyone?' he asked, one eyebrow arched.

I shook my head. 'Not personally but have you heard of a man called Bill Gates? I hear he's got a bob or two going spare.'

'Yes, I suppose. The last time he made me an offer, I wasn't ready to let it go but perhaps you're right.'

'Come again?' I did a double-take as Al gave his beard a good, contemplative scratch.

Pushing himself up and out of the deckchair, he turned away and strolled towards a sturdy-looking tree with long, curving limbs that swept down towards the grass before reaching upwards. Carefully, he sat back down on one of the lowest branches, testing its strength before committing to a proper sit.

'Tell me about yourself, Angela Clark,' Al said from his seat in the tree. Between the beard and the suit and the unreal backdrop, it was like something out of *Mary Poppins*. Original more than the remake, although I thought that was good too. 'What do you do?'

'I'm a writer?' I replied, following him down the lawn.

Al frowned and rapped his knuckles against the trunk of the tree.

'You don't sound entirely sure about that.'

'No, I definitely am,' I said, rubbing my thumb against the back of my engagement ring. 'I write for a website called Recherché. My website, actually. And I'm working on a book.'

'That's very exciting,' he said. 'What's the book about?'

I looked down at my laptop and frowned. 'Haven't got that far yet,' I admitted. 'Any ideas?'

Al made a huffing sound and scratched at his chin under his beard.

'You're writing a book but you don't know what the book is about?'

I confirmed with a sharp nod.

'Then why are you writing a book?'

'It's complicated,' I said, a tight feeling spreading across my chest when I thought about my impending, unrequested deadline. 'But someone I don't know very well thought they were doing me a favour and told a publisher I *did* have an idea and now they want to see my proposal and, well, I was hoping I'd have come up with something by now.'

His bushy eyebrows rose slowly as he took it all in. 'That's a very big favour from someone you don't know very well. You must have made quite an impression on them.'

'She's part of this very exclusive parenting group,' I explained. 'And they want me to join. I think she thinks this will persuade me.'

'Do you want to write a book?' asked Al.

'I do,' I replied. 'I've always wanted to.'

'Then what's stopping you from wanting to join this woman's group?'

I plucked a blade of grass and began tearing it up into tiny pieces. 'That's even more complicated than the book itself,' I laughed. 'I don't think it's for me. All the members are either rich or powerful or they have incredible jobs and they're all gorgeous and they all live in Brooklyn and they hang out with celebrities and—'

'Where do you live, Angela?'

I paused and cleared my throat.

'Brooklyn.'

'And didn't I see that actor chap is with you all this weekend?'

'He's an old friend?' I muttered.

'Ah, I see,' Al replied. 'Now, I haven't delved into your finances or realms of professional influence, but it sounds to me as though you're rather successful in your own right, are you not?'

I didn't bother to answer that one because I had an idea of where he was going.

'Perhaps this group want you to join because they think you'd be a good fit,' he suggested. 'They clearly think a lot of you or they wouldn't have asked you to join, now would they?'

I'd been intimidated by Perry Dickson and her

immaculately groomed lackeys from the moment she'd opened her front door but I hadn't once asked myself why.

'I think it's because she's got a crush on my husband,' I said, wincing as I said the words. 'And yes, I'm very aware of how stupid that sounds when I say it out loud.'

'Not for me to say.' Al held up his hand and dipped his head. 'I've seen it all around here but it does seem to me that most people wouldn't bother to do big favours for you or invite you to join their exclusive club if they'd got their eye on your chap. Have you stopped to consider the possibility they might simply believe you'd be a valuable addition?'

'No,' I said in a small voice. 'I don't think I have.'

'There aren't many advantages to getting to my age but I know a thing or two about a thing or two,' he smiled. 'The problem is, no one believes you until they've been through it all themselves.'

'I will take any and all advice,' I assured him. 'Ever since I had my daughter, I'm realizing I know absolutely bugger all about anything. I worry so much more than I used to, about work, about what other people think, about everything. I really haven't felt like myself since I had Alice.'

'Maybe you don't feel like yourself because you're not yourself.'

I looked back at him, not quite sure what to say.

'Not the same person you were before, I mean,' he said. 'Things change when you have a child. Not that I'm one to offer parenting tips but I can help out with some of the tried and true classics. Trust your gut, ask for help when you need it and always believe the people who love you. And what was it Janey always used to say? Oh yes, go for the thing that keeps you awake at night.'

'At the moment that's my baby,' I said, starting to smile again.

Even though we both laughed, I knew exactly what he meant. When Alex was working on new music, he would sit locked in his tiny studio until daybreak, playing the same song over and over and over for hours, not stopping until it was perfect. Before Alice, I'd have done the same thing with my writing but I felt like caring too much about my work made me a bad mum.

'You want to write a book, don't you?' Al asked.

'I do,' I confirmed.

'Then you must.'

'It all sounds very simple when you put it like that,' I told him, looking down at the grass and seeing a shiny pair of Oxfords underneath the tree with a pair of black socks neatly tucked away inside. Al was barefoot.

'At the risk of showing my age again, I think your generation has things a lot harder than mine did,' he said, scratching his neck underneath his neat, white collar. 'Yes, you've a lot more opportunities these days but there's a damn sight more expectation. I work with a lot of women and they're so bloody hard on themselves. Much more so than the men. There's a girl called Amy who works for me. When she had her baby, she was back at work before we'd even had a chance to notice she was gone.'

'It's not easy,' I agreed. 'But I can't imagine it any other way.'

Because if I could change it, would I? Alice was my

heart and soul. I could sit and stare at her face for hours and never get bored. I knew every freckle, every eyelash, every hair on her head, and I loved every single one of them, but that didn't mean I couldn't love my job as well. Even if I was exhausted and my hair looked shit and I accidentally wore two completely different shoes to the supermarket that one time, I wanted Alice and my writing in my life. And, god forbid, maybe even Perry Dickson and her friends? Well, perhaps this wasn't the time to be making dramatic decisions.

'I think this might be my last visit here,' Al said, thumbs hooked in his jacket pockets and a smile blooming under his beard. 'It's been so nice to share it with friends for the last few weeks. Lovely to have Camilla over one last time. Kekipi can stay to close things up and then I think we're done.'

'Ah, I forgot you were friends with Camilla,' I said, watching as his eyes glazed over, glassy with memories. I wondered what he was thinking about.

'Oh, she's an old friend of Janey's,' he explained, eyes still misty. 'Millie used to be an assistant for Mary Quant, you know. The three of them could get quite rowdy when they wanted to.'

'I believe you,' I said, pinching my toes together in the cool grass, feeling like I was intruding once again. 'I wish I could have been there.'

Al continued to stare at something I couldn't ever hope to see with a smile on his face that made me think he was happy, wherever he was.

'I should get back to my villa,' I said, picking up my laptop. It was time to leave him alone. 'I'll leave you to say your goodbyes in peace.'

'On an island full of beautiful things, this garden is perhaps the most magical thing of all,' Al said, weaving in and out of his memories before focusing back on me. 'Do you have a photo of your Al? I should like to see my almost-namesake.'

I patted myself down for my phone before I remembered.

'You know, I don't,' I confessed. 'They're all on my phone and my phone broke. Well, I dropped my phone and then a horse broke it. I'd say it's a long story but that's more or less it.'

Al considered me for a moment with a pleasantly confused look on his face.

'Do you know Tess Brookes and Amy Smith? Because if you don't, I really must introduce you.'

'Thank you for all your advice,' I said as he stood to his feet. I reached out to shake his hand goodbye but, instead, he beckoned me in for a hug and I wondered whether or not he was in the market for a part-time goddaughter. Surely Delia and Cici would share? Well, maybe not Cici. 'And thank you again for letting us stay here. I can't imagine a more beautiful place in all the world.'

'I don't think there is one,' he replied, looking around the garden and smiling. 'Very pleased to have met you, Angela Clark.'

'Likewise,' I said as I left him and his memories in the garden. 'I hope I'll see you again.'

And I very much meant it.

# CHAPTER EIGHTEEN

'I want to thank you all for joining us on such a beautiful journey.' Camilla Rose raised a glass of champagne
at the end of dinner on our final night, and, all along
the table, everyone followed suit. 'I'm so glad to have
shared it with so many new friends.'

James leaned in from my left with a huge fake smile
on his face.

'Why do I feel compelled to tell her the mascara is
a bag of shite?' he asked under his breath.

'Because you're no longer bound by your fears?' I
suggested. 'Or you're drunk. One or the other.'

'Both,' he said, tapping his champagne coupe against
mine. 'I think it's both.'

I dug my toes into the sand underneath the table.
For our last supper, Jenny had outdone herself. The
dining table from the main house had been moved
down to the beach, close enough to the ocean so we
could hear the waves washing in and out but far enough
away for our feet to stay dry. As well as the most delicious food, the table was covered in a rainbow of

Hawaiian flowers, just like the ones in Jane Bennett's garden. Even though I missed Alice so much, I knew I would be so sad to say goodbye to this place, especially if Bertie Bennett was seriously considering selling up. It was almost cruel to bring someone to a place so perfect and then break it to them that they could literally never return. I hadn't felt so betrayed since Cadbury discontinued Spira bars. Bloody loved a Spira.

We sat down just as the blue sky started to turn pink, laughing and joking and, most importantly, eating, until the sun was completely swallowed up by the ocean. What seemed like a hundred candles of tiki torches glowed in the sand and the moon rose above the water, keen to show us she wasn't afraid of a little flashy competition. It was a perfect night.

At one end of the table, Jenny was holding court, managing everyone beautifully. Not a trace of her worries appeared on her face. I hated to be so helpless when she was in need but, short of convincing James to sort her out with some slightly more active sperm, I didn't know what else to do – and after everything he had drunk during the trip, I wasn't sure that was a terribly workable idea anyway. God only knew what he was packing down there.

'Angela, Angela, Angela,' Louisa sang, resting her head on my shoulder, flowers in her hair and a smile on her face. 'I love you so much.'

'I love you too,' I said, smoothing a stray strand of blonde hair away from my drunk friend's face. She'd been tipsy for a straight twenty-four hours and was not going to enjoy the plane ride home. Flying hungover was the absolute worst. 'Are you excited to go home and see Gracie?'

She frowned and pulled a face. 'Perhaps you could pop her on a plane and send her to me instead?'

'What about Tim?' I asked, trying not to smile.

'No, he should probably stay in London,' she said, eyes fixed on one of the shirtless waiters I assumed Jenny had hired. 'Take care of the dog.'

I laughed but at the same time I really hoped she was joking. Tim and Louisa had been through their fair share of marital strife but I always hoped in my heart of hearts that they were happy.

'No, I can't stay here, the food's too good and I have no self-control. I'm getting fat,' Lou poked herself in her not even slightly fat stomach. 'But it's been nice to have some time off. I can't tell you how much better I feel for not watching *Frozen* in five straight days. '

'I don't think I've turned on the TV the entire time we've been here,' I breathed. 'This place really is magic.'

Louisa sipped her champagne and looked out to sea. 'I might have watched a couple of episodes of *Elena of Avalor* in the bath earlier. I suppose I do miss her a bit.'

'You know what you said earlier,' I said, filling up her glass. This was a delicate conversation that would doubtlessly go better if well lubricated. Like so many things in life. 'In the garden.'

'About what?'

'You said your life was boring,' I filled up my glass too, just to be on the safe side. 'You don't really think that, do you?'

She made a thinking noise and rapped her finger-nails against the stem of her glass. Louisa's nails were bright red, just like Jenny's, but short and neat rather than long and lethal. Someone out there would make a killing if they could make a video on how to change nappies with acrylics but it was not going to be me or Lou.

'Sometimes I do,' she admitted. 'But only when I compare myself to other people. We all have our off days, don't we? I bet even Meghan Markle gets pissed off sometimes. There's all these people out there going, "Oh, I wish *I* was a princess", but how many times in the last few years has that woman woke up, looked at the papers and thought, "Fuck all this, I just want to get in the car and go to yoga", but she can't, can she?'

She was right. To a million people, I had the perfect life but how many times had I lain awake, feeling like I wasn't enough?

'Seems like Lily is the only one of us who has achieved total transcendence,' I said, nodding across the table where the UK's leading beauty blogger was pouting into her phone screen, attempting to get the perfect selfie without any of us plebs messing up the background.

'No, she's just a dickhead,' Louisa replied. 'And I promised I'd meet up with her in London when we get back. Remind me to delete all my social media before we leave.'

'She doesn't deserve you,' I told her, picking a bit of frosting off one of the pink velvet cupcakes that had been our dessert. 'You, Louisa, are the closest thing this world has to a perfect human. You're a good mum, a brilliant wife, an awesome friend and you've always got one of those little blue blocks in the toilet.'

'Don't set me off crying,' she laughed, delighted.

263

'We both know this mascara won't hold up. Angela Clark, I will never forgive New York for stealing you away. Life would be so much easier if you were back at home. Every time either of us was starting to feel a flicker of FOMO, I'd come round with a bottle of wine and we'd slag off everyone on *Love Island* until we felt better.'

'Maybe I can convince Alex we need to spend a summer at home,' I said with a grin. 'Because that does sound nice.'

'What sounds nice?' Paige asked, hopping into James's empty seat on my left. I looked up to see him charging up and down the beach with Eva on his shoulders, apparently no longer concerned about using humour to push people away.

'Bottle of wine, slagging people off, *Love Island*,' I repeated.

'Oh *fuck*,' Paige looked stricken. 'I hadn't even thought about that. Do they even show it in America?'

I shook my head and emptied the bottle of champagne into Paige's glass as she choked back a sob.

'It's not too late for you to change your mind,' I told her. 'There isn't a single soul who wouldn't understand.'

'Except Cici,' she replied.

'There isn't a single person who has a soul who wouldn't understand,' I corrected.

She breathed in deeply before taking a drink. 'I have heard some horror stories about her but she's only been nice to me. I was just as worried about meeting you, to be honest.'

'Me?' I asked with surprise. 'Why would you be worried about meeting me?'

'You've already run your own magazine,' she said, lifting her perfectly groomed brows. 'I wasn't sure how happy you'd be about someone coming in above you.'

Which was entirely fair because I hadn't been that happy about it at all.

'I've been meaning to speak to you about something you mentioned the other night,' she said, putting down her glass. 'It's been bothering me and I think we should get it out the way before we start working together properly.'

Oh god, oh god, oh god. What did I say, I wondered, desperately trying to work out what she was referring to.

'Only you said something about me doing the job better than you could've and that threw me a little. It's better that we're honest with each other. Did you apply for the job?'

'No,' I said. 'I'm honestly very happy you got the job. I think you'll be amazing at it.'

'Thank you,' she said, still staring directly at me. Her ability to stay calm under pressure only made me flap more. There was nothing like someone who kept their powder dry to send my verbal diarrhoea into overdrive.

'It was actually Cici who mentioned something to me about someone in HR suggesting I would be good for the job but I certainly didn't apply for it because I've got more than enough on, haven't I? Launching Recherché and a new baby and now this book proposal as well – that's more than enough for one person.'

Paige licked her lips and took a sip of her drink.

'Besides, I really wouldn't want to do that kind of overseeing management job again,' I insisted. 'I really want to be more hands-on creative, writing, editing, telling stories, more that kind of thing.'

Still she said nothing.

'So I'm incredibly glad you're here, grateful in fact, because I know Cici doesn't care about the day-to-day editorial direction of Besson and I think you'll do a bloody good job of it and we British girls have got to stick together and I'm a Libra and I hate confrontation and everything's all right, isn't it?'

Paige nodded and picked up her glass.

'A-OK, AC,' she said, pushing back her chair and walking away with a wink.

'What was that all about?' Louisa asked.

'Why do you allow me to drink?' I groaned, head in my hands. 'Or talk? Or breathe?'

'There, there,' she said as she rubbed small reassuring circles on my back. 'It'll all come out in the wash.'

When Cici said she saw a lot of herself in Paige, I'd thought she was referring to the fact they were both hot blondes with hot bods who liked a nice frock but maybe Cici had seen something I'd missed. What if they had more in common that I realized?

'Hey, everyone,' Jenny clambered up on her chair, a champagne coupe full of sparkling water held aloft. 'We have one last surprise, courtesy of our host, Bertie Bennett, so if you'd all like to take out your phones, Instagram at the ready, and look over thatta way, we'll be starting any second.'

A rally of whoops and cheers came next and the entire table grabbed for their phones and cameras and, in a couple of instances, both.

'I should have asked, you don't think anyone is going to be sensitive to fireworks, do you?' Jenny asked, dropping herself directly into my lap and kicking her legs across Louisa's knees. 'I heard someone sued the city last year because the explosions gave their dogs PTSD.'

Louisa and I looked at each other.

'Lily?' she asked.

'Lily,' I agreed.

'Fuck Lily,' Jenny said after less than a second's consideration, leaning forward to take the tiniest sip from my champagne glass. 'I freaking love fireworks.'

'Me too,' Louisa said, holding up her phone in preparation. 'It always seems like such a shame that we only get them in winter at home.'

'And we only get them in summer,' I replied. 'And I mostly avoid the Fourth of July, don't I, Jenny?'

Lou gave her a questioning look.

'Jesus, it only happened one time,' she sighed dramatically. 'This guy I was dating asked Angela why she was celebrating America's independence from the UK and it got kind of heated.'

'He did not ask why I was celebrating, he screamed, "Why are you here, red coat?" over and over in my face,' I replied, not enjoying the memory at all. 'And then he sang "God Save the Queen" with some interesting new lyrics and showed me his arse.'

'He was a fun guy,' Jenny said, twirling a curl around her fingers as she gazed off into the distance with a small smile on her face. 'Billy, right? His name was Billy. I wonder what happened to him.'

'He's in prison,' I reminded her.

'Oh that's right,' she grinned. 'Man, he was such a good time.'

It was moments like this that I was very grateful

she was married. Before I could reply, the first firework blew up over the roof of Hala Lanai, lighting up the skyline with a shower of white sparks.

'Look, it's starting!'

'I fucking love fireworks.' James Jacobs strode over, plucked Jenny off my lap and placed her on top of his broad shoulders. 'I've got to say, Lopez, you've really pulled this off. When you emailed me, my first thought was "Uh-oh, Fyre Fest 2.0" but this has been a fantastic weekend.'

'And no one had to exchange sexual favours for Evian!' I cheered.

Jenny cupped her hands around her mouth and whooped loudly. James anchored her legs to his chest as we all cheered, dozens of fireworks exploding overhead.

'I gotta confess, this was Bertie's idea,' she said over the chorus of oohs and ahhs. 'He had them left from some other party and Kekipi organized the entire thing. I'm just glad they worked – looking at the boxes, they seemed pretty old.'

'Um, not to be a party pooper,' Louisa said, pointing off into the distance. 'But do we know where that smoke is coming from?'

We all followed her finger to see a thin stream of grey smoke rising from behind the main house.

'That's definitely supposed to be there, right?' Jenny slid down off James's shoulders. 'Like, there's been smoke every night and we just haven't noticed?'

No one said anything, the rest of the group distracted by the fireworks that continued above our heads.

'Maybe I should go check,' she said. 'I'm sure it's nothing.'

'I'm sure it's nothing,' I agreed, almost believing it. Until we heard an explosion that definitely was not a firework going off.

'It's OK!' Jenny shouted at the top of her voice as people on the beach began to whisper. 'It's all part of the firework display, no one panic!'

Louisa sniffed at the air, an expression on her face that directly contravened Jenny's orders.

'Something is on fire,' she whispered urgently. 'What if it's the house? What if we get stuck here on the beach?'

'The house isn't on fire and we aren't going to get stuck on the beach,' I insisted, even though I was sure of nothing. What if my villa was on fire? My passport? My laptop? And then a horrible thought occurred to me, what if I'd left my straighteners on? What if I'd burned down Bertie Bennett's Lanai estate because I'd been too lazy to blow-dry my hair properly and had run the straighteners through it instead?

'Everyone stay where they are!' shouted Sumi, as if a group of social media influencers were about to roll up their sleeves and put the fire out themselves. 'No one panic!'

At the end of the table, I saw Jenny talking to Camilla Rose, an animated exchange that did not seem to be going terribly well.

'It's all part of the display,' she yelled. 'This is all part of the plan, it's a traditional Hawaiian house burning. What a fucking treat, right?'

'See,' James said, picking up another bottle of champagne as orange flames began to rise from whatever we were watching. 'This is why we can't have nice things.'

As the sound of sirens serenaded us down on the beach and Bertie Bennett's vintage fireworks boomed overhead, James popped the champagne and filled everyone's glasses.

'Why aren't you worried?' I asked as Louisa tapped out a tearful text message to Tim and the rest of the girls live-streamed the disaster to their various social media platforms.

'Please,' he said, drinking straight out the bottle. 'You can't call yourself a Hollywood actor until you've seen at least one party end in a house burning down. And I've seen three. Nine times out of ten it's caused by fireworks. The first one was a heartbreaker, I don't think Leo ever got over losing that place.'

'I'm sure Jenny has it under control,' I said, hugging Louisa to me and watching the flames lick the sky as more sirens sounded somewhere out of sight. 'Who else would you want in charge of an emergency?'

'Exactly,' James said, watching Jenny race across the sand and back up the staircase, her assistants close behind her. 'But it does call for a new toast. A memorable end to a memorable trip.'

As the first arc of water from the fire engine rose into the air, I took a sip, one arm around Lou's shoulders, the other around James's waist.

A memorable end to a memorable trip?

It certainly had been that.

# CHAPTER NINETEEN

I let myself into the house as quietly as possible.

It was eight in the evening and even though Alice should have been asleep for at least an hour, I didn't want to take any chances. After all the drama of the fire, everyone had trickled away from Hala Lanai over the course of the evening and into the next morning. Disappearing in pink Jeeps until all that was left was me, Louisa and a very crestfallen Jenny. There was a slight chance the trip hadn't gone quite as well as she'd planned but over all, other than a bruised coccyx, a two-day hangover and the fact everything in my suitcase smelled like I'd been smoking fifty a day, I'd really had quite a nice time.

The hallway was silent, the living room empty as I wheeled my suitcase inside, locked the door behind me and checked the fridge for milk. Old habits die hard. Alex had to be downstairs in the studio and his mother had to be gone, proof that miracles could happen. Shrugging off my coat, I carefully, carefully, carefully opened the door to Al's room. Motherhood had made a ninja out of me. I knew if I pushed all my weight down on the handle, the door wouldn't creak, and if I took two steps to the left before I walked over to her cot, I could avoid the squeaky floorboard we still hadn't got round to replacing. Ducking under the mobile so as not to set off the flying duck that just loved to blast out a verse of 'Clair de Lune' if you so much as looked at it, I peeped down at my little girl.

She was fast asleep, flat on her back with her thumb in her mouth, doubtlessly traumatized by a long weekend of elaborate headwear. Annette Clark would certainly have something to say about the thumb-sucking but I was a woman who chose her battles wisely and it was not the hill I intended to die on that evening.

After a quick wee and spritz of Old Spice deodorant, I following the softened sounds of Alex's guitar as I made my way down the short staircase that led to his studio. He'd tried to teach me to play so many times but I could never get further than my crowd-pleasing acoustic cover of 'Umbrella'. And by crowd-pleasing, I meant Angela-pleasing. But to Alex, playing guitar was the easiest thing next to breathing. He only had to hear a song once before he could play it perfectly. I loved to sit on the stairs and listen to him play without him knowing I was there. Jenny and Louisa both complained about their husbands' silent moods but I never needed to practise my mind-reading skills with Alex, not when he had a guitar in his hands.

Tonight he was playing something quiet and gentle that wouldn't wake the baby. I didn't recognize the tune and I couldn't make out the words he whispered as he played it but it sounded like something he had written. I could tell an Alex Reid original from the first three notes these days. I spotted the baby monitor on his mixing desk and smiled. Night-vision Alice, still sound asleep. Holding myself back on the stairs, I revelled in my stolen moments. This was what Al had been talking about in Janey's garden. Alex's eyes were closed, his long fringe was tucked behind one ear and he strummed his new Martin guitar, the one he'd brought home with wild eyes and refused to tell me how much it cost because 'you couldn't put a price on love'.

Standing there and watching him play, I understood what he meant.

Five days was the longest we'd been apart since Alice was born and now that I was only three feet away from him, I realized it was five days too many. Knocking gently on the door, I held up my hand in a wave. The moment was too perfect to ruin with words. Alex rubbed his eyes as he came out of his songwriting stupor, looking at me as though he was dreaming. And then he smiled. That same slow smile I'd first seen all those years ago, in a diner that didn't exist any more.

'Hey,' Alex said, resting his hands on top of his guitar and tilting his face upwards for a kiss, not at all surprised to see me. I pressed my lips to his, eyes closed, and knew I was home.

'Hey yourself,' I said as I ran my hand through his thick, black hair. I loved it long, he liked it shorter, but I definitely hadn't accidentally-on-purpose forgotten to make him an appointment with my stylist friend twice in the last month.

'It's getting long.' He tucked it back behind his

ear as I felt unexpected butterflies flutter into life in my stomach. 'I gotta get it cut before the show on Friday.'

I smiled, resting my bum on the mixing desk and taking a moment to wonder just how I'd got so lucky.

'What's up, nothing to say?' Alex asked, pressing his hands to his pale cheeks. 'Did you lose your voice? Or has an entire weekend with Louisa and Lopez at the same time worn out your vocal cords?'

'A woman can't fly five thousand miles to take another look at her husband?' I asked.

His hair fell in front of his face as he set his guitar in its stand but when he brushed it back, he was smiling.

'You watched *A Star Is Born* on the plane, huh?'

'Yes I did,' I replied. 'And it remains glorious.'

'How was the weekend?'

'Completely amazing until Jenny put on a firework display and accidentally burned down two buildings.'

'She's never house-sitting for us. Ever,' he said, slicing the air with his palm.

Alex reached out for my hand and pulled me into his lap. I straddled him carefully, wrapping my arms around his neck, cradling his face in my hands and leaning in for another kiss.

'We missed you,' he said softly. 'I missed you.'

'I missed you too,' I whispered. 'Was everything OK? How was Al? How's your ankle?'

'Ankle's fine,' he mumbled, my forehead resting against his forehead. I curled my fingers in the hair at the nape of his neck and breathed in. 'Alice was gorgeous. There was a minor incident when I accidentally washed Sophie the Giraffe but she seems over it now. She's going to be so happy you're home. She loves her mummy.'

We kissed in a way we hadn't in what felt like forever. Alex's mouth was hot against mine and he held me as though he was trying to make me a part of him, his hands moving up and down my back, snatching up handfuls of my hair, proving to himself that I was really there. He buried his face in my neck as I closed my eyes and revelled in his touch and the lean muscles in his broad shoulders as they moved under my hands, my legs wrapped around his narrow waist. He slid his hands underneath my sweater and then the T-shirt under that and pushed them both up over my head. Warm hands on cold skin. I shook off my clothes, tossing them across the room and watching them land on the head of his guitar from the corner of my eye.

'Angela,' he gasped as I pulled his head backwards.

'Alex,' I moaned, kissing his throat.

'Are you wearing my deodorant?' he asked.

'Shut up,' I ordered, kissing him hard and deep and fast. He scooped me up, my legs still wrapped around his waist, and I felt the cold, hard wall against my back as he tore his own T-shirt over his head and fumbled with the button fly of his jeans. My feet found the floor as I tugged at my own zip, wondering if it had ever been so difficult to remove my clothes before. Hot, sweaty, my breath coming harder with every passing moment, I looked up for just a second and caught his gaze. It was just us. I didn't just want him, I needed him.

Things had changed since our first encounter. I cried when Erin told me Manatus, the cute little neighbourhood restaurant where we met, had closed but that was New York, always changing. Just because you loved something, didn't mean it was forever. Everything came and went over time, especially if you forgot to give it your attention. I hadn't been to Manatus in years and then I was surprised when it closed . . . Didn't really make any sense when I thought about it.

But sometimes, if you were very, very lucky, you found something else, something different to what you started out with. It would be a lie to say things were exactly the same as they were when Alex and I first met because they weren't.

They were even better.

# CHAPTER TWENTY

'Good morning.'

Jetlag was a monster.

I woke up, groggy, dazed, confused and wondering why the soothing sounds of the ocean had been replaced with honking horns and angry voices. The sun was streaming in through our bedroom window.

'Alice, look who's home.'

And then it all made sense.

'Gimme, gimme, gimme,' I said, scuttling my bum backwards until I was almost upright, nestled in a pile of pillows and holding my arms out for Alice. 'Oh my god, she's bigger. She's definitely bigger. Alex, don't you think she's grown?'

'No,' he said, handing over the precious cargo. 'I don't.'

'Mummy missed you,' I whispered, clutching her so tightly she'd be complaining about this moment in therapy as an adult. Without warning, my eyes began to prickle, my nose started to burn and that was it, I was off.

'Don't cry!' Alex yelled quietly, climbing onto the

bed and folding both me and Alice into a hug. 'You'll set her off. What's wrong?'

'I just missed her so much,' I sobbed. 'And I didn't even realize until now.'

'Then this might not be the best time for this,' he said, reaching under the bed to pull out a large, black box.

'What is it?' I asked, choking back more tears as Alice reached out to wipe the wetness from my face. I caught hold of her hand and nibbled on her fingers, bottom lip still trembling.

'Open it and see.' Alex sat back on the bed. 'Actually, give her to me. This could get messy.'

Lifting the lid from the box, I stared at the contents for a moment before a fresh set of overemotional sobs took me over. It was my bag. My Marc Jacobs satchel, stitched back together and sporting a brand new leather strap.

'Alex,' I wailed, picking up the bag and holding it to my chest, right where Alice had been only moments before. 'I love it so much.'

'Hal, the guy who makes my custom guitar straps, put it back together so it should be pretty sturdy,' he explained while Alice writhed, stretching her hand for the box. 'And this . . .' he ran a finger along the new shoulder strap, 'is the strap from the guitar I played the very first time you came to see me play.'

I didn't know if it was hormones, jetlag or the residual hangover from my weekend in Lanai but I couldn't stop crying.

'Is this a bad time to point out where they stitched a piece of the blanket we brought Alice home in into the lining?' he asked.

'Yes,' I wept, crawling across the bed and melting into a bag, baby, husband group hug. 'I love it so much. I love you so much.'

'We're a good team,' Alex whispered into my hair. 'And even the best teams have bumpy moments.'

'I'm going to remind you of that the next time you get mad at me for not sorting the recycling,' I said, a smile breaking through my tears as Alice curled her fingers around the strap of my bag and jerked it up and down until the buckles jingled.

'Like mother like daughter,' Alex said with a happy sigh. 'I think we need to get to work on giving her a little brother sooner rather than later.'

Swallowing back my tears, I scoffed, taking my daughter back into my arms and resting my cheek on her glossy black hair. 'My uterus would like at least another year off,' I said. 'But we should probably start practising more often, just so we don't forget how.'

'I'm gonna hold you to that.' He jumped off the bed and stretched his long, lean body until he touched the top of the doorframe with his fingertips. 'Pancakes for breakfast?'

'Yes, please,' I replied, all eyes on Alice and my new old bag, even more precious than ever.

'And then I want to hear all about Jenny burning this hotel to the ground,' he called as he wandered off towards the kitchen.

'It wasn't the entire place,' I said to Alice, bumping her up and down on my knees. 'It was just two outhouse buildings and a garage, wasn't it? Wasn't it?'

Alice did not seem able to confirm or deny.

Holding her again felt like plugging myself in at the socket. Maybe I was like my laptop, I needed to drain the battery completely before I could get the best out of a full recharge? So many mums had told me they didn't feel whole until they'd had their children, that they were the final piece of the puzzle they hadn't realized was missing, but it didn't feel that way for me. To me, Alice was like Alex. Impossibly wonderful additions to my life that I couldn't imagine living another day without. Things had been wonderful before I knew them but they were even better now. They didn't complete me, they helped me become the best version of me. At least, when I wasn't being insecure and neurotic and utterly convinced I was failing at every part of my life. But that's what my friends were for, wasn't it? To pick up the pieces Alex and Alice fumbled; no one person could juggle everything.

They say it takes a village to raise a child, I thought as I watched my own try to bury herself face first in a bag I had bought before I even knew her dad existed, but I felt 'it takes an army to keep a mother together' was far more accurate.

I'd planned to work from home on Wednesday but my conversation with Paige was running over and over in my head and sitting on it wasn't going to make me feel any better about the way I'd handled things. Yes, we'd had a great time in Hawaii but she was still my boss. Maybe not a whip-cracking overlord but, still, the person who ultimately decided whether or not I got paid at the end of the month and I really wanted us to get off on the right foot.

Leaving Alice happily hanging out with the nanny and Alex deeply preoccupied with his upcoming gig, I took myself off to the office, a bit tired, a bit emotional but entirely certain of what I wanted to say. Dodging a man wearing a monocle as I walked down Bedford Avenue, I heard my phone ringing. My third phone in as many weeks. I was making do with an ancient handset, equipped with a SIM card from the newsagent at the airport, until my new iPhone arrived at the end of the week and the only people who knew the number were Alex, Louisa, Jenny and, of course, my mother.

'Hello,' I said, checking both directions before I crossed the road. I refused to lose any more bloody phones or bags this month. 'What's up?'

'Why are you changing phones so often?' Mum grumbled. 'I don't like it and neither does your father.'

'I love it!' I heard him call in the background. 'Keeps me on my toes!'

'It's because I'm secretly a drug kingpin,' I replied, smiling happily at the sight of a yellow taxi. It was good to be home. And three and a half thousand miles from my mum. 'This is my burner. If anyone calls and asks you anything, tell them you've never even heard of me.'

'Ha ha, Angela, very droll,' she said with a theatrical sigh. 'Where are you now? Australia? Japan? Timbuktu?'

'I'm on my way to work.' I loitered at the edge of the pavement, eyeing an Apple Store that used to be a bagel place and Whole Foods that had replaced . . . I couldn't remember what. 'Alice is with the nanny who she now calls mum and Alex has run off with his mistress.'

'You're not funny, you know,' she replied, her voice clipped and prim. 'Karen, who runs the knitting shop in the village, her daughter married this man and he was completely besotted with her. Whisked her off her feet, ran off to Gretna Green to get married, pregnant on the honeymoon, the whole job. And then she started working at the little Asda on the high street and guess what happened then?'

'They lived happily ever after and never had so much as a cross word?'

'She found out he was gay and having it away with a fella at the service station up in Bingley.'

Mum really did have excellent timing. The stand-up comedy world had missed out on this one.

'Seems to me there's a slim chance that had more to do with her husband being gay than her taking a job at Asda,' I said. 'And why did they run off to Gretna Green? How long ago was this?'

'A while ago,' she said, non-committal as she always was when facts didn't necessarily support her story. 'Regardless, you know what I'm saying.'

'I do,' I agreed, nodding hello to the man who ran the street meat cart on the corner of Metropolitan. 'And I am honestly saying this with love because I don't want to argue with you but the way Alex and I do things works for us.'

Most of the time, I added silently. Which was still better than a lot of people managed.

'I'm sure it does,' Mum replied. 'I don't want to argue about it. If you want strangers raising Alice, then that's up to you.'

I hovered on the edge of the road, tiptoes clinging to the edge of the kerb as I took a deep breath in and let it out slowly.

'I really wish you lived closer,' I said calmly. 'I'm sure she'd love to have Granny Annette looking after her more often.'

I waited patiently for a response. Was that a sniff I heard down the line?

'Yes, well,' she said with a slight wobble in her voice. 'You will insist on staying in that godforsaken country and keeping our only grandchild thousands and thousands and thousands of miles away, won't you?'

So that was it. I'd been so stressed out defending myself, I really hadn't put any effort into working out what had upset her so much in the first place. She wasn't angry I was working and I very much doubted she cared about me having a nanny, having spent a great deal of my childhood loudly wishing for 'bloody Mary Poppins to appear out the bloody chimney so I can have five minutes' peace'. She just wanted to spend more time with Alice. I couldn't blame Mum; my daughter was the best baby ever.

'I was thinking.' I started talking quickly before I could second-guess myself. 'Why don't you come out for Alice's birthday?'

'We were already coming out for her birthday!' Mum bellowed, nearly taking my ear off. 'Did you think I was going to miss my only grandchild's first birthday? Not likely. We'll be there. We've already got her present. Have Alex's lot already got something? I bet they haven't. I was about to ask what you were doing for Christmas. Your dad wants to book a table at the Coach & Horses but if you're all coming over, I'd rather we were at home.'

It would serve me right for trying to do something nice.

'Can I let you know tonight?' I asked as I ran across the road against the light. Why wasn't there a Hawaiian horse around to step on your phone when you needed one? 'I should check with Alex.'

She really was testing my new-found commitment to being kind and finding the truth and all that shit. Another word and she was getting a tube of Précis mascara for her birthday.

'I'll let you get back to work, dear. Do you want to have a word with your dad?'

'Is he behaving himself?' I asked.

'She says are you behaving yourself?' Mum shouted across the living room.

'Do I ever?' he shouted back. 'You know me, Angela, always up to no good.'

'He's fighting with the neighbours over the apple tree at the bottom of the garden. They say the roots are on their property but your dad is insistent it stays.'

'It's my bloody tree and they're my bloody apples,' he called. 'If they want to cut it down, they can buy me a new, fully mature bloody tree and plant it six feet over. Or they can buy me a bag of apples every week for the rest of my life. Entirely up to them.'

'He's fine then,' I smiled softly. As long as he wasn't blowing up the microwave or ending up in hospital from one too many accidental weed brownies, I was happy. 'I really have got to go, I'm almost at the office. Love you, Mum.'

'We love you too,' she replied, in her grudging but certain way. 'Give Alice a squeeze from us when you get home.'

Well, I thought, dropping the phone in my impossibly wonderful new bag and fishing around for my key card to get into the building. Now I was very tired, extremely emotional and staring down the barrel of two parental visits in the next six months.

But at least my mum was happy.

One day Alice will think like this about you, whispered the voice in my head.

I shuddered at the very idea. Alice would never think of me the way I thought of my mum.

I was definitely going to be worse.

Going back into the office after any time away was always a pain in the arse. It was the only real time I missed my school days, that first day back after a fortnight in Minorca, armed with a shitty friendship bracelet for Louisa, long plastic strips of weird boiled sweets for the rest of the class and a breathless story about how I'd held hands with a Geordie called Nicholas at the kids' club disco on my last night. You were never more popular or exotic than that one Monday. Now I had zero friendship bracelets, we were banned from bringing anything in for the rest of the class in case it upset someone's allergies and the only story that left me breathless was almost being thrown from a horse.

'Angela!'

I spotted Paige as soon as I walked inside, stuck in the hot desk farm with the rest of us. I had wondered whether or not she'd be given a spot up on Cici's executive floor but that would have meant Cici getting rid of her personal pedicure station so it did seem unlikely.

'I wasn't expecting you in today,' she said. Her blonde hair was piled up on top of her head and the neon green of her midi-length floral dress would have made me look like I'd been at a tablecloth with a pack of highlighters, but on Paige, it set off her perfect tan and her worn-in Doc Martens and just looked cool.

'I know,' I replied, twisting the ends of my ponytail before throwing it over my shoulder. Note to self, get your bloody hair cut. 'I wanted to talk to you.'

'It's brilliant timing actually.' Paige picked up a cup of coffee in one hand, gripped her phone in the other, tucked an iPad under her arm. 'I'm on my way to show Cici the intro video we've put together for Recherché.'

Either she hadn't heard what I said or she didn't care.

'That was bloody quick,' I said, following her as she walked back towards the lifts.

Quick and weird. Shouldn't I be the first person to see the video for my website?

'The team here are amazing,' she replied with a nod. Paige didn't think it was weird, clearly. 'I was sending stuff through while we were in Lanai and last night I couldn't sleep at all so I stayed up and wrote the basic script. I'm sure you were the same?'

I nodded weakly as we zoomed up to the penthouse. Work hadn't even crossed my mind.

'You're going to love the vid,' Paige promised. 'There are still a couple of technical touches I want to add, a few flourishes to really make it feel slick, but it absolutely screams Recherché dot com.'

Slapping on my brightest smile, I pushed up my sleeves and followed her into the boss's office.

'You don't look like you've been to Hawaii,' Cici said without taking her eyes off her phone screen. Her assistant was sitting in the next chair, quivering every time she raised her hand.

'Why?' I asked, taking a seat as far away as my

British-born manners would allow. 'What does someone who went to Hawaii look like?'

'They look tan.' She looked up at me and waved a hand in front of her face. 'They look relaxed.'

'I wouldn't describe it as an especially relaxing trip,' I replied, already regretting my decision to come into the office. 'But it was amazing. Lanai is gorgeous.'

'It used to be much nicer,' she sniffed. 'It's gotten so commercial now.'

Paige and I shared a glance.

'But aren't there only three thousand people there?' I said. 'And two hotels?'

'Ha,' Cici scoffed. 'When I used to go to Lanai, there was only one hotel.'

They probably built the second one when they knew Cici had stopped coming, I thought to myself.

Two people I recognized from the main floor of the office but didn't yet know walked into the room, carrying their laptops.

'While Angela and I were away, Ember and Tennyson were working on an intro video for Recherché,' Paige announced as the duo tapped away at their computers. I jumped out of my skin as a projector screen whirred out of the ceiling, covering the floor-to-ceiling windows and casting the room into darkness.

'Think of this as a promo for your site, AC,' she went on. 'We want to connect with all the potential readers out there, let them know who you are and what they can expect from their new favourite site.'

A rush of either excitement or sugar from the Pop-Tart I'd eaten for breakfast ran through me as the screen lit up and a shot of the New York City skyline filled the screen.

'My name is Angela Clark.'

The sound of my voice filled the room.

The video cut from New York to a slow-motion video of me posing by the pool in Hawaii.

'I'm a mom, I'm a wife and I'm a career woman. You're probably wondering, how does she manage to have it all?'

I suddenly came over very queasy. Christ, I thought as I watched myself throwing shapes in front of Jenny and Louisa. What a complete tit. I swallowed. Definitely should have had more than a Pop-Tart for breakfast.

The video of our photoshoot cut to images of me that I hadn't seen in years. Photos Jenny took when I first arrived in New York, pictures of me, Alex and Alice from last Christmas, me and Louisa together in Paris, hanging out with James in LA, me, Jenny and Sadie in Vegas. They'd all been taken from my Facebook page, which would teach me not to accept a friend request until I got to know someone better.

'You're probably wondering,' the voiceover said as we cut to a video of me in the office, wearing a stripy T-shirt I'd had on last week. But I didn't remember being filmed . . . 'How does she do it?'

Another fast cut, filtering through more pictures, more clips pulled from social media. A quick clip of me laughing at the luau, a video of Jenny pulling me out of the pool after James pushed me in and a very attractive shot of me passed out on the plane, complete with my eye mask askew and mouth open wide.

'The truth is, I'm just like you.'

It was then I realized I had my hands over my face, as though I was watching a horror movie. And it kind of felt like I was.

'Follow my adventures on Recherché dot com to see my real life, my amazing friends, gorgeous husband and see what motherhood in New York is really like . . . Fabulous.'

The last photo of me, wearing the ice-blue sequined Elie Saab gown and looking back over my shoulder, laughing at something Tess had said, faded away and was replaced with the Recherche.com logo and a heavily retouched photo of my giant face.

The film ended, the screen rolled up and Paige sat back in her seat, so satisfied she looked as though she needed a cigarette, while Ember and Tennyson stared at Cici like a pair of golden retrievers waiting for a treat.

Cici looked over at me.

'Angela,' she said. 'What do you think?'

All eyes turned my way.

'It's awful,' I said, blinking as my eyes readjusted to daylight.

'Sorry, what?' Paige said, the smile frozen on her face.

Oh god, it was too much pressure. I definitely should have had more than just a Pop-Tart for breakfast and I definitely should have bloody well stayed at home.

'OK, not awful, sorry,' I said, looking around for a shovel to dig myself out of this giant hole. 'But it's not me, is it?'

'What do you mean, it's not you?' Cici pointed at my huge, gurning face on the screen. 'That's literally you. In great lighting. On your best day.'

'Would I be right in thinking there was some editing on the voiceover?' I glanced at Ember and Tennyson and saw nothing but pride on their faces.

'If I may, I'd like to add some context to the video,' Paige said, focusing on Cici and ignoring me entirely. 'Without wanting to be confrontational, I talked about this with Angela. I think her ideas for Recherché are fantastic but they're hardly original, are they?'

Even though I didn't say anything, I felt my eyes open wide and my head turned very, very slowly towards my vice president of content.

'There are already a million mommy bloggers out there, showing everyone all the boring everyday stuff. We wanted to give this a Besson Media slant, make it sexy and cool while still keeping her humour and honesty.'

'But it's not honest,' I blurted out.

'It's honest enough,' Paige argued. 'I can't sell *this* Angela, can I? Take your ego out of the equation and ask yourself, who would want to read about you?'

Welp, here we go, I thought, chucking the metaphorical shovel out the window before I bashed Paige in the head with it.

'This is the problem we've got,' I told her. 'We're not on the same page about this at all. I don't want to write about myself, I want to write about the things I care about, about the things women like me care about. If I was me, sitting at home or on my way to work, scrolling through my phone with a spare five minutes, this wouldn't make me feel good about myself.'

'It should,' Cici said. 'You looked great in that last photo.'

'Well, obviously me looking great in a photo makes me feel good,' I said with a sigh. 'I mean, as a random human being, it wouldn't make me feel better. Why would I want to hear what that woman has to say about anything? She sounds like a complete tit.'

'She's right about that part,' Cici nodded. 'When she fell in the pool, I was hoping she wouldn't get back out.'

'Thank you for the constructive input,' I said. 'My point is, I wouldn't want to watch this and, if I did force myself through it, I'd be hate-watching. None of this is real, all this video does is create another way to make women – all women, not just mums – feel like they're not good enough. It says you should be glamorous and sexy and perfect all the time. Isn't that the opposite of what we talked about in Hawaii?'

'I think you're wrong,' Paige said, crossing her arms and staring dead ahead. 'I think this promo is exactly what we need to make noise for you. This will get eyes on the site.'

'Have you not heard a single word I've been saying?' I asked. She fussed with a button on her sleeve and refused to make eye contact. 'You can't have forgotten what happened in the garden?'

'You guys,' Cici said, leaning forwards with a salacious smile on her face. 'Just what exactly happened in Hawaii?'

'I'm not saying this isn't gorgeous,' I said, giving Ember and Tennyson a thumbs up, even though they were already looking at their phones and really didn't give a fuck. 'But it's not me, it's not what I want to do and, as much as I want that to be my life, it isn't. I'm sorry, Paige. I don't feel comfortable going forward with this.'

Two tiny red spots appeared in the centre of Paige's perfectly porcelain cheeks.

'Authenticity is really hot right now . . .' Cici mused out loud. 'Angela could be onto something.'

'I don't want to jump on a trend,' I argued, thinking of Louisa sitting at home, flicking through Instagram stories on the sofa. 'I want to be real. We're so used to only having beautiful things pushed down our throats, we don't know what real life is any more. That's why we all get depressed when our own life doesn't look like an episode of *Keeping Up with the Kardashians*.'

'Ew,' Cici gasped.

'No one watches that any more,' Paige muttered.

'Kendall is the only cool one,' Ember whispered.

I flicked my hand in irritation. 'The point is, I don't think we should be promoting a website designed to make women feel better about the world by putting out videos that make other women feel like shit,' I said, trying to control my voice, trying not to lose my temper. Trying, not necessarily succeeding. 'I'm sorry for all the work that went into this but I don't want it out there with my name, my website or something approximating my face on it.'

Cici forced all her energy into her left eyebrow and raised it by roughly three millimetres.

'Are you finished?' she asked.

I glanced over at Paige whose entire face was now bright red. And that did not go with her neon green dress *at all*.

'Yes.'

'Great,' Cici said, laying her hands flat on her desk. Her manicure looked especially nice, I thought as I hid my chipped nails between my thighs. 'Here's what I think. Paige is right. Real life is boring, people like investing in a fantasy and, Angela, you could be this

292

version of you if you wanted to be. With the right amount of airbrushing. Like, a lot of it.'

She paused and turned her attention to Paige.

'But Angela is also right. I hired her to write the things she's good at because she's good at them and, for whatever reason, people love her stuff. If this isn't what she wants to do, we shouldn't be trying to force it on her. Find someone else to fill this slot if you really believe in it.'

It was the closest she'd ever come to genuinely complimenting me.

'These are teething problems I don't need to be part of,' she said, flashing her eyes at Don the assistant. He immediately scooped up her coffee cup and ran out the room. 'The promo video is a genius idea but this isn't it. I want a final version live by Friday and the two of you need to figure it out.'

'Yeah, I mean, absolutely,' I confirmed, flush with something like victory. 'Not a problem.'

'OK.' She looked at the two of us, seemingly confused. 'So, you know, go away?'

'Still working on those interpersonal skills,' I muttered as I pushed my chair back across the wooden floor. 'Thanks, Cici.'

'Thanks for pulling that together so quickly,' Paige said to Ember and Tennyson as we all barrelled back into the lift. 'We'll get notes on version two over to you ASAP.'

They nodded, pupils contracted from spending too much time staring at a screen, and the doors closed. We stood in silence for the entire ten-second ride but the tension coming off Paige was even louder than her frock.

293

'Thanks for throwing me under the bus,' she said, the moment the doors opened and the others ran back to their desks. 'I can't believe you did that.'

'You should have shown me the video before you played it for Cici,' I said, refusing to back down. My natural setting was apologize and make life easy but I was so certain I was right this time, caving in was not an option. 'I don't really know what else to say. I should have seen it, Paige.'

'There wasn't time,' she sniffed, busily flicking at her iPad to avoid looking at me.

'Well, this time we're going to work on it together.' If I could fix things with Alex and fix things with my mum, I was sure as shit going out of here with a win on the work front as well. 'There was tons of stuff I loved about that version, it's just tweaks really.'

And by tweaks, I meant delete all the voiceover, take out the retouching and that one photo of me asleep on the plane and completely rearrange all the videos, I added silently. This was the time to get her on side, not make her hate me even more.

'You could have said that in there instead of making me look like a knob in front of my boss,' she replied, softening by a fraction.

I threw my hands up in the air and sighed. 'And you could have shown me the video before you showed it to Cici and, oh look, we're right back at the beginning and I'm going completely mad.'

'Doesn't matter now, does it? We've got two days to get something worked out,' Paige said, opening up her calendar to check her schedule, a nail tapping on the keyboard. 'Can you get notes to me today on what you want the video to say? And I'll have Ember and Tennyson work on it all tomorrow.'

'I can,' I replied. I stopped myself from agreeing madly and offering all kinds of compromises, biting my cheek to stay silent. Paige frowned at her iPad before looking up at me with a satisfied nod. Mentally I added 'I stood up for myself at work and it didn't go horribly wrong' to my list of accomplishments alongside 'Moved to New York' and 'Didn't try to lick Daniel Craig that one time I stood behind him in the sandwich shop'.

'We're going to ace it,' I promised. 'Teamwork makes the dream work!'

'Never say that to me again,' she warned as she walked away. 'Ever.'

'And that's why you can't try to sell me as someone cool,' I said, shooting double finger guns in her direction as I bumbled back over to the field of desks. 'No one would ever believe it.'

# CHAPTER TWENTY-ONE

'So, in the end, it was just an unused garage and some old storage shed,' Jenny said, licking her spoon at Max Brenner on Thursday morning. 'Nothing valuable got destroyed, no major damage was done to the main estate, their insurance is gonna cover the whole thing.'

It was really far too warm for hot chocolate but when a craving came calling, what could a girl do? Not that my sugar addiction really counted as a craving when I wasn't pregnant but Max Brenner's was one of the few things that had been in New York when I first arrived that had managed to stick around and I'd learned my lesson from Manatus, use it or lose it, and I would lose a leg before I lost these hot chocolates. Possibly to diabetes, but still. It was the best in the world.

'And do they know how the fire started?' I asked. 'Was it the fireworks?'

'It was,' she nodded. 'But nothing went haywire. For some reason, a couple of the rockets had been pointed in the wrong direction, right at the buildings.'

'Inside job?' I asked, lowering my voice at the possible scandal.

'I don't think Bertie is the kind of guy to do that but . . .'

'Kekipi is?' I finished for her.

'Who knows?' She tore off a piece of her croissant and nibbled it carefully to avoid smudging her lipstick. 'I'm just grateful Camilla Rose wasn't hot about it and I didn't get fired. Can you imagine how bad it could have been?'

'I imagined we all tried to swim out to sea to get away from the blazing inferno and I was eaten by a shark,' I replied, helping myself to her pastry. 'So, yes. Also, you burned down two buildings. That's still pretty bad.'

Jenny seemed unconcerned.

'Thanks for coming with me today.' She pushed the rest of the croissant across the table towards me. 'I hate doing these check-up appointments on my own. It's so freaking sad.'

'Of course,' I nodded with a supportive smile. 'It must be really hard. Dr Laura's optimistic, though, you said? Should all be pretty straightforward once they get the eggs next week?'

'I feel like a goddamn chicken,' she muttered, clutching her swollen stomach. 'She says they're only getting maybe four extra eggs out of me but it feels like there are at least forty-five thousand in there already. And it's not me I feel sad for, this is gonna sound awful, but it's all the people crying in the waiting room. I feel bad because I never thought this would apply to me, then I feel even worse because I'm not the one who has a problem, then I feel like

297

I'm being disloyal to Mason, which makes me feel even worse again, and I don't even have a baby yet, how am I going to cope?'

'I've only been a mum for a bit,' I said, trying to sound reassuring. 'But at least forty-eight percent of it is feeling guilty about things that are completely beyond your control so I'd say you're off to a brilliant start.'

She smiled and carried on stirring her hot chocolate. She hadn't taken so much as a sip.

'Have you talked to Erin yet?' I asked.

The look on her face answered my question.

'OK, moving on. What about the podcast? What's the latest with "Tell Me About It with Jenny Lopez"?'

'It's actually going really well,' she said, brightening up at least for a moment. 'I have a meeting at a studio, right by our old place. It looks like I can go in, record and they'll do everything else for me. And James agreed to be my first guest!'

I gasped in mock horror.

'I thought I was going to be your first guest?'

'James then you,' she said quickly. 'James, then Sadie, then you. And maybe Eva. But you're definitely a shoo-in for the first season.'

'As long as you're happy, I'm happy,' I assured her. 'I'm sure James has enough stories to tell to fill an entire season. Maybe I can just be your number one cheerleader.'

Jenny smiled and pulled a napkin out of the dispenser on the table, reaching across to wipe some-thing away from the corner of my mouth.

'Doll,' she said with a grin. 'You already are.'

Grabbing the napkin out her hand, I wolfed down

the rest of the croissant before wiping my mouth properly.

'What are you doing after this?' she asked. 'Do you want to get something real to eat or do you have to go straight to work?'

'I have a meeting,' I said, not ready to share any more details until said meeting was done. I tapped her mug to hurry her up. 'Come on, we ought to get going. You don't want to be late.'

'You just want to see the inside of my uterus,' she pouted, ignoring the mug and throwing a twenty-dollar bill on the table.

'After everything we've been through, I'm almost positive I've already seen it,' I replied as I added a five for the tip. 'And I'm certain it's gorgeous.'

'Damn right,' she shouted. 'And so is yours. We have beautiful uteruses.'

'Uteruses? Uteri? Feels like it should be uteri?' I pondered before making eye contact with a horri-fied-looking old gent at the next table, pushing away his breakfast. 'Oh god, I'm sorry.'

'Do you know?' Jenny asked him, hooking her arm through mine. 'I think she's right on the money with uteri.'

'Both are correct,' he said, reaching into his breast pocket for a business card. 'Uteruses is more commonly used. I'm a gynecologist.'

'Goddamn, I love this city,' she yelled as I took the card and smiled politely on our way out the restaurant. 'You never know who you're going to meet.'

Holding Jenny's hand while Dr Laura performed what my father affectionately referred to as 'fanny mechanics' took longer than I'd expected and I was out of breath by the time I arrived back in Park Slope for my next appointment. Pressing the buzzer outside 585 11th Street, I squeezed the strap of my bag for good luck and waited to be summoned inside.

'Angela, darling.'

Perry Dickson opened the door with a smile on her face so wide, I had to wonder what she'd been doing before I arrived. I also had to wonder if I'd got my dates wrong because she was wearing what appeared to be a hand-painted, silk kimono.

'Perry,' I said, leaning forward for three kisses on alternating cheeks. 'Is this a bad time?'

'Not at all,' she insisted, leading me back through the front room I remembered so clearly, past the all-white chamber of judgement and through into what looked like a cross between a six-star hotel suite and an impossibly fancy spa.

'When you called, I was so determined to make time to talk to you, I had to move some things around in my diary.' She passed through the door and waved at a woman in a pale grey uniform. 'Anika comes to see us once a month or so. She's an angel, as I'm sure you'll find out for yourself.'

'We really can reschedule,' I said, looking down to see my white knuckles clinging to the doorframe. 'This can wait.'

'Can it, Angela?' Perry asked with intense eyes. 'Can it?'

'Yes,' I said, quite sure.

'Nonsense, this won't take more than two minutes and then we'll have a coffee while the redness goes down,' she replied.

'Redness?' I asked as Anika rolled a device over to the squishy-looking treatment bed.

It's a facial, I reassured myself. It's definitely a facial and not electro-shock therapy and you can leave any time you like and no one is going to force you to have it done and yes this all feels a bit *Handmaid's Tale* but everything is going to be OK.

'There's a little residual soreness but it's entirely worth it,' she said, untying the kimono and letting it fall to the floor.

Oh good, now I had to gouge out my eyes on the way home as well. Ten a.m. on a Thursday morning and I'd already seen three women's vulvas that weren't mine. At least one had been my daughter's.

'I wanted to say thank you so much for introducing me to Luka,' I wasn't sure where to look as she climbed up onto the treatment bed. 'I couldn't be more grateful.'

'But of course,' Perry said, smiling at me as she raised her knees and dropped them out to the side. What I hadn't seen before, I'd certainly seen now. 'Angela, we love your writing. The M.O.B. thinks you have limitless potential and we always work together to push our members to the highest of heights.'

How was it possible for her body to be completely hairless? I hadn't shaved above the knee since I'd given birth and I'd just come back from a long weekend in Hawaii. Why was everyone else suddenly so chill with their nether regions? I felt like a maiden aunt with no idea where to look. 'That's what I wanted to talk to you about,' I replied, eyes on the very nicely restored tin ceiling. What on earth were they doing? 'Can I ask, what made you get in touch with me in the first place?'

'Well,' she settled back against the bed as Anika

pulled on a pair of goggles and slipped her hands into a pair of latex gloves. 'Our group keeps an eye on birth announcements in the neighbourhood and we've a couple of members who worked at Spencer Media when you were there. They spoke highly of you, your work ethic, your dedication. Then we heard you were moving to Besson and of course the Spencer family are very well respected so that was enough to get you in for a chat. Also, you're British and we don't have any British members at the moment.'

'Really? That was one of the reasons?' I switched my view from the ceiling to the floor in one quick flick of the eyes.

'We have a sister organization on the West Coast, Mothers of Beverly Hills? And they're forever bragging about that awful Vanderpump woman. Clearly we wouldn't even consider admitting someone from reality television but we did discuss whether or not it might be a boon to diversify our membership somehow.'

Not the time to tell her I'd binge-watched eight seasons of *Vanderpump Rules* while pregnant. I didn't have a book deal yet.

'We approached you because we thought you would be good for us and we could be good for you,' she said simply. 'You're clearly hard-working, you're bright and you're an upstanding Brooklyn resident. At least, we couldn't find any legal records suggesting otherwise.'

'It's not just because of Alex then?' I asked with a deep breath in.

'This serves me right for getting overexcited when we first met, doesn't it?' Perry said, covering her face with her hands. Now she was going to be embarrassed? 'We don't look at a woman's partner when we're considering her for membership. He, she or they are not part of the group and, as long as they aren't involved in any criminal activity or could potentially damage our reputation or, again, I imagine reality TV would be an issue, they don't come into the equation. Really, Angela, the women who are part of our group are capable of more than enough in their own right without bringing their husbands into it. Most of us are here to get away from them, although you didn't hear that from me.'

I breathed out, shaking my head at myself. I'd been so certain they were trying to stitch me up or use me to get something from Alex, the idea that The Mothers of Brooklyn might genuinely be interested in having me, a mother who lived in Brooklyn, join their gang hadn't really hadn't occurred to me until Al had suggested it.

'We're a group of like-minded women, looking for a place to come together and make sense of things,' she went on. 'I don't know about you but my world was turned upside down when I had my kids and none of the mother and baby groups I went to felt like a good fit for me.'

That much I could agree with.

'I hate to admit it but I was jealous of the mothers who took to it all so easily. So many women made it look simple but I missed my job, I missed the inter-action with my colleagues and friends. And so I created The M.O.B. to find new ones. It has, admittedly, grown a little beyond its humble beginnings but when Hillary said she was heading back upstate and didn't need this space any more and we could have it for next to nothing, it seemed churlish to look a gift horse in the mouth.'

'Hillary?' I repeated quietly.

'We'd love to have you join us, Angela. I offer my most profound apologies if we were unwelcoming on your first visit. I was having a terrible day.'

'Happens to the best of us,' I replied as Anika fired up her machine. 'Perry, can I ask what it is you're doing right now?'

'Vaginal rejuvenation,' she answered, casual as you liked. 'We use a $CO_2$ fractional laser to tighten the skin of the vulva and vagina.'

I had to ask.

'I really don't want to sound ungrateful but I've got such a lot happening at the moment, would it be all right if I think about it for a few days and let you know in a week or so?' I winced as the laser made snapping noises in a place where neither lasers nor snapping were supposed to be.

'Not a problem,' she replied, her voice utterly even. Her vag was being lasered and she didn't even flinch. What a woman. 'Whenever you're ready. We're not the Mafia, you know.'

'No, of course not,' I muttered. Was that burning I could smell? Jesus H . . . 'Oh, and I put you on the guest list for tomorrow night, at Alex's show. I did a plus one but if you need more tickets just let me know.'

'That is so lovely of you!' Perry curled her upper body upwards with core control I could only dream off. 'But entirely unnecessary. It turns out one of our members actually owns the concert venue so I had her get us all tickets. We'll see you there.'

'Right, I'm going to go and let you get on with your . . .' I paused, words escaping me at the worst time as usual. 'Rejuvenation, and I'll see you tomorrow night. You'll have to meet Alex and the boys.'

'I'd love to,' she replied with what seemed like a genuine smile. 'Anika, I know we were just doing downstairs today but we might have to tighten up the face as well.'

'I really hope she's got a different attachment for that,' I muttered as I waved goodbye and let myself out.

# CHAPTER TWENTY-TWO

'Does this look good?'

Alex strode into the middle of the living room on Friday morning with arms outstretched, and gave me a spin. I looked him up and down; black leather hightops, ancient jeans that looked as though they'd been made just for him, an untucked white button-down shirt that actually had been made just for him and his favourite vintage blazer. He looked almost exactly the same as he did the day I met him.

'It looks amazing,' I confirmed from the floor of the middle of the living room where Alice was busy discovering a stuffed duck that had an especially irritating crinkly bill and made a quacking sound every time she stomped on its belly. Which she did every three minutes. I started off thinking it was worth it to hear her delighted giggles of joy. I was no longer sure. She clung to the edge of the sofa, wobbly on her new legs, before falling onto her bum and laughing her back off. My daughter was mental and I loved her.

'You don't think it's kinda dated?' he asked, wind-milling his arms to confirm it was an appropriate outfit for a rockstar. 'I've had it forever, I must have worn it to a hundred shows.'

'Then it must be good,' I said as I tried to steal away the cursed duck. 'You look like you, I like it.'

'Yeah,' he said, raising his voice as he disappeared back into the bedroom. 'But tonight is a big deal. It's the first time we've played New York in forever and we're trying a ton of new stuff. Should I be wearing the same stuff I wore a decade ago? I don't want to look like me, trying to look like me. What about this?'

He reappeared, having swapped the blazer and the shirt for a tissue-thin black T-shirt that hung from his broad shoulders and just met the waistband of his jeans.

'Your belly is going to show when you play,' I said, pointing at the hint of bare skin.

'My belly?' With a look of alarm, he turned to look in the mirror and slapped his firm, flat stomach. 'I don't have a belly?'

'Not that kind of belly,' I said, rolling my eyes at Alice as she pulled up her tiny T-shirt to demonstrate her own belly action. 'I meant, there's going to be some bare flesh action. But that might be what you want, trying to get by on your looks again, you monster.'

'Hey, it works for that Maroon 5 dude,' Alex replied.

'You know his name is Adam Levine and you're only pretending you don't to annoy me.' I rolled a light-up ball towards Alice, seizing the opportunity to grab the duck and hurl it behind the settee. 'What are Graham and Craig wearing?'

'I didn't even think to ask them,' he said, manically

patting himself down for his phone. Happy to be the level-headed spouse for once, I reached over to grab it from the coffee table, where it had been all morning, and handed it to him.

'Thanks.'

He stooped down to kiss the top of my head before hitting number one on his speed dial and heading back into the bedroom. Number one was Graham, number two was Craig. I was number six, after the pizza place on Bedford Avenue, Northside Cars and his hairdresser.

'Hey, it's me,' I heard him as the door closed. 'What are you wearing tonight? A suit? What do you mean, you're wearing a suit! We didn't talk about suits!'

'Don't worry about Daddy,' I said as Alice tried to eat the light-up ball. 'He just wants to look pretty for his special night with his friends.'

She looked back at me, drooling onto the floor as my phone began to vibrate somewhere nearby.

'Yeah, I know,' I said, resting my back against the settee. 'He looks amazing in everything. It's very annoying . . . Hello, Angela Clark speaking?'

'It's me,' Paige answered on the other end. 'New version of the video is done, I'm sending it to you right now. Do you want to look at it again? Cici wants it out this afternoon.'

'What's new on this version?' I asked, scrambling for my laptop. Technically, it was a Friday so I was working from home but it was also eleven a.m., I was still in my pyjamas and the only work-related thing I'd managed so far was opening the blank document that was my book proposal for Luka. Which was due on Monday.

'Nothing major,' she said. 'It's the same as the one you saw last night with the new music added at the end. I haven't snuck in any photos of you looking ravishing or anything like that. Tennyson added some more footage from Hawaii just to spice up the pacing but that's about it. We put in some of the audio to give it more of a real-life feel. It works really well with everyone laughing and having a good time.'

Hmm. Whatever could everyone be laughing at?

'Is the part where I fall in the pool still in it?'

'And we added a bit where the horse ran off,' she admitted. 'But in Tennyson's defence, it is really funny. We really need to get it out today, Cici's going spare.'

'If that's it, I don't need to see it again,' I replied, my epic to-do list running through my mind. One less thing to think about. 'Let's get it out. I can't believe we got it done so quickly, I should get Ember and Tennyson doughnuts or something.'

'Ooh, that's a good idea,' Paige said. 'I found a brilliant little vegan bakeshop that's just opened next to the office. No dairy, coeliac friendly. They're so much better than you'd think they're going to be.'

'Good god, woman, you've been here, what, three weeks?' I said with a sad little sigh. 'And you're already fully converted. Shame on you, get yourself down to Krispy Kreme and get me a dozen original glazed and we'll forget this ever happened.'

She cackled down the line.

'You've been away from England too long, my love. You wouldn't recognize east London if it bit you on your perfectly Pilates-toned bottom. We're all food-conscious these days.'

'It's time to go and live in a cave,' I declared, rolling

onto all fours to follow Alice as she scooted off behind the sofa but I was too late. *Quack quack quack quack.* 'And you're coming tonight, aren't you?'

'Can't wait,' she replied. 'My ex is over from London for work stuff, I'm going to bring him, if that's OK?'

I nodded as I tried to bribe Alice away from that bloody duck with a half-empty packet of Wotsits. Her lack of interest in British snacks was worrying. The child was rejecting her heritage.

'Totally, sounds like a brilliant idea and not in any way a huge mistake.'

'Piss off, I'll talk to you later,' Paige said happily. 'Thanks, babe.'

'Your boss is coming tonight?' Alex walked back in wearing his suit, swooping down to scoop Alice up into his arms.

'Boss and friend,' I replied. Damn he looked good. I really did have to start putting on people clothes as soon as I got up in the morning. 'Although yes, she is my boss. I still need to learn boundaries.'

'Good for you,' he said, messing with his hair in the mirror. 'I'm gonna head down to BAM, run through the sound check. Graham said there are a couple of interviewers coming by so I don't know if I'll get back before the show. Do you want to come over and eat with us? The guys would love to see Al.'

He threw Alice up into the air, almost letting go as she reached the top and bounced her all the way back down again. She shrieked with laughter every single time, as though it had never happened to her before, reaching out for his face, his hair, his shirt, anything she could get her pudgy little claws into. That little girl was so in love with her daddy.

'I would but I've got a ton of work to do.' I clicked on Paige's link and started downloading the video. 'I'll call you when we're on our way.'

Alex pointed over at a square cardboard box on the dresser by the door. 'Don't forget her ear defenders. Can't have my baby messing up her hearing at Daddy's show.'

'Are they the ones Gwyneth used?' I asked, my heart pounding.

'They are,' he nodded. 'I called Chris to make sure. You're Goop-approved.'

There it was, confirmation he was actually perfect.

'And did I tell you my mom and dad are coming?'

Almost perfect.

'No, you did not.'

'Yeah, they haven't been to a show since . . . you know, I don't think they've ever been to a show. You'll hang out with them backstage, right?' he asked, lowering a devastated Alice back down to the floor. She lay at his feet, gazing up at him in despair before opening her mouth, taking a very deep breath and screaming as loudly as humanly possible. According to our upstairs neighbours, that was very loud indeed.

Alex stepped over the screaming baby and leaned over to give me a real kiss.

'Remember that time she screamed so long she turned blue?' he said, looking at his wailing daughter with love only a father could feel.

'Pretty sure I'll remember that until the day I die,' I replied, picking her up and resting her on a hip, letting her snuggle into my neck until she stopped crying. According to my mum, this was bad parenting and children should be left to cry but her only child, me, ran away to America and never came back so I wasn't totally sure her tips were one hundred percent reliable.

'Call me if you need anything,' Alex said, checking himself for his phone, his keys and, nope, that was it because he was a man. 'It's supposed to rain so I got her duck boots out.'

His mother had bought them. They were actually pretty cute but it would be a cold day in hell before I put them on my daughter.

'We love you!' I called, holding Al at arm's length and bouncing her up and down on my knees. A dry nappy didn't feel that squishy and bouncing a dirty nappy up and down was not about to make the next five minutes of my life any more pleasant.

'Love you too,' Alex replied as I sniffed Alice's bum for confirmation of her dirty protest at her father's leaving.

I retched, she giggled and the front door slammed shut.

'Brilliant timing,' I muttered, holding her aloft and keeping the offending butt area as far away from me as possible as we made our way into the nursery.

Three hours and four cups of tea later, Alice was fast asleep and I had answered three emails, written two articles and now I finally felt ready to face the book proposal. I tightened my ponytail and stared at the computer, willing a brilliant idea to make its way from my brain directly onto the page. I couldn't work out why it was so hard. I wrote words every day, I had a million stories I could tell that would all make good books (or at least that's what Jenny said), so why was

I hitting a brick wall every time I tried to commit them to paper?

Everything I'd come up with so far could be best described as complete toss and now Alice had gone down for her nap, all I wanted to do was copy her. But there was no time for sleep, I had to come up with something. This could be my one and only chance to have an actual book, actually published. All I needed was one fantastic idea . . .

I wasn't sure which came first, the ringing doorbell or the pounding on the living room window, but I did know Alice screaming the house down followed only split seconds behind. Leaping out of my chair, I sprinted for the door, dodging the ankle-shattering stuffed toys that lay littered around the living room, and wrenched it open, ready to kill.

'Jenny?'

My best friend was standing on the doorstep, mascara running down her face and fury burning in her eyes. This was the first time in the entirety of our friendship she hadn't immediately let herself into my house and made herself at home. Something was very wrong.

'Jen?' I said again, actually afraid. 'What's wrong?'

'What's wrong?' she repeated from the doorstep. 'Are you for real?'

'I don't know what's happening,' I said, looking back over my shoulder. Alice had quietened down but was still grumbling away in the background. She enjoyed being woken up from a nap about as much as I did. 'But can you come in and stop banging on things? Alice is having a nap.'

'No, I can't,' Jenny shook her head. 'Because you

just ruined my life so I don't especially care about your precious daughter's naptime.' She thrust her phone in my face.

I stepped backwards to avoid getting punched in the nose with a giant iPhone and stared at the cracked screen.

'Did I break your phone?' I asked, taking a step backwards.

'Not the screen, genius, what's on the screen.'

It was my video.

'OK, I'm a bit confused.' The cold dread in my stomach suggested this wasn't Jenny's very dramatic way of telling me how much she had enjoyed it. 'What's wrong with the video?'

'The video is great,' she said, pulling her arm back and scrolling through to what I hoped was her favourite part. Maybe I was wrong? Maybe I'd ruined her life by being really great?

'Super high production values, perfectly pitched to your readers, and I think the best part, and this is only my humble opinion, is when you say the mascara that paid for your trip to Hawaii completely fucking sucks. And then I agree.'

She pushed the phone back into my face and pressed play. Paige – or Ember and Tennyson more likely – hadn't only included the video of me being pushed into the pool, they'd added the audio. I watched the screen in horror as a laughing Jenny hoisted me out of the pool, both of us with mascara tracks running down our faces, merrily slagging off Précis Cosmetics without a care in the world.

'Oh god, Jenny,' I whispered, barely hearing Alice's screams any more. Not hearing anything but me telling the entire world just how bad the new Précis mascara exactly was. And leading Jenny into agreeing. 'I am so sorry, I'll get it taken down right away. Let me call Paige.'

'Oh, OK, if you're sorry then that's totally fine,' Jenny declared, restarting the video all over again. 'You call Paige and I'll call Camilla Rose, tell her it was a huge mistake and then she'll give us back the Précis account, stop threatening to sue and I'm sure she'll put in another call to Bertie Bennett and tell him not to cancel his AJB contract with us too.'

The cold dread in my stomach blossomed into immobilizing fear.

'I'll get it taken down right now,' I said quietly. 'Let me call Paige.'

'Cool, cool,' she said, curly hair flying everywhere, still utterly manic. 'Then could you call Erin and ask for my job back? I'm sure she won't mind the fact her entire business is at risk because *you're sorry.*'

'Erin sacked you?'

For a second, I really thought I was going to throw up.

'Does it sound like the kind of thing I'd make up?' Jenny bellowed. 'How could you, Angie? How could you do this?'

'I didn't do it on purpose,' I said, knocking her phone away from my face. I really didn't need to see the video again. 'I didn't even know, I haven't seen the final video. I'm—'

'So help me god, if you say you're sorry one more time,' she warned, pointing a sharp, red fingernail in my face. 'What the fuck, Angela, what the actual fuck.'

I didn't know what to do. I wanted to hug her, I

wanted to punch myself, I wanted to reach into her phone and yank that video off the internet with my bare hands, but none of those options would help Jenny. Well, punching myself in the face might be a start but, from the look in her eyes, I could tell she'd much rather do that herself.

'What can I do? Tell me what to do.'

'No,' she said, her voice this close to breaking. 'I can't fix this for you this time. You really screwed up.'

'I don't know what else to say.' I bit my lip and looked down at my feet, unable to meet her tearful eyes. The weight of my guilt was so heavy I couldn't even raise my head to look at her. 'There's been so much going on with work and Alex and the book and—'

'And I was the last thing you considered, as usual,' she finished for me. 'Because everything is more important than me. Alex, Alice, your job, your little British besties, your mommy friends. No room left for ol' No Babies Jenny.'

'You know that's not true,' I said as Alice began to scream louder. 'Come inside. I'm going to call Paige right away and have it taken down then I'll call Erin and explain. And I'll call Camilla and Al and whoever else I need to speak to. I can fix this, I promise I can fix it.'

'Only you can't.' Jenny's rage finally exploded into a flood of tears. 'It's done. You can't take something like this off the internet. People are already posting about it. And Camilla knows everyone, we'll have lost every account by the end of the day, then it won't only be me who's unemployed, it'll be the entire staff. How are you going to fix that?'

'I'm sorry,' I whispered but the words had lost all meaning. 'I hate myself right now.'

'Good,' she said, giving me one last heartbroken look before she turned and stormed off down the street. 'You should.'

I watched as she went, pausing only for a second before stuffing my feet into the trainers I kept beside the door for emergency bin visits. I was down the steps and on the pavement before I stopped. Alice. I couldn't leave her to chase after Hurricane Jenny. And by the time I'd got her awake, changed and dressed, Jenny would be long gone. I hovered in the street, stamping my feet in frustration. As Jenny disappeared out of view, I turned back to the apartment, a plan of action forming in my head. First things first. I would call Paige, get the video removed, call Erin and explain how this was all my fault. Then I'd get Camilla's number and give her my best grovelling apology and, after that, Alice and I would trawl the streets of New York City, hunt down Jenny Lopez and find a way to make her forgive me. No matter what Jenny said, nothing was impossible. There had to be a way to make this right and I was going to find it.

Or at least I would if I hadn't locked myself out of the apartment.

'Do not freak out,' I told myself as I immediately started to freak out. What if the house burned down? What if Alice got out of her cot? What if I'd left my curling iron on? I hadn't used it in about three years but what if it'd been on for three whole years?

'People say these things will never happen but it literally *just happened*,' I whispered to myself, gripping

317

the door handle so tightly and shaking it so hard, my fingers turned white. Nothing.

And if things weren't bad enough, I heard a rumble of thunder overhead. I looked up and saw the sky was heavy with dark clouds. Fantastic. A summer storm was just what I needed.

I pressed the doorbell for our upstairs neighbours, holding it down and fighting back tears. It was still raining, I didn't have my phone and Alice was screaming inside the apartment but there was nothing to be done, no one was home. All out of other options, I ran around the side of the building and climbed over the assorted shit that had made itself a home in the alleyway between our building and the next. Plastic crates, an abandoned office chair and bottle upon bottle upon bottle. I stretched as far as I could without doing myself a mischief, as my dad would say, trying not to look down at whatever was crawling around underneath all the junk. They said you were never more than six feet away from a rat in New York but six feet felt very generous at that exact moment in time.

'This won't traumatize her at all,' I whispered, dusting off the dirt and cobwebs from my baggy sweatpants, I Heart NY T-shirt and neon pink hoodie, finally finding myself in what passed for our backyard. Alice's bedroom window was just a few feet up, all I had to do was pop the screen, slide open the window, climb inside and reset the alarm before it went off and automatically called the police.

Easy.

Dragging a dustbin over to the window, I climbed up on shaky legs, the rain still pouring down. I was worried that if I didn't get inside, Alice would scream herself sick, but I was also worried that if I tripped, fell and broke my neck, not only would she have to grow up motherless, I would have to spend eternity knowing my own mother walked around my funeral telling everyone how her idiot daughter died climbing on a dustbin in the rain while breaking into her own apartment.

'We just pop the screen,' I muttered to myself, jamming what was left of my fingernails between the metal edges of the screen and the window frame as Alice's wails grew louder. I'd done this once before, when Jenny and I locked ourselves out of a summer house we'd rented in the Hamptons that turned out to be about as glamorous as a student house in Leicester. We'd paid a fortune for a shithole but still had the best time. I wiped away a fresh run of tears with my upper arm as I focused on getting the screen out the window.

'Fuck,' I exclaimed as the nail on my middle finger bent then snapped. Ignoring the pain, I refused to let go of the screen, I was almost there, almost there . . . 'Yes!'

The screen popped and I tossed it on the floor behind me where it landed with a clatter. Now to work on the window. Our apartment was two floors of an old townhouse and, as far as I could tell, the windows hadn't been replaced since it was built. The wooden frames swelled in winter and shrank in summer, providing natural climate control, but now, fat and heavy with the rain, it was almost impossible to get them to budge. My fingers filled with splinters as I forced the windowpane upwards, throwing my entire weight behind it, determined to get back inside.

Finally, just as I was about to give up trying to open the window and simply put my forehead straight through the glass, I felt it give. It was just an inch but an inch was enough. I slid my fingers into the crack and shuffled the window upwards, side to side, up and down, shaking it loose as I went.

'Mummy's coming, Alice,' I cooed as soon as I'd created enough room to get my head through the window. 'Don't cry, Mummy's coming.'

'Excuse me, Ma'am?'

With my head and one arm through the window I glanced back under my armpit to see two of New York's finest looking back at me. I made a mental note to tell Alex our alarm service was definitely worth the monthly expense and decided this was not a good time to tell them most women prefer 'Miss' to 'Ma'am'.

'Hello, Officers,' I said as I shuffled back out through the window, propping it open with one of Alice's board books and beaming happily. 'This isn't what it looks like.'

'It never is, Ma'am,' he replied, tucking his thumbs into his belt. Right next to his gun. 'It never is.'

# CHAPTER TWENTY-THREE

In the NYPD's defence, this wasn't my first run-in with them but it was the nicest. I never would have expected their training to cover hysterical women trying to break into their own homes but, within, fifteen minutes, we were all standing in my kitchen while the younger officer prepared a perfect brew and the older one happily bounced Alice up and down in the air, just like her dad. The contrary madam gurgled happily while I paced the living room on my phone, explaining the Jenny situation to Paige before the babysitters had to leave and fight actual crime. Predictably, Cici was ecstatic with the Précis drama.

'She's an actual demon,' Paige whispered. 'She's literally refreshing your page over and over, watching the views and the comments rack up. I don't know how I'm going to get it down.'

'Can you replace it with a version that doesn't have me destroying my friend's life without her noticing?' I suggested. 'Paige, it's got to come down.'

'Agreed,' she replied. 'Précis is a big advertiser for

Besson Media. Cici'll change her tune if they pull all their money. We'll both be for the chop then.'

'Is there anyone I can't get sacked?' I groaned when Officer Russo appeared in the living room. 'OK, got to run, text me when it's done.'

'I know I've apologized already but honestly, Angela, I'm so sorry. I was so desperate to get it done, I just didn't think. But I'll take care of it right now, I swear,' she said before hanging up.

'Uh, Ms Clark, we gotta go,' the policeman said while Officer Dixon spoke into his radio. 'Will everything be all right or would you like us to call your husband?'

'Everything is fine,' I replied as I hung up, wondering what exactly they thought Alex was going to do to improve my situation. 'Thank you so much for your help.'

'Hope you get things figured out with your pal,' Officer Dixon said as I showed them to the front door, my keys held tightly in my hand, just in case.

'Me too,' I said, waving them away into the suddenly sunny afternoon. 'Me too.'

Turning back to Alice, safely smiling at me from her highchair, I wiped a filthy hand over my tear-stained face.

'We should go and find Aunt Jenny,' I said, planting my hands on my hips. 'What do you say? Afternoon adventure in Brooklyn?'

Alice opened her mouth and burbled until she arrived at something that sounded an awful lot like 'No.'

'I'm going to say that was not your first word.' I grabbed the papoose from the coat rack and strapped it on over my coat, Alice muttering away to herself, knowing full well what this meant. 'And I would appreciate a little more positivity from you, right now.'

She blew a loud raspberry and yanked on my hair, protesting as I strapped her into the papoose. You never knew how she was going to react to the thing, sometimes she loved it and sometimes she tried to claw your eyes out if you so much as brought it into the room but, quite frankly, I was in a pickle and she was shit out of luck.

'Please don't cry,' I crooned, slipping her little bear hat on top of her head and reaching for the closest baby bag which I greatly hoped was fully stocked. 'We won't be out long. Mummy just needs to talk to Aunt Erin then find Aunt Jenny and beg her forgiveness and then we're going to see Daddy make music and then Mummy is going to sleep for three days. Deal?'

She blinked back at me with huge, clear green eyes and farted.

'Good enough,' I replied, throwing the pink ear defenders Alex had bought into the baby bag just in case we didn't have time to come back. 'Let's go.'

By the time I reached the subway, Paige had the video down and somehow found me a direct phone number for Camilla Rose. Strangely enough, she didn't answer my call and her voicemail cut me off three minutes into my grovelling apology but at least I was one down when I arrived at Erin's house. I couldn't have been more relieved that she was working from home and I didn't have to go into the office. Jenny's girls would have torn me limb from limb if I'd so much as tried to cross the threshold.

And so I moved onto my next target.

'I understand what you're saying,' Erin said with a frustrated sigh after my considerably-longer-than-three-minute apology. 'But my hands are tied. There's nothing either of us can do.'

Defeated, my head drooped down towards Erin's gorgeous rug. I'd paced back and forth so many times since I arrived, I was amazed the carpet wasn't thread-bare.

'But it's my fault,' I argued, not ready to give in just yet. 'Why is Jenny getting fired?'

'Angela.' She leaned forward across the desk in her home office, all the diamonds on her fingers glinting in the carefully designed lighting. 'Even if you hadn't included the part where the person supposedly in charge of promoting the waterproof mascara *agreed* that said waterproof mascara was the worst on the planet, I would still have had to fire her. Précis keeps the lights on at that place. Even when things are going well, they're our biggest client and they pay on time. Do you know how many of those fashion brands we look after literally never pay their invoices? Not a week goes by when we aren't sending out polite but threatening letters. Even if I can't keep Camilla, I have to be seen to be doing something about this. Jenny understands.'

'But she's your friend,' I said, refusing to be distracted by all of Erin's beautiful things. A royal-blue tufted velvet chair, stunning floor-to-ceiling drapes that framed her view out into the West Village. The ornate, antique mirror on the far wall was easier to avoid, given the state of me. 'There has to be another way.'

'It's for the best,' Erin answered with her mind made

up. 'It was time for Jenny to move on. She only ever meant to work for me as a stop-gap. This could end up being the best thing that ever happened to her. And maybe me too.'

'That's the kind of thing people say when they're trying to convince you a shitty thing is secretly brilliant,' I replied, covering Alice's ears when I swore. 'Everyone knows it isn't true.'

'Then why do we have the saying, when god closes a door he opens a window?' she asked.

'Would you like me to tell you how much more difficult it is to get into a house through a window than it is through a door?' I asked, holding up my bruised and broken hand. 'Wait, what do you mean, it's good for you too?'

Erin sighed and picked a brazen bobble from her otherwise flawless ivory cashmere sweater. 'I'm not going to London,' she replied. 'I'm going to stay here and run the company.'

'You're not going to London?'

She shook her head.

'What about Thomas?'

'What *about* Thomas?'

I really didn't know what to say.

'You can't make someone stay if they don't want to,' she said, tripping lightly over her words. 'And if I'm being entirely honest, I don't want to stay either. Or rather, I don't want to go. We're taking a break for a while and we'll see where we're at after that.'

'Erin, I'm so sorry,' I said, finally walking over behind the desk and offering up an awkward Alice-in-the-middle hug. She took it gladly, albeit briefly, before sitting back down in her chair.

'I can't pretend you're my favourite person on earth today,' she said, sounding like a stern school ma'am. 'But I appreciate what you're trying to do. And I appreciate that mascara really is terrible.'

'Is there any chance you can convince Camilla Rose not to fire you?' I asked.

Erin pinched her thumb and forefinger until they were almost touching.

'The tiniest chance. She isn't going to sue at least. I'm trying to convince her this is a good opportunity. We can say the press samples weren't final quality product and get out in front of people to talk about the rest of the brand,' she stopped to give me a pointed look. 'And discuss the integrity of the media.'

'If there's anything I can do, just say the word,' I said, picking up my phone and seeing a missed call from Paige. I'd asked her to let me know if she was able to get hold of Jenny since my best friend had blocked my number.

'I'd say you've done more than enough,' Erin assured me. 'But thank you for the offer. If the "no publicity is bad publicity" line takes hold with her, I'll let you know.'

'Again, very, very, very beyond sorry,' I said, scanning a text as it came in. 'About all of it.'

'It might not always feel like it but I do believe things usually work out for the best,' she replied. 'It always does, one way or another.'

'I hope you're right,' I told her as I kissed her goodbye. 'I'll talk to you later.'

'For sure,' Erin replied. 'And I absolutely get that you're stressing out right now but can I at least give you a real jacket? You look like a drug addict from an episode of *Law & Order*.'

'Thanks Erin,' I replied, declining her offer as I raced out to find a taxi.

Fully aware of the state of me, that was more or less a compliment.

The on and off rain was very much on again as I pulled my hood up over my head and started down the street. No one could argue that the West Village wasn't one of the most beautiful parts of New York but it certainly left a lot to be desired when it came to public transport. There were no useful subway lines anywhere near Erin's townhouse, presumably because people who could afford townhouses could also afford town cars. Unfortunately, I was still in an apartment and beholden to the MTA. Thanks to the weather, there wasn't a single taxi to be found and the Uber surcharge was so high, I was sure even Louisa had heard my shriek when I saw exactly how much they wanted to get me from one side of the city to the other.

Paige had spoken to one of Jenny's co-workers, who had spoken to Jenny and reported that she was going in to collect her things. Even though it felt like an impossibly stupid thing to do, I made my way from Erin's house to the office. Because how could my walking into the office of a company I almost accidentally destroyed possibly go badly?

'Thank god I brought you,' I whispered to Alice, letting her squeeze my finger as tightly as she liked. As long as I was in pain, I knew the EWPR girls wouldn't tear me limb from limb.

Erin had kept the same offices for years, expanding to the floor upstairs as the company grew, and I'd spent almost as much time in here as I had in my own workplace. But, for the first time in a long time, I was afraid to go inside. Walking into reception with Alice face outwards in her papoose, I watched the receptionist's face fall. Her blinding welcome smile turned into something altogether more threatening, somewhere between a snarl and a scowl, and nothing I ever wanted to see again.

'Hi, Kaci,' I said, waving Alice's arms up and down in front of me. 'Is Jenny here?'

'No,' she replied. 'Because you got her fired.'

'Right, should have expected that,' I said. Slowly, the rest of the office seemed to sense my arrival and I saw them gathering, one by one, beyond the glass wall that led to the office proper. 'Do you know where she is?'

'Unemployment office?' she snarked. 'A homeless shelter? The *gutter*?'

'OK, that one might be a bit much,' I replied as the mass of women on the other side of the wall began to move all together. It was like something out of a very well-groomed zombie movie. 'Just so you know, none of this was on purpose and I am trying to fix it so please don't have a contract taken out on me or anything.'

'Can't make any promises,' she said, her fingers clicking away on her keyboard. Fuckity fuck fuck fuck, why would I go and give her an idea like that? 'Also, you're banned from the office. Would you like me to show you the way out?'

'I've got a baby with me.' I pointed down at Alice and began to back away towards the front door. 'If you see Jenny, please tell her I'm looking for her.'

'Shan't,' she sang. 'Please leave.'

'Yes, fair enough,' I mumbled as the glass door to the office began to creak open. 'Nice to see you, speak soon.'

I was back on the street before the torrent of abuse could reach little Alice's delicate ears.

'I wish I had a pair of ear defenders,' I said, falling back out onto Lexington and moving quickly away from the building. I couldn't imagine any of those women willingly walking outside in the rain but they were so loyal to Jenny, you never really knew. 'OK, she's not at work and I don't think she's in the gutter. Where next?'

Alice looked up at me as though the answer were obvious.

'Quite right,' I agreed. 'Got to be worth a try.'

# CHAPTER TWENTY-FOUR

I let myself in to Jenny's building through the back door, taking it as a good sign that she hadn't changed the access code to her building. I smiled at the supposed security guard on reception on the way to the lifts and he waved at Alice, asking zero questions. I picked up her chunky little arm and waved back. No one worried about your intentions if you had a baby. If I'd tried trotting inside this building in the same state without a child attached to my body, I'd have been explaining myself to the cops for the second time in one day before I'd even crossed the threshold.

By the time we made it up to Jenny and Mason's floor, Alice was starting to get fidgety.

'Give me half an hour,' I begged her, switching the baby bag from one shoulder to the other, fighting the fatigue that was starting to pull on the edges of my already frayed nerves. 'Half an hour to beg Aunt Jenny not to have us killed and then we'll go home, have something to eat and go and see Daddy's band. Then

Mummy can google cilice belts, indulge in a little self-flagellation and everyone will be happy.'

I'd chosen the worst time to watch *The Da Vinci Code* on TNT but what could I do? I was a sucker for Tom Hanks.

Knocking politely on the door, I waited.

Nothing.

I knocked again and held Alice up to the peephole, hoping her little face would convince Jenny to open up, but there was still nothing. It was almost five thirty; if she wasn't home and she wasn't at work, I didn't know where she would be.

After one more knock, I gave up and walked back towards the lifts, my heart sinking. I had no idea what the next part of the plan was but I did know it involved me having a wee because I'd drunk a lot of tea and I really should have gone before I left Erin's house.

'Angela, hey!'

The lift doors opened to reveal Mason, Jenny's husband. He gave me a grin and immediately reached out to squeeze Alice's cheek.

'Mason, hi,' I said, manically combing my tangled hair behind my ears. Even though he was my best friend's husband and I was very happily married, Mason had the kind of intense six-foot-something masculinity that made you come over all flustered, even when I was on a manhunt for his wife.

'Going out on a limb here,' he asked, cocking his head for me to follow him back to the apartment. 'You're looking for Jen?'

'I am,' I said, following him inside and looking longingly at their guest toilet. 'I'm going to go out on a limb and guess that you've spoken to her.'

'Um, yes,' he said before taking a long pause. 'I don't think we're going to make the show tonight.'

I covered my face with my hands and groaned.

'I really need to talk to her,' I said from inside my literal face palm. 'You know I didn't do it on purpose, don't you?'

'Listen, I know and so does Jen.' Mason rested a supportive and actually massive hand on my shoulder. 'But there's no talking to her when she's in this kind of a state, you should know that better than anyone.'

He was right, of course. I was being selfish. I wanted Jenny to feel better but, more than anything, I wanted her to forgive me, tell me she knew I wasn't responsible for the pain she was in. But in the end, I was. The best thing I could do was to try and dig us both out of the mess I'd created and give her some space.

That would be the sensitive, mature and sensible thing to do.

'She's going to be fine,' Mason insisted. 'I got Monday off of work, we're going to go away for the weekend, give her some time and space to calm down.'

'Yeah, it's not good for her to be stressed right now,' I replied, thinking of everything Dr Laura had said. And immediately remembering I wasn't supposed to know anything that Dr Laura had said. 'In general, you know, because the world is so stressful and, man, you've only got to pick up a newspaper for your blood pressure to go through the roof and—'

Mason held his hands out towards Alice.

'May I?'

'You may,' I confirmed, easing her out of the papoose and into her uncle's arms.

'I know you know,' he said, eyes on the baby. 'It's cool. I thought she would have told you right at the beginning. It was dumb of me to say we shouldn't talk to anyone about it.'

'Not dumb,' I said, even though I definitely thought it was at least a little bit dumb. Misguided, perhaps. 'She just needed to talk to someone about it. Some people do, some people don't.'

'Man, I want one of these so bad,' Mason whispered, bopping Alice on the nose and then snatching his hand away over and over. 'I never thought it would be this hard. My brother has four kids, none of this hassle.'

'You just never know,' I told him, dancing back and forth on the spot. I really was desperate for a wee. 'My doctors told me I was going to have problems and Al was a complete surprise. Who knows if it'll be as easy the second time.'

'You're going for number two?' he asked, grinning through his beard.

'At some point,' I replied. 'Not yet.'

'But how great would it be if we had kids the same age?'

'So great I think I might wet myself,' I said, wondering if he'd been speaking to Alex. 'Is it all right if I use your loo before I go?'

'Uh-huh,' he nodded, not even offering to give up Alice. 'You know she calls it the loo as well?'

'Really? She always made fun of me for it.'

'You're more her wife than she is mine,' he replied, laughing. 'That's why you guys always make up in the end.'

I nodded weakly before locking myself in the bathroom.

If only I believed him.

No matter how many of Alex's shows I attended, I'd always been so excited to slap on an Access All Areas pass and go backstage before the show. At least I had until tonight. By the time we trotted up, the dressing room was already busy, crowded with friends and people from the venue and well-wishers and, knowing Craig, at least one girl he'd met on Tinder the night before. Such was the burden of the only single man left in a successful band. I saw Graham had taken one for the team and was sitting in a corner looking very suave in his suit and talking to Alex's overdressed parents. They looked like they were going for a night at the opera, which I hoped they were. They'd shown their faces, no need to stay.

'Hey.' Alex stood as soon as we entered, kissing me quickly and taking Alice out of my arms as her overloaded baby bag dropped off my shoulder and into the crook of my elbow. Babies were so small, why were their things so heavy? He guided me over to a slack, spring-less settee, covered with a blue blanket. Even in nice venues, the backstage amenities had usually seen better days.

'Hey,' I said, bottom lip trembling. 'Ready for the big show?'

'What's wrong?' he asked as I curled into his chest and burst into tears. 'Don't cry.'

'We uploaded a video at work and it got Jenny fired and it's all my fault and now she hates me,' I said. 'There's a longer version where I locked myself out and had to break in and the police came but we can do that one when I don't feel like I'm about to pass out.'

'I was gone for half a day,' Alex replied, his eyebrows furrowing together and he switched his concern from me to Alice and back again. 'I thought you were gonna say you've been stressing about your proposal.'

'My proposal?' I collapsed backwards on the settee, somewhere between laughter and tears. 'I haven't even looked at my proposal.'

Alex brushed my hair back from my face while I whimpered, staring at the ceiling. It was really very nice. Then I remembered Perry Dickson's ceiling and Perry Dickson's vulva and the fact I'd be seeing the rest of Perry Dickson here tonight.

'What time do you go on stage?' I asked, closing my eyes. 'I still need to send Camilla flowers and eat and shoot myself in the head.'

He pulled down the zip on my hoodie to reveal my I Heart New York T-shirt and promptly zipped it back up.

'Open your eyes and look at me,' he ordered.

Using my last reserves of strength, I forced open an eyelid and peeked at him through my left eye.

'I say this with complete love and adoration,' Alex said. 'You're a mess, go home.'

'No,' I replied, trying to sit up straight. 'It's your big show. I'll be all right in a bit. I'll just have a Diet Coke or a coffee or something. Or both. Can you put a 5-hour ENERGY shot in coffee or will that kill you?'

But Alex remained unconvinced.

'If by Diet Coke you mean cocaine, then maybe you'd be able to make it through the rest of the night,' he said. 'But I don't think that's a great idea.'

'You know I won't do cocaine,' I wept, looking around the room to make sure no one had heard him. 'What if my heart explodes and my dad finds out? He'd be so disappointed.'

'Your dad went to hospital because he OD'd on weed brownies,' Alex reminded me. 'And I'm serious. There will be more shows and I will feel better knowing you're taking care of you instead of worrying that you're back here about to have a heart attack. You brought the baby bag, my mom can look after Al. They don't want to see us play anyway. They can take her back to the apartment. You need to rest, or work on your proposal or go find Lopez, whatever it is that you're actually gonna do when you leave here. Although I don't think I can recommend the resting option strongly enough. Also maybe taking a shower.'

My heart began to pound as I looked back at my husband, the love of my life and father of the year.

'Are you sure?' I asked, swallowing back my sobs.

'Go,' Alex said, pulling his head away slightly as Alice slapped his face happily. 'You won't be happy until you've talked to her.'

'But Mason said I should leave her alone,' I said quietly. 'And that does seem like the sensible thing to do.'

'And since when did you and Lopez ever do the sensible thing?' he asked, a crooked half-smile softening his eyes. 'Who loves a dramatic gesture more than Lopez? We don't go on until ten, you might be back by then. Or I'll see you after the show. I don't need you to be here to prove that you love me.'

'I don't think there is a way for me to prove how

much I love you,' I said as I pried myself off the sofa. 'You're incredible, you know.'

He grinned, standing and pulling my hood up over my head.

'I do know. But it's always nice to hear it.'

I put my arms around him and Alice and squeezed as tightly as I dared, feeding on the combination of her sweet baby powder scent and the pure and unmistakable smell of Alex Reid. If I could bottle the two of them, I'd douse myself in it and never shower again. Although he was right, I realized, giving myself a sniff, I definitely could use a shower right now.

'I'm going.' I pressed my lips against his while Alice squeezed my finger tightly. 'I'd say break a leg but definitely don't.'

'Wasn't planning on it,' he said, kicking me softly in the shin. 'I love you.'

'There you are!'

I turned to see Mr and Mrs Reid blocking my exit.

'We've been waiting all night,' Janet said to her husband. 'I thought perhaps you weren't coming.'

'Here I am,' I said, my second wind gaining momentum now I was upright again. 'And I'd love to stay and chat but I'm not going to.'

Blowing right by them, I legged it for the door and pelted full speed down the corridor and out onto the street. Alex was right, I wouldn't be happy until I'd talked to Jenny. She was free to ignore me but she was definitely going to listen to what I had to say.

Just as soon as I worked out what that was.

People loved to talk shit about Millennials but if there was one thing we were good at, it was finding everything out about a human being using the internet. Give us a technological inch and we will hunt you down like dogs, I thought, following the pin on the Google Map Paige had sent. She'd blocked my number but not Paige's and, with just five minutes of Google's help, we had a location.

It took me almost an hour to get there but when I turned the corner onto Lexington Avenue and peered through the steamy window, I saw Jenny slouched against the wall in our booth, an untouched plate of food in front of her and the saddest look on her face.

'Hello, English Girl!' the large mustachioed man behind the counter said when I pushed open the door and shook down my hood. 'We don't see you in months and now both of you in one night. I am so honoured.'

'Hi, Scottie,' I said, mustering a smile before walking over to Jenny.

'My name isn't Scottie, it's Igor,' he thundered as he stuffed white paper napkins into the dispenser on the counter. 'I give up with you two.'

Jenny looked up, as though she had been waiting for me, before turning her entire body away to face the wall.

'I don't want to talk to you.'

'I know,' I said, shuffling into the booth to sit opposite her. 'But I wanted to make sure you were OK.'

'Just peachy,' Jenny rolled her eyes and grabbed the salt shaker, knocking it back and forth across the table. 'So you can go.'

'I might get something to eat, actually,' I said. Twisting against the plastic booth, I waved at Not Scottie. 'Could I get a bacon, egg and cheese?'

'Bacon, egg and cheese on an English muffin for the

338

English girl,' he replied, throwing me an OK sign. 'Coming right up.'

'Shouldn't you be at the show?' she asked, tossing her head dramatically.

'Maybe,' I said lightly.

And then I sat, in silence, waiting for the rest of it.

And then the rest of it came.

'Today was the worst day of my life,' Jenny said, gripping the salt shaker so tightly, it was a wonder it didn't shatter in her hand. 'I lost my job, I got threatened with a lawsuit and the entire industry is laughing at me. And all because one supposed friend fired me because of something my supposed *best* friend posted "without thinking". My stomach is swollen, I'm full of fucking hormones, I've never been so hurt or humiliated but, sure, let's talk about it.'

I mean, where to start?

'You know I would never do anything to intentionally hurt you.' I reached across the table to take her hand but she pulled it away before I could touch her. 'And I'm doing my best to make it right.'

'This time your best isn't good enough.' She pulled a bunch of bills out of her pocket and tossed them on the table as she stood to leave. 'I know you don't believe me but I'm done. This is a real wake-up call. When I look at all the drama in my life over the last few years, who's at the centre of it, every time? You.'

'That's not fair,' I protested as she pulled her hair out the back of her jacket. 'And you know it isn't.'

'I don't care,' she said, not angry, not swearing, just sad. 'Leave me alone, Angela. Unless there's some other way you want to ruin my life then, by all means, give it your best shot. If everything goes OK, I have my egg retrieval appointment on Wednesday. You could find some wacky way to stop me getting there on time, fuck this up too?'

She breathed out and shook her head, looking ready to deliver her final blow.

'I'm done,' she said simply, digging her hands in her pockets. 'Bye, Angela.'

And then she left.

'Bacon, egg and cheese,' Not Scottie said as he delivered my dinner to the table. 'English girl, why you cry?'

'I've had a fight with my friend,' I said, fully aware of how pathetic I sounded.

'You girls, always with the drama,' he sighed, sliding into Jenny's vacated seat. 'For years you come in here late at night with the fighting and the screaming. Today, you're not even drunk, the other one either. How come with the tears?'

'Because I don't know how to fix it,' I replied, poking at my greasy sandwich. 'I've really fucked up.'

'One thing I don't like is the language,' he said, handing me a napkin. 'Another thing, you think too much. Best way to fix things? Go home, work hard, problems fix themselves. You don't have better things to think about? Come on.' He slid back out the booth and snatched up my sandwich. 'I wrap this up and you take it to go. No good sitting here and being sad. Go away, do something else, you will find an answer.'

I watched him shuffle back behind the counter, wiping his hands on his stained apron. He tipped my sandwich into a waiting stack of greaseproof paper, wrapping it once, twice, turning it deftly in his hands before tossing it into a brown paper bag, looking up to check the weather. Rain flickered in an orange halo in front of the streetlight outside and he nodded to himself, dropping the brown paper bag into a white plastic one, printed over and over with the words 'thank you'.

'Off you go,' he said, holding out the bag. 'And I'll see you two next time.'

'Thanks, Scottie,' I said, with something like renewed hope and an improved appetite. 'I mean, Igor.'

'That's what I'm here for,' he said as I pulled my hood up against the weather. 'Advice and sandwiches. You don't get that from the McDonald's people. Tell your friends!'

There was still time for me to get back to BAM in time for Alex's show but something else drove me back towards the apartment and it wasn't just the thought of relieving Alex's parents of their babysitting duties or the smell of my delicious sandwich. These were the streets I'd walked when I first arrived in New York and I felt a million memories run up and down my skin, the hairs on my arms prickling with nostalgia. Mine and Jenny's apartment had been just a block away from Scottie's Diner and I couldn't stop myself from walking down to stand outside it and stare.

My entire body shivered from head to toe as the ghosts of me and Jenny, me and Alex, Erin and James, Craig and Louisa and all our other friends poured past me, laughing, singing, crying. Over the years we'd done our share of it all. The longer I stared at the building the more I felt it. Life passed by so quickly. There hadn't been a single day since I'd arrived in this city that I hadn't had a thousand things to do, and ever since Alice arrived, it was at least a thousand and one. But I never took the time to register a single second of it and here it was, all rushing back, all at once, and it was overwhelming. I half expected to turn around and see a younger version of myself hopping out of a cab on the corner or running down the street with a Duane Reade bag in one hand, my keys in the other, moments away from another adventure. I had never loved anything like I loved this place. New York, New York, so good they named it twice. The city that never sleeps but always dreams.

With a heavy sigh, I tore myself away, pushing on down the street, passing people as they peeled the plastic off a new drugstore umbrella they would leave in the back of a cab within a week. Others strode by without any such protection. Either they knew the rain would stop soon enough or they didn't care. New York had a good number of both kinds of people. Of all kinds of people. And Jenny was all of them wrapped up in one. I remembered days when we had run home in the rain, laughing so hard I could barely breathe, let alone worry about the weather, and others when she had screamed the whole way home, holding a plastic bag over her hair to try to keep her curls dry.

Jenny was my New York. You could keep the Statue of Liberty and the Empire State Building and your exceptionally good bagels, without Jenny Lopez, this city had nothing and no number of bacon, egg and cheese sandwiches (that I suddenly realized I had not paid for) could change that.

# CHAPTER TWENTY-FIVE

'Angela?'

I woke with a start and no idea where I was. This was not my bed. Ow. This was not any bed.

'Babe, you OK?'

Turning my aching neck I saw Alex standing in the doorway of our living room, looking worried.

'I don't know,' I said, feeling around the settee cushions for my phone. What time was it? Why was I in the living room? Instead of my phone, I felt something hard and sharp digging into my hip. It was my laptop.

'I told you to come to bed when you finished,' Alex whispered, walking over to take the laptop out my hands. 'Go to bed, get some sleep. I'll deal with Alice.'

'What time is it?' I asked as the events of the evening slowly filtered back into place.

'Almost six,' he said softly as he set the computer on the dining room table next to a stack of paper.

'Is Alice awake?'

'Not yet.'

I rubbed my eyes and rocked my head from side to side, my neck was so tight. This really was a settee that needed to be reserved for naps only. My eyes rested on the stack of paper.

'I printed it out,' I said, my voice croaky as the final pieces fell into place. 'I have to take it over now.'

'Take it over?' Alex asked, puzzled. 'To the publisher? Babe, it's a Saturday. Please go to bed.'

After Jenny had left the diner, I'd walked almost the length of Manhattan and, just before I got to the F train stop at Delancey, it had hit me. I knew what my book would be about. And I spent the rest of the night writing the proposal.

'I can't,' I said. 'I've got to go now, before they leave.'

'I don't want to say you're starting to scare me but you're kind of starting to scare me,' Alex said, kneeling down in front of me and placing his hands on either side of my face. 'Do I need to stage an intervention? I never thought I'd have to beg you to get some sleep.'

'I swear I'm OK.' I leaned forward to plant a quick kiss on his lips, wishing I'd brushed my teeth before I did. 'There's just one more thing I have to do and then I'm going to sleep for so long, you may need medical assistance to wake me.'

'None this sounds like a dream come true,' he replied. 'I don't think I've ever seen you up and awake before seven a.m. unless it's Alice or you're on your way to an airport.'

'Time to add one more reason to the list,' I assured him, stuffing my arms through the sleeves of my coat and slipping the pages of my proposal into my satchel. 'I'll be back before you know it.'

'Bring pastries,' he called as I let myself out the front door. 'Or I'll know for sure you've been possessed by aliens.'

The city was beautiful early in the morning. At night, it was sexy and in the day, electric, but first thing in the morning, New York seemed shiny and new, its empty streets filled with possibilities. I exchanged a smile and a nod with the postman as I flagged down a cab, watching him push his little mail cart down the next street. People were happier first thing in the morning. There was more optimism to go around at sunrise than there was at sunset.

'Pearl and Cedar,' I said, bundling myself into the back seat.

'You got it,' the driver replied as we tore away from the kerb.

Before the weekend rush hour had a chance to kick in, we raced through Brooklyn, only stopping for red lights and one particularly foolhardy pigeon who thought it a good idea to test the brakes of a yellow cab.

'You can't just hit 'em,' the driver explained as I braced myself against the Perspex partition. 'If they hit the grille, they'll be stinking up the car for days. At first it ain't so bad, smells like chicken, but a couple of days in, after a twelve-hour shift, you better believe you're thinking, "If only I hadn't hit that damn bird."'

'No problem,' I replied, fastening my seatbelt and clutching my bag tightly against my chest.

'So, the tunnel is closed and we gotta take the bridge,' he added. 'Probably faster this time of day.'

'That's fine,' I said. All I wanted was to get to Jenny's place. I'd sent Mason a text, asking what time they were leaving, but he hadn't replied, either because they were still asleep or because Jenny had seen my name come up on the screen and tossed his phone down the building's trash chute, I didn't know which.

We passed the big hotel at the entrance ramp to Brooklyn Bridge and began to slow down, a sea of bright red brake lights ahead of us.

'Is something wrong?' I asked as a police car zoomed past us on the opposite side of the road, sirens blaring. It was never a good sign when a police car was going the wrong way on a main road, this much I knew.

'Don't look good,' he grunted. 'We might be here for a while.'

I stayed buckled in, tapping my fingers against my thighs. We wouldn't be here for long. No matter what was going on, traffic would start moving again any minute. I'd be at Jenny's in fifteen minutes flat. Twenty, tops.

And then two more police cruisers followed the other, followed by a fire engine, followed by an ambulance.

'Nyaah, shit,' the taxi driver groaned. 'That's it. We're fucked.'

'Can't you turn around and go another way?' I asked, craning my neck to look at the lengthy line of cars sitting behind us.

'Can you magically make the car fly?' he replied. 'No, I can't turn around.'

'OK, I don't have time to wait, I'm in a rush.' I unbuckled my seatbelt, threw the strap of my bag over my head and fished two twenty-dollar bills out of my wallet. The meter only read eighteen dollars but I had a feeling he was going to be sitting there for a while. 'Here you go.'

'Forty bucks? To sit in traffic for an hour? Forget about it, lady, you're looking at a hundred,' he said as he snatched them through the tiny slot in the Perspex partition.

'I don't have any more,' I lied, my mother's influence coming through. Actually, no, she wouldn't have even given him the extra twenty. My mum didn't believe in tipping as a concept. 'Sorry.'

Before he could lock me in, I opened the cab door and took off in a run, ignoring the blaring car horns as I scooted in front of cabs and trucks and miserable-looking commuters to find myself on the pavement. OK, fifteen minutes away by car couldn't be more than half an hour on foot, I told myself, running as fast as I could, for as long as I could.

But it wasn't long enough. I'd only gone a few hundred yards when I realized the footpath of Brooklyn Bridge was a steady incline until you reached the middle. I was so out of breath, I'd be lucky if I made it to Jenny's apartment by Christmas.

'Christ,' I gasped, pushing my arm into my side to stretch away the stitch that threatened to slow me down even more. 'I really have got to start going to the gym.'

But I kept going, one foot in front of the other as the sun rose over the city. It would have been a beautiful photo if I trusted myself to stop and take it but I knew, the second I stopped moving, it was all over. Eventually, I wheezed my way over the halfway point and began to pick up speed again.

'Thank god for gravity,' I panted, studiously ignoring the dozens of runners who were overtaking me, especially the ones pushing prams that carried judgemental babies. I wasn't sure what they were looking so smug about, it wasn't as though they were running themselves.

After what felt like forever but was really much closer to forty painful, sweaty minutes, I let myself in through the back door of Jenny's building. I couldn't guarantee the same security guard would be around and, if Erin thought I looked like an extra from *Law & Order* the night before, she really ought to get a glimpse of me now.

The lift buzzed up to the twenty-third floor while I caught my breath. It didn't matter that I didn't know what to say this time. I had it all written down. Crossing my fingers for luck, I found myself outside Jenny's apartment for the second time in twelve hours, hoping against hope that this time she would be home. Closing my eyes, I knocked.

And knocked again.

And again.

Eventually, I heard a door slam and footsteps, followed by a muffle of swearing that definitely sounded like Jenny.

Bollocks. I winced and pressed myself against the wall so she wouldn't see me. I'd expected Mason to come to the door with it being so early in the morning, damn my internalized misogyny. There was no way Jenny would let me in.

'Angela,' I heard her say through the door.

'No?' I replied in a fake American accent. 'It's your neighbour, uh, Lucy.'

'No, it's you,' Jenny replied. 'We have a camera above the door. I can see your dumb ass.'

'Then let me in,' I pleaded, searching for the camera as I fussed with my hair. 'I want to show you something.'

'I told you yesterday, I'm done,' she said. 'Go away.'

'Wait,' I shouted, battering my fists against the door one more time. 'Wait, I want you to read this.'

I dropped to my knees and fished the printed pages out of my bag. I slid the first page halfway under the door and waited. After what felt like an eternity, it disappeared, snatched up on the other side.

I pressed my palm against the door, my heart thudding in my ears. I tried to breathe slowly, counting to ten before every exhale.

'Is there another page or is this it?' Jenny said, finally.

'There's another page,' I confirmed, pushing the rest of it under the door, page by page. 'A few more actually.'

The white paper slipped out of my view as I squatted on the floor, leaning against Jenny's front door, cold, tired and, once again, desperate for a wee. When would I learn to go before I left the house?

As the first lock clicked inside the door, I tried to stand up but my tired, aching legs betrayed me, wobbling with the effort and sending me backwards to land hard on my bum as Jenny's face appeared above me.

'Why are you on the floor?' she asked, her face tear-stained, her hair tied up on top of her head.

'Because I'm a dickhead,' I replied.

'Get your ass inside, dickhead,' she said, brushing away a fresh tear with the back of one hand, the other pressing my pages against her chest.

'Are you going to burn that if I go for a wee first?' I asked, scrambling to my feet.

'Maybe,' she sniffed. 'Let's find out.'

She moved to the side and I hurtled into the apartment before she could change her mind, dropping my satchel on her sofa and shutting the toilet door without locking it.

When I emerged, she was standing at the kitchen island, the kettle boiling on the hob behind her while she read through the pages. She'd spread them all out on the marble counter top, stark white rectangles against the black and white.

'When did you write this?' she asked. She pulled her dressing gown tightly around her and I noticed she was wearing the same T-shirt she'd been wearing the day before. I wasn't the only one who had slept in her clothes and, according to the blankets on the settee, not the only one who had spent the night on the sofa.

'Last night,' I said, lingering in the living area of her open-plan apartment. Behind me, the sun was stretching all the way across Brooklyn, stretching across the city like a warm yellow blanket. It was a beautiful sight to see but it wasn't what I was there for. 'It's my book proposal.'

'It's not really long enough to be a book proposal,' she said. 'You need three chapters and a synopsis.'

I gave her a look before walking over to the cupboard and taking out two mugs. When she didn't tell me to get the fuck out of her kitchen, I opened the next cupboard, looking for the Tetley teabags I kept in there.

'The writing is good,' she said, opening the fridge

and taking out the milk. 'I like this Jessie character, she seems like a real stand-up gal.'

'Much better than the Anna character,' I agreed. 'Who is basically useless.'

'Total asshole,' she agreed. 'I don't know what Anna sees in her.'

'It's a love story,' I explained, my eyes darting over my own words, rereading them for the first time since they'd come pouring out. 'Only it's not about a boy and a girl, it's about two soulmates who find each other in New York when they need each other most and all the adventures they go on together.'

Jenny set her features in a pout, determined to look unmoved.

'Because that's what best friends are,' I added before picking up the boiling kettle. 'Soulmates.'

'You're being incredibly cheesy right now,' she said as her air conditioning kicked in to make the pages dance around on the counter top. 'Is this for real?'

'Yes.' I wiped away a tear as I poured out hot water through blurry eyes. The one thing I could do blind-folded was make tea. 'Because sometimes friends cock up but, when they're meant to be, they're meant to be. I can't imagine not having my best friend in my life so I thought I ought to write a story about that.'

She passed me the sugar bowl.

'Did you write the part where one of the friends makes an absolutely colossal fuck-up and costs the other friend everything?'

'Not yet,' I replied. 'Might save it for the sequel.'

Jenny wrapped her arms around herself and stared at the floor. 'Then you'd better put in all the times the other friend was a totally selfish dick who put the other friend through hell,' she said, a single tear trickling down her cheek. 'And the times the same friend said really nasty shit because she was angry and upset and, like, literally full of hormones. Literally injecting herself with them every day and making herself crazy.'

'I think I'm going to concentrate on all the brilliant things they did together,' I told her, tears prickling behind my own eyes. 'And all the times that other friend made the first friend realize what she was capable of and how she could do anything if she tried hard enough and—'

'OK, quit it, quit it, I'm totally lost,' Jenny roared, throwing her arms around my neck and wailing loudly. 'I get it, I'm sorry and I love you, you asshat.'

'I love you too,' I cried. 'And I'm sorry.'

'What is going on out here?' Mason padded in from the living room in a pair of pyjama bottoms and nothing else. His eyes were still full of sleep and his hair was absolutely everywhere but it was very hard to concentrate on anything but his abs. That was the last time I wanted to hear Jenny complain about being a CrossFit widow.

'It's OK, it's OK,' Jenny sniffed. 'Angela is writing a book and we're friends again.'

Mason looked at us both like we were mad before turning around and traipsing right back into the bedroom.

'He's happy, really,' she said.

'I am as well,' I said, resting my head on her shoulder. 'And sorry if I smell, I didn't have a shower last night and yesterday was quite the day.'

'I didn't want to say anything,' she replied, her voice

thick with unshed tears. 'But you really do. You can shower here if you want, there are a bunch of your clothes on the spare bed. I was gonna burn them.'

'You were going to burn my clothes?'

'Yeah, I mean, I probably wouldn't have,' she sighed, turning her attention back to our tea. 'Where can you burn shit in New York without getting into trouble anyway? They even put a smoke detector in our bathroom.'

'Thanks,' I said, accepting the piping hot tea, made just the way I liked it. 'Did you talk to Erin again?'

She nodded, blowing on her mug before she took a sip.

'Last night, for like, ever. She's giving me a severance package and she says she'll give me a reference if I want to apply for another PR job.'

'And do you?'

'I don't know,' she replied. 'I didn't think I'd have to make this decision right now. But between the severance she's giving me and the money I've saved, I think this is my opportunity to shoot my shot. I might go back to school, take a couple of psychology courses. I know people think it's dumb but I really want to focus on the podcast. But I'm scared.'

'Of course you're scared,' I told her, wrapping my hands around my mug. 'You don't have what I had when I had to make big, life-changing decisions.'

'And what's that?' she asked, her jaw set, ready to fight.

I smiled at my best friend.

'You.'

Jenny raised an eyebrow and tutted before looking down at the floor.

'I can't believe I'm friends with the next Oprah,' I said sipping my tea. 'How mad is that?'

'As if there was ever any doubt,' she muttered, taking in my emergency bin trainers, my jogging bottoms, my scrappy T-shirt and grubby sweater. 'Angie. I'm sorry about all the things I said. I know you have a lot going on. I don't mean to be selfish, I just miss you sometimes is all. I miss us.'

'I miss us too,' I said, determined not to cry again. 'I don't think I realized how much until last night. There's just so much going on all the time, I don't know how to handle it.'

'No one does,' she said. 'But you're not on your own. I can help more – hell, I don't have a job, I can help all the damn time.'

'I was thinking I might ask if I can work from home more.' I pulled a face, imagining Cici's reaction. 'Otherwise, I don't know. Maybe I'll have to look for something else. Turns out there's no such thing as having it all.'

'No, there is,' she countered. 'Only what they don't tell you is the "it" part stands for millions of dollars. Then you just buy your way out of all of this stress.'

'So I just need to make millions of dollars,' I sighed with mock relief. 'Thank you for figuring that out. Maybe this isn't the right time to give up work.'

'Or maybe this book is going to be a huge bestseller and you'll be able to sit at home, eating bonbons all day, living a life of luxury,' she said, slapping the pages of my proposal with the back of her hand. 'You gotta get this written, doll.'

'You really think it's good?' I asked, skimming the words I barely remembered writing.

'I think it's fucking awesome,' she replied. 'You got a title?'

I took a deep breath in and blew it out through my nose. 'Not yet. I really want it to be something people get right away, something that lets you know it's a book about how two girls really love each other. What do you think?'

She pinched together her features, her official thinking face. 'But it's not just about the girls,' she said, running her finger down the pages as she scanned it again. 'It's about their lives, their friends, their boyfriends, living in the city. You know, it seems to me like it's about how much Anna loves New York as much as anything.'

'You're right,' I agreed. 'But I still have absolutely no idea.'

Jenny looked at me, a strange almost-smile on her face.

'I got it,' she said, tapping her finger against the logo on my chest. 'How about, *I Heart New York*?'

I looked up with a bright smile on my face. 'It's perfect. You think they'll like it?'

'I think they'll love it,' she replied before pulling a face. 'I mean, as long as it doesn't suck. This is just a proposal and you don't even have enough chapters. It's a good proposal but still.'

'Thanks, thank you,' I said, rolling my eyes. A classic Jenny shit sandwich. 'You're the best.'

She stretched her arms over her head as she yawned, both of us resting our backs against the kitchen counter, my head on her shoulder as we stared out the window. From here, I could see the Statue of Liberty, waving hello, the Williamsburg, Manhattan and Brooklyn

Bridges rising up over the water and the bright orange Staten Island ferry sailing back and forth across the water, like a little bath toy. To the east, I saw the sun's reach stretching further and further across Brooklyn, tinting everything a primrose yellow and glinting off the fancy new developments downtown. Even the docks looked romantic at sunrise and, having been there once for a secret fashion show party Jenny got us into, I knew full well there was nothing romantic about those docks. But that was how you knew it was true when they said New York was the city that never slept. No one looked this good when they first woke up.

'You wanna get breakfast?' Jenny asked. 'There's an awesome twenty-four-hour diner around the corner that's not so bad. I'm freaking starving.'

'Always,' I replied, tearing my eyes away from the love of my life and smiling at my best friend. 'Let's go.'

Life was rarely simple and relationships never were, I thought to myself as Jenny traded her dressing gown for a bright red blazer and picked up her keys. And the only thing I knew was absolutely true was that I really didn't know anything. New York was a city that was always changing and growing, sometimes for the better and sometimes for the worse. Just because I didn't like that new coffee shop on 7th Avenue didn't mean someone else couldn't love it. Maybe they'd meet their future husband in there, or it might be where their best friend would tell them they were engaged or maybe they'd even write a bestselling book at one of those tables. The most important thing was to keep the things you loved close and take care of them always. I had the subway and Bloomingdale's and round-the-clock pizza. I had that guy on the corner of 14th and 1st who performed Taylor Swift songs with sock puppets and always gave me a wink when I dropped a dollar into his hat. I had my home, my health, my job. My family back in England and another family, right here. I had Jenny, I had Alex, I had my Alice.

I had New York.

And it was more than I ever could have wished for.

# EPILOGUE

One year later . . .

'She lives!' my dad bellowed from behind the paper at the kitchen table. 'I thought I was going to have to get you going with the jump leads for a minute. I even brought the car round back.'

'What you two do in your own time is up to you,' I replied, sitting down beside him. 'Please leave me out of it.'

'Less of that cheek,' Mum said, clipping me round the back of the head and placing another steaming cup of tea in front of me. It didn't matter which teabags I took back to New York with me, or how much I paid in the little English shop in the West Village, there was nothing like a proper cup of tea made at home.

'Right, as soon as you've had your breakfast, I want you upstairs, showered and dressed,' she went on, opening cupboards, pulling out pots and pans, bacon, eggs and seemingly every single other item in the kitchen. 'What time do we need to be where?'

'I can't remember,' I lied. I knew, I was just too scared to think about it. 'I'll check my phone in a bit.'

Dad closed up the paper with a flourish, folding it once, twice, with knife-sharp creases. 'How are you feeling?' he asked. 'Nervous?'

'Petrified,' I replied. 'Anything exciting going on in the news?'

'We're all going to hell in a handbasket,' he replied jovially. 'Haven't you heard?'

'He only reads it for the telly listings,' Mum muttered, cracking half a dozen eggs into a sizzling frying pan. Apparently she was feeding the five thousand rather than one very queasy daughter. I wasn't even hungry.

Wait. I wasn't hungry. That really was a bad sign.

'You shouldn't be nervous,' Dad said, checking his fingers for newsprint even though I was fairly certain the ink didn't come off newspapers any more. Or did it? It was that long since I'd picked up a newspaper. Certainly didn't come off *Heat* magazine, that much I knew. 'I'm sure it's all going to be very simple, very straightforward. It'll be over before you know it and then you'll wonder why you made such a fuss, sitting up until all hours and rattling on to yourself.'

'You heard me?' I asked, sipping my tea. It was perfect.

'When you get to my age, you're up to the loo at least twice in the night,' he nodded. 'I didn't like to disturb you.'

'She's disturbed enough already,' Mum muttered to the eggs. 'Gets it from your side.'

'All I'm trying to say is, what's done is done. The meeting went well enough yesterday, didn't it?'

I nodded.

'And you can't change anything now, can you?'

I shook my head.

'So relax and enjoy it! What's the point in getting all worked up? It's out there now, people will make of it what they will.'

'Thanks,' I said, scratching at the faded Dairy Milk logo on my mug. It came with an Easter Egg god only knew how many moons ago but my mother never threw anything away. 'I think?'

'Knock knock, Clarks!'

As always, we heard her before we saw her.

'Here's my girlfriend!' Dad leapt up from his seat to welcome Jenny with a giant hug as she blew into the kitchen. 'Look at you! I don't know how to feel about this. I'm really quite jealous.'

Jenny grinned, rubbing a hand over her six-month pregnant belly.

'What could I do, David? I knew Annette would never give up a stud like you.'

'You only needed to ask, dear,' Mum said, holding her at arm's length to get a proper look at her bump. 'I still don't think you should be flying but I'm very happy to see you. Get sat down and I'll make you some chamomile tea.'

'I would kill for a coffee, Annette.' Jenny grabbed my face with both hands and kissed me square on the lips. 'She's not going to give me coffee, is she?'

'There's a Starbucks on the high street,' I whispered. Mum didn't approve of Starbucks. Only Costa. No real reason, just Mum. 'We'll get you one in a bit.'

'And where's that gorgeous man of yours?' Mum asked as she fished through the cupboards for Jenny's specially bought tea.

'I hope you're talking about me.'

Alex. Alex, Alex, Alex. I leapt out of my seat and bolted across the kitchen.

'I thought you weren't getting in until this afternoon,' I said, covering his face in kisses before carefully unloading his most precious cargo. 'Hi, hi, hi!'

'Mummy!' Alice screamed with joy as I bounced her up onto my hip. My own mummy immediately stopped what she was doing, Jenny bumped immediately into second place by the arrival of her granddaughter, and ran over to snatch her up.

'There she is,' Mum cooed, holding her over Dad's head so he could at least grab hold of a foot. 'Alex, you should have told us you were coming earlier, we'd have come to get you from the airport.'

'You didn't offer to pick me up from the airport,' Jenny commented, clutching her perfectly fine back as she lowered herself into a kitchen chair.

'I managed to move a couple of things around and get on the same flight as these guys since you ditched me,' Alex brushed my hair away from my face and gave me a lazy smile.

'Don't say I ditched you!' I said, incapable of stealing another kiss while my father made forced retching sounds across the table. 'I had my meeting! And you had your meeting! And you said you would bring her!'

'I'm joking,' he said as Mason stumbled through the door, carrying what looked like every suitcase on the plane. Jenny never had been good with the concept of travelling light. 'We had fun flying with Aunt Jen, didn't we, Alice?'

Alice maintained a dignified silence.

'And what a treat it was for me,' Jenny said, taking

a surreptitious sip of my tea. 'An overnight flight with a toddler. I wish we'd done it before I dropped nearly thirty grand on cooking up this one.'

'She's joking,' Mason walked up behind his wife, pinching her neck in a cross between a massage and a Vulcan death grip. 'Alice was amazing.'

'Mason brought noise-cancelling headphones and slept for most of the flight while she screamed all the way through *The Avengers*,' Jenny countered. 'And that shit is three hours long.'

'She was a little rowdy during the turbulence,' Alex admitted. But my parents were not listening, and did not care. All that mattered was their precious grand-daughter.

'So,' Jenny slapped her hand on the table. 'You ready? You excited? You know what you're wearing? Come on Angie, I'm dying over here.'

'Not ready, mostly scared and I have three potential outfits, all of which you're going to hate,' I told her. Jenny clapped happily.

'And that's why I have an extra suitcase of clothes, just for you,' she said, waving a hand at her mountain of luggage. 'You gotta show out tonight, Angie. It's not every day a girl publishes her first novel.'

'That is true,' I agreed. 'Fuck.'

'Angela,' Mum snapped, covering Alice's ears. 'Language.'

'She hasn't read the book, huh?' Mason asked quietly.

The book. I'd written a book.

An actual book in actual shops for actual people to read with their actual eyes. Or ears if they went for the audiobook, I wasn't fussy as long as they read it. I'd spent the last month doing interviews, answering questions and generally not quite believing what was happening. But today was the actual day it came out and every time I thought about it, I wanted to dance and puke at the same time. Kind of reminded me of our Hawaii trip, now that I thought about it.

'I talked to Delia and she's going to be at the venue this evening,' Jenny carried on talking while I stared at the copy of my book I'd picked up from Cooper & Bow UK along with a giant bouquet of flowers during my visit to their offices the morning before. 'Everything should be set up when we get there so we literally don't need to do a single thing but show up and be awesome, which, you know, is a given.'

It turned out Erin had been right about firing Jenny (as usual). Determined not to give up, she'd thrown everything she had at her podcast and, within three months, she'd signed to Spencer Media's podcast network and was doing so well, she'd already interviewed four out of five of the boys from *Queer Eye*. She even let me sit in the studio during the recordings, cementing our friendship for all eternity.

And tonight we were celebrating the publication of my book as part of the Gloss Magazine Festival, recording a special episode of "Tell Me About It" live. I was finally going to be on the podcast and only one year and two seasons later than promised.

'Hello, is anyone home? The door is open.'

'We're in here,' I shouted to Louisa, watching as giant man Mason attempted to orient himself in my mother's chintzy kitchen. It doesn't matter how many times you open that cupboard door, I thought to myself, you're not going to find a single protein powder, my friend.

'Oh, everyone's arrived,' Lou said, car keys dangling from her hand. 'I just dropped Gracie off at school. I was going to see if Angela wanted to pop for a coffee.'

'I want to pop for a coffee!' Jenny cried, standing up a lot faster than she'd sat down. Six months pregnant or not, nothing was going to keep that woman from her caffeine fix. 'Let's go before Annette chains me to the kitchen sink.'

'Angela?' Lou asked, tilting her head for Alex's kiss on the cheek.

'I'm OK.' I shook my head.

'And still in her PJs,' my dad pointed out. 'Alice, can you say hello to Auntie Louisa?'

My little girl concentrated on the vaguely familiar blonde standing in the kitchen doorway.

'Yes,' she replied before returning to her very important task of showing my mother her new teeth.

'Like mother, like daughter,' Dad smirked. 'You were a little smartarse too.'

'David,' Mum snapped.

'Yes, I know, I know,' he said, slapping the newspaper on the table before standing up. 'Let's get these suitcases upstairs before I trip over them and break my neck. I'm sure you could use a hand, Mason.'

'Uh, sure,' he replied, carefully putting the smallest, lightest suitcase out of the three down in front of my dad. 'Thanks Mr C.'

'You want anything from the coffee shop, Angie?' Jenny asked as she practically dragged Louisa out the door.

'No, I'm fine,' I said, eyeing the half-cooked eggs Mum had abandoned on the hob. Good job I really wasn't hungry. 'Thank you!'

'Go wee,' Alice demanded, turning her attention from her teeth to grabbing at her crotch.

Before I could stand, Mum was sailing off to the downstairs bathroom, Alice grinning as she began to realize just what she had stumbled into. An adoring and willing slave. The front door slammed on Jenny and Louisa, Mason and Dad headed upstairs and Mum and Alice were locked in the loo, leaving just me and Alex in the kitchen.

He settled into the seat next to mine. Even with his hair rumpled from the plane, his eyes red-rimmed and bloodshot, I couldn't think of a time I'd been happier to see him.

'Last time we were here together, we almost got married,' he said, looking around the room. It had barely changed since I was sixteen so I couldn't imagine it was that different to the last time he was there. 'What kind of trouble are you planning to get me into this time?'

'Well, we can't get married again,' I waved my wedding ring in his face. 'And we agreed no baby talk until the new year, so I don't know. What does that leave us?'

He shrugged off his leather jacket and cracked his neck with a happy groan.

'I don't know,' he admitted. 'But I'm kind of excited to find out.'

I leaned in for a kiss, taking hold of his hand to feel for his wedding ring.

'Masochist,' I whispered just before our lips met.

'You're the one who wanted to stay at your mom's instead of at a hotel.'

He had me there.

'I know you're stressed about this,' Alex said, pushing my hair back from my face. I resisted the urge to curl up in his lap and purr. It was already after nine and I had to get this show on the road. 'But it's gonna be awesome. You're excited, right? Because you should be.'

'I am,' I replied, smiling. 'It's scary but good scary, if that makes sense. I'm more excited now you're all here.'

'My wife, the author.' He brought his face to mine for one more perfect kiss. 'I'm so fucking proud of you.'

As I kissed him back, I realized it wasn't a lie. I *was* excited. About the book, about Alice turning into a toddler terror. I was excited for Jenny and Mason's baby and her inevitable world domination and I was excited for everything I didn't even know about yet. When I thought about all things that had happened since I'd walked out my mum's front door on my way to Louisa's wedding all those years ago, none of it seemed real. Meeting Jenny, meeting Alex, getting married, having a baby – how many little tiny things had to fall into place for even one of those things to happen? What if Jenny had been in the loo when I checked in at my hotel? What if Alex hadn't stopped into Manatus for a drink? It could all have been so different. The only thing that had stayed the same was the fact that I'd had no idea what I was doing back then and – being completely honest with myself – I had even less of an idea now.

But that was OK, we had the rest of our lives to figure out what came next.

And I couldn't wait.

# ACKNOWLEDGEMENTS

Jesus, this one could go on for a while – do you want to go and get a cup of tea? No? OK, let's just get started. First things first, without Lynne Drew, there would be no book in your hands today and there is no version of this written thank you that could adequately show my appreciation for all that you've done. I owe millions of thank yous to my friends at HarperCollins and we'll need more pages if I'm going to get everyone but special shout-outs to Martha Ashby, Kate Elton, Charlie Redmayne, Lucy Vanderbilt, Damon Greeney, Eleanor Goymer, Liz Dawson and everyone in sales, marketing, design and production who has worked on, worked with or been forced to endure either this book or any of the others that came before. Thank you to my publishing family around the world, especially Jean Marie Kelly, Leo McDonald and Kimberley Allsop – you have all endured, you are all owed. And of course, a special thanks to Felicity Denham for keeping me in pizza and booze and nice hotels. I've never seen anyone handle a Post-It Note quite like you, champ.

Rowan Lawton. You are the greatest agent I could ever have asked for (and I didn't even ask for one! How lucky am I?). Without your wisdom, support and well-timed cocktails, I'm not sure how I would cope. A lot of the time, this is a weird, uncomfortable and stressful job and I would not want to do it without you in my corner.

If I was going to thank all the friends who made this book possible, I'd get RSI from typing, and that's just *I Heart Hawaii*, let alone the rest of them. So I will name and shame those who kept my head above the water and the rest of you will just have to know the part you played in keeping me sane in your hearts. Della Bolat, Terri White, Kevin Dickson, Harriet Hadfield, Emma Gunavardhana, Danielle Radford, this one is for you. Oh, and Jeff Israel because even though we share a home and a cat family and adult sleepovers, you're still my friend and for that, I love you more than anything else. Even if you probably won't read this part of the book (or any other TBH). Special *I Heart* props for ten years of support from Rebecca Alimena, Ana Mercedes Cardenas, Ryan Child, Sarah Donovan, Jackie Dunning, Catherine Ellis, Georgia Fraser, Emma Ingram, James McKnight, Erin Stein, Beth Ziemacki and man, I really want to name all the terrible dudes who gave me great ideas for the books but I won't. Big author buddy thanks to my beloveds: Paige Toon (and her hot husband, Greg), Giovanna Fletcher (and her invisible husband, Tom), Louise Pentland, Sarra Manning, Rosie Walsh, Mhairi McFarlane, Rowan Coleman, Julie Cohen, Lucy Knott, Miranda Dickson, Isabelle Broom, and god, there are so many more writers who have talked me off a ledge, even if they didn't know it at the time. Thank you for making me feel like I have a handle on this, even when I don't.

Most of all, thank you to you. If you read this far, you need a medal but the simple truth is, if you hadn't picked up any of my books, I wouldn't be thanking these people for anything because I wouldn't be writing. It's been a mad ten years and I don't have the words to thank you properly. Which is dead embarrassing because writing is my job.

Thank you, thank you, thank you. You made all my dreams come true.

# Q&A with Lindsey

**1. *I Heart Hawaii* marks the end of the *I Heart* series (\*sob\*) – how do you feel? (Spoiler: we are in mourning.)**

When I decided to finish the series, I was so very certain it was absolutely the right thing to do. I've always said I wouldn't drag it out but now it's all over, I'm so sad! Writing 'the end' is never really the end of the writing process – you've got the edits and proofreading and then the marketing, PR and all the rest of it. Usually by the end, you're glad to see the back of the book so you can get on with the next one but this has been heartbreak after heartbreak. I can't believe Angela, Alex, Jenny and the gang are really gone. Oh god, and now I'm crying again… I truly feel as though I have lost some of my best friends and it's incredibly hard.

**2. *I Heart* has spanned eight books and ten years – how do you think Angela has changed over that period? And – more importantly – how have you changed?**

We both changed so much! When I first started writing *I Heart New York*, Angela was so heavily based on me. She had my personality, my preferences, even my hair. But as the books went on and our lives went in different directions, she became her own person, which was such a lovely surprise. I learned a ton about her, about writing and about myself. I think we've both learned the importance of communication and the problems you can face if you're not clear about what you mean, what you want and what you need. We've also learned the importance of taking chances and trusting the people who love you.

I was also living in London at the time, bored in my job and unhappy in my relationship. In the decade since, I broke up with my ex, sold our house, moved to New York where I lived for six years and then moved to LA. I fell in and out of love more than once, lost family members and made friends I will know for the rest of my life. If you'd told me any of this would have happened on the day I sat down with my computer and started writing the first story, I never would have believed you.

### 3. How did you know this was the right time to say goodbye to Angela and her friends?

It's like anything else in life, you just know. Before now, I've always had a million stories for Angela and her friends to tell. They get into your head and started tapping at the inside of your skull until you sit down and tell them but more and more, I've found the stories I want to tell belong to other people. Maybe ten years from now a story will start screaming at me and I'll know it's Angela's to tell but for now, there are new stories that need my attention.

### 4. What do you think the future holds for Angela et al? Or are you happy for readers to draw their own conclusions?

Oh absolutely. Send me your fanfic, please! But really, I think they're all happy. They've worked really hard to get where they are – a true, honest place, doing work they care about, surrounded by people they love. What could be better than that?

### 5. Do you have any favourite places you'd love to go back to? And is there anywhere you would have liked to take Angela but couldn't quite make it work?

New York is my forever love. Even though I don't live there anymore, it's truly my soulmate city and I go back as often as I possibly can. Actually I love all the *I Heart* destinations! London, Paris and LA, obviously, and anyone who follows me on social media knows I can't keep away from Las Vegas. The two places I would have loved to take Angela but I just couldn't make it work are Tokyo and Australia. The *I Heart* gang has so many friends in Australia, I'd have loved for her to have an adventure there and I'm obsessed with Japan so that would have been entirely selfish. Maybe one day…

### 6. Taking a step away from *I Heart*, your professional life has evolved over the last ten years, and now you have your finger in many other different pies too. Is there anything you haven't tried yet that you'd like to do?

Everything in the last ten years has been bonkers. I never thought I would get to write for a living, let alone write books for adults and children, write for magazines and websites I love *and* make podcasts about some of my favourite subjects. That said, there are a million other things I'd like to do. Everyone always asks me about making a TV show or a movie out of one of my books and I think that would be super fun, or maybe I could write an original script or work on a TV show. Ultimately, I think of myself as a storyteller and TV and movies are just another way of telling stories. And you know I still have time to make my debut as a professional wrestler…

**7. Keen fans of your Twitter and Instagram will be familiar with your cats, BelleBelle and Anderson Cooper. Can I ask how you named them? And will they ever make an appearance in any of your books?**

Man, they're going to be so smug they got a question all of their own. They actually had their names when I adopted them, so I can take zero credit. Anderson was a tiny bundle of silver fluff with big blue eyes which is how he got his name, while BelleBelle actually started out as Belle and her name expanded. She had a brother named Sebastian, so they were named after the band, but someone else adopted him and left her all on her lonesome. Luckily, she bonded with Anderson and I couldn't bear the thought of taking one without the other and they've been inseparable ever since! They haven't appeared in any of the books as yet but my boyfriend, Jeff, is a TV editor and he has used their meows on some of his shows so I think that's fame enough. I don't want them going all Hollywood on me…

**8. What's next??**

I don't know, a nap? Actually that seems unlikely. I have my children's series, *Cinders & Sparks*, out in the world which I'm very excited about and of course I'm working on more adult books. I've also got Full Coverage, my beauty podcast which just won a best podcast award at the J&J Beauty Awards, and Tights & Fights, my wrestling podcast. Oh, and I'm currently making a documentary with two awesome filmmakers about being a female wrestling fan, plus I'm always hanging out on social media *and* I'm working on other assorted secret projects I can't even talk about just yet! So that nap seems a little bit unlikely but I'm not complaining. I never was very good at taking it easy, anyway.

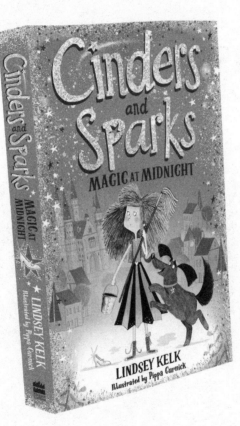

# DISCOVER LINDSEY'S

# I heart SERIES

There are lots of ways
to keep up-to-date with
Lindsey's news and views:

lindseykelk.com

facebook.com/LindseyKelk

@LindseyKelk

@LindseyKelk

Or sign up to Lindsey's newsletter here
smarturl.it/LindseyNewsletter